Marge - than'
for taking
I hope I have
to reciprocate.
Rachel

NATURE'S KISS

A ROMANTIC FANTASY

(AND MORE)

BOOK ONE OF THE NATURE SERIES

By Rachel Crosby

Published by
Orange Leaf on Midnight Snow
Harwich, MA

ISBN 10: 1543262791
ISBN 13: 978-1543262797

For more information or to contact the author:
Rachel Crosby
c/o Orange Leaf on Midnight Snow
13 Haromar Heath Road
Harwich, MA 02645
bemindful22@comcast.net
https://risingtidewriters.jimdo.com/rachel-crosby/

Cover designs by Rachel Crosby

Acknowledgements

I must first acknowledge the unwavering support and guidance given me by the **Rising Tide Writers Group** of Harwich, MA. By observing the dedication and drive of the members and by reading and listening to their wonderful weekly works submitted to the group for critique, I found the courage to try and write this novel. For more about the Rising Tide Writers, please visit their website: https://risingtidewriters.jimdo.com/

Of the many members of the Rising Tide Writers, several have been unfailing in their support, encouragement (and criticism). They are: Joe Cromarty, Lee Doty, Marge Frith, Barbara Leedom, Elizabeth Moisan, Sebastian Mudry, Bill Richmond, Ingrid Stabins, Bob Surrette, and Francoise Webb.

I also want to acknowledge the **friends** who have consistently inquired after the novel's progress and have even read selected chapters. Thank you to Rhoda Auerbach, Eric Ekstrom, Sandy Fay, Flo Ann Femling, Sue Fleming Gerry Kinahan, Cindy Mather and Dorothy Strauss.

Finally, a huge shout of appreciation goes to my **Beta Readers**, who found all the typos, missing words, grammatical errors, etc. and also provided insight into how to improve the content of the novel and make it ready for publication:

This book is dedicated to my sister Candace, who has always been there for me in so many ways. She is truly a part of me.

Pertinent Quotes

The first draft of the novel had a quote at the start of each chapter which, while editing, seemed a bit much. So I deleted them. A few of the best were too good to leave behind.

"The soul should always stand ajar, ready to welcome the ecstatic experience." — Emily Dickinson

"Adopt the pace of nature; her secret is patience. Sometimes you don't need the things you 'need' to enjoy the simple things, quiet times, friends, family." - Amish proverb

"It is easier to guard a sack full of fleas than a girl in love." - Jewish Proverb

"Life is a series of natural and spontaneous changes. Don't resist them - that only creates sorrow. Let reality be reality. Let things flow naturally forward in whatever way they like." - Lao Tzu

"If I weren't doing what I'm doing today... I'd be traveling around the world on the back of a motorcycle." - Donna Karan

Table of Contents

Chapter One

High school English teacher Faye Bloomberg despised mandatory standardized school tests. ~~And Her attitude was extra negative when~~ proctoring such a test on a warm and sunny Friday afternoon in late May on Cape Cod. Despite a school-wide rehab a decade previous, the classroom looked much the ~~way it had~~ when ~~Faye had been~~ a student ~~here~~. Some days, standing in front of the "smart board" and behind her streamlined, mostly plastic, "teacher's module," ~~she~~ swore she could still smell the chalk dust and hear the thwack of Mrs. Cooke's wooden pointer on her massive oak desk. Faye often wondered what ~~had~~ happened to that worthy piece of pedantic furniture.

On normal school days Faye's classroom hummed with the suppressed excitement only a group of restless teenagers could generate. But today the mood was dampened by widespread anxiety and desperation. The 10th graders, ~~most of them 15 or barely 16~~, were sweating, fidgeting, chewing their pencils and muttering to themselves, while sneaking peeks through the windows at the glow of spring a few tantalizing yards away. Faye had opened the room's windows and the bird calls and bee buzzes wafted in, along with the delicious scent of new growth, all announcing that, after a typical wet Cape Cod spring, nature was finally in labor to birth summer.

The majority of the exam takers were pressured by the test time limit and glared at the clock every couple of minutes. A few sat motionless, overwhelmed by the number and complexity of the ~~test~~ questions, staring at an answer sheet filled with endless rows of empty little circles.

Faye scanned the room to provide at least the illusion she was doing her job as proctor. Her gaze stopped at Ariella Cardona, sitting as usual at the end of the front row next to the windows. What an interesting, but strange girl, Faye thought, not for the first time. Ariella, often referred to in the teacher's lounge as "The Dreamer," wasn't showing any signs of anxiety nor any real interest in the test. She wasn't ignoring the questions, because every two minutes or so she bent over the exam booklet for fifteen seconds and made a mark on the answer sheet. Then she'd raise her head and gaze out the window, her hands folded together on the desk, her legs crossed just so at the ankles. Faye often wondered if the girl was stoned.

Ariella was in one of Faye's 10th grade English Composition and Literature classes and had attracted everyone's attention when she'd arrived as a new transfer in September. Every day Ariella wore vintage, black patent leather Mary Jane shoes with white ankle socks. Unlike the other girls, she always wore an ironed dress or blouse and skirt. And the skirt was invariably full and bell-like and fell below her knees. Faye had even caught a glimpse of petticoats. Ariella's tops were simple, usually a solid pastel color, often with a Peter Pan collar and cap sleeves. When the weather was cold, Ariella added a demure white cardigan which she draped over her shoulders. She was tall for her age, which also made her stand out. Faye was 5 feet 8 inches and Ariella was just an inch shorter.

After her astonishing green eyes, Ariella's thick, long, reddish-blonde tresses were her best feature. Her hair was always neat, either up in a complicated chignon or in two long, thick braids, often tied off with neon-colored electrical wire. The jewelry pieces she wore were small and delicate, with the exception of a gold ring set with a large green stone and worn on the third finger of her left hand. But her makeup was unexpected. She used startling near-white foundation, reminiscent of Kabuki actors, with poppy red clownish rouge spots on her cheeks, and bright pink or purple on her lips. Small beauty marks made with black eyeliner appeared above both corners of her mouth, and, on her lids, pastel colors coordinated with her blouse or dress. She reminded Faye of a china doll, updated to the 21st century.

Faye knew Ariella wasn't stupid because the homework she turned in was well-written and thoughtful, if a bit predictable. In fact, the girl wrote as if she were trying to sound like an ordinary, smart 10th grader. Plus, she always behaved in class and was responsive when called upon, never seemed to be bummed or angry and often had a quirky, enigmatic smile on her lips. And

Ariella liked Emily Dickinson and quoted the poet in her essays. This endeared the girl to Faye, ~~as she herself was~~ who was also a Fan of Emily D. ~~D.~~

Faye knew she wasn't alone in singling Ariella out. Both boys and girls were always sneaking glances and even staring, but Ariella never took notice. She did none of the in-class primping, flirting or gossiping which preoccupied many of the other girls. Faye couldn't tell if Ariella had a boyfriend or even a best friend. Like the teachers, students also had nicknames for Ariella. "Spooky Kabuki" was almost funny and "Airy Fairy" wasn't as vicious as it sounded because the girl *was* ethereal. However, a 10th grade boy had written a suggestive song called "Let Me Tell Ya, 'Bout My Girl Ariella." The video of him playing the guitar and singing the song on YouTube was the talk of the school for a week. The lyrics' teasing and sexual innuendos were softened by the song's last lines:

"Ariella, Ariella, don' want to hem and haw,

Got's ta tell ya, Ariella, yeah, I really love ya."

But Ariella never complained about the video to anyone in authority and took no less or more interest in the boy. And the expected outraged phone call from her parents didn't happen, so the gossip and speculation was allowed to run its course. If anything, Ariella seemed pleased by the extra attention she got.

Faye understood while the students made fun of Ariella, they also granted her minor celebrity status. Her peers recognized she was making a statement, even if they didn't understand what it was. So, having Ariella at your cafeteria lunch table was a social plus, like owning the latest cell phone. In a peculiar way, the girl was popular, never in the center but never excluded. She seemed to float along, part of the action, but remained at the edge of the jostling herd.

Faye envied Ariella, because in high school she had been a tall and geeky Plain Jane Nobody who kept her head down in the halls and hugged books to her chest. She actually had had a nice figure (and still did, plus 10 pounds) but, like Ariella, had hidden her curves beneath clothes. Her hair, black and curly, gave her a gypsy look when unbound, but in high school she had minimized its allure by pinning it back severely. And her mouth, when it wasn't pursed into a tight line, was full and sensuous.

Faye hadn't been repulsed by boys, but got tense and silent when one tried to talk to her. Her scalp would start to tingle, her facial muscles would tighten and her hands became ice cold. She'd hunch her shoulders to make herself shorter and looked at anything but the boy. Her mind would fill with a paralyzing blankness through which her thoughts darted randomly or not at all. If she tried to force herself to speak, she wound up stammering, so she generally just walked away without speaking. The boys, and even the girls, thought she was rude and stuck-up.

By the time Faye was a sophomore in college and desperate for a social life, she went to a therapist and was told her freezing-up was caused by an unconscious fear she was going to be compared to her four-years older sister Clara, who had cut a wide swath through the high school. Clara had been super popular, was class valedictorian, editor of the school paper, captain of the soccer and tennis teams, dated only the smartest, most athletic, gorgeous boys and had the coolest girlfriends. Clara had graduated the June before Faye started 9th grade and throughout Faye's entire time in high school, teachers and students repeatedly asked after Clara.

Even now, at age 36, despite various coping mechanisms, Faye could still go into stasis and be unable to talk or, at best, manage a few spastic bursts of words when she was in an intimidating situation. She likened the phenomenon to the instinctive reaction of some animals to play dead when in the clutches of a predator.

Faye dragged her attention back to the classroom and turned to see Ariella, who had a small smile bowing her pink lips, staring at her. Faye immediately glanced away and went back to scanning the other exam takers, ostensibly to watch for cheaters. She didn't care if the kids shared a few answers and if she noticed small signs of suspicious behavior she tried to ignore them. Or, if the cheating was blatant, she glared at the offending students until their faces got red and they stared down at their test papers.

Faye was deeply resentful of the assumptions behind the standardized tests, assumptions based upon the belief that the sole goal of public education was to produce graduates equipped with skills needed to meet the "demands of the modern workplace." That phrase irritated her no end, implying the school was little more than a factory designed to turn out skilled workers whose only aim in life was to be functional, productive and "successful." Successful at what? Fitting into some corporate slot where they got treated like a proverbial cog in the machine? What about their hearts and feelings? What about their appreciation for beauty and nature? What about learning what it is to lead a good life and about philosophy and ethics? What about learning to read for enjoyment and insight?" Most of her colleagues ignored her on this issue.

Faye fought back by being lenient when proctoring the exams. Not only did she not prosecute students she spotted cheating, she also bent the rules in how she answered their questions. When the situation indicated, she used the Socratic method to focus their thinking. She would lean down, get close to the student's ear and began whispering questions designed to nudge them toward the correct answer.

Today was no different and, as the exam time reached the halfway point, raised hands appeared like long stemmed flowers blossoming all over the room. Faye was kept on her feet, all the while delighting in the thrill of her secret rebellion. As she sat down after one successful "proctor response," she saw a pale, slender arm, with its hand at an artful angle, go up. It was Ariella, which was unusual, because in English Lit class she almost never asked a question. Faye hurried over to Ariella's desk, being careful to put herself between the girl and the rest of the students.

She leaned down and whispered, "Yes, Ariella, how can I help you?"

Ariella looked up with eyes so green Faye had often thought they might be contact lenses, though she was pretty sure the gold flecks in the girl's irises couldn't be faked. Faye had a sudden vision of how she might look with eyes as green as Ariella's. Her own were a muddy brownish hazel. Would life be better, different, more exciting with green eyes?

"I lost my pencil," Ariella said at normal volume. Faye twitched as if stuck with a thorn and whispered, "Oh, you did?"

Ariella continued at ordinary volume, "Yes," and her unreadable smile curled her lips. She waved the hand with the large green stone ring in Faye's direction as if she was at a loss about where the pencil had gone.

"Please try to whisper, dear, so as to not disturb the others," Faye managed to say and realized she felt a little lightheaded. She reminded herself to eat the lunch she had packed.

"They can't hear me," said Ariella. In fact, Faye saw none of the students were looking their way.

"Huh!" Faye tried to focus. "Where's your pencil then?"

"I don't know, it just vanished."

"Well, it can't have 'just vanished'." Teenage girls can be so dramatic, Faye thought. "It must be somewhere. Did you drop it? Did it roll away? Didn't you bring another one?"

"No, I only had one and I don't know where it went. I need your help to find it." Ariella fluttered her left hand again.

Faye, having bent down to whisper, felt her face go hot. Then there was a twang in her head and she put her hand over her mouth to stifle a gasp, sensing a shift of something important, like a glacier calving from an ice shelf. She forced herself to look away from Ariella and, glancing to the side and down, saw a bit of yellow beneath the nearby baseboard heater. Without thinking, she got down on her hands and knees, crawled over and coaxed out a dusty pencil with teeth marks all along its stubby length. She straightened, holding up the pencil as if it were a prize and exclaimed, "Here it is! It was right here! I found it!"

Now the students did turn their way but, ignoring their curious looks, Faye allowed a big, sappy grin to capture her face. She beamed at Ariella and repeated, "I found it!"

"That's not my pencil."

Faye frowned. Surely this had to be the pencil. "Well, I'm afraid it must suffice, my dear," she said, proud in an odd way of how deliberate and normal she sounded, despite the squirrelly sensation in her head. She was aware she and Ariella now had the full attention of the other students. "Time is running out."

"I don't think it will work." Faye studied the pencil and realized the point was broken. Her mind went blank like an actor's who had forgotten her lines.

Finally, Ariella shrugged and said, "Can I at least sharpen it?"

Faye clutched the pencil tight. "No, no, I should do that." Faye watched herself, as if from a distance, walk to her desk and, her hand wavering, stick the pencil into the electric sharpener. The buzz from the sharpener was sudden and sharp and pop! Faye's dizziness left. She pulled the pencil out and examined its point with exaggerated care, before walking back and handing it to Ariella with what she hoped was confidence.

"Everything okay now?" Faye understood she was also asking herself the question.

Ariella examined the pencil and seemed in turn fascinated. "I guess so."

Faye marched back to her desk module, sat down with a bump and yanked her lunch bag from her purse on the floor. She unwrapped the pita bread sandwich of organic humus, lettuce and tomato and devoured it in quick bites, feeling deserving and righteous, but also still a bit quivery. What was it about that girl? Having eaten the sandwich, she felt not energized but exhausted like she did after one of her infrequent gym workouts. She struggled against the need to put her head down on the desk. Checking the time, she saw an hour and a quarter remained before she had to call a halt to the exam. Not long at all, surely she could hang in there. She leaned back in her ergonomic desk chair and her eyes closed. *I'll just rest for a moment. . .*

Chapter Two

"Ms Bloomberg?" Faye heard a distant voice. "Ms Bloomberg?" With effort Faye opened her eyes and knew she had dozed off. She searched out the wall clock. Oh no! She had been out for ten minutes. She wondered how many students had noticed her sleeping. Had she snored? She smiled to herself. Well, if they took advantage and did some real cheating, so what?

"Ms Bloomberg?" Faye realized the voice was right next to her. She turned and saw Ariella looking down at her. Faye sat up and managed to ask in her teacher voice, "Yes, Ariella, what is it?" She ignored the fact the girl was supposed to stay in her seat unless given permission.

"I need to go to the bathroom."

"Okay, let's get the hall monitor to take you." Faye stood, but avoided looking directly at Ariella.

"I don't feel well. Can you take me?"

At this, Faye did face Ariella. For once, the girl wasn't smiling and her eyes were flat and expressionless. Even under her pale makeup, her face was drawn and she was clutching hard at her backpack. When Faye tried to look closer, the girl dropped her head, making her braids fall forward like thick tentacles. Faye also looked down and started. Was blood oozing down Ariella's leg? Was blood staining the top of Ariella's white sock?

Faye gently took the girl by the arm and guided her toward the door. Opening it with a jerk, she propelled Ariella ahead of her. Faye stuck her head into the hallway, careful to keep most of her body in the classroom, not wanting the other students to think she was going to leave them unattended, not after nodding off. She called to the monitor at the next corridor intersection, "Sarah! Can you watch my room for a few minutes? I need to escort this young lady to the restroom."

Ariella was quiet as they walked side-by-side through the halls. When they entered the bathroom, she dropped her backpack into a sink and began rummaging through it. She pulled out a small white jar.

"What's that?" Faye asked.

"It's some healing cream of my mother's."

"May I please see it?" Faye turned the jar over in her hands. It appeared to be a recycled face cream container, with the original label mostly scraped off. Someone had scrawled "Healing" on it with a black magic marker. She unscrewed the lid and saw the jar was half-full of a greenish jelly with leaf fragments and other planty bits mixed in. Its scent was earthy but not offensive. It reminded Faye of walks in the deep woods on misty mornings. She had moment of longing for something ineffable and started to drift like she had in the classroom. Struggling to maintain composure, Faye said, "Your mom makes this stuff?" and gave the jar back. Ariella nodded and turned toward the stalls.

"Wait, don't you need a tampon or pad?"

Ariella stopped with her back to Faye and said, "I don't have my period," and reached for the stall door.

"Hold on," Faye said with more emphasis. "Then you need to tell me why blood is running down your leg and into your sock. If that's not from your period, where's it coming from?"

Without turning around, Ariella reached behind her and lifted the hem of her dress, exposing the backs of her thighs and the long red welts crisscrossing them. Most of the welts had scabbed over but a few were leaking blood. Blood that had dribbled down Ariella's leg and stained her sock.

Faye stared in disbelief. Somebody had whipped or cut Ariella! She tried to say something, to ask who, what and why, but the girl let her dress fall back into place, went into the stall and locked the door. Faye spun around, wondering if anyone had overheard them. Had she violated the girl's privacy? No, a quick glance showed no feet under the other stall doors.

She couldn't ignore this. She had a responsibility to . . . . to what? Should she report a possible child abuse incident or try to talk to the girl first? She caught her reflection in the mirror above one of the sinks and saw a tense, not-young, woman whose hair was frizzed out, blouse rumpled, and with some dried sleep drool at the corner of her mouth. *These kids must think I'm a total ditz, nodding off during the test. But, what else is new? What's more important is what I do now about Ariella.* She pulled her hair back and secured it with a hair band, the fluorescent light highlighting a few new gray hairs. She straightened and tucked in her blouse and wiped the gunk from the corner of her mouth.

Ariella emerged from the stall and the pain was gone from her face. I gotta try that cream, thought Faye, then mentally slapped herself upside the head. *Focus, Faye, focus!* Ariella picked up her backpack and dropped the jar and her bloody socks into it. She started for the bathroom door.

"Wait a minute, Ariella, we need to talk about what's going on with you. I need to know how those . . . ", Faye searched for the right word, "wounds on your legs got there."

Ariella gave Faye an unreadable look. She frowned, but then she rolled her green eyes and said, "Right now?"

"No, not right now. You need to get back to the test. Later, maybe." Faye paused, thinking it was Friday and everyone was about to flee the school once the test was over. Could she make the girl stay and wait until all the exams were turned in and she had completed all the proctor paperwork? No, that would be awkward, plus Ariella might have a bus to catch home.

"Is there any way we can talk over the weekend? Maybe on the phone?"

Unexpectedly, Ariella dropped into a perfect curtsy, holding the her dress out to the sides so she looked like a big, beautiful flower. "Sure!"

They pulled out their phones and typed in each other's numbers. Faye was startled to see Ariella didn't own some big-screen smart phone but rather a much older flip-open model with duct tape across the back, apparently to hold in the battery.

Faye was pleased, but not surprised, at Ariella's quick agreement to talk on the phone. Faye had, over the years, cultivated a reputation of being a teacher the kids could come to with their problems. Ariella no doubt knew Ms Bloomberg was someone safe and easy to talk to, someone who could keep a secret.

After they returned to the classroom, Ariella went directly to her desk and sat down without any apparent discomfort. Faye thanked the hall monitor and resumed her place at her teacher's module. The clock showed only 55 minutes of exam time remained. A boy in the back was waving his hand at her. Three minutes later, after whispering several leading questions into his ear and seeing a light go on in his eyes, she straightened up and saw Ariella drop her exam papers on the teacher's module's desk and head for the door.

"Ariella!" she exclaimed without thinking. The girl glanced back, flashed her brilliant smile and held her hand to her ear with the thumb and little finger extended. *"Call me,"* she mouthed and slipped out the door. Faye hustled up to the desk and picked up Ariella's papers. They were all there, but when she took a closer look she saw almost half of the multiple-choice questions had not been answered. Shocked, she turned toward the classroom door, feeling a strong impulse to run after the girl. She took one step and stopped. Several students had their heads up, watching her with quizzical expressions.

Okay! This has to end! Ariella's test still in her hand Faye sat down hard in her chair. She was trembling with the need to do something, anything. But what? Ariella was gone, no way to go after her. She glowered at all the blank, empty boxes. The test was an abomination, but Ariella was going to fail it and might not get a normal diploma. Faye took deep breaths, closed her eyes, and tried to put herself in the quiet place she often reached when she meditated. She hoped the kids wouldn't think she had fallen asleep again. All that had happened in the last 45 minutes skittered through her mind in a herky-jerky movie – flashes of brilliant, emerald green eyes, a yellow, tooth-marked and dusty pencil, the dizzy disorientation, blood staining a white sock, ugly red stripes on the back of tender, white thighs, an inscrutable smile which both asked a question and offered an answer, the blank, blank answer sheet, and the buzz of the pencil sharpener.

Faye's eyes leapt open and she grabbed a pencil, centered the girl's answer sheet in front of her, and began to fill in the multiple-choice circles of the unanswered questions. Her movements were quick, as she made random choices from the five lettered circles per question. She quickly fell into a rhythm. On and on she went until every last question had a circle filled in. When she stopped there were still 30 minutes exam time left. She sat back, her heart thumping. *Well, Ariella might have done that herself. Just random choices. Surely no harm in that.* By the time the last minute ticked off, Faye had calmed down.

"Time! Please close your booklets and put down your pencils," she called out in a clear, firm voice. "Pack up your papers and form a line in front of my desk." She paused, then said, "Good luck to you all!"

When the classroom was finally empty of students, Faye slumped. *What did I do? Am I nuts to mess with Ariella's exam? I could so be fired for this.* She reminded herself how much she hated these tests and her nostrils flared. Screw it! She had done it on principle, not because she particularly cared about Ariella. One small action, one small gesture - it might not make a difference in the big picture, but it mattered to Faye. Gathering the papers into a neat stack, she again rationalized that, in reality, the answers she had filled in at random could, at best, only add a few points to Ariella's score.

Faye stood, straightened her spine, picked up her bag and the papers and strode into the hall. Locking the classroom door behind her, she marched toward the Administration wing to log in the exams.

Chapter Three

Faye had majored in English Literature at Brown University where, by her own admission, she had been a mediocre student. After she struggled to a Master's degree, she concluded she was only interested in reading and immersing herself in works of fiction. She wasn't motivated to discuss themes, plot lines or the author's hidden meanings. All she asked for was a good story capable of taking her away from her ordinary life. Her especial passions were for fantasy/alternative reality novels and romantic comedies.

Faye's love of fiction and fantasy began when she met a girl in 6th grade after Faye's parents moved the family from Boston to the Cape. Wanda Eldridge was a true Cape Codder, having the requisite double set of grandparents buried on the peninsula. She was, like most of the other Cape-born kids, scornful of "washashores" like Faye. Though Wanda was a de-facto member of the native kids' clique, she wasn't popular, mostly because she was a tomboy and tended to be bossy. And her need to go on about magic and dragons, strange realms and other dimensions marginalized her further. Wanda saw Faye as a potential fellow fantasy nerd. Things clicked between the two girls and, within a few months, they were inseparable.

Wanda took Faye to quiet, isolated beaches where they waded through tidal marshes as small fish darted and hermit crabs skittered away. They kayaked in the tangles of small rivers and streams which wound through wetlands and ponds populated by herons, frogs, turtles, fish and dragonflies. When it was hot enough, they would swim naked. And occasionally, when saturated with idyll, they lay on the sandy bank of a pond and kissed, just for fun, and called each other fantasy names of endearment, before dozing entwined under the summer sun.

They spent hours discussing the merits of various kinds of unicorns and which was worse: getting captured by a troll or an ogre. They also debated what to name their personal dragons (of course, they each had one) and what their enchanted powers were. And they argued over whether they could ever be enticed to break their white magic vows and use black spells on a particularly nasty person - Faye said she never could and Wanda said she absolutely would.

As an adult, Faye felt no embarrassment about maintaining her love of fantasy and romance. In fact, she often livened things up by pretending she was a character from one of the novels to point where their mannerisms and way of talking leaked out into her conversations. More importantly, she could often deflect a freeze up by shifting into a fantasy persona. As time passed, she developed a repeating cast of characters, such as the Posh Brit, the Southern Belle, the Fairy Princess and the Cowgirl.

After graduate school, Faye had moved to Boston intending to find a position as an assistant editor at one of the local publishing houses, but her just average transcript and her tendency become monosyllabic or shift into one of her personas in the middle of an interview led to zero job offers. Desperate, she took a job as a sales clerk in a major chain bookstore, primarily because it provided her ample opportunities to read. Two years drifted by and no other literary job opportunities materialized.

She did endure several tepid affairs with bookish men she met in the store. Men who, thankfully, enjoyed sitting around reading as much as they did having sex. One of these men, Stanley, was also into role-playing. With him, she went to several RPG Conventions to participate in cosplay, to dress up as a character from a game, book, TV show or film. Behind a mask or elaborate make-up, Faye was free of her social phobias. But Stanley moved to the West Coast and without him she hadn't the courage to cosplay by herself.

Her mother, Rhoda, who had continued teaching math in the same high school Faye and Clara had attended, suggested, with frequent use of the phrase "it's important to be realistic," Faye try teaching. At first Faye ignored her mother, if only because she hated the idea of having to be realistic. She did, however, understand she needed to start some sort of a "career" or risk sinking further into the family role of littler, and lesser, sister. Of course, Clara, with her successful practice as a Doctor of Internal Medicine, had continued as the family star. She had married another doctor and already had two children, which thrilled both pairs of grandparents. After another six months at the bookstore Faye gave in to Rhoda, especially as she imagined part of an English teacher's job would be to read a lot.

Because Faye had a Master's degree all she had to do was pass a competency exam to qualify for a teaching license. A month later, Rhoda told her of an opening for an English teacher at the high school where she was teaching. The job interview quickly became cozy and friendly once the two women administrators realized Rhoda was Faye's mom. And Faye didn't freeze up, but chatted with the women as if they were old friends. She felt an unexpected sense of belonging which was both welcome and confining.

Being a high school English teacher didn't compare to Clara's career, but it did provide Faye focus and purpose. Also, it provided her a real income – magnificent compared to what she had been making as a bookstore clerk. And she found she liked teaching. Not only was she able to offer literary knowledge to young minds, but she had a non-fantasy role of importance and authority in the same school where she had been invisible as a student. She could look the most beautiful, slender girls in the eye as she talked about books. And she could converse easily with the handsome, popular boys.

Faye lived with her parents for her first two years of teaching, but then her father died and her mother decided to retire and downsize to a one-bedroom condo in a senior living complex. So Faye, 30 and single, took the plunge and bought a small two-bedroom Cape in a woodsy development where the houses were on good-sized lots, yet near enough for neighbors to say 'hi' when going to the mail box. A year later she met rakishly handsome Drake Hershfeld, another Cape Cod teacher (of Social Studies) at a teacher's conference. To Faye's amazement, their attraction was mutual and they became a couple.

She and Drake had talked marriage and children, but those discussions, while civil enough, never went anywhere. Drake always suggested they "think on it." Five years later, at 36, Faye struggled to accept she might never be a mother. But, as she put it, "the alarm on my biological clock appears to be broken." Instead of obsessing about having children, she devoted herself to becoming the best possible teacher and advisor to her students. When asked by her friends about motherhood, she said being with teenagers five days a week gave her all the youthful sparkle she could handle.

Chapter Four

When Faye got home after the exam on Friday, she thought to call Ariella but instead flopped onto the couch and fell asleep. At 6:30 she awakened to the sound of her front door opening. Someone walked toward the couch. Crap! She had totally forgotten Drake was coming over. And she was supposed to make dinner. She struggled to her feet and, seeing the question in Drake's eyes, went to him and wrapped her arms around him in part embrace and part leaning-in for support.

Drake was tall and lean as befit a long distance runner. He had been a star cross-country racer in high school and college. And he was so handsome. His prominent nose, broken in a lacrosse pick-up game, gave his face a pleasing asymmetry. Like Faye, his lips were full and sensuous, and he had dark, almost onyx eyes, which, combined with his longish black hair and daily five-o'clock shadow, made him look like a sophisticated gangster, though his rimless glasses added a scholarly touch. She teased him often, saying he had missed his calling, he was male model quality and the last place he belonged was in a Social Studies classroom.

They made an attractive couple. They were both taller than average, he was 6' 2" and she was 5' 8" and they both had curly, black, untamable hair and striking features. And Faye's tendency to slight plumpness contrasted well with Drake's spare frame. People always told them their children would be both beautiful and intelligent. At this, they would turn, lock eyes on each other and smile. Faye was, however, often left confused and couldn't say for sure at what she and Drake were smiling.

The fact they were both Jewish was more coincidence than deliberate choice. They both were secular in their approach to their faith, observing some of the holy days, but viewing them more as opportunities to visit their respective families. Luckily, neither Faye's mother nor Drake's parents (who lived close to Boston) ever nagged about grandchildren or marriage. Despite the fact their relationship hadn't advanced to any definite commitment,

Faye felt she was lucky to be with Drake. Certainly, he was the most attractive man she had ever dated. And he was certainly her best lover. Drake had transformed sex for her from a generally pleasant experience into a stimulating and exciting thrill ride.

Over take-out Chinese, she told him about her weird time with Ariella, only leaving out the part where she had filled in the blanks on the girl's answer sheet.

"You've got to report what you saw! It could be evidence of abuse!" Drake exclaimed. "No matter how she got those 'wounds,' as you call them, this needs official attention. If you don't do something, you're putting yourself at risk."

Faye gazed at Drake. For a gangster look-alike hot lover, sometimes he could be so damn scrupulous, practical and self-righteous. "What if they were self-inflicted?" she countered. "What if I raise a big outcry and it turns out to be some sort of teenage joke? It's possible they're fake! I didn't get right up close and examine them, you know. And Ariella certainly seemed pretty blasé about them, though she was definitely in pain. What if I wind up embarrassing myself and her and lose her trust completely?"

Drake rolled his eyes as if she had suggested some new, exotic sexual fantasy which involved him dressing in a pirate costume and singing a sea chanty. "Faye," he said after a long pause, "No matter what, you can't ignore this. And I don't think you should take this on by yourself. You're an English teacher, not a therapist, not a guidance counselor and not a mother. Turn this over to the professionals and be done with it."

Faye felt a familiar surge of frustration. Was he saying she couldn't handle this situation? Why couldn't she, a teacher with years of experience, deal with a teenage girl with some scratches on her legs? Why did Drake always humor or devalue her? Why was she being shoved away from the action like some clumsy schmo? She felt her face flush and a hint of the day's earlier dizziness returned. She sat forward to steady herself and saw Drake flinch away. He knew she had a temper.

"I think you may be overreacting, Drake," Faye said, in what she hoped was a rational and competent tone. "I think the best idea is for me to talk to Ariella, find out what's going on and then decide if the situation warrants more extreme measures. How will it look if this all turns out to be a big joke or a hoax? I'll be the laughing stock of not only the student body, but the other teachers and administration as well."

Drake, who prided himself on being methodical and organized and always, always following the rules, took his time answering. He seemed to be looking at her breasts as he thought, a characteristic Faye found endearing. All of a sudden, she was horny, feeling a strong twinge in the nether regions, so to speak. She smiled. She liked the phrase "nether regions."

She saw Drake's face relax and knew he'd realized her mood had changed. She also knew he was thinking he might ease his way through this issue without appearing to back down. The plan had been for him to stay overnight and an unpleasant squabble could nix that. Drake was much the pragmatist. And, if she was honest, she wanted him to stay.

"Okay," he said, as if granting permission, "What you're saying makes some sense. You should definitely get more facts before making this into a big deal. But promise me if you discover Ariella is being abused, you'll report it?"

"Well, thank you Drake, for that lukewarm endorsement. And, of course, I'll make a report if it's necessary and when the time is right," Faye gave him a under-the-eyelashes look and watched the spark of comprehension grow in his eyes. "I'd love to continue this discussion but, honestly, it's been a long day and I think I'm ready for bed." She stretched and her smile turned lascivious and her twinge became a twang. "Maybe we can continue communicating in another venue? Maybe we could engage in a heated discussion in the bedroom? Maybe I could convince you to change your endorsement from lukewarm to boiling hot?" Faye's passion for the language of bodice-rippers often surfaced when she was trying to be seductive. Without saying another word, Drake grinned like a maniac, jumped to his feet, grabbed Faye's outstretched hand and led her to the bedroom.

Faye's disorientation resurfaced while they were in the throes of lovemaking, but it wasn't a bad thing. As her sense of self started to drift, she felt a loss of control which wasn't scary, but liberating. She fantasized herself as an Earth Mother from whom new spring growth was emerging. The growth brought with it greater confidence and a willingness to take risks. She felt anything was possible, as if she had tapped into a magic, wild energy. Reckless power surged and her hip thrusts became more enthusiastic, more urgent, more demanding. She heard herself grunting loudly and was reminded of some tennis players who cried out each time they hit the ball. Dragging her fingernails across Drake's back and butt, she wanted to rip off his skin and devour him. And Drake, as accustomed as he was to Faye's quirks, seemed surprised at her intensity. But, he rallied and soon lost himself in the storm she was stirring up. For endless minutes, they rode and rode and rode each other until oblivion washed them into nothingness.

Much later, Drake went to shower while Faye lay on her side in bed, her hair splayed out. I'm stunned, she thought, her eyes half-closed and unfocused. Absolutely stunned. As if I've been tased but with pleasure, not pain.

Just then Drake came out of the bathroom with an odd smile on his face. "I have a clue as to how Ariella got her scratches," he said and turned to show his back to Faye. She gaped when she saw the multiple parallel, long and vivid red welts that striped Drake's back from neck to buttocks. One was even leaking a runnel of blood which had reached his thigh and was meandering toward the floor.

"Wh . . . what," she stammered. "What happened?"

Drake turned around and laughed at the expression on her face. "You mean you don't know your own artwork? Don't you recognize the precision of the slanting red parallels, so symbolic of the ethos of your creative work, mixing organic material – in this case flesh and blood – with the precise geometry of straight lines?"

Faye sat up fast and tried to speak but nothing came out.

Grinning, Drake went on, "And, of course, your choice of tools and canvas are so archetypical! Simple fingernails applied vigorously to a nice blank human back! A more violent and painful variation on finger-painting." She continued to gawk at him. "We should get it photographed before it starts to fade, don't you think? Do you want to sign it?"

"Fingernails!," Faye finally got it and examined her hands, giving a gasp in horror at the dried blood on and under her nails. "I did that? Really?" She fell back on the bed, her hands over her mouth.

"Don't worry, darling, it will heal," Drake said and turned toward the bath, "and I'll take care of the first aid. And the photos," he continued with an airy wave over his shoulder, stopping to pick up his camera phone. "You just relax and contemplate your new ability to create passionate, sexual art. Just warn me next time I'm the chosen canvas."

Chapter Five

In the morning, Drake did more teasing and threatened to post photos of his lacerated back to his Facebook page.

"Go right ahead," Faye sniffed. "It will only add to my wild woman reputation. There will be candidate lovers lined up in the driveway!"

Drake took her into his arms and gave her a kiss that made her knees go wobbly. She threw her arms around him and he cried out, "Ow! My back! No more, no more!" and he pulled away as if in extreme pain.

Her laugh was loud and unrestrained in a way that was new to her. "Ha! If you can't take the heat, get out of the kitchen," she said, pushing him in the chest. She saw a telltale glint in Drake's eyes and, instead of thinking of all the chores she had planned to do, she glinted right back at him.

"I've got a tennis match in 45 minutes . . ."

"Plenty of time!" the new Faye said.

If anything, their lovemaking was even better this time, despite the fact Faye had to restrain herself from raking his back again. At one point, when she lost control and put her arms around him, he winced and grabbed her hands and pinned them over her head. Being even a little restricted kicked Faye into overdrive and she bucked and thrashed like a wild mare being ridden for the first time.

Half an hour later, Drake got unsteadily out of bed, fumbled into shorts and T-shirt, then bent over to kiss her tenderly. "Later, wild woman," he said and tottered out the door.

Faye didn't get up for another hour. Her mind and body were so suffused with pleasure and the zing of her new intensity, she just wanted to savor, savor, savor it for as long as possible. She toyed with the idea she could make a living having sex with Drake. Why work when such stunning pleasure was readily available? And being a porn star, with Drake as her partner, wouldn't be at all bad.

Finally she began thinking about the rest of the day. She had housework, some gardening to do and, of course, she would call Ariella. Ariella. An image of the girl floated in front of her, wearing her odd clothes and with her unique smile bright in her pale face. Did the weirdness with Ariella Friday afternoon have anything to do with Faye's unprecedented explosions of sexual energy? She had felt odd around the girl but that didn't mean there was a connection, did it?

She decided to meditate before she did anything else. The morning was warm and bright, so she brought her cushion, a rug for her knees, a timer, and a cup of coffee out onto the back deck. She hoped Yellowfoot, the Squirrel of the Future, might show up. Yellowfoot had caught her attention months before because he, unlike the other squirrels, who didn't come within four feet of her even when she had peanuts in her hand, bounded toward her as if they had been best friends for years. If she was indoors, he leapt onto the sliding door screen and displayed his furry tummy. Hanging by his back feet on the screen, he grabbed not one, but two peanuts, from her hand and somehow stuffed them both in his mouth. Yellowfoot was the Squirrel of the Future, clearly possessing genetic traits which made him smarter, stronger and faster. He was winning the struggle to survive, to be the fittest and to successfully mate, over and over again.

She sat cross-legged facing more or less toward the east, so the morning sun flickered over her as it passed through the trees. A light breeze tickled the back of her neck and she settled with a sigh into her meditation. At first she just focused on all that was happening in her immediate bubble of awareness: the calls of the birds, the distant hum of a lawnmower, children laughing a few backyards away, the black ant which was meticulously exploring the nearby rhododendron leaves, the slight stiffness in her left knee and that chronic hitch in left shoulder. And, of course, the contented purr in her nether regions.

Suddenly Faye imagined Yellowfoot mating, rutting away in some treetop nest, his willing female partner and mother of many offspring squealing in delight as he thrust and thrust and thrust into her. Faye saw the leaves of the tree around the nest waving in time to Yellowfoot's rhythm, she felt the sun on his back, she felt them start to climax. Faye began to pant. It was so very realistic! The passion and unbridled lust she had felt with Drake returned and she gasped as shiver after shiver ran up and down her spine, almost like she was orgasming again. *This is all really, really weird. Weird and exciting and I love it! But why now?*

With effort, Faye returned her attention to the present and her body. Her heartbeat slowed and her breathing became steady. She tried to stay in calm observer mode, but wasn't surprised when memories of what happened during the exam yesterday surfaced and swam about. *What am I going to say to Ariella when we talk? How will I be able tell from a phone call whether she's being honest with me? And what should I do if I suspect there is more to know than what her answers reveal?* Faye took a sip of coffee and adjusted her legs to avoid getting a cramp. *Drake is right, this is a delicate situation and I should just tell Ariella's guidance counselor.*

After 30 minutes of sitting, she got creakily to her feet and brought her things inside. She refreshed her coffee, picked up her cell phone, went back out onto the deck and settled into a comfortable chair. Ariella answered on the third ring, which Faye thought was unusual for a teenager at 10 AM on a Saturday morning.

"Ariella, it's Ms Bloomberg," Faye began, "your English teacher," she added even though she knew it wasn't necessary.

"Hey, Ms B, thanks for calling! Great morning, huh?"

"It *is* a beautiful morning!" Faye paused, for some reason she wanted to tell Ariella about her meditation. She brushed the impulse aside and instead got right to it. "Yesterday, in the bathroom, we agreed I would call and we would talk about those injuries to your thighs."

"Oh, they're much better, thank you! They don't hurt at all and you almost can't see them anymore."

"Well, that's great. Glad to hear it. But my reason for calling is to find out how they got on your thighs in the first place." When Ariella didn't say anything, Faye asked, "Did someone hit you with something?"

There was a long silence and Faye realized Ariella had put her hand over the phone's microphone and was talking to someone else.

"Ariella? Can you hear me?"

"Sorry, Ms B, I was talking to my mother."

"Oh! How is she?"

"Just a moment, Ms B, she's still talking."

Faye had met Mrs. Cardona just once at a parent-teacher conference the previous autumn. She remembered the woman as intelligent and adequately concerned about Ariella's education. Mrs. Cardona's appearance, on the other hand, was extraordinary. The words "pagan," "funky," and "non-conformist" had passed through Faye's mind as they talked. Mrs. Cardona's hair was long, luxurious, unbound and reddish-blonde like her daughter's. Faye could easily picture it interlaced with flowers. Her face bore no visible traces of make-up but it's slim, elfin shape and pale, almost translucent skin, high-cheekbones and big green eyes gave it a theatrical impact. Faye wondered if the woman had ever done any acting. Mrs. Cardona wore sensible low heel sandals, but her top and skirt were made of silk or some almost transparent, light cotton or exotic synthetic. Faye had to restrain herself from reaching across the desk to feel the fabric. The garments, which were clearly designer made, seemed to float around Mrs. Cardona's body, and responded to her every movement, so it was difficult for Faye to tell if she was slender or just average. Her vibe, as Faye remembered it, was otherworldly, but with a strong undertone of earthy and musky. Mrs. Cardona had not offered her first name, but Faye had glanced down at Ariella's data profile and saw it was Calista. And the father's name was listed as Alberte Cardona.

"Ms B? Are you still there?" Ariella said, "My mom wants to know if you and she could talk."

This was a surprise. "Why? Is this about the injuries to your thighs?"

"Yeah, maybe. But there are other things she wants to talk about."

"You mean, right now, on the phone?"

"No, she was wondering if you could come over, like tomorrow?"

"To your house?" Faye knew she sounded befuddled, "Tomorrow? Sunday?"

"Yeah."

"Well, let me think for a moment," Faye wanted to get this conversation back on track. "Can you first tell me how your thighs got injured? Or do you want to let your mom tell me?"

"Oh, was nada. We were just playing our parts, you know, acting in a sorta morality play, and it got a little too real. But it was meant to be humorous. Kind of like reality-fantasy TV, I guess. We even had scripts and costumes."

"So, you got whipped or hit during a performance and it was okay with you?" Faye's voice went up in pitch.

"Uh, yeah, sort of. It was no biggee. It was part of the act."

"So why did you get real injuries if you were acting?"

"I was being punished."

"Punished! For what?"

"Well, it was kind of a Cinderella thing. I was like the daughter all the other sisters hated. And I got some power and did something bad and so I had to be punished."

"So another. . . uh, actor hit you with a stick or whip?"

"Actually it was a willow branch and it has mystical significance or something. It was supposed to cleanse me of my evil ways." Ariella giggled. "But, I think both the girl whipping me and I got sort of carried away, if you know what I mean. It hurt but it was okay because it helped me get into character. Everyone afterwards said I was really good."

Faye sighed. "Did anyone else get hurt?"

Ariella paused. "Mmmm. Maybe. It was hard to tell. There were a lot of people on stage."

"Where and when did this reality-fantasy thing take place? Were other students involved?"

Another pause, then Ariella said in an it's-not-important tone, "It was earlier this week, I think Wednesday or Thursday night, and we were out in the Punkhorn near a pond."

The Punkhorn was a large forested and mostly unpopulated tract of land in the Mid-Cape area containing lots of ponds and dirt roads and unnamed trails which wandered like animal paths. It was easy to find privacy in the Punkhorn, but also easy to get lost.

"You don't remember which night it was?" Faye's voice went up again.

"Oh, well, it was the night of the full moon, whenever that was."

"Okay, were there any other students there? Were any adults present?"

"Adults? Yup, my mom was there, but Moira was the leader and she set it all up for us. She provided the costumes and arranged for the music and told us what to do and what to say. We couldn't talk to anyone unless it was part of the script, and because everyone was in costume, I couldn't tell who was who. I'm not sure other kids from school were there. Maybe. I dunno. And we didn't want to do anything that might break the spell for the audience."

"Moira is an adult? And there was an audience?"

"Oh yeah! Moira's way old."

"Does Moira have a last name? Where's she from?"

"Not sure of her last name, but lots of people know her and she has lots of friends." Ariella sounded if amused at the cross-examination. "My mom knows her very well. And I'm not sure where she lives. She travels a lot and she's really . . . uh . . . cool."

Faye noticed Ariella's obvious attempt to use her teacher's

slang. "You think Moira lives in the woods?"

"Maybe. But we do! You'll see when you come to my house."

"Ah, about tomorrow," Faye paused to be certain of her decision. "What time was your mother thinking about? Can I talk to her real quick?"

"She's not here. She left. Disappeared somewhere. She does that a lot."

"Is that so?" Faye wondered about a teenage girl's reality in which pencils and people "disappeared."

"Well, I just checked and she took the car. She just said she was going, didn't give me any deets."

"Deets?"

"Oh, sorry. Details."

"Well, should I tell you the time I'll stop by tomorrow? Or do I need to talk to your mom?"

"Yes, please tell me. I'll tell her later."

"Okay, tell your mom I'll arrive around 4:00 PM. And tell her to call me if the time isn't good for her." Faye shivered as if a cold wind had blown up. Agreeing to meet felt like the right thing, but she was definitely entering new territory. Plus, Drake was sure to give her a hard time, though she figured she could pacify him by promising to talk to Ariella's guidance counselor. And a conversation with Ariella's Mom should yield more information about Ariella's injuries and this Moira character.

Ariella gave directions to her house which were long and complex, but clear. She concluded by saying, "If you get lost or don't see the oak tree with the star carved into it at the head of the drive, call me."

Faye studied what she had written and asked, "So, if I dead end at a pond, it means I've gone too far?"

"Yup! Just be happy you're not coming when it's dark. We actually had one guy drive into the pond on a cloudy night!" Ariella paused. "So, we're all set? I can't talk too long because my mom gave me all these chores to do before I can go out tonight."

Faye wanted to ask what Ariella's plans were and if they involved more happenings in the moonlight, but instead decided to broach her other important issue.

"Ariella, before you go, I want to ask you one more question."

"What's that, Ms B? I gotta bounce soon."

"The test yesterday. You didn't answer more than half of the questions. You didn't even guess at the answers. What happened?"

"Oh, that." Ariella's tone was flat. And then her voice harshened. "I just wasn't feeling it. It just seemed kind of wack and I couldn't keep it real, know what I mean? I mean, so it was my bad, but the questions were so bogus and 'trocious."

Faye knew the girl's shift into street slang was an indication she was feeling defensive and defiant, so she said, "Well, you know you'll probably fail the exam and you'll need to pass it eventually if you want to graduate with a regular diploma. You do know you can take it again, right?"

Faye waited, but Ariella was silent, so she continued, "I'm not going to argue with you about the test questions being bogus or atrocious, but I'm sure someone with your intelligence could easily get enough correct to pass. And, don't forget all your test results will be on your transcript and could affect your chances to get into a good college." Faye despised herself for giving the mandatory test so much importance, but she couldn't let her bias influence a student's choices.

After another silence, Ariella said, "You think I'm intelligent?"

"Why, yes, of course I do! You're not like the other kids, but you're different in a very good way. You're being true to yourself and are obviously smart, creative, caring and sensitive," Faye finished in a rush, though she wanted to add 'and you're beautiful'.

"Ms B, thank you so much! It's so awesome and dench and gnarly and all for you to say that! You're the dope, Ms B!"

Faye cheeks flushed. Teenagers were so insecure, a few positive words could turn their world around. "You know it's true, Ariella. And I want you to promise me you'll make a real effort when you take the retest. If you want, we can get together after-school to do some extra exam prep."

"That would be off the chain!"

After they hung up, Faye sat in the warming sunshine, musing at how different Ariella was. She heard familiar scrabbling on the deck and turned her head to see Yellowfoot, the Squirrel of the Future, doing his "I wanna peanut, gimme a peanut" shuffle. Now, here was a familiar happening. She went inside, reached into the jumbo bag she kept under the kitchen counter and selected two good-sized peanuts. When he saw her returning, Yellowfoot leapt onto the screen, splaying himself out so his furry belly and impressive genitals faced her. She carefully slid the screen open so as to not dislodge him and reached out with both peanuts held just so in one hand, telling him in a low voice how evolved he was and how his offspring would rule the trees. Yellowfoot took the peanuts one at a time and somehow stuffed them both in his mouth. Before scampering away, he gave her his signature glance with his big, black almond-shaped eyes.

"Yes, Yellowfoot, you're very intelligent, too."

Faye was quite pleased with how this day was going.

Chapter Six

That evening, Drake arrived with pizza and a DVD of the documentary "Bully", which depicted the real life experiences of five students, their parents and teachers, all struggling to deal with the chronic problem of kids abusing other kids. Both she and Drake knew bullying took place in their respective high schools and they wanted to learn more about the larger context. The film called bullying an "American crisis" and that 18 million kids had been bullied the previous year, making it the most common form of violence experienced by young people in the U.S.

Despite having to pause the movie a couple of times because their kissing and fondling got too intense, they did watch to the end. And, as the credits rolled, Faye insisted Drake move to a chair while she stayed on the couch and they managed to talk about the film and what they, as teachers, could do in their classrooms. But, after a half-hour of being intellectual and objective, the tension between them became unbearable and they grabbed at each other like animals, stripping off clothes and falling onto the rug. Frenzied passion again gripped them. Faye had a stray thought that if this was to become their new normal, they both needed to rearrange their schedules. Their usual "most every weekend" routine was just not going to cut it. Then the release of her first orgasm took her and she was lost again in pleasure. Later, in the warm, gooey, post-coital bliss, she told Drake about her phone conversation with Ariella. She thought it better, however, to wait to tell him about her plan to meet with Mrs. Cardona the next afternoon.

Drake gave a little sigh and said, "Well, so it was all part of some goofy thing the kids were doing in the woods. I'm glad we didn't get all worked up and report it."

Faye studied him. "You no longer think I should tell somebody?"

"Well, I'm not sure it will do any good, especially if Ariella pooh-poohs it."

Relieved, Faye said, "I agree!" And began kissing him again.

Sunday morning they didn't wake until Drake got up to pee. On his way back to bed, he glanced at the bedside clock, then rushed about gathering his clothing. Faye half-sat up in bed and admired his bare butt as he struggled into his tennis shorts. *Ummmm, going commando.* She was about to say something salacious, but Drake ran toward the door and shouted over his shoulder, "Really late for tennis. See you later. Love ya!"

Faye closed her eyes. Memories of last night washed over her in warm, gentle waves. Too bad Drake had to leave. They didn't usually get together on school nights, but could she justify going to his place this evening? The warmth and intensity of the pleasure waves increased. She was developing an itch which needed scratching. *Why did Drake leave? For a stupid tennis game? He should still be here.* She rolled restlessly onto her side and squeezed a pillow between her thighs and that felt good. She found if she squirmed her legs just right she felt even better. "Mmmm," she purred. Her hand strayed, almost sauntered down her belly, then wriggled between her legs. Ahh, that was so nice. As her fingers worked, her purr grew into a growl and, eyes closed tight, she started rolling from side to side. But, she couldn't quite make it happen.

Damnit! Where is that man? I need him. Now! She tried to imagine Drake in bed with her and it helped, but not enough. Then a cool breeze flitted over her heated body and she smelt a damp, earthy odor overlaid with the scent of lilacs and roses. Behind her eyelids a bright circle opened like the iris of a camera. The brightness faded to reveal what appeared to be a forest glade in moonlight. The wind was blowing and the branches and leaves were in restless motion. A tall, slender figure, she knew somehow it was a man, had his back to her. *Is that Drake? It must be Drake. He's lean and tall.* She tried to call out his name but only a weak whimper came out. *Am I dreaming? I can't be dreaming! I'm at home in bed, aren't I?* She stopped her hand and legs and lay still, her breath coming in quick gasps.

The man began to turn around and she saw, her eyes still closed, it was definitely not Drake. Drake was handsome, but this guy was beautiful, though his skin had a greenish cast, maybe reflected from all the vegetation. He had a pale, heart-shaped, almost feminine face, a perfectly straight nose, but with narrow slanted nostrils similar to a cat's, and full, wet lips parted as if about to say something. Black brows and emerald green eyes tilted upward at the corners, eyes that now were gazing at her, while the perfect, so kissable mouth began to smile. The guy beckoned her toward him. His fingers were impossibly long and slender. His clothes fit him like a wet suit, but were dappled, browns and greens, similar to camouflage, she couldn't tell for sure. She heard a chiming and tinkling reminiscent of wind chimes. She smelled lilacs and roses. *This is just like a scene from one of my fantasy novels,* she thought.

Then he said her name.

Faye gave a little scream, popped her eyes open and sat straight up in bed. She scanned her bedroom in part terror, part exhilaration. She grabbed the covers and yanked them to her chin with both hands, one of which was still slick with her juices. The room was quiet and empty. She was alone, but her body was vibrating like a plucked bass string. It felt as if she had been straining forward against some sort of tether, but had been snapped back just before release. *What was that? Did I experience some sort of 3D fantasy? Did I hallucinate?* She slowed her breathing and even crossed her legs beneath the covers in a loose meditation pose. After 15 minutes, she forced herself out of bed and, after a quick tour of the house to be sure nobody was lurking, got in the shower and tried to wash away the dream or whatever it was.

When Drake called in the early afternoon, she gave him a lighthearted, edited version of what had happened. She didn't say she had been masturbating, but rather she had been dozing when the vision occurred. She didn't emphasize how gorgeous the green guy had been,

"Isn't that the weirdest thing?" she said with a laugh, "I've never had anything like that happen. I mean, there were those couple of times I took mushrooms in my twenties and saw swirly stuff, but I knew it wasn't real. This felt very, very real, as if I could reach out and take his hand."

"Maybe it's because of all the hot sex we've had since Friday night?" Drake asked, "Maybe your system just got over-amped. I know I played tennis this morning like a demon, as if I was on fire."

"Huh. Well, you were certainly a demon on fire last night. Yeah, that's probably it. Too much of the good stuff! Guess I can't handle it the way I used to. Though, to be honest, I don't think I ever had it this good."

"Me either," Drake agreed, "But if it's freaking you out, it might be good to slow down or even take a break." His voice was plaintive, as if he was trying to be reasonable and, for once, not liking it.

"You think?" Then Faye felt an echo of the surging need she had felt earlier. "Well, maybe not. I'm okay and everything. No damage done, really, just kind of startled me, especially when the green guy said my name. But, I don't think we should stop, especially now it's so good. I say let's roll with it. In fact, I want to come over to your house this evening and see what happens!"

"But tonight's a school night," Drake protested, but Faye could tell he didn't mean it.

"Oh, c'mon, just for a little while. And we'll just talk. Really. With all this new sex stuff happening, we should talk, right?" Faye smiled and twirled a bit of her curly black hair between her fingers, imagining Drake feeling the same swell of desire she did. Her hand strayed toward her lap, toward that special spot, but she pulled back and picked at some crumbs on the table. *What am I doing? I've never been this sex obsessed!*

"Sounds good. Perhaps we can go for a walk while we talk?"

"Sure, whatever. I just want to see you." *Walk? Talk? I don't think so!*

Chapter Seven

Faye left for Ariella's house at 3:15, allowing extra time in case she got lost. She entered the Punkhorn from the south end as Ariella had suggested. Within a quarter mile, the pavement gave way to dirt road which quickly became much narrower, with branches scraping the side of her car and the road's surface filled with potholes alternating with bumps. Faye felt as if she was riding in a boat, bouncing over waves. But, Ariella's directions proved to be complete and precise and, before long, she saw the oak tree with the star incised into it.

Faye squeezed her Prius through a small opening between bushes and overhanging tree branches. Once she was through, she was surprised to find the dirt track wide and smooth. She wound her way through turn after turn, pleased it appeared the woods had been groomed or thinned. Sunlight angled down from the treetops. It was almost like driving through a park.

The Cardona cottage sat at the far side of an open field of wildflowers. Faye parked next to an older, dark-green Volvo, which had a "My Other Car is a Broom" bumpersticker. Cute, but passé, Faye thought, and checked her look in the mirror. She had gone with dressy casual – newer jeans and a pressed blouse, light makeup and a gold chain necklace with a small cloisonné book as a pendant. For this woodsy adventure, she had chosen tennis sneakers, though they were clean.

Faye found the footpath through the field Ariella had described and checked out the cottage as she meandered through the spring flowers. The cottage was rustic, with grey, sun-bleached cedar shingles on the sides, but its tall peaked roof was incongruously crowded with solar panels. A stone chimney protruded near the back with white smoke drifting from it. The small front porch was inviting with flowering pots hanging in several locations. There wasn't a doorbell, so Faye knocked on the screen, softly at first, but, when there was no response, with a bit of emphasis. She heard a rush of running steps and Ariella appeared, her green eyes glimmering with excitement.

"You're here! Yippee!" She swung the door wide and Faye saw, with surprise, Ariella wasn't wearing any makeup or jewelry. The girl's feet were bare and she wore gym shorts, a T-shirt with the PETA logo on it and a baseball cap turned sideways. Her hair hung messily from under the cap.

She looked so the average teenager, Faye had to say, "Well, don't you look nice!"

Ariella gave her a marvelous smile and stepped aside for Faye to enter a hallway that ran toward the back of the house. Faye looked to the right into a bright and airy room with plants everywhere and an elaborate, feathered dreamcatcher dangling from the ceiling. She thought it was probably someone's workroom, as it was dominated by a large table surrounded by shelves holding various pieces of neatly arranged equipment.

Ariella took Faye's hand and pulled her toward the back of the house. Faye caught a quick glimpse of through an open door on the left of another cozy room with vases of fresh flowers, comfortable stuffed chairs and overflowing bookcases. Three or four, Faye wasn't sure, large cats were curled up in a mass of fur in one of the chairs. Through a wide, many-paned window she saw what appeared to be a big and already flourishing garden.

"C'mon, my mom's in the kitchen. We baked special for you!"

"Something does smell good!" Faye agreed. The aromas evoked warm memories of times when Faye had gone with her parents to her grandmother's for Hanukkah and the house had been filled with the smell of homemade jelly donuts and potato pancakes.

Faye paused in the doorway, taken aback by the most interesting kitchen she could remember. It was out of an illustration in one of the books Faye had cherished as a child. Hansel and Gretel? Little Red Riding Hood? Sleeping Beauty? Wide plank flooring gleamed, as did the copper bottoms of a dozen cooking pots hanging from hooks in the low ceiling. Large oak cabinets had intricately hand-carved doors depicting what appeared to be woodland scenes. Stone countertops ran almost all the way around the room, with breaks for doorways and for a big, soot-stained, open fieldstone fireplace with a huge, blackened cookpot hanging from a swinging arm. A massive oak mantle supported a variety of old pewter tankards, plates and clay figurines. And, from all available ceiling space hung bunches of herbs and dried flowers, resembling an upside-down garden.

Mrs. Cardona, standing near the stove, gave Faye a big smile, put the spoon back in the steaming pot she'd been stirring and lifted her apron over her head. She came toward Faye with her hand outstretched. "Welcome to our home, Ms Bloomberg. Ariella has told me so many nice things about you."

To Faye's dismay, she froze up, as if she was an actor about to make her entrance onto an elaborate stage set and couldn't remember her lines. It wasn't until Mrs. Cardona had crossed the big room that Faye was able to take a stiff step forward and reach out to shake hands. Out of the corner of her eye she noticed Ariella give her an amused look.

"Uh, please, uh, to meet you!" Faye managed, "And, please call me, uh, Faye." She took a deep breath, gestured with her free hand toward the fireplace and succeeded, without stumbling, to say. "Do you actually cook on that?" And then without pause, "This is a wonderful house. It must be quite old?"

Laughing, Mrs. Cardona, let go of Faye's hand and looked to the fireplace. "Oh, yes, we use it all the time. There are some dishes for which it's the best. The house is over 300 years old and we like to think the energies of all the dozens of women who cooked over that open fire add something precious to the food. And please, call me Calista."

Faye was glad her dressy-casual outfit wasn't far off the mark, though she'd expected Ariella's mother to be draped in more of the mysterious fabric she'd worn to the parent-teacher conference. Instead, Calista was wearing a pair of tight-fitting, faded jeans, a forest green V-neck pullover and green ballet flats. Her hair was tied back in a relaxed ponytail and her enchanting face, as before, appeared free of make-up. She was as tall as Faye and she glided with a lithe grace reminiscent of a dancer or jungle cat. Given that Ariella was 15, Faye estimated Calista was in her thirties, though she looked twenty-five.

Calista took Faye's arm and walked her over to a handmade wooden table in the corner near the fireplace. A plate on the table was mounded with small pastries. "Come, sit down. We've baked some goodies for us to snack on. Would you like tea or coffee?"

Faye imagined Ariella sitting at the table doing her homework on a winter night, warmed by a bright fire in the fireplace. The image was so cozy Faye shivered, wishing there was a fire burning now.

Calista must have noticed the shiver. "We could start a fire if you like."

Startled, Faye wondered if the woman was some kind of psychic. Ariella turned and bent over the large woodbox next to the fireplace. Faye could see below her shorts the angry red stripes on her thighs had faded to pale pink.

As Ariella began picking pieces of wood from the box, Faye said, "No, really. Not necessary. I'm fine." But, then her face went hot and her thoughts swam like a fish in a bowl being watched by a cat. She grabbed the nearest chair at the table and sat down with a thump. She was aware of the concern on Calista and Ariella's faces.

"I'm dreadfully sorry. It's just that a lot has been happening and I'm going a bit bonkers. I've been distracted these past couple of days. I really need to get things sorted." Faye realized she had slipped into her faux British accent and glanced at Ariella and her mom to see if her phrasing had been noticed. But the two just gave her twin brilliant smiles.

"Let me get you some herb tea," Calista said and went toward the stove. Ariella sat opposite and, still smiling, took Faye's hands in hers. The girl's hands were warm and comforting. Faye gave them a squeeze and went to pull back, but Ariella held on.

"I'm so glad you're here!" she said, bouncing a little in her chair. "I can't wait to show you my room!" Faye tried to smile. This meeting wasn't going the way she expected. Calista returned to the table with two steaming mugs and gave one to Faye and one to Ariella. Faye cupped the mug in her hands and sniffed. The tea's aroma was rich and strong, full of enticing scents. She took a sip and tasted citrus, some allspice and perhaps cinnamon. And a strong, but pleasant, herbal undertone. Warmth spread through her and she leaned back with a sigh.

Calista sat down with cup for herself. "How do you like the tea?"

"It's excellent! Delicious and very soothing. What's in it?" Faye said, pleased her voice sounded normal.

"Some chamomile, some mint, a bit of dried orange peel, some common spices and, of course, one of my herb mixes."

"Herb mix?" Faye wondered if she would start to feel stoned in a few moments. And, if she did, what should she do? She knew she had to take control of this meeting. Some tea and chit-chat was fine, but she needed to ask questions about Ariella's injuries and the exam.

Faye had opened her mouth when Calista said, "Oh, didn't Ariella tell you I'm a professional herbalist? That's part of how I support us."

"She did say something the other day when she needed to treat her, uh, injuries. She had a cream you'd made. Oh, and about those injuries—"

"The healing salve. Of course. It works well for minor skin irritations and abrasions." Calista glanced down, paused, and then said, "And, for this tea, I used a mix which eases tensions, clarifies the mind and strengthens inner energy. Do you feel somewhat more at ease?"

Faye thought Calista seemed uncomfortable and decided to allow more polite conversation before asking her questions. "Definitely more at ease. So you sell herbs to people or stores?"

"Mostly to folks here in the Punkhorn and to select others

around the Cape who prefer alternative, homemade teas and herbal remedies. We grow most of the herbs in our garden or gather them from the woods nearby. Their native origins give the plants more efficacy, especially for locals. We also wholesale to a few health stores. As you can imagine, our quality is high and it all requires a lot of time, so our products are more expensive than commercial ones."

Faye was impressed by Calista's use of the word "efficacy," but wondered what kind of income could an herbalist generate? Were Calista and Ariella really poor?

"In case you're wondering, most of my earnings comes not from the herb business, but from working as a model and actress."

"Really!" Faye was surprised Calista had answered her unspoken question, but not not surprised at the news Calista was a model and actress. The woman had an exotic, youthful, but adult, beauty that fit well in many a fashion magazine or catalog.

"So, I assume you've been in Vogue?" Faye grinned to indicate she was joking.

Calista returned her grin. "Twice, in fact, though most of my work hasn't been in the US. The majority of my modeling assignments originate in Europe and most of my professional acting has been in small films and theatre productions in Canada and Central America. But now I've started to get offers from Japan, India and Southeast Asia, which means I could be away from home for even longer periods of time." She turned to Ariella, who smiled up at her. "But, enough about us. Please, have some of these. We made them especially for you." She slid the plate piled with cookies, muffins, and little cakes toward Faye.

"Yeah, Ms Bloomberg, I made the cookies!"

"You did? Well, I'll try one of those first." Faye bit into the cookie. It tasted as good as any she'd gotten at any bakery. It had just the right texture, chewy with a crunchy outside, and the flavor was complex with a delicate sweetness. Faye thought it might be wild honey, combined with nutty whole wheat, cinnamon, raisins and some fruit.

"Yummy!" Faye said, and took another big bite. "Is that banana I taste? And honey?"

"Yup!" Ariella grabbed a cookie and said, while chewing, "They're my special recipe! I got the honey from one of our neighbors. He has his own hives and I helped him harvest the honey combs."

"Really! I must say I'm quite impressed!" Watching the happy girl, for once without her pale Kabuki-style makeup, dressed like any teenager relaxing at home, Faye felt unexpected affection. How wonderful it would be to have a daughter like Ariella.

The three of them began chatting in earnest. They talked about recipes and ingredients and Faye learned both Calista and Ariella were accomplished cooks and gardeners. They all agreed locally grown, organic food was essential to good health. Calista gave more details of the films and theatrical productions she'd acted in and Faye pretended she had heard of some of them. Calista didn't seem fazed by Faye's abstraction, but mentioned several times how difficult it was for her to be away from Ariella and home.

After eating several more of the baked goodies and after being served a second cup of the herbal tea, Faye felt terrific. Her earlier anxiety and dizzy head had disappeared. Her mind was clear and energized, as if she had woken from a refreshing sleep. It was time to ask her questions.

Chapter Eight

"About Ariella's injuries, I was wondering—"

Calista held up her hand. "We can talk about all that in a moment. But first, I want to give you some context, so what I say later won't be alarming."

Faye wasn't upset her questions had been put off again. She found Calista to be one of the most fascinating people she'd met, like a fantasy character had come to life

Calista explained Ariella had been a "love child," that she and Ariella's father, Alberte, had met at an open-call audition in LA. They were both in their late teens and from the East Coast - she from the Boston area and Alberte from Cape Cod. They fell in love and created Ariella. Alberte found work as a stagehand and roustabout while Calista adjusted to life as a stay-at-home mom.

"Was that frustrating for you?" Faye asked.

"Not really. Ariella was a very, very quiet kid and we had friends who were happy to watch her once she was big enough. So, Alberte and I still managed to go on auditions. And really, I loved becoming a mother. I don't think there is a more important role for any woman."

Faye eyes went wide and her mouth dropped open. Calista had echoed the yearning she'd felt earlier. She stammered, "Were you . . . were you able to make enough money?"

Calista said her folks "back East" had mailed sizeable checks pretty regularly. But then, when Ariella was three, Alberte was offered a part with a travelling troupe. The pay was good and he sent most of it back to Calista, who had begun exploring natural healing and herbal medicine.

"I met an older woman, Hyacinth, who was an established herbalist and was selling her mixes and potions from her house up one of the canyons near LA," Calista said, "Ariella and I moved in with her and I became her apprentice and assistant. I was able to save money because she paid me in free rent. Plus, she fell in love with Ariella and was very happy to babysit when I went on auditions."

"How wonderful. It's like a fairy tale."

"Yes, those were special times," Calista said, "Everything seemed possible. In fact, that's where I met Moira, who jumpstarted my acting career. At first, she gave me small unpaid parts in some of her productions in California and later she introduced me to LA film and theatre people. Before I knew it, I was getting regular offers for paid acting.

"Sadly, Hyacinth, who was already well into her 80s, took a fall one day on a steep slope when she was collecting herbs and died of complications. Hyacinth's relatives were eager to sell her house, so we had to move. Alberte came back from tour right about then and said he needed to go back to Cape Cod to occupy his family's home. His parents were moving to Boston and none of his siblings wanted to relocate to the Cape. It was the perfect opportunity for us and came at just the right time. So, we packed up and moved to this house. Ariella has been essentially raised here."

"Growing up in a fairy tale cottage in the woods. How great!" Faye smiled at Ariella.

"So that's our story," Calista said. "Alberte's family stops by occasionally, but no one stays longer than a day or two. It's just Ariella and I most of the time. Except, of course, that changes when Moira and her people gather here." Calista sipped her tea and raised her eyebrows at Faye.

Faye realized this was her chance to get answers. "Can you tell me more about the full moon event and Ariella's injuries?"

Calista frowned. "Well, you know, the 'injuries,' as you call them, looked worse than they were. They stung for a day or two, but she's okay now. And I'm sure they weren't inflicted intentionally. Plus, the event was organized impeccably by Moira, who has done thousands of these productions. Did Ariella tell you about Moira, how she schedules and stages the full moon gatherings and dramas?"

"Ariella mentioned her, but didn't give me much detail. She

lives around here then?"

"Yes, you could say Cape Cod is a base for her, but she's not here full-time. She travels constantly, but shows up a few times each year, usually a week or so before a full moon. Moira was holding events on the Cape long before we moved from LA."

"It only takes her a week to put the plays together? That's amazing! Do you still act in the dramas?"

"Oh, I used to be in every production here until I started getting gigs outside the US."

"What does your husband think about what happened to Ariella on the full moon?"

Calista turned to her daughter and they both smiled. "Husband? Alberte and I aren't married and we're not in regular contact. He left with another touring troupe about four years ago, when Ariella was 11. But I'm sure he wouldn't be upset. As an actor he'd definitely understand what happened. He was many times in Moira's productions and, if I remember correctly, was bruised, sprained his ankle, and even scratched more than once."

"Have you heard from him recently?" Faye found it curious this beautiful woman was so comfortable with an absentee partner.

Ariella piped up, "My Dad's fine. We'd know if something happened to him, wouldn't we Mom?"

"Of course!" Calista brushed some hair off her daughter's forehead. "We get phone calls from time to time. In fact, we just heard from a friend that Alberte's found a place with a company in Peru. Near Machu Pichu."

Puzzled, Faye sat back. She bit into one of the little cakes which tasted so good she had an urge to stuff the whole thing into her mouth. Instead, she put the uneaten piece on her plate and tried another tack.

"I assume you know about Ariella's failure to answer all the questions on the big exam on Friday?" Glancing over, she saw Ariella's face darken.

"Oh, that," said Calista in a dismissive tone. "Yes, she told me, but I don't find it alarming. Ariella and I discussed these ridiculous exams when she insisted on going to public school rather than continuing her home schooling. I disapproved of public school then and I still do, though I must admit I have more free time now."

Faye hadn't known Ariella had been home-schooled, though it made a lot of sense and could explain why the girl never seemed to fit in. "So you don't care her future could be adversely affected by a failing exam grade? I mean, the scores will be on transcripts sent to colleges. And she won't be able to get a normal diploma from the high school without passing the tests." Faye knew she sounded like a proper School Marm and part of her squirmed. But, she was obligated to speak the truth.

Calista contemplated Faye for a long few seconds. "Well, Faye, I believe your personal attitude toward the test is more like mine than your role as a teacher allows you to express."

Faye started and sat upright. This mind reading thing was beginning to get spooky.

"Our family isn't like most of the other families with children in the high school," Calista said. "I think you understand that, don't you? We don't place much importance on our children becoming successful in modern society. We're more concerned with them becoming complete human beings so they can reach their full potential in ways the mainstream does not encourage or recognize.

"So we teach our children to not accept conventional standards or strictures, to never accept being denied something because of artificial rules. If Ariella wants to go to college, she will, I assure you. But, if she chooses not to go, that will be very much okay with us."

Faye couldn't think of what to say. Calista's words resonated with her and she wanted to tell her so, but hesitated. And who did Calista mean by "our" when she said "our family" or "our children?" Wasn't the family just she and her daughter?

"Calista, I understand completely what you're saying, but I want to be sure you and Ariella know what's at stake. As for my personal feelings about the test, I can't deny it bothers me and I don't like the focus public education places on it. However, if Ariella plans to stay at the high school and graduate, she should retake the test until she passes it. The diploma may not seem like a lot, but it will make things easier for her in the future, no matter what path she chooses. For example, my degrees made it relatively easy for me to become a teacher." Faye turned to Ariella. "Do you want to get a regular diploma from the high school?"

Ariella, who had been watching with interest the interchange between her mother and Faye, smiled and said, "Oh, for sure! And you're going to help me pass the test, right?"

Faye looked to Calista, who nodded her approval. "Yes, I thought we could start getting together after school on a regular basis. And then, once we get your test score, we can spend time focusing on the areas which gave you trouble."

Ariella giggled. "The whole stupid thing gave me trouble! But do we have to always get together at the school? Can we study here? Or maybe even at your house?"

"Why sure, why not? It would be more comfortable for both of us. I'm sure we can work something out. And we've got the whole long summer vacation coming up."

"Speaking of working things out," Calista broke in, "I'm grateful you've offered to help Ariella and I want to ask a connected favor of you. Feel free to say no, however. I certainly don't want to create any difficulty for you."

"A favor? From me?" This incredible woman needed Faye's help?

"Yes, you could make things much easier for us when I'm away on location." Calista paused and Faye couldn't imagine what it was she could do – tend the garden, feed the cats?

"You see, it's become increasingly hard to find someone with whom I can leave Ariella. Our Punkhorn neighbors are willing, but their homes are not healthy or safe for a teenage girl, if you know what I mean. And I don't know any other people nearby well enough to trust them. So, I was wondering if you might be interested in having her stay with you."

Faye had never been good at hiding her feelings and she knew her face had lit with startled pleasure. She began to express her delight, but Calista went on. "Ariella's been talking about you from almost the start of the school year - how nice you are, how all the students like and trust you, how you treat everyone the same. She was actually the one who suggested I ask if she could stay with you. And she's promised she will behave especially well."

Faye saw, in the corner of her eye, a large and brilliant smile beaming from Ariella. Faye wanted to blurt out that, of course, it was okay, but the thought of Drake's reaction restrained her.

"Well, I'm very flattered! I am, of course, willing to let Ariella stay with me on occasion. But, first I should check with the school. I'm pretty confident there isn't a regulation prohibiting teachers from having students stay with them, but I need to confirm that." Seeing the deflated expression on Ariella's face, Faye quickly added, "When were you thinking the first visit might be?"

Calista and Ariella contemplated each other and Faye could practically hear their unspoken communication. Calista turned to Faye, "We were actually hoping it could be this coming weekend. I'm flying to L.A. on Friday to meet with some film people from Japan. It's the three day Memorial Day weekend, so Ariella could be with you from Friday afternoon until Monday afternoon. I thought it was a manageable time period for both of you to see if it works. But, if that's too soon or if you've made plans, I can try to find an alternative."

"Alternative?" Faye said in a small voice, knowing she so wanted this visit to happen. "I don't think that'll be necessary. In fact, I think we should count on Ariella coming to my house next weekend." She paused, again thinking of the fuss Drake was likely to make. She resolved to keep him so happy he wouldn't have a chance to complain. "I don't have any plans and the school won't object to one weekend. And, you're right, it is Memorial Day weekend. With the extra day, I can be more relaxed about my time. There will be plenty of opportunities to hang out."

Faye was rewarded with happy expressions and bright eyes from mother and daughter. Glancing at her watch and seeing it was close to 6:00 PM, she said, "Wow! Look how late it is! I really must get going. I told my partner I'd meet him."

She started to get up, but Ariella jumped from her seat and ran around the table and stood in front of her. "I wanted to show you my room, Ms B! I want you to see how neat I am! Please, please, it'll just take a minute!"

Faye couldn't say no, the girl was so excited. She felt her heart swell. "Oh, okay," she laughed.

Chapter Nine

Ariella took Faye's hand and drew her into the hall and up a stairway Faye hadn't noticed on the way in. The stairs were narrow and steep, normal for a house this old. She caught glimpses of what appeared to be cracked oil paintings of women which, judging by their clothing, lived hundreds of years previous.

Upstairs was divided into two large rooms on either side of the landing, with a bathroom straight ahead. The room on the right, from the quick glance Faye managed before being tugged to the left by Ariella, looked to be Calista's. Ariella's room wasn't at all like a normal teenage girl's. There were two large mullioned windows on the far wall and brilliant sunshine slashed in to glint off sparkling articles on shelves and tables and also illuminate an ornate old crystal chandelier hanging in the middle of the room. The light flashes were dazzling and Faye felt as if she was straining to see through a shifting, shimmering brightness.

Squinting, she saw large pieces of furniture, all solid wood and handmade and obviously quite old. A four-poster bed, complete with a carved headboard and sheer lavender and gold drapes all the way around, dominated the room. The top of the posts supported carved winged figures, which Faye guessed were either dragons or eagles or even gryphons. Along one wall was an antique writing desk, with a fold-down writing surface and lots of pigeonholes. The desk was covered with school books and papers and Ariella's backpack was on the floor nearby. Between the two windows on the far wall, which had a wide view of the garden and forest beyond, was an old bureau crowned with a circular mirror. It's surface was cloudy and it's reflection distorted. The feet of the bed, the desk and the bureau were all sculpted into animal shapes. Lions? Cats? Wolves? There were bookcases on every wall and an enormous chest at the foot of the bed. On the wide planked floor were three large circular rugs, all quite old, but in excellent condition. The rugs' patterns were colorful and geometric, reminiscent of mandalas. Faye was startled by what appeared to be a working woodstove in the corner to the right of the windows. *Are they actually heating with wood? What about those solar panels on the roof?*

"Wow!" she exclaimed. "This is a fairy tale princess' room! Or even a queen's! Where did you get all this wonderful furniture and these rugs? And the chandelier is magnificent!"

Pleased, Ariella performed a graceful pirouette on one of the rugs, her outstretched arms taking in the entire room. "Most of it came with the cottage, but my mom inherited some pieces from her mother. And some came from my dad and his family. What do you think of my collections?" Ariella pointed at the contents of the various bookcases.

Faye stepped forward and realized the bookcase shelves displayed dozens of items in neat rows. There were bird's nests, pieces of wood twisted by the wind and sea, animal skulls and bones, large chunks of crystal, two huge pine cones, polished rocks, many shells, both large and small, dried flowers and leaves, pieces of bark, and dozens of smaller bits she couldn't identify at a distance. There was even a contorted bonsai tree.

"Ariella, I had no idea you were so into nature. It must have taken you years searching the forest and beaches for all these."

The girl seemed puzzled. "Well, yeah, I do spend a lot of time outdoors. But, most of these are gifts. I didn't go searching for them."

"Gifts? You mean people give them to you?"

"No, of course not!" Ariella's laugh was merry. "The nature spirits leave them where I'll find them. I always know when I've pleased them because I find a treasure right in my path."

"Nature spirits?" Faye suspected she was being teased.

"Oh, you know. They're all around here, but especially where there aren't a lot of houses or cars. Like here in the Punkhorn forest or on the beaches and dunes in the National Seashore."

"Really! That's so interesting!" Faye tried to sound sincere. "And amazing. Did you ever see a nature spirit?"

Ariella stared at Faye as if she had just asked who Emily Dickinson was. "We don't see them so much as feel them," she said, caution creeping into her voice. "I almost always can sense them nearby, except when I'm at school or riding in a car or doing stuff like that."

Faye was puzzled and opened her mouth to ask another question, but Ariella did more graceful pirouettes and somehow wound up right in front of Faye, laughing and grabbing her teacher's hands. Faye had the quick impression there was a glittering crown on her head.

"I'll get my mom to talk to you about it, okay? She can explain it better than I can. So, you like my room?"

"I think it's wonderful and amazing and, well, magical. And so neat. You're even more remarkable than I thought." Faye's heart warmed when Ariella's face lit up.

"I wish I'd had a room like this when I was your age. But, where's your computer? Where's the TV? Do you have a stereo?"

Ariella again contemplated at Faye as if she was saying something which made no sense. Her grip on Faye's hands loosened. "We don't allow anything like that in the house," she said, her expression uncertain, as if she wasn't sure what to say. "I thought you knew that."

Cautious, Faye scanned the room again, expecting to see a flat screen peeking out from behind the bed or a closed laptop under the papers on the desk. Ariella had to be joking. But the room was so neat and open, there wasn't anywhere a TV or computer could be concealed, unless in a closet.

"You're funning me, right?" Faye said, "They're just tucked away, right?"

Ariella gave a little shrug, let go of Faye's hands, dropped cross-legged to the floor and stared down at the carpet. "Okay, here are some of the deets. My mom has a thing about being too exposed to the influences of mainstream society. She feels this house should be an oasis of mostly natural things and natural energy." Her voice sounded solemn and adult, as if she were reciting a lesson.

"Kind of like the Amish?"

"No," Ariella began picking at loose threads in the carpet. "This is more about what my mom and Moira and all the rest know is really going on in the universe. I mean, she doesn't think the rest of the world is evil or anything and she does think technology can be useful. But, she believes we humans are like plants which need to be nurtured by nature if we want to grow and blossom. She says artificial things and environments don't provide the right natural and spiritual sustenance, so people often grow up crooked, or stunted, or might not even ever blossom."

After a pause, she continued. "But she thinks some techno stuff is okay in moderation. Like, she has a cell phone and she borrows a friend's laptop when she goes on a trip. We get electricity from the solar panels, but we only use it when we really need it."

Ariella looked up and Faye knew she needed to proceed with care to avoid making the girl feel uncomfortable. "How interesting," she said in a neutral tone, "Your mother is truly a unique and wonderful woman. I would love to hear more about her beliefs sometime."

"Yeah, she can talk about all that better than I can." Ariella jumped up and grabbed Faye's hands again.

"Can I use the computer at your house when I'm staying over? I mean, I work on computers at school all time and even stay after to type my papers and homework and all. So, I know how to use them and everything. I won't mess anything up, I promise."

"Sure, as long as your mom is cool with it, I don't see why not. But you better not spend all your time chatting online with some boy!" Faye grinned and squeezed Ariella's hands.

The girl wrenched her hands back as if she had been scalded. "I would never do that! Never!"

"No, of course you wouldn't. I understand. I was just joking."

But Faye didn't understand and wondered what raw nerve she'd touched. She wasn't going to press Ariella. She'd save the whole nature spirit, no computer, no TV business until she had a chance to talk alone with Calista.

"Why don't we go back downstairs and I'll say goodbye to your Mom, okay? I really should get going."

"Okay!" Ariella's smile reappeared like a spotlight snapping on.

Calista was sitting at the kitchen table leafing through an old, loosely bound book. Faye could see the pages were yellowed and many were rough-edged and smudged. Calista put a long black feather between the pages to mark her place and closed the stained and cracked leather cover.

Calista answered Faye's question before she could ask it, "It's a book of recipes, for both food and herbal potions, which has been handed down by the women who have lived in this house. I think the oldest entries date back to the 1600s. Almost every page has comments scribbled in the margins. The comments say how the recipe could be improved and confirm how well it worked or didn't. I love going through it, reading what the women had to say and envisioning the context in which they were living and writing. It's a combination history book and recipe book. And even a bit of a diary." Calista gave a little laugh. "Do you like to cook, Faye?"

Faye, who was repressing an urge to grab the book and begin reading, said, "Well, sort of. I'm not a gourmet or anything, but I do make an effort to make something from scratch a few times a week. I must admit, however, I'm very reliant on the microwave."

Calista shuddered, but then smiled and said, "Ariella is becoming quite the baker, as I'm sure you noticed. Perhaps next weekend when she comes to the cottage to feed the cats she could show you how to work the woodstove. Baking with wood heat is an art."

It took Faye a second to comprehend what Calista had said. It was at least a 30-minute drive from Faye's house to the cottage in the Punkhorn. Was Calista indirectly telling Faye chauffeuring her daughter about was part of the deal?

"That sounds great!" Faye said, understanding her normal weekend activities, which usually featured a lot of reading, naps, watching a movie or two, going to the beach, hanging out with Drake, and grading student papers, were going to be altered by the needs of her young houseguest.

Faye began her goodbye hugs and was pleased when Calista handed her a small cloth bag and explained it contained some of the herbal tea mixture Faye had enjoyed, a dozen of Ariella's cookies, a slip of paper with Calista's cell phone number, plus a " . . . few other things."

"The herbal tea will help you with the 'going bonkers' problem you mentioned earlier," Calista said in a perfect posh British accent, much better than Faye's. She smiled at Faye's reaction and said, "Well, I'm an actor, after all. Learning various accents and even other languages is part of the craft. I can even do a passable Cockney accent, if you prefer."

"Can you really, now?" said Faye, "Then it's too bad I've got to scarper, mate, cuz we could rabbit on for hours!"

Calista laughed. "You're a delight! Please come back soon!

Faye turned to Ariella and the girl jumped into her arms and held her tight in a long hug. Faye's cheeks pinked with pleasure and Calista gave her a knowing smile. Faye felt again the bittersweet pang she associated with her desire to be a mother.

On the way to Drake's house, she sang along with Bonnie Raitt's "Thing Called Love" on the radio, thinking how true it was we only see the world we make. It felt as if her entire body was tingling, electrified, perhaps due to the tea or energy leftover from the great sex with Drake. She didn't understand half of what was going on, but she did like the idea of changes happening, like waves washing the beach clean and depositing new shells, rocks and seaweed. It would be cool to learn more about Ariella and Calista's lifestyle and beliefs. Plus, she'd make new friends. It was as if she was travelling to a new country. As she drove and sang, she ate almost all of Ariella's cookies, saving only three for Drake.

Chapter Ten

She arrived at Drake's condo complex at 7:15. Twilight softened the two-story, identical buildings and no-nonsense landscaping, though she knew in bright light the complex had a barracks' look. Drake was pragmatic and economical in his choice of housing, car (he drove a ten-year old Honda Civic) and furnishings (some Ikea, but mostly a mixture of yard sale bargains and hand-me-downs). The inside of his small condo was painted off-white throughout and there were only a few prints and posters on the walls. His taste was all about function rather than beauty.

The hardwood floors were bare - no rugs, no piles of stuff from unfinished projects. There was little mess or clutter anywhere and Faye knew from experience it wasn't a good idea to leave papers or books or dishes about. Rather than tease him for his no-nonsense ways, Faye figured it was the same preference which made Drake pick her as his girlfriend. She knew she was definitely a pragmatic and economical choice. When they were out and saw some striking beauty, Drake would always mutter "high maintenance." If Faye was Drake's girlfriend because she was low maintenance, it was fine with her, especially as sex with him more than compensated.

As she let herself in, she heard the sounds of a tennis match on television. She called out to Drake, but didn't get a response, so she walked to the living room and saw him sprawled on his back on the couch, one leg hanging off and an arm up over his eyes. A book lay open on his stomach. He was snoring loud enough to be heard over the noise of the tennis. She allowed herself to drink in the sight of him - his long lean body, his dark hair spreading out around his head, and the blue-black stubble on his cheeks and chin which felt so wonderful on her skin. She tip-toed across the room and knelt beside the couch, her fingers twitching with the need to touch him, to rub him, to make him groan and squirm the way he did her. She fancied she was a panther about to pounce on her unsuspecting prey and could almost feel her tail swishing in agitation. Leaning over she gently brushed his lips with her hair and blew a warm breath into his nostrils. He stirred, shifted, but didn't wake.

Faye bent closer and touched the tip of her tongue to the space between his nose and upper lip, tasting him. She felt saliva form in her mouth and realized she might start drooling. Not being able to hold back any longer, she eased her body on top of his and began kissing him, losing any last bit of self-control in a surge of lust. Without opening his eyes, Drake responded. He wrapped his arms around her and lifted his groin to meet hers. Clothes went in all directions and soon Faye was astride Drake with him deep inside her. She gazed down into his now wide open eyes and felt how each movement she made affected him. She had been on top before, but never had understood how much power she had, how she could bring him so easily to the brink of orgasm and then, by going still, allow him a respite. She started timing her movements to the rhythm of the tennis ball thwacking on the racquets. Drake began making deep, guttural grunts, but held back and put his hands on her hips, almost limiting her movements. She knew he prided himself on waiting for her, but this time she wanted him to orgasm first.

With several sudden thrusts and an another squeeze or two and then leaning over to overwhelm his mouth with a kiss, she pushed him over the edge. Then she sat back and watched in fascination as he spasmed over and over. The crowd at the tennis match was cheering wildly. When he was still, he reached up and drew her down into a tight embrace. They lay still so long Faye thought he'd fallen asleep again.

"Thank you for that," he whispered in her ear and a tingle ran through her mind and body. She knew, in that moment, he was hers in a way she'd never before fathomed.

"Now you," he said in a husky voice, and he slid out from under her and onto the floor. He turned her on the couch so she was in a sitting position, then knelt in front of her and spread her legs. Faye began whimpering and gasping as soon as he started kissing the insides of her thighs, working his way inward. When he reached his goal, the touch of his tongue was so intense she could only bear it for a second. She bucked, knocking Drake's head back a foot.

"Whoa! Take it easy, darlin'. I need my teeth to eat other things, like food." He made a show of feeling his front teeth and licked his lips. The expression on his face was so funny, she couldn't stop herself from giggling, then snorting as he kept his tongue moving over his lips. His eyebrows went up.

"You know, it's weird, but you taste just like cinnamon and honey. I mean, you taste really good!" he said, "Did you do something? Put some lotion down there?"

"What!" Faye stopped laughing. "You're kidding, right?"

"No, I'm not. Here. Taste." Drake leaned forward and kissed her. She let her tongue explore his mouth and lips and, yes, there was the faint, but definite taste of cinnamon and honey, just like the cookies she'd been eating. She felt a jerk of disorientation, but it was quick and weak.

"Wow. That *is* weird," Faye said, "I wonder if . . . "

"What?"

She shook her head. "I'll tell you later."

Much, much later, after they had moved to Drake's bed and were lying even more satiated in each other's arms, Faye confessed to having gone to Ariella's house that afternoon. She described Ariella's remarkable room and told him about the herb tea and cookies. Mentioning the cookies, reminded her she had saved three and insisted on getting dressed enough to go out to her car and bring them back to Drake, who gobbled them and pronounced them excellent.

"Now you're going to taste like cinnamon and honey," Faye teased. She told him what she'd learned about Ariella's injuries and the full moon events.

"You're sure you don't still need to go to the guidance counselor or the principal?" he added, his voice drowsy.

"No, I don't think so. I really think it's a benign situation. I'm sure there wasn't any intent to hurt Ariella. I mean, they talked about other actors, including Ariella's father, getting injured at other times. Aside from the fact these plays or events or whatever you want to call them take place at the full moon in the woods, they sound like any other theatrical production. And, seeing Ariella in her home environment and getting to know her mother, who obviously loves her daughter, I'm convinced there's no need to worry."

Drake's eyes started to flutter closed. "Okay, whatever you think is best."

"I love you," Faye whispered. But Drake was asleep. She decided she'd wait to tell him about Ariella coming to stay with her. After all, she still had to make sure it was okay with the school. She'd let a sleeping Drake lie.

Faye woke just before midnight and saw the third quarter waning moon rising brightly above the trees. She gave Drake a gentle kiss on the nose, slipped out of bed, dressed quietly and drove home. She felt as refreshed and as invigorated as she had after drinking the tea that afternoon. In her driveway she stared up at the moon for a long while. The big, glowing crescent seemed to be glowing at her in a special way. Inside, she took a shower and changed into an oversize T-shirt and panties, her usual sleep wear. But, instead of climbing into bed, she took the bag Calista had given her into the living room and spilled its contents onto the coffee table.

There was the tea, of course, but the other items gave her pause. She picked up a gold locket shaped like a small scallop shell and opened it to find a black and white photo of a toddler, who she recognized as Ariella. There were also several acorns, still green, three dried flowers, and a tiny purple diamond shaped piece of what appeared to be amethyst. The biggest item was a circular dreamcatcher, about four inches across, constructed of bent twigs with an elaborate design woven into the center of the circle and little sparkly bits threaded on the weaving. She felt the reddish-golden weave and realized it was hair. Hair like both

Ariella's and Calista's. A tiny, delicate, glossy black feather dangled from the bottom of the dreamcatcher.

The last item was a yellowish coin slightly more than an inch and a half in diameter, old, begrimed and so well worn Faye could barely make out the dim outlines of a head on one side and some sort of winged bird or creature on the other. She hefted the coin, not sure what kind of metal it was. It was heavy and, as she held it, she thought she heard people whispering. She put the coin down and the whispering stopped.

Bemused, Faye shook her head and said to herself, "Enough for one day."

She left the items on the coffee table, stretched and went to her bedroom, where she sat and meditated until she got sleepy. Just before she drifted off she said to herself, "I want a child."

Chapter Eleven

Monday morning Faye bounced out of bed, did some yoga, meditated and had a light breakfast of homemade granola with fresh organic strawberries, yogurt, soy milk, and sweetened with organic maple syrup. She also had a big cup of the tea Calista had given her, savoring again its spicy yet soothing taste.

Yellowfoot, the Squirrel of the Future, leapt onto the deck's sliding screen door, his black eyes fixed on her. She handed him his two peanuts and then, just to see what he would do, dropped a third on the deck. He did try to fit the extra peanut in his mouth, but after several attempts, he gave up. He shot Faye a look of extreme exasperation and scampered off. She imagined him arriving a bit later at his nest and being greeted by the excited cries of his wife and kids and him so proud of the booty he had brought home. *Anthropomorphize much?* She laughed out loud, she felt so good.

Faye dressed in typical school day attire - a modest black skirt, tailored blouse and low-heel pumps - but was surprised at how radiant she looked in the mirror. She knew it didn't matter what she wore today, she was going to get noticed. She called Drake on her cell as she drove to school, knowing he, with his regular-as-clockwork schedule, was also on the road. They both had Bluetooth phones linked to their car stereos, so it was safe to talk while they drove.

"Hey," she said when he picked up.

"Hey, whassup babe?" He knew she liked him to live up to his gangsterish image.

"I love you."

"Ya do? Well, I gotta say I dono believe it. Not after ya almost knocked my teef out last night! It's getting' dangerous to dance wit ya dese days."

"Are you sure that's correct, Mr. Hershfeld?" Faye slipped into posh Brit. "I would say, my good man, you've exhibited an extraordinary ability to handle the special care I've bestowed upon you. If, however, you are saying you no longer wish to be my consort and general dogsbody, then I shall consider finding someone of better quality, if you grasp my meaning."

"Why no, no, no, Ma'am. I wuz just sayin' things have been extra excitin' recently. And I do relish a challenge, I do. Honest."

They went on in a similar vein for another five minutes, changing accents and dialects at whim. Faye realized she was approaching her exit on Route 6 and was only a minute from arriving at school.

"Seriously, I do love you and there's something I want to talk to you about."

"Well, I too am totally sincere in echoing your sentiments and saying I love you too," Drake replied, still with humor in his voice. "Do you want to tell me your topic now or can it wait?"

"Why don't I call you after-school or this evening? I know it's a week night and all, so we should probably stay in our respective corners."

"That's true," Drake sighed, "so, yes, let's talk on the phone later. But no veiled erotic suggestions allowed, because I must tell you, I don't think I can put up much resistance."

"Mmmm," Faye said, feeling the familiar heat rise unbidden, "I will do my best to keep it clean. Gotta go. See ya!"

The morning zipped by. Everything she did had an extra spark and lightness. It felt as if she was floating above it all, but also very much in control. Her enthusiasm was reflected back by her students, whom seemed eager to engage with her. She had her free period at 1:00 that afternoon and, having called ahead for an appointment, arrived at Principal Brendan Fitzgerald's office just as his previous visitor was leaving. Brendan waved her in with a big smile.

Principal Fitzgerald was considered a decent guy by most of the teachers, and both students and their parents loved him. He was Irish through and through, which wasn't unusual on Cape Cod, where you couldn't throw a clam shell without hitting somebody Irish. He was in his early fifties, with wavy light red hair shot through with white. His cheeks were ruddy and his smile wide. He still had a trace of a lovely brogue when he spoke. And his eyes were quite green.

"How are you Faye?" he asked, then gave her a once over. "Did you do something different with your hair? Lost some weight? I know it's not PC, but I must say you look quite the hottie!"

Faye gave him a modest smile and said, in her approximation of an Irish brogue, "No, me hair's the same and the weight, too." She caught his eye and added, "But me sex life's improved quite a bit!"

Faye and Brendan's friendship allowed for such easy, uncensored banter. Back when Faye had first been hired as a teacher and was trying to fit in, she had gone to every social event the teacher's union held. Around then, Principal Fitzgerald had been emerging from a painful divorce. At one of the events in the autumn of her first year, he had engaged Faye in conversation, and seemed to want to get to know her personally.

After a half-hour of Brendan's undivided attention and not wanting to press her luck, Faye said she was tired and was heading home. As she got to her car, Brendan materialized alongside. Somehow they wound up in her front seat, passing his small flask of Irish whiskey back and forth and telling each other their life stories. At one point, Brendan turned to her and said, in the solemn voice only alcohol can invoke, "You know, Faye, you're going to be a great teacher. You understand what it's like to be a nobody, so you won't be seduced by the Great High School Popularity Contest. You'll be fair and evenhanded."

Faye was unsure how to take that, so she smiled and said, "Why, Brendan, you silver-tongued devil, that's the nicest thing anyone has ever said to me."

She leaned over, intending to kiss him on his cheek, but he turned his face to her and their lips met. Rather than jumping back like a frightened fawn, Faye just let the kiss happen. The subsequent fumbling and groping, while trying to gain traction with the gear shift in the way, was both frustrating and tantalizing, until Brendan said in a hoarse voice, "The backseat. We could get back there, right? Make things a bit easier."

"You think?" Faye giggled. "Begosh and begorrah, Brendan, we're like two teenagers at the drive-in. Except I never went to the movies, much less the drive-in, with a boy in high school. This'll be a first."

"Well, me darlin', firsts come in all shapes and sizes," Brendan opened his door and got out. Faye stumbled into the crisp, autumn air and turned to open the back door, but, glancing over the top of her car, saw Brendan duck down and scuttle to the rear. A large crew of teachers were exiting the tavern and heading to the parking lot. Brendan whispered, "I think our drive-in party will have to wait. Sorry, darlin'." He met his second wife soon after that, but the fizz between them persisted over the years and they joke flirted with each other often.

"Yer sex life's improvin' is it? Well, I must say it's about time that Drake fella stepped up and made a real effort."

"Well, Brendan, me boy, I want you to know it's not Drake that's makin' the effort." She saw his surprise and added, "No, it's not another lover, though I certainly could have my pick, as ye know. No, it's me that's heated up the place."

They both burst into laughter. Finally, Brendan said, "You know I want to hear all about it, but you didn't stop by to flaunt your sex life and," he glanced at his wristwatch, "I've got an angry parent due in 10 minutes, so what's really on your mind?"

Faye gave him an edited version of what had happened with Ariella on Friday, that during the exam the girl seemed distracted and was, at one point, in a lot of pain and Faye had taken her to the bathroom. She didn't specify what caused Ariella's pain, but did say Ariella had been the first to turn in her exam paper. "I glanced at her answer sheet later and I don't think she did well on the exam." Faye explained she had called Ariella on Saturday and had expressed concern.

Brendan put up a hand to stop Faye and typed a little, hit

Enter and scanned the screen. Faye glanced around his office, noted the several framed photos of Brendan's kids, and thought he must be a great dad. She wondered how Drake would be as a dad.

"Oh, I know her. The kabuki kid. The one with the YouTube video about her." Brendan smiled and Faye knew he wasn't being disparaging. "She's got good grades, no discipline incidents, though she is tardy more than we like . . . " he paused to study the screen. "I see she was home-schooled before she came here for 10th grade and I met her mother when she first enrolled. Isn't the family some kind of hippies? Alternative types, sort of green crusaders or something? They live out in the woods somewhere?"

"Actually, the mother is an actress and an herbalist and, yes, they do live in the Punkhorn. I went there yesterday afternoon to talk to Calista, Mrs. Cardona. She seems very together, but, yes, her world view is definitely not mainstream. That's part of the reason why Ariella didn't take the test seriously, but she's excited about getting extra help from me."

"You went to a student's house? That's way beyond the call of duty. I always said you'd be a great teacher. You know you can work with Ariella after school whenever you want, so what is it you needed to see me about?"

"Brendan, we three hit it off yesterday and we all agreed I should tutor Ariella both in and out of school. But, the thing is, her mom asked if Ariella could stay with me next weekend because she's is going to the West Coast to talk to some film people. So, is it kosher for me to have Ariella as a houseguest for a few days?"

Brendan sat back. "That would be out of the norm, but there are precedents. Teachers occasionally volunteer to take at-risk kids into their homes when the Social Service options are pretty awful. This doesn't sound like it's as serious as that, though."

"No, I agree, but spending a few full days with Ariella will allow us to make quick progress. And I promise to give you a report afterward."

"Okay, the school can't stop you from having contact with

your students outside of the building. It might appear unusual to those who don't know the facts of the situation. Just be careful and tell Mrs. Cardona to confirm with me she wants Ariella to stay with you."

Ariella answered when Faye called around five that afternoon and the girl gave a little shriek of excitement and joy when she heard the Principal had given his okay. Faye could hear rhythmic thuds and realized Ariella was jumping up and down.

"Hey, cool it. I told you I was going to let you stay no matter what," Faye said. "This just means we can go places and not be worried about seeing people from school."

"Ms. Bloomberg, you just don't know how wonderful I feel. Yippee!"

"I'm happy, too, Ariella. We're going to have a fine time," Faye imagined all the mother-daughter talks and activities they'd enjoy. "Is your Mom around? I just need to talk to her for a few minutes." Ariella said yes and Faye could hear her running away from the phone, shouting for Calista, her voice squeaky with delight.

"Well, Faye, you certainly have made one of your students very happy. And me as well. Thank you so much."

"Calista, I must ask you. Why did you give me all those interesting things yesterday - the locket, the little purple star, the dreamcatcher?"

"Oh, I thought you understood. You need to place those items around your house and especially in the room Ariella will sleep in. They'll help settle her energy and make her feel at home."

"Any particular locations for specific items?" Faye pretended this was an everyday question.

"The dreamcatcher needs to be in the bedroom and preferably over the head of her bed. You can put the purple star anywhere. Just leave the locket where she'll find it - on a dresser for example - she'll know what to do with it. And put the rest of the things around the house, though I think the acorns will work best in the kitchen. Did Ariella tell you which of the cats were going to accompany her?"

"Cats?" said Faye, her voice creaky. "No, I didn't get a chance to talk to her today at school. So, no, no talk about cats. How many are there?"

Calista's snorted. "How many? What an interesting question. I'm going to state we have more than a few, but certainly less than a lot. Let's just say there are the right number of cats. Ariella began acquiring them when we first arrived from LA and they're quite devoted to her and generally well behaved. In fact, she doesn't really refer to them as cats, but rather as her furkids."

"That's good, right? Uh, with how many furkids does Ariella usually travel?"

"Oh she never brings more than an environment can tolerate. Don't worry, she's very considerate in such matters. Do you have any pets?"

"Nope, no pets at the moment. Unless you count Yellowfoot, the Squirrel of the Future!"

"Yes , Yellowfoot! Of course we've heard of Yellowfoot, though I think his real name is something a bit different. Our friends in the treetops use quite a communication system, you know, so even at a distance we've heard about this wonderful creature. Quite the showman, too, I understand, though perhaps his opinion of himself is somewhat inflated. No, don't worry, the cats and Yellowfoot will respect each other's presence."

Faye huffed. She was in her familiar, comfortable kitchen and the late afternoon sun was striping the deck. But, talking about cat's instead of dolls or other kids for playmates? Communicating with squirrels? Where was this all going? Faye made some agreeable sounds, remembered to tell Calista to send a note to Principal Fitzgerald, thanked her again for the tea and said goodbye. Then she went out to the deck with her meditation cushion and sat through the rest of the afternoon and into the evening twilight. Finally her phone's ringtone broke her concentration. It was Drake.

"Hey," he said, "I thought you were going to call."

Faye rubbed her forehead, then absently stroked the big gray cat who lay beside her. "I'm sorry. I decided to meditate and just didn't stop. I think . . ." she trailed off. Somehow the grand plan to tell Drake she wanted a child had lost its urgency. She became absorbed in scratching behind the cat's ears and it stretched out its front legs and began purring.

"Are you okay? You sound a little strange."

"I'm fine, really. The meditation was just so good and . . . deep, I guess. What time is it anyway?"

"It's almost 7:30." Drake's voice was a monotone. He'd never gotten why she meditated. "What did you want to talk about anyway?"

Faye stood and watched the gray cat also stand up, stretch again, glance back at her, and wander off the deck into the darkness of the backyard. She could hear Drake's breathing as clear as if he were beside her. She gathered herself, inhaled and, in a rush, said "Well, I know this is going to seem a bit out of the blue, but I've been thinking I really want a baby."

Drake gasped and she heard him push back his chair and start pacing. "That does come as a surprise. What exactly brought this on?"

"I honestly don't know. Perhaps hanging with Ariella and her Mom reminded me of old dreams. But I think the desire has been growing for some time and is now more like a need." Were those two yellow eyes she saw glimmering in the deepening dark?

"Drake, do you like cats?"

"What? Cats? Why are you asking me that? Are you saying you want a child *and* a cat?"

"No, I just want to know."

"Yeah, cats are okay, I guess. We had some when I was a kid. I didn't bond with them, if that's what you mean."

They were both silent. Faye could picture him, a deep frown

on his handsome face, his mouth a tight straight line. She knew what he was going to say.

"Faye, you know I love you and I want things to work out between us, maybe even for the rest of our lives, but I'm not sure about having a child. I mean, we would both be getting close to our sixties when it was time for college. Are you sure you want to tie up the next twenty years or more?"

She didn't need to think. "Yes, I do. I really do. I think it might be the most important thing I could do in those years." She heard him sigh.

"Okay. This is sudden. I'm not saying no. I just need some time."

"No problem," Faye said, "I love you. Talk to you tomorrow?"

"Yeah, sure, but I don't think I'll have a final answer by tomorrow." He didn't say he loved her before they said goodbye.

Faye dropped down onto the deck and lay back, staring up into the stars. The air had turned cool, but she didn't care. After a minute, she felt a weight on her stomach and looked up into the golden eyes of a cat, though this one was orange. She stroked it and it settled onto her chest, kneading her collarbones and purring.

Chapter Twelve

Faye awoke in her bed on Tuesday morning and realized she had been dreaming about cats. Big cats in many colors. They had seemed so real she could still feel their fur beneath her fingers. She remembered talking with Calista about Ariella's cats and she and Drake had discussed cats. It was no surprise she dreamed about them. She started to get out of bed, but stopped and looked down at herself. She was still wearing the same top and bottom she'd on the previous evening! And her sweater front was covered in gray and orange hairs.

Faye flashed on being outdoors at night on her back on the deck with a big orange cat on her chest. Did that really happen? Another memory flickered and she jumped up, ran out of the room down the hallway and skidded into the kitchen. An opened tin of tuna was on the counter and, on the floor near the slider to the deck, there were two saucers speckled with crumbs of dried tuna alongside two small bowls, each still containing a few drops of milk.

Bemused, she picked up the saucers and bowls, rinsed them off and put them in the dishwasher. Then she rinsed out the tuna tins and put them in the comingle recycling bin. After putting the kettle on to heat for tea, she walked to the slider and gently tugged it open. Moving with deliberation, she eased onto the deck and saw her meditation cushion and mat, wet with dew. Otherwise all seemed normal. She walked toward the rear of her scruffy lawn where it met the woods, but halted at a patch of bare dirt. There was one perfect feline paw print in the moist earth. Faye knelt and reached out to trace its ridges. The toes of the paw print were pointed toward her house.

She ran back to the deck, then into the kitchen, ignored the first tentative toots from the tea kettle and rushed to the hall and then to the doorway to the second, spare bedroom. The bedroom where Ariella would be staying. Her first impulse was to throw the door open and charge into the room, but instead she just rested her hand on the knob and slowly turned it.

As she inched the door open, she thought she heard two thumps, as if some things were landing on the floor. Then she felt a strong breeze from the room and heard the tinkle of bells. She pushed hard on the door and it swung open and slammed into the wall. Faye took two quick steps in and looked around. Nothing. She got down and peered under the bed and the dresser. Nothing. She threw open the closet door and rummaged through the boxes. Nothing. The room was empty or, at least, there weren't any cats. Then she noticed a rumpled, circular indentation in the bed covers. She put her hand on the spot. It was warm.

Faye backed out of the room, leaving the door wide open and went to the kitchen where the kettle was now screaming. She took it off the burner, got out her teapot, dropped in some bags of organic green tea and stood, trembling, one hand on the counter. She gazed without seeing out at the deck until the water in the kettle stopped boiling and she could pour it into the teapot. She went through the rest of her pre-work routine as if sleepwalking. It wasn't until she was in her car, halfway to school, she thought to call Drake. He didn't answer, and he didn't text, so she left him a voice message.

"Hey! Where are you? Something weird happened last night and again this morning. Something to do with cats, if you can believe it. Give me a call later and I'll tell you all about it."

The school day passed without incident, though Faye felt unsettled, like she had missed something important. Brandon Fitzgerald sent her an email saying he had received approval from Mrs. Cardona for Ariella's weekend stay. In class, Faye gave Ariella, who was again in full makeup and costume, an extra smile. The girl gave a little smirk in return, but otherwise was her usual enigmatic self. Faye noticed Ariella's backpack now had what appeared to be a cat stuffie attached to it. Ariella noticed her teacher's glances and, with another little smile, reached down and stroked the stuffie.

Faye was restless when she got home from school, so went out on the deck and did a thirty-minute yoga routine. She concluded with the savasana pose in which she just lay on her back with arms and legs outstretched for as long as she wanted. As expected, her breathing slowed and she slipped into a doze. Part of her wondered if a cat might appear. She was a bit disappointed when she heard her cell ringing in the kitchen. It was Drake.

"Mrs. Hershfeld, please?" he said with mock formality.

"Yes, that's me," she chuckled, "May I ask who's calling?"

"Uh, this is Mr. Drake Hershfeld, your husband, whom you may remember from the other evening? I was the one who did the taste test with you?"

"Why yes, I do remember you. How are you? How are your tastebuds?"

"Fine, fine, everything's fine," Drake replied in a fake gruff voice. "Yes, everything's just fine, tastebuds and all. Though I must admit I'm experiencing some strange physical sensations whenever I think of the taste test."

"Oh, really, Mr. Hershfeld? And which part of your body is experiencing these . . . sensations?"

"Well, I know you're my wife and all, but it's kind of embarrassing to talk about. Any possibility we could meet in person and I could show you?"

"I guess it depends." She wanted badly to see him, but knew they needed to talk without drooling with desire for each other.

"Depends on what?"

"Whether you've been thinking about my wish for a child. And, if so, what are your thoughts?"

"Ah, the child question. And wasn't there also a cat question?" Drake paused, but Faye just waited. "Guess I'd better shift gears and put my physical sensations aside, if I can, while we talk. Yes?" His voice had lost all pretense of humor.

"That would be appropriate," said Faye.

"Okay then, I have questions."

"Ask away."

Drake cleared his throat. "Does having a child together mean we'll get married? And live together? Share finances? And all that stuff?"

"Get married? I thought we already were. Didn't you just call me Mrs. Hershfeld? But, seriously, no, no and not necessarily. I don't expect you to marry me just because we produce a child. Nor is it necessary to live together, though I'm assuming you'll take some interest in the child. And finances? Well, financial support from you would be appreciated and possibly needed. Kids are expensive, you know. But I'm pretty sure I can swing it on my own."

She heard Drake huff out a held-in breath, so she went on, "My desire for a child is just that. I know it's only mine and that's okay. I'm comfortable with the idea of being a single mom. But I also want you to know I love you and hope our connection can continue, even with a kid in the picture."

Drake was quiet and she waited. Finally, he said, "Look, this isn't my final answer, but what would happen if I simply told you I didn't want to be a father, no matter how little responsibility I had to take on? Would we stay together? Would you find some other guy to be the father?"

It was Faye's turn to be quiet. She felt a tight ache grow between her breasts. "I don't know the answers to those questions. I guess I figured you'd want to be the father, especially if all you had to do was engage in unprotected sex with me. I mean, it would be no-strings attached. Really."

"The problem is I don't think I can be a no-strings father. I've avoided having children until now, but I always knew if I did, I would go all out. And that's what is scaring me. I mean, I'm 42 and happy with my life as it is. And a child will change that. I think when we talked before about children I was clear about my viewpoint."

"I see," said Faye. "And, yes you did make yourself clear. I just thought if it meant minimal commitment from you, you would be okay with it. I just thought—"

"Faye, I'm getting truly uncomfortable. Can we take a time-out and talk again, like tomorrow?"

"Sure, sure. I certainly don't want to make you feel uncomfortable, especially not if you're already having those weird physical sensations." Faye tried to laugh.

"No, I don't want to complicate our physical stuff with this. Talk to you tomorrow?"

"For sure. I love you."

"I love you too, Faye, I really do. Bye"

The afternoon warmth was cooling and Faye shivered, gathered up her yoga mat and meditation cushion and went into the house. She poured herself a cup of the tea leftover from the morning and popped it in the microwave, imagining how Calista would cringe.

Drake wasn't jumping on her bandwagon, that was obvious. And her bandwagon couldn't move without him. Or at least not in the direction she wanted. She needed to step back, get some objective distance and see the big picture.

This whole desire-for-a-child thing had not even been at the forefront until this past weekend. But she knew how certain how she had felt since Sunday evening. *What happened? Are suppressed parts of me emerging along with the sexual eruptions?* She had a vision of things falling off walls and shelves during an volcanic explosion. Was her desire for a child strong enough for her to seek out another man? She shuddered at the prospect. *Ugh, it would take forever to get over Drake and a long time to find somebody with whom I would be so comfortable. And, by then, I probably would be too old to be a mother. Of course, I could try artificial insemination.* She thought about that for a minute. *No, it has to be Drake. I'm going to find a way to convince him.*

She picked up the fantasy novel she had neglected the past four days, grabbed some organic corn tortillas and some red pepper hummus, poured herself a large glass of chilled Chardonnay, and flopped onto the couch. The novel was good because the fantasy element was strong, but not dominant. The main characters were mostly human and the story focused on their interactions with creatures from fantasy realms. Faye slid into the book's world, where magic and magical beings were taken for granted, but humans still had ordinary concerns. Hours passed and she only stirred to go to the bathroom or to get more snacks. When the print on the page became blurry, she went to bed. As she slipped under the soft blanket of sleep, she reminded herself to tell Drake about her weird cat experience and about Ariella's upcoming weekend visit.

Chapter Thirteen

On both of the next two days, Faye thought about cats right after waking. She wondered if she should put some tuna on a plate on the deck, but knew it would attract all sorts of other critters. No matter, she was going to formally meet Ariella's cats this weekend.

Both mornings she drank a big cup of Calista's spicy herbal tea and relished its satisfying warmth and tingle. On Wednesday morning, despite the tea, she felt abstracted, as if she were watching herself in a video. She knew she wasn't being present when, after giving Yellowfoot one peanut, he stayed and stared up at her. Faye glimpsed her reflection in his black eyes and snapped back into the moment. Of course! She quickly handed him another nut and then poured a handful on the deck. Yellowfoot glanced back at this bounty, then at her. She could swear he was asking if she was okay.

At school, events progressed in an odd, linear fashion, as if on a railroad track. She imagined herself the conductor in a railway car which stopped at the start of each class period to pick up and disgorge student passengers. She, like the conductor taking tickets, moved among them during the 50 minute period/ride, announcing things they should know and answering their questions. It all went like clockwork, which was eerie, because she couldn't remember a day when some event or emergency or rambunctious student hadn't disrupted the schedule. But no, today the students sat quietly in their seats, reading or writing and occasionally talking with her. She imagined time flowing smoothly by, like scenery scene through a rail car's windows.

After school Faye didn't want to wait for Drake to call so she rang him when she got home. "Is this Mr. Hershfeld hyphen Bloomberg?"

"Yup." Drake made his voice hoarse and a little nasal.

"How are you Mr. H hyphen B?"

"Ahm fine, Ma'am. How be you?"

"I'm smooth and easy," Faye said, dropping her voice into a lower register.

"Izzat right? Well, ahl be right over."

"Really?" Faye said, and felt a pleasure twang.

"Why sure, Ma'am, your wish is my command."

"Are you a sharecropper, Mr. H hyphen B?"

"I might be. I kin tell you all about it when I git over to your place."

"Hmmm. I dunno."

"Remember Ma'am, your wish is my command. Any wish atall."

"Well, I'm not sure I want to make a wish right this minute. Can we talk for a bit?"

"Of course." Drake dropped the accent.

"So, last night you said you wanted to think about things and—"

Drake cut her off, his voice now agitated and tense. "Yes. I did think about things - a lot - and I must admit I'm still not understanding and only partially believing this sudden desire for a child. Is this some fantasy you read where a character is pregnant or wants to get pregnant?"

Faye was taken aback and a little stung, though he knew well her predilection for role-playing. Before she could reply, Drake continued.

"I mean, is this possibly some passing fancy? And, don't you think you should first try something which isn't so much of an all-in commitment? How about babysitting? And if that goes well, maybe even foster a kid?"

"Babysitting? Really? Why would I want to babysit? Oh wait, I get it. Then I'll realize how much I really don't like babies? Is that what you're saying?" Faye felt an escalating burn which had nothing to do with sex.

"No, no, please! That's not what I meant. I just want to be sure you know what you're getting into. I mean, you're signing up for the next 21 years or more of child care. And, as I'm sure you realize, being a parent isn't a part-time job. And it continues even when they're grown and gone."

"Duh! You think? Like I haven't already thought all that through?" Faye realized as she spoke she *did* know what she was doing. "This may seem sudden to you, but the desire to be a mother has been growing in me for a long time. I'm a woman and, of course, women give birth to babies and raise them. What could be more important? And right now my body and spirit feel it's time to give birth. And doing that will give meaning to the rest of my life. A meaning I believe is missing. Can you understand that?"

There was a painful silence. It seemed as if Faye's words echoed and reechoed between them. This was the strongest statement she'd ever made to him, or to anyone for that matter, about having children. And she knew it was all true, even if she hadn't known it in her heart completely until now.

"Of course I get it. I know you're sincere. " Drake finally said, his voice low and rough, his breathing uneven. Was he crying?

"Drake? You okay?"

"I'm, I'm fine," he said, but there was a catch in his voice.

"Listen. Perhaps we should change the subject for a bit. Did I tell you about my cat experience?"

"No."

It sounded as if Drake had the phone away from his mouth. Could he actually be crying? She imagined him rubbing his runny nose and teary eyes with his sleeve like a little kid. She forged ahead and told him all about the cats she believed had visited her. And how she had wakened the next morning and tried to catch them in the spare bedroom.

"And they disappeared! Like the Cheshire Cat or something."

"Did you see them at all?"

"Well, I think I saw them Monday evening, but now that whole time period is hazy. I'm pretty sure one cat was grey and the other was orange. They're supposedly Ariella's cats, so I guess I'll meet them formally and learn all about them this weekend when she stays over. She's going to bring some of her cats with her."

"What did you say? Ariella's staying at your house this weekend?"

"Oh yeah, guess I forgot to tell you. It wasn't a big deal compared to the other stuff we've been talking about."

"Not a big deal? I thought we were going to spend this weekend together."

"Oh, we still can. How about you come over Saturday evening?"

"That's it? One night?"

Faye dithered. Was she short-changing Drake? More important, might it weird out Ariella if Drake stayed the night? Calista had made it sound as if Ariella's home life had been worldly and progressive, but the girl had reacted with aversion when Faye had mentioned using the computer to chat with a boy.

"Well, Friday night will be her first night at my house and I want to give her my undivided attention. So —"

"Hold up! How did this even happen? Why is she staying at your house in the first place? Why am I hearing about this now?"

Faye kept calm and explained how Calista was in a bind about finding a place for Ariella to stay. She also emphasized she wanted to get to know Ariella better so she could help the girl with her exam prep. "And, honestly, I like both of them and want to see if we can become friends. And yes, I am looking forward to playing mom to Ariella's kid. So what?"

"So, I am getting bumped by a 15 year-old who wears funny clothes and clown make-up? I guess I shouldn't be surprised. You've never been a big fan of ordinary reality. And now you're feeding cats who might or might not be real? And having visions of green men? Don't you think this has gone far enough?"

"Drake, that's harsh. I understand you're upset, but it isn't that big a deal. It's only one weekend and you and I will still get to see each other." Faye decided to try another tack. She lowered her voice and did a passable Mae West imitation. "You know, Mr. H hyphen B Sharecropper, you only need one night with me to make the crops grow. And that won't be a corn cob in your pocket."

"Okay, okay. I'm sorry for being harsh, as you put it. But I must admit all these sudden changes are alarming. I mean, you've gone through some weird stuff since last week and I'm not convinced you know what you're doing. I want to talk more about this, okay?"

"Sure. And I'm sorry for not telling you about the Ariella visit sooner. Why don't you come over for dinner on Saturday, say around seven? You can get to know Ariella and later let me know what you think. She's truly one-of-a-kind and can be delightful when she's away from school."

After she hung up, Faye was swept up by a mini-tornado of questions and doubts. Drake was going to continue to challenge her and the situation with Ariella could blow up if Saturday evening went awry. But she loved she was developing a new sense of purpose and drive. Purpose and drive made life more vivid, somehow both bigger and liberating at the same time. And the new energy, while sometimes disorienting and leaving her spaced out, was exhilarating. It felt like a new dimension had opened inside her, a dimension filled with enormous potential. Change felt good. Very good. Cheshire Cats and green men were not going to frighten her off.

Ariella came by Faye's classroom after school on Thursday. The girl was definitely in character. She danced into the room, twirling around so her bell skirt flared and smiled her wonderful smile, her green eyes sparking in her pale face. Faye felt as if she was in on some special secret, a secret only she and Ariella shared.

"Hey you," Faye grinned. "Are you excited about the weekend?"

"Totally!" Ariella said with another twirl. "It's going to be so epic, Mrs. B!"

"You know, Ariella, you can call me Faye when it's just the two of us. But not when anyone from school is around."

"Okay, Faye! Whatever you say, Faye. I'll do it your way. All day. Every day."

Faye couldn't help it, she burst out laughing. The girl was adorable!

Pleased, Ariella adopted a formal pose like an old-time orator – one hand held out in front of her, palm up and the other on her hip. "I'm a poet and don't know it. But my feet show it 'cause they're Longfellow's!" She did a quick shuffle step, glancing down at her Mary Janes.

"Ariella, you're too much! But that's an old one."

The girl grinned, did a little hip-hop move, and changed her stance to one reminiscent of a rapper. She gave a mock scowl, her voice deepened, and she began to chant. "I know a girl name Risqué Faye, who loves to play and play. But she don't play no croquet, and she don't eat no soufflé. She ain't goin' to work for the CIA and she ain't goin' to join the KKK. She loves her Edna St. V. Millay, a poet from the U.S. of A. and Emily D. is too way okay. No, my girl Faye's cool as Beyonce, and I say okay, hooray!"

Ariella was gesturing with her hands like rappers Faye had seen on MTV. She remembered reading something about certain hand signs having a connection to the Illuminati, an old secret society which was still reputed to influence governments and culture.

Ariella continued, "To Faye it's all just child's play, like goin' to a soiree and eatin' raspberry sorbet. She's the one who points the way and she's the one I will obey. If I don't listen to what she say, I know I'll have to pay or maybe get sent far away, to Guadeloupe, Uruguay or even passé Bombay."

Ariella stopped, the her face pink beneath the pasty white makeup. Faye clapped and hooted like she was at a rock concert. "Wow! Ariella, I don't know what to say except that was awesome! Did you make that all up on the spot or what?"

The girl's eyes were glowing and Faye thought Ariella probably didn't have anyone with whom to goof off and just be silly. Calista didn't seem the type to appreciate a cool rap and Faye doubted Ariella had many close friends at school. There might be Punkhorn kids for her to hang out with, but given the cottage's isolated location, Faye doubted it.

"I've been working on it all week Ms. B., I mean Faye. I just knew you would 'preciate it. I've got even more words if you want to hear them."

"Let's wait for the weekend, okay? Maybe we can do a duet or something?"

Ariella nodded, clapped her hands and spun around once more and sat down at a nearby desk. "What else are we going to do this weekend? Can we go to the mall? Can we go out dancing?"

Faye held up her hands. "Whoa! Let's not get too ahead of ourselves. Why don't we just spend Friday night hanging out, just us girls, and we can plan what we'll do on Saturday. I'm sure there will be plenty of places we can go to have fun. And, if you remember Cyndi Lauper, you know 'Girls Just Want to Have Fun.'

"Was that song on her album 'She's So Unusual'? The one that had all the hits?" Ariella's face was now still and serious.

"Uh, yes, I think so and I'm surprised you know that. There was even a song on it called 'He's So Unusual' or 'She's So Unusual.' "

Ariella studied the floor. "Some of the kids at school sing that when I walk by."

Faye was surprised. She didn't think Ariella was at all fazed by what the other students said or thought about her. "Well, you know Cyndi was celebrating people who dare to be different. She, herself, was pretty unusual for her time, back in the mid-1980s. I'd be flattered if I were compared to her."

"Yeah, I know I appear different on the outside, but I sometimes I think I'm not so different on the inside."

Faye stared at Ariella, startled by her apparent vulnerability. "If you think you are more ordinary than you appear, why do you go to so much trouble with the way you dress and do your makeup? Isn't it easier to just try and fit in?"

Ariella considered Faye for a beat. "It's important for me to dress this way and act different when I'm at school. It's part of my training."

"Your training? For what? To be an actress like your mom or something?"

"No, not exactly. It's for my future work for the nature spirits." Ariella grabbed her backpack. "I've got to zoom if I want to catch my ride. I'll tell you more this weekend."

"Ariella, wait. I wanted to ask you about your cats. Your mom said you're going to bring some with you and I was wondering how many. By the way, I think I met two of them the other night."

"Oh yeah, Fog and Leaf. They liked you and they checked out my room at your house, too."

"Fog and Leaf? Of course. Fog is gray and Leaf is orange, right?"

"Yup. Did you like them?"

"Well, I was pretty sleepy the evening they hung out with me on the deck, though I guess I fed them some tuna. And the next morning I thought they were in the guest bedroom, the one which will be your room. But they weren't there. It was like they disappeared. How do they do that?"

Ariella glanced away, a small frown on her face. "It's kind of complicated. Can I tell you on the weekend?"

"Sure, but before you go, just tell me how many cats are coming. I want to buy enough tuna or cat food."

"Well, Fog and Leaf maybe. Snow and Midnight are interested, but they're waiting to see what I say. A bunch of others are curious, but I'm going to discourage them. Four is plenty."

"Let me guess, Snow is white and Midnight is black? Fog must the gray one. But what color is Leaf?"

"Leaf is orange and yup, all the cats' names are related to nature, mostly because they're always hanging with the spirits."

"Really? Wow, we do have a lot to talk about. But go ahead and get going." Ariella turned toward the door. Faye called after her, "Don't forget I'm driving you to your house tomorrow to pick up your stuff. And, by the way, my boyfriend is coming for dinner on Saturday night and he'll probably stay over. He's very nice. He's a teacher too."

The girl gave Faye an odd look. Then she said, "Okay!" and was gone.

Faye slumped back into her ergonomic chair. There was so much going on with Ariella and her mother. Their lives were exotic compared with Faye's. What did Ariella mean by '. . . future work for the nature spirits'? Once again Faye went over all that had happened since the exam last Friday. Weird and unusual stuff, to say the least but, compared to the content of her fantasy novels, it could be ordinary. So why was she worried? She knew her meditation teacher would say she needed to first accept things as they were, to give up any expectations or attachments to preferred outcomes. Just let it be and work with it. But wasn't there a point where you had to ask yourself if perhaps things were getting a bit too crazy?

The weekend was going to be interesting, that much was sure. Ariella was so hilarious with her poetry and her rapping. Especially the rapping. Amazing she could memorize all that and then deliver it flawlessly. But how had Ariella known Faye was going to tell her to call her by her first name when she composed her rap days earlier?

Chapter Fourteen

At home, Faye had just put her books and papers down when her cell rang. Caller ID said it was Drake and she was tempted to let it go to voice mail. She wanted time to sit on the deck, drink tea and think. The phone rang again. Twice. Three times. She caved.

"Hey Mr. Sharecropper. How grow your crops?"

"Listen Faye, I've got a last minute tennis match in half an hour. And we're going out for beers after, and I don't think I should talk when I'm rushed or had something to drink. Plus, I got really worked up during our phone call yesterday. So I just sent you an email. It says all the things I'm not sure I can talk about calmly. Is that okay?"

This didn't sound good. "Sure, who are you playing with?"

"Some people who need a fourth."

Faye felt a tickle of intuition. "Is it mixed doubles?"

"In fact, it is. A couple I know from school needed a partner for a friend of theirs. Supposedly she's a good player."

"Really. How nice for you. A good woman player and beers too."

Drake had tried many times to get Faye to play tennis, but she found it much too intense and competitive. She didn't mind watching the matches on TV, but couldn't understand why Drake was so fanatic about playing. Her idea of a fun exercise was to crank up the stereo and dance in her living room. Making love burned lots of calories too.

"Now, Faye, you know it's not like that."

"Do I? Sometimes I wonder."

"C'mon, you know I love you."

"You say you do."

There was a long silence.

"Okay, Faye. I'm getting uncomfortable again. Let's talk tomorrow?"

"Ariella will be with me from after school on, but I am sure there will be time to talk." Faye was about to say goodbye when on impulse she said, "What's the name of the woman you're going to be partners with?"

"Shandra Cohen, why?"

"You're kidding? Shandra Cohen who teaches at my school? No way."

Shandra was a Physical Education teacher and she was young, extremely fit and had looks verging on beautiful. She'd reportedly been a star soccer player in high school and college. All the male staff members went silent whenever Shandra walked by.

"I didn't know she taught at your school. What's she like?"

"Well, she's teaches PE and I've heard she is a total athlete. Probably an excellent tennis player."

"Oh, that's good. I've been hoping for a strong partner."

"She's also beautiful." Faye waited, but Drake didn't say anything, so she added, "But she's way too young for you."

Drake didn't react.

"And she's a real bitch. She's broken more hearts than Madonna. So watch out!" Faye was trying to tease, but it came out all serious. She knew, in fact, Shandra didn't take advantage of her beauty and was something of a feminist. She was also a dedicated teacher.

"Well, thanks for the much unneeded info, Faye. I'll call you tomorrow," Drake said and hung up.

Faye again felt that tight, painful knot near her between her breasts. She was definitely going to have to be extra nice to Drake this weekend. He was getting quite irritated with her. She was torn between going out onto the deck to relax and nap in the late afternoon sun and reading Drake's email. The email won. She went to the kitchen and made a cup of tea, grabbed a banana, then fired up her laptop and sat in an armchair in the living room.

"Woman of My Life," the email began, "I first want to tell you how much I love you and how important you've become to me over the years. We've been so good together I was actually thinking we might talk about a commitment of some sort. I know you've never advocated for anything like that and I appreciate it. But, as we've comfortably settled in with each other, I thought it was the right thing to do. Maybe we could vow to be lifetime partners and then fine tune the details of whether we live together or what. I might even go so far as to say marriage is not out of the question.

And I know you are probably thinking I'm mentioning all this now because of the child question, but that's simply not the case. I genuinely had been thinking that way before now. And especially this past weekend when we were so right together."

Faye felt her eyes start to sting with the salt of imminent tears. She got up, grabbed a tissue, wiped her eyes and resumed reading.

"But, this having a child business has kind of put a stick in the spokes. You've never before expressed a strong desire for children. Or at least you've never made it sound like it had to happen for you to be happy.

"The problem is I very much want to make you happy. But not at the cost of my own happiness. And therein lies the rub.

"I've gotten to this ripe old age of 42 by making life choices carefully and, as you know, often based upon practical considerations. For example, I chose to be with you because I knew you weren't high maintenance and liked sex as much as I do. Plus, you're a really good friend. I know that sounds cold, but I want you to understand that my practical thinking also allowed me to fall in love with you."

Faye stood up again, went to the couch, picked up a pillow and threw it across the room. Then she stared at the laptop screen, took a big sip of tea and a bite of banana. She removed the hair tie holding back her unruly black curls and waggled her head like a dog shaking off water. With her fingertips, she scrubbed her scalp until her hair stood out from her head like a halo. Finally she sat down and again turned the screen toward her.

"I don't think I told you, but I had opportunities to father children before we met. But each time the opportunities veered toward reality, I veered away. I was even the willing partner in two abortions. I'm not proud of that, but I don't really regret my choices, though I am sorry for any pain the women involved felt. My proof of the validity of my choices is that my sense of personal happiness has remained strong.

"And before you label me as self-centered, I want to remind you I work hard and devote my life to educating young people. There were many other career paths open to me, but I chose teaching because I wanted to make a contribution and because I'm making a contribution as a teacher, I think it justifies my choice to not produce offspring. And I thought you had made the same choice."

Faye slammed the laptop cover down. "Bastard. Jerk. Cretin."

She drank the rest of her tea and ate the rest of the banana. Then she went out to the deck, did her yoga routine and meditated. It was dark when she came in. She turned the laptop back on.

"Faye, by now you're probably feeling pretty emotional and I don't blame you. I want to keep this discussion going. Let's talk and email as much as is necessary. However, we need to face the fact I'm not going to be the father of your child. And I can't imagine ever changing my mind.

"But I will support your efforts, even if it means losing you to another man. That's hard for me to think of and even harder to write. And I know I will probably regret even mentioning it.

"I hope we remain close, wherever the future leads us.

"See you Saturday. I'll bring some wine."

At the end of the email there was a little smiley icon with a question mark next to it. Faye got up from the armchair and set the laptop down on the nearby table as if it was extremely fragile.

She found its charger and plugged it in. Her hand was shaking. She walked over to the pile of stuff she had brought home from school and dug out the laptop she had cadged from the school's IT Director, saying she was tutoring a student over the weekend. As she carried it down the hall to the spare bedroom, tears started streaming down her face. The ache between her breasts was throbbing.

Another man! He had said he could support her being with another man! How could he even say that? In the spare bedroom, Faye put the school's laptop on the desk and sat heavily on the edge of the bed. Tears had dribbled off her chin and her blouse was wet. She didn't try to wipe the tears away. She needed to cry. What was she going to do? Was the pain of losing Drake worth the joy she imagined a child would bring? There must be a way to both keep Drake and birth a child. She had created this dilemma and now she had to find a way to deal with it. Some compromise must be possible.

She kept crying, making little whiny noises in the back of her throat. Dizzy, she leaned forward and brought her head between her knees. She might never stop crying. Drake would come over and she would cry the whole time. Then he would see. She mentally flailed about like someone drowning, trying to find a life preserver to cling to, trying to think of some idea or plan. Her tears dropped onto the carpet. Some calm part of her mind focused on the pattern the drops made. She began her deep breathing exercise. In, pause, then out, pause again and in again. It was hard to do the exercise while doubled over.

She remembered reading a book by an early 20th Century spiritual leader called Krishnamurti, who said it was pointless to agonize over a choice, because it was best to simply wait for "choiceless clarity." She recalled her father, who was fond of Jewish proverbs, saying "What one has, one doesn't want, and what one wants, one doesn't have." And her mother, who had picked up her husband's habit, saying "Don't sell the sun to buy a candle." What would Rhoda make of the mess her daughter was in now?

Faye hiccupped and smiled, imagining telling her mom about green men and Cheshire Cats. The old math teacher would scoff and say something like, "Well, Faye, you know it just doesn't add up." And then she'd snort at her pun. Why not call her mom? Or Wanda? Her friend's reaction would be harsh and critical of Drake and she wasn't sure she could handle that. She'd wait until tomorrow to make any calls.

Faye straightened, wiped her eyes with the back of her hand. *I made him cry and now he made me cry.* She sniffled and went into the bathroom and splashed cold water on her face. Her eyes in the mirror seemed greener somehow. The pain between her breasts had subsided to an ache. She imagined again what Wanda would say and suddenly the ache became a burn of anger. *Bastard. Ignominious wretch. What a schmuck. Literally. How could he? And in a fucking email! Bastard.*

In the living room Faye picked up the other items Calista said should be placed about the house to make Ariella comfortable. The green acorns and three dried flowers she put on shelves in the living room. The diamond shaped amethyst went on a table near the front door. And she hung the dreamcatcher over Ariella's bed, the tiny, delicate, glossy black feather swaying in some unfelt breeze. The old, begrimed coin she left in the pouch, not wanting to chance hearing whispering voices. She put the scallop shell gold locket on her bedroom dresser. She'd wear it tomorrow to show solidarity with Ariella.

When all the items had been situated, Faye grabbed a half-full bottle of wine from the refrigerator and went out on the deck. The stars were bright, competing with and complementing the first quarter moon. A strong wind moved the tree limbs like dancers' arms. She took two big swigs of wine, then coughed and choked. Then she cried a little more. And she drank some more. When the wine was gone she lay down on the deck and stared up into the night. She wasn't surprised when she felt the delicate brush of a cat's tail against her arm. And she didn't protest when two front paws gently kneaded her chest, right on the sore spot between her breasts. And it felt right to look up and see an orange cat with somber golden eyes gazing down at her. She knew his name. Leaf. He was Leaf.

Chapter Fifteen

Faye awoke on Friday still in the shorts and t-shirt she'd worn the previous evening. As she had been the last time cats visited her, she was in her bed and, like the last time, she couldn't remember coming in from the deck. She did remember putting an empty wine bottle in the recycling bin and her mouth now tasted sour. She opened her eyes slowly to see if the sunlight spilling through the windows would trigger a hangover. Nope, she was good. She gazed at the ceiling and wondered how a dreamcatcher would look above her bed.

What had happened last night? Drake's email. Yes, of course. Crying. A lot of crying. And the ache in her chest. Wine on the deck. A whole half bottle? And the cat. The cat! The wonderful cat! She sat up and was surprised to see not an orange cat but a big black one curled up on the bedspread near her knees.

"Midnight? Is that you? Where's Leaf?"

The cat opened its eyes, raised its head and turned to give Faye a cool, green-eyed gaze. It blinked once before lowering its head back onto its paws. Faye realized she didn't know which of Ariella's cats were males or females. But she was pretty sure Midnight was male.

"Would you like some food?" Midnight didn't move. Faye reached out her hand and, with great care, rested it on the cat's silky black flank. A small shiver ran up her arm. It felt as if her hand was immersed in something bubbly and tingling. Midnight didn't twitch.

In small increments, Faye began stroking the cat's back and side and was rewarded with an immediate burst of purring. When she gently scratched behind Midnight's ears, the purring became a steady rumble. The sense of energy flowing between them increased and Faye spirits rose. After a minute or two of scratching and stroking, she had the urge to pick up Midnight and hold him in her arms. She wanted to clutch him tight to her chest. She wanted all the energy he could give. Was it possible she could settle for a cat instead of a child? Drake would be okay with a cat. But, when she reached with both hands, Midnight jumped down from the bed and left the bedroom.

"Wait! I'm sorry. I didn't mean to . . . I thought you liked me," Faye called as she hurried after the cat. She felt a bit of the heart wrench which had gotten her crying last night. Her eyes smarted again. Midnight was standing at the sliding door to the deck staring through the glass at an equally large white cat staring back at him. Faye skidded to a stop and grabbed the back of a kitchen chair to keep from falling.

"Oh, Snow is here. Is she your girlfriend? I have a boyfriend. Or, I think I do."

She collapsed into the chair and sniffled back some tears. Midnight turned and glanced at her before walking over to rub against her bare legs. Faye felt a tickle of the same energy she had when petting him on the bed. She reached down to scratch his head and the energy flow swelled. In a minute she realized she again felt better. Why was she weepy? Things would work out with Drake for sure. They had to. She would make him see they could both be happy with a child. He loved her. He said so in his email. Midnight bumped against her ankle and she saw he was focused on the deck where Snow was waiting.

"Okay, okay, I get it. You want to be with your girlfriend? I bet you're a good boyfriend, aren't you. Do you have any children?" If Midnight and Snow had children, then certainly Faye was entitled to at least one. She was going to point that out to Drake.

When she opened the slider, Midnight darted out and the pair went down the steps and headed across the lawn toward the woods. Faye watched them go, feeling something akin to envy. Just before the two cats entered the trees, Midnight stopped and glanced back. Faye waved and they disappeared into the shadows.

"Well, at least I am getting on with cats." Certainly, this was a good sign. She dressed for work with care, choosing a loose-fitting, high-waisted, dark lavender print dress with a scoop neckline and velvet trim. Faye thought of it as her hippie dress. Black tights, ballet flats, the scallop shell pendant from Calista on an extra gold chain and her hair worn loose completed what she hoped was a look recognizable to Ariella. She added some delicate gold filigree hanging earrings in the shape of leaves. After approving of what she saw in the mirror, she glanced at the clock, saw she had time and called her mom.

"Well, daughter of mine, to what do I owe the honor?" Rhoda's voice was always a bit louder than necessary. Decades of trying to get teenagers to pay attention to geometry and algebra had given her a permanent semi-shout.

"Oh, just had a few minutes before work and thought I would say hi."

Her mom gave a snort. "You've never called me at this time on a workday. In fact, you almost never call me on a workday. I'm lucky if you can spare 15 minutes on the weekends. But, who am I with my expectations? Just your mother, that's who. Though I guess I was a pretty crummy mother, going by the little time you and your sister give me."

Faye opened her mouth to protest, but Rhoda continued, "What is it, Faye Evelyn?" Her mother never used Faye's middle name unless she was upset or serious. "It's that Drake boy, isn't it? What has he done? I always told you he was too good looking to be trusted. He could be a gangster for all we know. He and Sean Penn could be brothers. Bad boys to the bone, if you ask me. Did he do something to you? Hit you? Make you take drugs? Pimp you out?" Her mother snorted again.

"Mom! Stop. Yes, I'm upset over Drake, but it's not because he's been a 'bad boy.' It's just that I want a child." Faye sniffled a little.

"What? Are you crying? What did you say? You want a child? At your age?"

"Yes, yes I do want —"

"Well, of course you want a child. Why not? Lots of women your age and older become mothers. And that fershtinkiner Drake isn't cooperating? Give me his phone number. I'll straighten him out right away. You've given him, what, five or six years of your life and he can't even help you create a child? What a schmuck. Better yet, give me his mother's number." There was a pause, then, "And stop sniveling. We can solve this."

Faye took a deep breath, dabbed at her eyes with a tissue and said, "Mom, I'm glad you're supportive, but I don't want you to intervene. I think I can handle this. I just wanted to talk to you and let you know what's been happening. All I need is a sympathetic ear."

"What's to know? The guy's being a putz. You're better off without him. But, go ahead, tell me how things got this way."

Faye tried to summarize all that had happened in the past week. She even told her mom about the incredible sex, though she blushed as she did so. She tried to make the business with the cats and the whispering coin sound funny, but her voice got quivery. The only part she left out was her filling in the blanks on Ariella's answer sheet.

Rhoda responded with her usual dry and logical analysis, as if she was explaining a complicated, but solvable math problem. "Let's review. This weird girl gets you involved in her life and you think the connection gave you some energy. Said energy manifested in great sex with Drake, the schmuck. And then you have a creepy green guy vision when you're half-asleep. The girl's mother is some kind of movie star and she and her daughter live in an old, old fairy tale house in the woods. They don't own a TV or a computer. The mom makes a big impression on you and sweet talks you into taking care of her daughter while she gallivants off to LA. And somehow this all makes you think you need to make a child right now. Oh, and there are magical cats visiting your house and giving you yet more energy. Have I got all that right so far?"

"Yes, but —"

And Drakee boy decides he's too old to be a father, but he still loves you and, no doubt, wants more fabulous sex?"

"Sort of, but —"

"Faye, my darling girl, let me be blunt. You're going through a phase. Nothing more. I think, at age 36, you're getting those 'is this all there is?' thoughts. You're feeling like you want something more out of life, that you deserve something more. But, sweetie, you've *always* wanted more than you thought you were getting. And this is more of the same. Remember when you were little, you always tried to keep up with Clara, making up imaginary friends and telling us incredible stories of what you did with them?

"Now, I think we have to face the fact this affair, relationship, whatever you want to call it, with Drake has reached a dead end. He's never going to commit to anything but what makes him happy. The minute you start making your wishes known, he twitches back like a scalded cat. Pardon the pun." Her mother snorted.

"He says he loves me."

"Of course he does! You're the perfect woman for him. Convenient, compliant and good in bed. The question you need to ask is does he truly love *you* or the way you've molded your life to his? And you need to ask whether you really love him or just the fantasy of having a cool, sexy boyfriend?"

Faye was astonished. Rhoda had always been a straight shooter, but this was something else. She would have expected ruthless words from Wanda, but her mother? No way!

"Faye Evelyn, I think the bubble has burst and reality is rushing in. Or what you, with your love of fantasy, call reality. Disappearing cats? Come on! Visions of green men? You had those when you were thirteen. That girl Ariella and her mother have given you a glimpse of a different way of being which is good, but It's time you stop fantasizing about green men and start thinking about a career change. And definitely a boyfriend change."

"Mom, you're the one who encouraged me to become a teacher. And you kind of approved of Drake."

"I know, I know, but at the time you needed something or

someone to hang onto, to get you going in a direction. And you needed someone to make you feel loved. You were floundering worse than a flounder." Another snort.

"I know you only wanted a sympathetic ear, but I'm your mother and I still get to give my opinion. And you're too old for me to just kiss your boo-boo and tell you it's going to be okay. I believe all the craziness you've been experiencing is a symptom of your growing need to make a change. Your subconscious is working hard to get you to listen, fabricating all these scenarios and visions to shake you out of the rut you've been in. And so you now realize you want a child, which is one of the biggest changes of all. Does that make sense?"

"Mom, I don't know what to say. Things seem to be changing, for sure. But I don't think it's all coming from within me. I mean, the cats are real cats. I was petting one an hour ago. Really."

"Faye, you used to bring home the neighbors' cats and tell us they were your magical friends. And sometimes it was bugs and even worms. One time you showed me a dead dragonfly and were convinced it was a sleeping fairy. And what about all those years you and Wanda spent dreaming of unicorns and ogres? Do you remember?"

"Yes, but —"

"Okay dear, I must go. I'm going to be late for an appointment. Think about things and call me later?"

"Sure. Thanks mom. I love you."

"And I love you. Call your friend Wanda. She's got a good head on her shoulders." There was a pause, then, "I'm sure things seem confusing and don't add up for you right now, but it will all work out, wait and see."

After she hung up, Faye erupted into laughter. In the end, Rhoda had said exactly what Faye predicted she would. Few people were as dependable as her mom.

As was usual on Fridays, time at school moved both fast

and slow. The kids were excited about both the upcoming long weekend and the end of the school year, which was only two weeks away. Their fizz was contagious and Faye became fidgety as the day wound down. The last period seemed to take forever and, when the final bell rang, she practically chased the kids out the classroom door. Fifteen minutes later she and Ariella were buckled in and waiting in a line of cars to leave the school parking lot.

"Want to listen to some music?" Faye asked.

"Sure."

"Any suggestions?"

Ariella didn't turn to face Faye, but kept gazing down at her lap or out the window. Some kids in her class were walking nearby and looked in their direction. Faye saw Ariella start to squish down in her seat, but then straighten up.

"What kind of music do you like?" Faye tried again.

"Oh, just play whatever you want, okay?" Ariella waved her hand in the general direction of the car's stereo.

"All right then." Faye popped in a Bonnie Raitt CD and "Something to Talk About" kicked in as they swung out onto the road. Faye was relieved when Ariella started tapping time on her backpack. She snuck glances at the girl, who wasn't her usual bright self. Perhaps it was apprehension about the weekend, but Faye thought Ariella might be a bit sad.

"Is anything troubling you?"

"I miss my mom."

Faye studied Ariella, who again gazed out her open window. The wind had blown some of her hair loose from her braids. *Wait a minute! What are those squirmy green things holding the braids together?* Ariella usually had colored electrical wire or bits of yarn to secure her braids. But today there were green strands starting at both braids' ends and woven up into their length. It seemed like the strands had little leaves on them and these were moving. Faye wanted to take a closer look, but had to keep her eyes on the road. When she had a another chance to check on Ariella, she had faced forward with her braids down her back and hidden. Her green eyes were gleaming, but whether from unshed tears or some inner light, Faye couldn't tell.

"You know we can call your mom from my house. Or we could even text her."

"I know, I know. But you know what's really wack? She's probably going to get this big part. And that means she'll be gone for weeks or even months. And I'll get stuck staying with my derpy neighbors." Ariella's voice rose in anger. "Or worse, she'll ship me off to my grandparents in Boston. "I'll die if I have to live in a city all summer! I'll lose touch with the nature spirits. And it will be much longer before I'm ready. It's not fair!" Ariella threw her backpack onto the floor in front of her seat and kicked at it. Her foot caught the stuffed cat toy and it skewed sideways and hung at an awkward angle.

Whoa, this was sudden. Less than five minutes into the weekend and Faye's houseguest was having a tantrum. What had happened to the happy rapper of yesterday? Faye kept her attention on her driving while she planned her response.

They stopped for a red light and she said, "Ariella, you know your future is yours to create. You imagine what *could* happen, but that doesn't mean you can't change how things turn out. And you know, nothing is forever. Everything changes and what seems horrible now can turn into a funny memory years down the road."

"Yeah, I know. The nature spirits are always going on about being patient, that true growth always takes time and you can't make a flower bloom before it is ready." The girl fiddled with her backpack, rearranged the stuffed cat and gave it a half-hearted pat.

"So, you should listen to them, right? They sound wise to me. How lucky you are to have them give you such good advice."

"You don't understand, do you? You don't get it! You don't know what they're planning for me or how important it is to me to be ready for those plans." Ariella's anger was back. "You probably think I'm just another teenage girl with fantasies, except mine are about "nature spirits" rather than horses or boys or unicorns. Do you know how hard I work to remain true to myself? Do you know the burden they put on me? I'm always worried I'll screw things up."

Faye shifted into full "I'm Your Friend, but I'm Also an Adult and Your Teacher" mode. She pulled the car to the side of the road and turned off the motor. Ariella was now scowling, tears seeping from her eyes and making tracks across her pale makeup. She had her pack in her lap and was obsessively grooming the stuffed cat.

"Ariella, I like you and want to understand you. That's why I agreed you could stay with me. There will be plenty of opportunities for long talks these next few days. You can tell me as much as you want about what's going on with you, with your mom and with . . . the nature spirits. There's some stuff I want to share, too."

Faye couldn't tell if her words were having a positive or negative effect. Or any effect at all. Ariella kept her head down and was running her left hand over the stuffed cat. She began humming. Faye lowered her window and sniffed the warm, late spring air. She glanced in the rear view mirror and saw her hair was still nicely tumbled around her shoulders, rather than just frizzed out.

After a minute, Faye said, "Are we good to go?" and started the car. Ariella slid her eyes to Faye and her face wore a strange mixture of affection and amusement.

"Sure thing, Faye, whatever you say Faye." Ariella sat back, put her feet up on the dash and laughed. Faye started to pull onto the road, but stopped and looked at the girl again and her eyes went wide. While the girl's left hand still stroked the stuffed cat, her right hand had slid under the hem of her dress and was busy up in her crotch. Faye realized what she thought was rhythmic hummings were actually low groans of pleasure. Ariella's had closed her eyes and her eyebrows drawn together and down in concentration. She was grinning.

Faye tried to think of something to say, but came up blank. She merged with traffic and concentrated on driving. She had a vision of her mom saying "things just don't add up."

Yes, there was going to be a lot to talk about this weekend.

Chapter Sixteen

Faye was proud she was able to navigate all the way to Ariella's cottage without once asking for directions - through the maze of dirt roads in the Punkhorn, then into the shrouded entrance to the park-like woods surrounding the cottage. Ariella hadn't spoken, not even when Faye had to pause at a fork in the road to choose the right way.

About 10 minutes previous, Ariella had let out a loud sigh and collapsed further into her seat, the backpack sliding out of her grasp and onto the floor. Her eyes were closed and her lips were parted with a tiny drop of drool at the corner of her mouth. Her off-white makeup was streaked with tear tracks and the flush of her skin showed through, rivaling the bright rouge circles on her cheekbones. Her hair was windblown and her mascara smudged. Faye thought she looked adorable. Like a funky doll come to life.

Now, as they sat in the car at the edge of the wildflower meadow spreading out from the cottage, Faye watched Ariella, who appeared to be asleep. The girl was so different, was it crazy for Faye to think she could help? Did Ariella really need help? And did this fit with Faye's mom saying it was time for a change?

Ariella stirred, and murmured, ". . . not mine . . . talk to Moira . . . full moon . . . ," then she quieted again into sleep. Faye opened her door slowly and didn't close it. There was no need to wake Ariella. She took a few steps into the meadow, her hands trailing through the tallest flower stalks. The air was warm, the late afternoon sun still bright and bees buzzed all around. There was a sweetish, planty, earthy scent in the air. She felt at ease, relaxed even. And her mind began to quiet, though she felt dreamy, and visioned herself as a character in a tale about enchanted cats, ancient cottages in the deep woods, nature spirits, and full moon gatherings. She twirled around a few times, her purple print dress opening into a circle and catching on the flowers nearby. Faye knew she had worn the exact right outfit for this fantasy. She took deep, rhythmic breaths of the scented air, feeling her body relax further.

It was remarkable the way Ariella had pleasured herself, doing it when she needed, without any pretense or modesty. As she continued to twirl through the meadow, Faye wondered if she could ever be so uninhibited. She imagined her adult restraints detaching and spinning away and had the sudden urge to take off all her clothes and dance naked through the meadow, to roll about in the flowers and grasses, to stain her skin with plant juice and dig her fingers into the moist, fertile earth. The image was powerful and enticing, and without giving herself time to doubt, she kicked off her shoes and yanked down her tights and panties. The warm air rushed in under her dress like a lover's caress and she gave a gasp of pleasure, then reached up behind her neck and started to unbutton her dress. She heard a noise behind her and froze.

"Go ahead, Faye, you know it's way okay." Ariella was rubbing her eyes and smiling.

Faye blushed and picked up her shoes and underthings and clutched them to her chest. "Uh, maybe later. "I thought you were sleeping."

"Hey, c'mon. It's just us. No one else around. Why not go au naturel? YOLO!"

Why not? Faye thought. Why not just go with the flow? Let it happen. Scratch that itch. But what did YOLO mean? Trying for laid-back adult, she said, "Ariella, listen. I'm your English teacher. No matter what, I've got to keep that fact in mind. I want us to be friends, but even friends need to have boundaries. Right?"

"Whatever!" Ariella laughed and skipped past Faye down the path through the field. Faye stumbled after, hopping on one foot as she tried and failed to put on her panties. The grass now felt spiky and the path was full of unseen sharp pebbles which jabbed at her bare feet before she managed to slip on her ballet flats.

Ariella waited for her on the porch, damnable smile lighting her face. "Do you want to come in? We've got some fresh lemonade or I could fix some tea."

Faye gestured with the hand holding her clothes, and one

leg of her tights flew free and fluttered like a narrow black banner. "No, you go ahead. I'm going to stay out here and enjoy the sun for a bit. Unless you need my help?"

"No, I'm good. You go ahead and chill. I'll be about half an hour or so, getting changed and packed and feeding the beasties and all. There's some chairs out back near the gardens if you want to catch some rays." With that, Ariella disappeared into the darkness of the house, the screen door closing lazily behind her.

Faye wandered toward the backyard and marveled how much the cottage was like something in a Disney movie. All it needed was a few elves or fairies poking their heads out the mullioned windows. The rear lawn, which was bordered by vegetable and flower gardens, was tidy, with two large, old, handmade wooden tables on either side and a variety of wooden chairs and smaller tables scattered about. She picked an Adirondack-style chair that could open into a chaise lounge, pivoted it around to face the afternoon sun, and lay back. After a few minutes, it was too hot and she slid the skirt of her dress up to the tops of her thighs. This helped for a bit, but then sweat began beading between her breasts. Sitting up, she glanced around and knew, the way one does, there was no one around. Standing, she grabbed her panties and drew them on, being careful to keep her dress down. Then, she reached back, unbuttoned the dress to her waist, and quickly drew it over her head.

Little breezes delighted her bare skin and made the hairs raise up on her arms. She dismissed the urge to take off her bra. Instead, she let out a big breath and reveled in the feel of the sun on her skin. She wondered idly where all the cats were, what herbs or flowers were making the air smell so great, whether it would be a good time to call Drake, or even Wanda. She thought about all the questions she had for Ariella. She fell asleep.

Faye woke to feel fingers in her hair, stroking it back from her forehead. Ariella's intent green-eyed gaze was difficult to interpret. Humor was evident, yes, and affection, but there was something more, reminiscent of the appraising way her mother looked at her, as if adding up all the pluses and minuses in Faye's life.

"Guess you needed sleep, too," Ariella said, "I brought out some goodies. Is it all right if we hang here a while longer?" On a low table nearby was a tray with a pitcher of lemonade, glasses and a plate of cookies.

Faye's wristwatch showed 40 minutes had passed since they'd arrived. She gave her body a quick once over and was pretty sure she hadn't overdone the sunbathing. Her Mediterranean heritage made it easy for her to tan and difficult to burn. Then she fully realized she was in her underwear in front of her student and reached for her dress. And stopped. Certainly she was more covered than if she'd been wearing a bikini. So, it was no big deal. Both Calista and Ariella probably sunbathed nude in this private green oasis.

Ariella now wore an oversize, designer-quality, khaki, double-pocket long-sleeve shirt with the sleeves rolled up to her elbows. The shirttails were knotted in front, exposing her taut midriff, the sight of which made Faye glance down at her own small kangaroo pouch. Ariella had on matching khaki, cargo-style, multi-pocketed shorts and had rolled the legs up to mid-thigh. On her feet she had ankle-high hiking books with tan, knee-high wooly socks. She topped it all off with an Indiana Jones style hat that was too large for her, though the fullness of her cascading hair held it in place. Her face was clean of makeup and her only jewelry was a necklace with a scallop-shaped pendant matching the one Faye wore. She looked like a junior archaeologist or, from another angle, a model ready for a photo shoot.

"Chillin' sounds wonderful," Faye said, taking two cookies and pouring them both a tall, cool glass of lemonade. The cookies had the unique aroma she remembered from Sunday, combining cinnamon, honey and some herb she didn't recognize. And the lemonade was obviously fresh-squeezed. She smacked her lips at the perfect combination of tart and sweet. Ariella sat in the grass near the chaise and they munched and drank in silence. Faye lay back and tried to find the ease she'd felt before she fell asleep, but questions yammered at her.

"I like your bra. Where'd you get it?" Ariella asked.

Faye glanced down at her matching purple bra and panties. The set had been a gift from Drake and, while they were edged with lace and expensive, they reflected his practical taste in that they were well-made, the straps were sturdy and the seams triple stitched.

"Oh, they were a gift."

"Your boyfriend?"

"Yup."

"Yup? You sound like me!" Ariella laughed. "Guess we're going to learn from each other, huh?"

"For sure," Faye grinned.

"For real, can we go to the mall or somewhere and get a bra for me? Like yours? I've got money."

"Yup, tomorrow afternoon we can go cruise the Cape Cod Mall. What size do you take?"

"I dunno. I don't have any bras." Ariella plucked at the grass. "My mom says bras were invented to make women's breasts stick out more to attract men. She says I don't need a bra. That I'm too young. She gets upset when I say I want one to wear to school."

Faye glanced up and saw a gull float by, white against blue. *What do I say now?*

Ariella unbuttoned her shirt. "Can you tell what size I take?" She held the shirt open to reveal two small breasts, about the size of large lemons, with delicate pink nipples.

Faye felt a strong spasm of discomfort. She had wanted a mother-daughter experience, but this was unexpected. On the other hand, wouldn't a mother counsel her daughter about things like bras?

"Well, you can try on bras at the store and the women who work there can give you some advice. You might just need a training bra." Faye paused. "But, is your mom going to be angry? I don't want her to think I'm breaking her rules or anything."

"No, no. Don't worry about that. She's big on personal freedom and she always encourages me to make my own decisions. But we get into some heavy discussions and we don't always agree, like about me going to public school. But, if I stand my ground, she relents. So, she won't help me if she thinks I'm wrong, like about getting a bra, but she won't stop me. The only times she insists on her way is when she thinks I'm doing something dangerous." Ariella giggled. "And I don't think anyone would consider a bra dangerous."

"Okay then. We'll go to the Mall and, if you find a bra that works for you, get it."

Ariella buttoned her shirt, leaped to her feet and jumped around saying, "Yippee! Yippee!" over and over. So young, so very young, Faye thought, and yet . . .

"Can we continue our discussion on the way to my house?" Faye said, "I need to get out of the sun and I want to change into something less dressy. Like shorts and a t-shirt."

She stood and picked up her dress, but paused to give Ariella a mock, up-and-down scan. "Speaking of outfits, may I ask if there is a reason you're dressed for the African veld?" Ariella seemed puzzled and didn't reply, so Faye tugged the dress over her head, buttoned just enough in the back so it wouldn't gape open, and sat to put on her flats. No need for the tights.

"Oh, I get it. Good vocab word, Ms English Teacher! Veld, like in Africa, the plains or something. Where lions live. And gazelles and zebras and elephants, right?"

"Yup, that's pretty much it. So, why the safari look?"

"Cause we're going for a hike later, aren't we? I always go for a hike after a trying day at school."

Faye smiled. Again the adolescent yippeeing had been replaced by surprising maturity. "Now that you mention it, a hike does sound good, though I think I would prefer something more

like a sedate walk. Where will this hike and/or walk take place?"
They were at the back door of the cottage, carrying their glasses,
the empty pitcher and the cookie plate.

"There's lots of places I like, especially in the deep woods or
on deserted beaches where I can hear and feel the nature spirits.
But, let's go somewhere you like this first time."

Faye considered her many favorite spots. "Okay, there's a
beach on Nantucket Sound in Chatham near the border with
Harwich that's usually pretty empty of people at this time of year.
And you can walk and walk and get to where it's just you, the wind
and the waves. Not sure about nature spirits, but from what you
said, I bet there might be some around."

"Perfect! And walking on the beach is also such a good
place for meaningful conversations."

Faye looked away, suppressing a laugh. "Are you all
packed?"

"Yup, my duffel bag is ready and I just need to rouse the
beasties and say goodbye to the ones who are staying."

"Ah, the feline entities, the mysterious, wonderful felinities."

There were what appeared to be large piles of multi-colored
fur in each of the four comfortable chairs around the ancient,
blackened stone fireplace in the room off the hallway. In the
mullion-filtered sunlight, Faye saw combinations of black and
white, multiple shades of brown, orange and white, and an
individual whose fur had a bluish sheen. Multiple pairs of green,
gold and even a pair of one blue and one brown eye opened and
contemplated them. With the abundance of lush green plants and
flowers on almost every available surface, the overall effect was of
deep jungle inhabited by a troupe of felines. Ariella ran to the
nearest chair and began petting and talking softly to its occupants.
Faye could hear purrs and mews in response.

"How many are there?"

Ariella paused and counted. "Sixteen here and I think there
are two or three more outside, standing guard." Her expression

was one of mixed pride and doubt. "Do you think that's too many?"

"No, if you're happy and your mom is okay with it, then why not? I mean, the cats love you and you love them. But, how do you keep them fed? And where's their litter box? Or, should I say, boxes?"

"Oh, feeding them is easy. They pretty much eat what we do. And they all go outside to pee and poop. They have a special sandy spot in the woods."

"They eat what you do? I thought you were a vegetarian? You were wearing a PETA shirt the last time I was here."

"Yeah, I am most of the time. But my mom isn't. Though she only eats fish on a regular basis."

"So the cats eat veggies and fish?"

"Yup. And road kill. My mom is always bringing home recently dead animals she finds on the roads. The cats certainly like those."

"But you and your mom don't eat road kill, do you?"

"Not usually. The animals she finds are pretty small, so they go to the cats. But once she found a baby deer, so we all had a feast." Ariella turned and clapped her hands and two cats, one black and one white, jumped down from the chairs and came to sit at her feet.

"So only Midnight and Snow are coming to my house?"

"Yup. They like you and they've already visited your house, so I'm ready to go if you are." Ariella picked up her backpack and a duffel bag Faye hadn't noticed. The bag bulged and tinkled when Ariella swung it onto her shoulder.

"They better like the canned cat food I bought, cause I'm not cruising for road kill," Faye said as they went out the front door and headed into the meadow. "Aren't you going to lock the door?" she added as Ariella strode ahead. Faye noticed the welts on the back of the girl's thighs had completely disappeared. *I gotta get some of that healing cream.*

"Nope. Nobody will bother this place. Plus, the cats do a

good job of guarding it when we're away."

Faye shook her head. When in Rome, don't question everything. Gathering her tights into a crumpled ball, she reached to stow them in her handbag and get out her car keys. And realized her bag wasn't on her shoulder.

"Wait. Where's my handbag? Is it in the backyard? Did I bring it from the car?"

Ariella turned and smirked at Faye. "Did you take a ganja break while I was getting ready?"

"A what? Oh, me? No. No ganja. I simply don't know where my bag is. I don't remember carrying it to the backyard, so I hope it's in the car." In her mind's eye Faye saw the driver's door hanging open. Of course, she hadn't closed it because she didn't want to wake Ariella. Faye took off running through the meadow toward the car, remembering she had put her handbag in the backseat when Ariella got in. She heard the teenager snort as she galloped by. When she got to the car, a quick glimpse into the back told her the bag wasn't where she'd left it. She peered into the front seat and gave a sigh of relief. The bag was on the driver's seat, but it was slightly open and something bright green was sticking up from it. The green thing was a paper card, bigger than a business card and shaped like a diamond, with "Viridis Glas Productions by Moira" embossed in big, fancy, black calligraphic letters. But there wasn't a phone number or address. Faye turned the card over and saw a handwritten note addressed to her.

"My dear Faye," the note said, "I hear so much good about you. We meet sometime soon. I think you be perfect for next full moon!"

Faye set the card on the dashboard and peered into her bag. On top of her wallet, checkbook, brush, makeup and the multiplicity of the little things that accumulate, was a beautiful bunch of small, delicate flowers, their stems tied with green ribbon. She recognized violets and primroses, but not two others, both bell-shaped, one in a vivid shade of purplish-blue and the other in a rich blend of pink and red.

"I guess Moira's been here."

Faye whirled round to see Ariella standing close behind her. The usual impish grin and shining green eyes defused Faye's fright and she fell into the driver's seat, willing her heart to slow. Snow and Midnight sat on either side of Ariella's feet, and gave Faye the feline thousand-yard stare, like they saw something she never could.

"I guess she did. And she opened and moved my bag. But why didn't she come to the cottage and introduce herself? And what does this card mean?" Faye handed the green diamond to Ariella, who glanced at it and gave it back.

"This means you've been invited to the next full moon event and she'll meet you beforehand to get you ready. And she didn't come to the cottage because she knew you and I were chillin' and wanted privacy."

"She knew that? And how is she going to 'get me ready'? What if I don't want to be part of this event or production or whatever?" Faye knew she sounded truculent, but didn't care. She started pawing through her bag again to see if anything was missing. "Moira wouldn't take anything, would she? What kind of person is she anyway? Does she live around here? And what kind of flowers are these blue and pink ones?"

Ariella smiled. "Moira take anything? I don't think so. She's got so much cheese, she could buy Cape Cod and have enough left over to take a bite out of Boston. Her family has been super wealthy for a very long time, like centuries, when they did business all over Africa, Europe, Asia - everywhere. And she has this huge crib here in the Punkhorn, but it's so private nobody ever finds it unless they get permission." Ariella gave Faye a considering look. "No, Moira wouldn't take anything from your bag or car. I think she wants what you don't even know you have to give."

Faye closed her eyes. She so wanted to believe Ariella and her family and friends were for real. But her bullshit meter, never quick to respond, started to quiver. Was she being taken in by an insecure, lonely teenager with an overactive imagination? An outsider girl left alone by her mother and so desperate for friends she would create an elaborate fantasy world and then invite her favorite teacher to play in it with her? Or worse, Faye could be the mark in an elaborate scam and would eventually be drained of her savings and home by a team of cons who were using Ariella as bait. *Could Ariella have planted the card and flowers in the bag while I was prancing and twirling in the meadow or dozing in the backyard?* Faye shivered despite the warm air. *One step at a time, one small step at a time. Wait for choiceless clarity. I can always back out after this weekend.*

Faye sighed. "C'mon, let's bounce. I really need to get home. Put your beasties wherever you like." With a bit of force, she yanked her door shut.

Ariella threw her duffel bag in the back, got in, buckled up, put her backpack on the floor and patted her lap. The cats jumped in and began kneading her thighs while looking around and sniffing, their nostrils and whiskers quivering. Snow stepped daintily around the gear shift and onto Faye's lap, where she resumed kneading. Midnight had settled and was curled up watching Snow. Slowly, Faye let her hand fall on Snow's back and her touch, as it had with Midnight, started the purring, though Snow's sounded more like distant thunder. As Faye began stroking, a tingling, warming sensation filled her. Leaning back, she exhaled and rubbed her eyes.

"Are you okay?" Ariella asked.

"Yeah, just a bit tired. Too much excitement, I guess. Feeling overwhelmed. I might nap when we get to my house."

"Sorry if I startled you. You just acted so cray-cray about your purse and I knew there was nothing to worry about. Not out here. For sure, you need to moss more. And those flowers are Bluebells and Foxglove, just so you know."

"Whatever. Sometime soon you're going to catch me up on all the latest slang, okay?" She picked up Snow and put her back on Ariella's lap, started the car, turned it around and headed for home.

Chapter Seventeen

As they bumped through the dirt roads out of the Punkhorn, Faye realized she was not only tired, but also a bit blue and she might be getting a headache. It was clear Ariella was attempting to bridge two completely different ways of being – from the home schooled kid isolated in the woods to the weird student at a bustling public high school. *Wouldn't it be better for Ariella to consult a life coach or work with a therapist rather than me, her well-meaning, but confused, teacher?*

As she had on the drive to the cottage, Ariella was again rhythmically stroking a cat, though this time the cat, Snow, was alive. *Oh no is it possible she's at it again? Is the girl hypersexual? Am I going to interrupt this time? Yes, I absolutely should.*

Faye envisioned herself saying, "Excuse me, are you masturbating again?" but that would sound so weird. After a careful check of the road ahead, Faye risked a longer look at her passenger and let out the breath she hadn't known she was holding. Yes, Ariella was stroking, but this time both hands were in view, one for each of the cats stretched out on her thighs like black and white sphinxes. She was crooning a melody as she caressed the cats, a melody Faye found familiar, but couldn't place in memory.

"So, what were those green things in your braids today?"

Ariella stopped singing and stroking. "Before you start asking me lots of questions, you've got to agree to let me ask you questions."

"What?"

"Yeah, this has to be a two-way street. I wanna know about you as much as you wanna know about me."

"What kind of stuff do you want to know about me?"

"Prolly the same you wanna hear from me. What makes you happy, what makes you sad. What are your dreams. Why your hair is the way it is. How you think the world works. All that stuff."

Ariella made it sound so simple and obvious. How could

Faye not agree? Yet the girl was also complex to the core. One step at a time.

"Okay, that sounds fair. But we should each reserve the right to not answer a question and not explain why. And let's take turns. We each ask three questions and then the other gets to ask three questions."

"Deal!" Ariella laughed and stuck out her hand for Faye to shake. Faye took her right hand off the wheel and reached out. Just before their palms touched, there was an audible snap and a small flash of green sparked between their hands. It didn't hurt, so Faye didn't pull back. Ariella's hand was also still outstretched, though she was staring at the spot where the spark happened.

"Hey, Cat Power! That was crunk, dope and off the chain!" Ariella's reached further, their hands touched, they shook.

"So, what were those green hair things?"

"They're a variety of South American fern vine. You can uproot a plant, put the roots in water in a little glass vial like the ones used for cut flowers and they do fine for a day or two. I just hide the vial in the end of my braid and then weave the vine in and out of my hair. The vine naturally wants to wind around things, so it stretches up the length of my braid. And the little ferny leaves are very, very sensitive and will move, open or shut with a change in wind, light, warmth or even loud voices."

"So that's why they were squirming. Wow. That's so cool. Really awesome."

"Yup. Cool and wow and awesome. All of that. Next question?"

"Okay, that was an easy one. How about . . . " Faye stopped to think. There were so many questions. "How about . . . you tell me more about Moira. Who she is, where she's from, why she coordinates these full moon productions and so on. From her note I'm guessing she doesn't possess a great grasp of the English language, so . . . "

"You're going to meet her soon, so I prolly should let her tell you herself. But, you're right, she isn't fluent in English, either speaking or writing. But she always gets her meaning across. The spirits link everything and everybody together, and Moira is always in sync with them. And, because I'm often in sync, I can hear her inside me, like she's speaking with my voice. She's one of the Old Growth members of the Viridis Glas Luminasti. She and her family supply a lot of the money for the VGL, too."

"Viridis Glas Luminasti? That's on her card." Faye gestured to the green paper diamond still sticking up from her bag.

"Yup. They're a worldwide group dedicated to keeping humanity aware of and connected to nature. And to preserving nature. Many of them are either super rich or well-known artists, writers and spiritual leaders. Some are even in politics. My mom claims the group began during the early days of the Roman Empire and Moira says the VGL were the inspiration for another group, The Illuminati, who started in Bavaria around the time of the American Revolution." Ariella sounded like she'd memorized this little speech.

"You know, I heard something about the Illuminati and the hand signs rappers use," Faye said. "But the VGL is different?"

"Fer sure. The VGL started long before the Illuminati, but they've stayed way out of the spotlight. You can't find any mention of them on the Internet or anything. The Illuminati tried to publicly oppose ideas and practices they didn't like, but the VGL are way more subtle in the way they do things. Moira once said the Illuminati were a splinter group, some VGL members who wanted to be more public." Ariella pulled a wrinkled piece of paper from her backpack. Faye could see there were handwritten notes on it.

"Here's what my mom said to tell you about the VGL. 'The Viridis' Gas . . . oops, I mean 'Glas Luminasti' work behind the scenes to guide humanity to return to a healthy relationship with nature, to acknowledge that all life is interconnected and human life is dependent on those interconnections. The VGL also wants to make it clear that so much of what we humans do or think can be attributed to the fact our existence, our behavior, our instincts are derived from capital 'N' Nature which is the source all life and, in fact, all things in the universe."

Ariella cleared her throat and kept reading. "In other words, humanity stands at the apex of the evolutionary pyramid nature spirits have built on this planet over millions of years. The VGL has helped, in various ways, to make these connections and dependencies part of the general human consciousness, so everyone, in every place, no matter how remote or urban, can see themselves not so much as an individual but more a product and part of nature and will act to preserve the nature which birthed them and now supports them."

"Whew, I had no idea," Faye said, "It all sounds interesting. But tell me more about the nature spirits. And what's the work you're training to do for the them?"

"Yeah, that's where I need to draw the line about what I can say. At least for now." Ariella sounded so serious, Faye couldn't help letting out a bark of laughter.

"No, for real. I can't tell you more until you meet Moira. She and the NSA would be upset."

"What? The NSA? You don't mean the National Security Agency, do you? Are they involved in all this?"

Ariella giggled. "That's right, didn't I tell you my mom was a federal agent? She actually went to LA to report to some heavy-duty government people."

Faye eyes widened and her eyebrows turned into upside-down U's until the grin appeared on the girl's face. Faye gave Ariella's leg a playful swat, which brought a baleful stare from Snow.

"You . . . you're . . . ," Faye tried to think of some current hip thing to say. "You're punking me, right?"

"Hey, Faye, I'm keeping it real, but you're such a prep sometimes, I can't help myself. Okay?"

"All right, okay. You've, uh, schooled me. So, c'mon, tell me more."

"We read about the NSA - the government agency - in Social Studies one day and I realized the initials could also stand for 'Nature Spirits of America.' My mom hates it when I say 'NSA.' Sometimes she and Moira get all serious and I just can't get that jacked up. I mean I believe in all of it, but I think it's supposed to be fun some of the time. The spirits I know are always playing. At least the nice ones are."

Faye was about to agree maintaining a sense of humor was important, when Ariella's phone rang. The girl dug into her backpack and pulled out her beat-up phone, poking at the duct-taped back to be sure the battery stayed put.

"Hey, Mom, you called!" She turned to Faye and said, "It's my mom."

Faye thought Ariella would prefer some privacy. She spotted a donut shop and decided a cup of coffee and a nice big glazed cruller would both perk her up and get her out of the car. She could also get some water for Moira's flowers. She mimed she was stopping for something to drink and eat and pointed at Ariella, who had not said another word to her mother after her initial greeting. The girl glanced up and shook her head. Ten minutes later when Faye emerged with her coffee and pastry she saw Ariella was now speaking with intensity, her free arm waving about for emphasis. Faye sat on a nearby bench, took a couple of bites of the sugary cruller and called Drake.

"How was your day?" she asked without saying hello and while still chewing.

"Oh, you know, Fridays are like trying to stop a buffalo stampede with a butterfly net. Today, with the good weather, it was more like trying to stop an avalanche. Otherwise, normal day at school. How did things go for you?"

"Wild, weird and wonderful, as usual." She took another big bite of the cruller and almost groaned at its perfect sweetness.

"I bet. Though it would take something pretty crazy to top your past week. Did anything happen to you or did you do something so wacky it deserves mention? Any talking cats or green men calling you into another dimension?" Drake chuckled, but Faye knew he was serious.

"Well, what do you think of me trying to dance naked in a field of wildflowers?"

"You what? You're kidding, right?"

"Nope."

"You danced naked in a field? Did anyone see you? Whatever possessed you to do that?"

"I didn't actually take everything off, but I was about to when Ariella brought me back from the brink. Or, I should say, she was encouraging me to get naked and that's what made me realize I was going too far."

"Ariella? You were with Ariella? Oh, right. Of course." He hesitated and Faye knew she wasn't going to like what came next. "You know, Faye, I think you should talk to someone very soon and get some advice, before you do or say something that will ruin your life."

"For your information, I did talk to someone. And she advised me it was time for some big changes. And that I should explore opportunities" She popped the last bite of cruller into her mouth.

"Your mother, right?"

"Uh, yes, she, in fact, gave me the straight-shootin' truth, that I was letting my chances slip away and I needed to embrace the new before I got any older."

"Don't tell me. She told you to dump me, right? Because of the baby thing?"

Faye dithered. Rhoda had been blunt and had said she thought Drake was taking advantage of Faye. But did Drake need to hear that, especially as she was expecting him to come over tomorrow night for dinner and some hot monkey sex?

"Faye? Don't lie to me. I know your mother thinks I'm some kind of womanizing, domineering gangster who only keeps you around for convenience."

"She did say you don't appreciate me enough and . . ." Again Faye hesitated as the memory of their incredible lovemaking last weekend made her inhale sharply and squeeze her thighs together.

"And what?"

"and . . . and . . . that I should try harder to get you to see my point of view." Faye finished in a rush, knowing full well how lame she sounded. She glanced over at the car and saw Ariella was now off the phone and had her head down on the dashboard. "Drake, I've got to go in another minute or two. I think Ariella is in crisis because of something her mother just told her on the phone."

"Shore, shore, ma'am, ain't no problem at'all." Drake had switched to his sharecropper voice, which Faye now found annoying. "But," and he started singing in a whiny voice, "Ariella, Ariella, don' want to hem and ha, got's ta tell ya, Ariella, yeah, I really love ya."

"That's from the video the boy made about her! Where did you hear that?"

"That Goggle look-see is pretty amazin', specially seein' as they own YouTube."

"Well . . . fine! That will make introductions so much easier at dinner tomorrow." Faye thought it was somehow indecent for Drake to quote from that nasty video.

"Yup, it shore will. Bye, babe . . . er . . . ma'am."

"No, wait, we need to talk about —" But he had hung-up. She held the phone away from her ear and stared at it as if it were a grenade and she needed to throw it before it blew up. I'm the one that's going to explode, she thought. What an irritating, insufferable, insensitive bastard he could be! A real arsehole. She jammed the phone in her handbag, licked the last bit of sugar off her fingers, and picked up her coffee and water. Ariella's head was up off the dashboard and she was looking at Faye with an unreadable expression.

As she slid into the driver's seat, Faye asked, "How did the talk with your mom go?" She noticed the cats were now curled together in the backseat.

"Bad, real bad. How'd the talk with your boyfriend go?"

"How did you know I was talking to Drake? That's his name by the way."

"You had real sappy expression on your face, like the girls at school when they're getting all weird about boys."

"Really. Well that's observant of you." Faye decided talking about Drake with Ariella was "most inappropriate," as her Posh Brit character would say. "First, tell me what your mom said."

"She's going to get the part. They're just working out the financial details. She's very excited." Ariella spoke in flat, uninflected tones.

"And that means you're going to have to find a place to stay for longer periods of time." They both knew this wasn't a question.

"Yup. I'm either going to live with my ancient grandparents in Boston in their ancient Beacon Hill mausoleum which smells like old people and where I won't be able to sync with the spirits, or I'll get stuck with those Punkhorn weirdo anarchist perverts. I told my mom I'm not going be cooperative, that I was going to run away and she just said we'll talk about it when she gets back and everything will work out."

Ariella and Faye regarded each other. The girl looked so sad, like she was going to start crying, and Faye understood again how difficult her young life was. A sympathetic dull ache formed between Faye's breasts, just like it had when she had wept after Drake said no to being a father. She couldn't cry now, could she? *I need to be strong for Ariella. That's what mothers do. They're strong for their kids, even when they're falling apart inside. And mothers and their kids don't usually participate in mutual weeping sessions, do they?*

"Well, listen to your Mom. Things *will* work out. If you get all stubborn and rigid, then you won't be able to take advantage of the opportunities when they do come up. I mean, your Mom wants you to be happy. She's not going to abandon you or anything."

"Yeah, I guess so. But it just feels so unfair all this is happening right now when I genuinely need her around. After all, I'm in the critical part of my all-important teenage years. Without her around, I could get influenced by some evil creepoids and wind up smoking crack and selling my body!"

They gaped at each other until grins cracked their faces and both started laughing without restraint.

"That sounded pretty good, huh?" Ariella managed to squeak out.

"Oh, totally good! 'All-important teenage years.' Smoking crack with evil creeps and selling your body. I love it!" Faye snorted, then began laughing so hard she started to hiccup and Ariella tried, between giggles, to pat her on the back. Faye felt tears start to come, but they were the tears of hilarity, the good kind, and she let them flow. She glanced at Ariella and wasn't surprised to see she also had wet, brimming eyes. When Faye finally got herself under control, she reached across the center console with her arms wide. Ariella came willingly into her embrace and they held each other, still snickering and snuffling, and wiping at their eyes.

"You're almost like my mom. But different in a way I like," Ariella said as she drew away. "I'm having a good time already and we're not even at your house yet."

"I'm having a very good time, too, Ariella. Let's just enjoy the weekend and put our worries away for now. Yes?"

"Yup. Whatever you say, Faye, I know you know the way."

They chatted like best friends for the rest of the drive and Faye was so entertained she didn't realize her hiccups had stopped.

Chapter Eighteen

Faye held her front door open for Ariella, who lugged in her backpack plus the bulky duffel and was followed closely by Midnight and Snow. Ariella walked to the middle of the living room and turned slowly around like a tourist in a historic house. Faye tried to see her home the way Ariella might. Narrow plank oak floors – she knew those would meet with approval – with a few handmade, southwestern Indian scatter rugs, also good. The prints and paintings on the wall were a mix of Cape Cod scenes: beaches, boats, marshes, plus a few posters from the fantasy conventions Faye had attended. Mostly nature scenes, though, which should appeal. Then Ariella stopped and stared at the 42" hi-def digital TV.

Faye coughed and said, "Oh, I bought that because Drake always complained when he tried to watch tennis on my ten year old set, even though it worked fine for me. Good news is I put the old set in your bedroom and I get lots of cable channels."

Ariella gave Faye a brief, but bright smile and kept looking around. The combined living and dining area was at the front of the house and faced west, so the windows had tables and stands in front of them to hold Faye's mismatched and eccentric collection of houseplants. Shelves along other walls were crammed with books and magazines, comingled with shell and rock finds, though nothing like the plethora in Ariella's room. The couch was old, claimed when Faye's mom had downsized to the condo, but was still comfy and good for naps and cuddling. A coffee table was strewn with books and papers brought home from school. Three tired, but serviceable, upholstered chairs, also from her mom, circled around and made the living room cozy. The adjacent dining area was bare except for a large unfinished wood table Faye used as a work surface and a few scruffy, mismatched dinner chairs purchased at yard sales.

Ariella gave a little nod. "Nice house! I like the plants. Where's my room?"

Faye was pleased Ariella said "my room." She felt another

mothering twinge. Probably impossible, but perhaps the girl could become a frequent guest? If things continued to go well, she might suggest that to Ariella, especially now Calista expected to be gone for long periods. She led Ariella down the hallway to the spare bedroom. The girl stepped in first and did a slow, deliberate twirl, taking it all in. The cats immediately jumped onto the double bed and started grooming themselves and each other, preparatory for overdue naps. Ariella did one more twirl, this time even slower, before spinning her hat onto the bed, and dumping her backpack and duffel in the general direction of the closet. She walked over to the desk and ran her fingers over the laptop.

"It's okay for me to use this 'puter?"

"Yup, I borrowed it from school for the weekend."

"Thank you!" Ariella said with touching sincerity, "And I can watch TV too?"

"For sure! You can watch the TV and use the laptop as much as your little heart desires. But I want to be sure you get your homework done. Do you have a lot?"

Ariella had already picked up the remote and was pointing it at the TV and pressing buttons. "Uh, no, not too much and most of it is easy. Some reading for science and social studies. We've got a pop quiz on Tuesday in Social. Some math problems and, of course, the essay my English teacher assigned. I think it's supposed to be about 'What I Will Do This Summer to Improve Myself and/or the World'. Can you believe it?"

Faye smiled. "Well, I think your English teacher is 'right on' with that assignment."

"Oh, she's the dope, that's for sure." Ariella had succeeded in turning on the TV and was flicking through channels. "This is sick! You've got so many channels. Do you get Animal Planet or HBO?"

"I'm pretty sure I get Animal Planet, but I think HBO costs extra. What are you other favorite shows?" Ariella didn't respond, but kept clicking the channel selector. "So, you're going to write your English essay on how watching TV improved you and made the world a better place? And how great your English teacher is?"

Faye wasn't surprised when the girl didn't look up, but just nodded and said, "Fer sure."

"Okay then, I'm going to go get changed and do some stuff. It's about six o'clock, so let's go on our walk around 6:45? Sunset is around 8:00."

"Okay. See ya later." Ariella was leaning into the TV, giving focused attention to what appeared to be one of the news channels. After half a minute she finally realized Faye hadn't left.

"Wassup?" she said without looking away from the screen.

"Nothing. I guess I'm just surprised at how quickly you became engrossed in television."

"This is interesting! And I haven't watched TV in like weeks. GMAB."

"What? GMAB?" Talking with Ariella was like communicating with a person who threw in phrases from other languages.

Ariella smiled and said, "Give me a break."

"What? Why should I give you a break? What did you do?"

"That's what GMAB means. Give . . . Me . . . A . . . Break. Everyone uses it when they text." Ariella's smile wavered as she saw Faye's frown and she said, "Okay, I'm sorry I'm so inscrutable to you. I'll try harder, I promise."

"All right then. Whatever you say. Carry on." Faye went to the living room, collected her handbag and the paper coffee cup holding the flowers. Once in her bedroom, she closed the door tight and sat on the bed, bent over with her elbows on her thighs and her face in her hands. The afternoon had become like a music video, with camera angles and sets and characters changing every few seconds. Confusing and happening too fast. She picked up her handbag, took out the green paper diamond and reread the message:

"My dear Faye. I hear so much good about you. We meet sometime soon. I think you be perfect for next full moon!"

When is the next full moon anyway? Faye got up and

checked the wall calendar near her dresser. Full moon was in 18 days. Right after the last real work week at school. As she turned back to the bed, she glanced in the mirror above the dresser and stopped, startled, seeing a character who could be from A Midsummer's Night Dream. Wild black hair exploded out from her face which was already lightly toasted by the sun. And her eyes glowed. Her purple dress had stretched down in front because the back buttons weren't all fastened and showed the top of her lacy purple bra and more than a little cleavage. Faye gave her reflection a wicked grin. *How would Drake react if he could see me now?*

Perked up, Faye found a little vase in her closet, put Moira's flowers in and added water. She set the bouquet on her night table and contemplated it. It was actually quite sweet and brightened the room. She wanted to call Wanda and talk things through, curious how her friend would react to the news Ariella was staying with her for the weekend. But it was close to dinner time at Wanda's house, so she texted first.

"*Things r weird. Almost unbelievable. Need 2 talk 2 u. R u busy?*"

Wanda's reply text said, "*Feeding the brood. Magic spell didn't work, still a housewife! Will call in a bit. Stay strong. Remember the good times.*"

Faye lay on her bed and thought about her long, bumpy friendship with Wanda. In middle school, Faye had tried hard to be just like the native Cape Codder. From late spring to mid-autumn, the two were either in bathing suits or shorts and t-shirt and they rarely wore any footwear other than flip-flops. Like Wanda and the other native girls her age, Faye let her hair grow long and wore it loose. She was always outdoors and her skin was always brown, even in winter. Faye's mother, at first worried her bookish, introverted younger daughter was being transformed into an untamed nature child, soon relaxed. Rhoda had taught high school math to both of Wanda's older siblings and knew the Eldridge family well. She was confident the friendship with Wanda was a good thing. Faye had certainly never seemed so consistently happy.

The two girls had a secret club, based upon all things fantasy. They built a thatched hut from tree branches, driftwood, bent-over saplings, leaves and rocks in the middle of a large patch of woods on oceanfront land owned by Wanda's family. Here, in the warmer months, they could spin and indulge their imaginings and visions without interruption or criticism from either adults or other kids. When it was too cold to go to the hut, they would closet themselves in one of their bedrooms and watch fantasy movies and TV shows, or read to each other from their favorite books.

Through Wanda, Faye gained entrée to a social circle, which consisted mostly of other kids from long-time Cape families. In 6th, 7th and 8th grades, the group played along when Faye and Wanda acted out fantasy roles. But, in 9th grade, the group's interest turned to dating, sports, cars, and popularity games. Wanda and Faye were still included in beach parties and the like, but were referred to as the Fantastic Two. They were also each given a nickname: Wanda the Witch and Queen of the Faye-ries. But they took pride in being different and declared to each other in posh voices the other kids were of "rough nature" and "decidedly unaware."

When, in 10th grade, Brian Hopkins started to tag around with them, they found it amusing and teased him and often dumped him. Brian's family were also deeply rooted Cape Codders and claimed their lineage went back to the Mayflower. Brian and Wanda had been friends since pre-school and their families socialized often, so they had grown up in each other's house and backyard. Brian was tall and attractive in a blunt way. His features were regular, and he had a bland, pleasant oval of a face. His blond hair was always uncombed and ragged and he allowed it to grow long so the front thatch often fell over his eyes. He didn't talk a lot and tended to stay at the fringe of any activity, which was where Faye and Wanda were usually found.

Wanda dismissed Brian by saying, "Oh, he's had a crush on

me since first grade. He used to follow me around everywhere. The other kids said he was my dog."

"Do you like him?" Faye had asked, feeling a sudden shiver.

"He's okay. He can be fun sometimes."

"But you like me better, right?"

"Of course, he's just a boy."

Faye expected Wanda would make it clear to Brian he wasn't welcome, especially when Faye was with her. But, increasingly, The Fantastic Two became The Unlikely Three. Then, one hot summer afternoon, Faye had surprised Wanda making out with Brian in the hut on the bed of leaves, moss and ferns the two girls had built. Wanda just smiled like it was no big deal, but Faye knew her own face showed only shock and disappointment. She felt naked and alone and her eyes had a peculiar feeling they got when she was about to cry. But she wouldn't cry. She wouldn't.

"You said you were going to be spell casting! You love him, don't you!"

"Don't be silly. We're just role-playing. Anyway, it was Brian's idea." Wanda glared with obvious fake irritation at Brian, whose face wore a big smile.

"Yeah, it was all my idea. Sorry, Faye." Brian smirked.

Faye felt foolish, wrong-footed and more than ever like she needed to run away. She whirled around toward the door, but heard Wanda say, "And you were just leaving, weren't you Bri?"

Faye glanced back and saw the smile Wanda gave Brian and knew, despite Wanda's dismissive words, life had shifted, and not in Faye's favor.

Three weeks later it was official. Wanda was dating Brian and began to spend all her time with him. Faye quickly reverted to the shy, books-clutched-to-chest girl she bitterly accepted she was destined to be. The kids who had been nice because she was Wanda's friend weren't rude or anything, they just seemed to stop seeing her. It was as if she had become invisible. Which, Faye had thought with sour amusement, was a cool spell to cast upon oneself.

Chapter Nineteen

Faye went on to a four-year college and Wanda chose instead to take some pre-nursing courses at Cape Cod Community College. Wanda grew tall, even taller than Faye, and transformed into a graceful, slim, clean-limbed, blue-eyed, beautiful young woman whose auburn hair fell smoothly past her shoulders and gleamed like polished wood. Over the years, Faye heard through the grapevine Wanda had broken up with Brian and was dating this or that hot summer guy, but Brian always reappeared, just like he had in high school.

One summer, however, no one was sure where Wanda was or with whom she was hanging out. Somebody said she was going to Ptown every weekend to dance and someone else said they saw her walking down Commercial Street holding hands with another girl. But, by the first snowfall she and Brian were again an item. When she was twenty-five, Wanda married Brian, who had by then worked up to a manager's position in his father's large landscaping business. Two years later Wanda had the first of what was to be a brood of four children.

It wasn't until Faye came back to the Cape at age 28 to teach English that Wanda reached out and made it clear she wanted their friendship to resume. Faye was reluctant, but Wanda, always the bossy one, didn't give up. After a few meetings for coffee, they began going for walks, most often on weekends when Faye was free and Brian could take care of the kids. On one of the walks, Wanda apologized for how she had treated Faye when she took up with Brian in high school.

Faye laughed and said, "Oh, you and I were only a school girl thing. Who could take it serious? It wasn't like we were lovers or anything." She thought this sounded funny and sophisticated and let Wanda know she was now a woman of the world. She peeked at her friend and was surprised to see Wanda grimacing and frowning so hard white creases showed through her tan and her lips were pouted, like she was going to cry.

"Wanda, what is it? What's wrong?"

"Faye, I did love you. I sincerely did. Letting you slip out of my life was stupid. I've learned to regret it."

Faye felt her heart skip a beat. Wanda stared at Faye, her eyes blazing with a fierce intensity. Then she opened her arms and engulfed Faye in a long hug which drove away any fears or doubts Faye had about their becoming friends again. As Wanda drew back and gazed down into Faye's moist eyes, she said, in her husky French Ingénue voice, "Mon cheri, 'ow I have missed you." And she bent forward and gave Faye a passionate full on the lips kiss.

When Faye mindlessly responded, Wanda's tongue began a delicate, insistent probing. This was nothing like the kisses they had exchanged as young girls. But Wanda had always been the leader, the one who showed Faye the way. Perhaps this was a more elaborate, more realistic, more adult-style role-playing? Faye gave herself to the kiss, opening her mouth to the teasing tongue, while imagining Wanda was a tall, elegant prince with long flowing hair. A prince who had just decided she, a mere peasant girl, was to be his bride. Her head started to wobble. Actually, it was more like being thrown without warning on a Tilt-a-Whirl which was running out of control. A heat filled her sex and a pulse began to beat there.

She was about to say, "Oh, Monsieur, you are too kind to this poor maid. I am so unworthy," when she felt Wanda's hands slide under her t-shirt and start moving up her ribcage. She grabbed both of Wanda's wrists and took a large step back, trembling and panting, gaping at her friend, wanting an explanation.

Wanda only burst out laughing and said, "You should see yourself right now. You're so beautiful when you're aroused. You were fantasizing I was a guy, weren't you?"

"I was not! And I'm not aroused. I was just 'role-playing,' like you were with Brian that time in the hut." Faye managed a little laugh of her own. "Pretty good, huh? Pretty realistic, right?"

Wanda laughed even harder and Faye, after an few more

moments of indignation, joined in. The two women sat down side-by-side, laughing and laughing, letting the ridiculousness of their situation wash them clean of any remaining tension.

As they walked home later, hand-in-hand as they had as teenagers, they were quiet, just enjoying the closeness and camaraderie of their refound friendship. Faye squelched an urge to press Wanda about the kiss and the hands roving toward her breasts. She didn't want to disturb the happiness she felt. After that they took up as if nothing had ever gone wrong. Each week, they talked on the phone for at least half an hour, exchanged multiple texts and met regularly for walks and talks. Faye was surprised at how eager Wanda was to hear about her life away from the Cape, what it was like to be able to read every day and to daydream. Wanda also demanded names and descriptions of books Faye thought were good. When they said goodbye at the end of a walk or in-person visit, they kissed each other full on the lips. But these kisses, to Faye's relief, contained little heat and none of the irresistible tongue.

Her cell rang and she saw it was Wanda. It was 6:35, so she only had about 10 minutes to talk before going walking with Ariella. Faye had another insight into how a mother's life must bend around the needs of children.

"So, tell me all about the 'weird' and 'unbelievable', " Wanda demanded.

"I will, I will." Faye chuckled. "But how are you?"

"Never mind about me. Just think of the old woman who lived in the shoe and that'll do it. Though, in addition to having too many children, I've got this lunk of a husband who's going through a ridiculous mid-life crisis."

"Brian? A mid-life crisis?"

"Yeah, who woulda thought? Good old, easygoing, always smiling Brian is now becoming temperamental, cranky, introspective, not-happy-with-anything Brian. He's currently debating between hiking the Appalachian Trail for three months, moving us all to a cabin on a lake in Maine he saw on the net, or buying a 1968 Dodge Charger muscle car."

"1968? We weren't even born in 1968, though buying the car sounds like the least disruptive choice."

"I guess. Anyway, what's happening with you? I've almost wet myself waiting to hear what the Queen of the Faye-ries would consider unbelievable."

Faye took a deep breath and launched into a full recap of all that had happened in the past seven days. When she got to the part about Drake declining to be a father, she heard Wanda mutter "Toad on a toadstool!" which had been one of their favorite descriptors for some of the boys they had known in high school. And when Faye relayed what her mother had said about Drake, Wanda laughed and said, "Right on, Rhoda."

"So, what do you think?" Faye asked.

"Well, dahlin," Like Faye, Wanda did a good Southern Belle. "As I see it, ya'll got two issues, or no, could be even three. One, you got this teenager taking over yore life. Two, you got some strange goin' ons which shook things loose in your usual reality. I'm talkin' bout the disappearin' cats, the fairy tale cottage in the woods, Punkhorn Calista and the sexy green man and all. And three, you, outta the blue, up and decide you want a child and that has put a major cramp in your thing with Drake the Rake." Wanda thought Drake was "so hot" and was always teasing Faye with the idea the two couples should do a "man swap."

"So, here's what I think you should do. First, get rid of the teenage nightmare. Now. Before you get sucked in any deeper. I know that girl and I know her mother. These are not people with whom you want to get involved. It won't end well, believe me." All traces of southern accent were gone from Wanda's voice.

"You know Ariella and Calista?"

"You may find this hard to believe, but about nine years ago I was approached by Calista and asked to be in the full moon 'productions.' Though I call them farces and consider them borderline legal. Somebody ought to investigate them. Cape Codders don't take kindly to fakes. Or tricksters."

"What? You're kidding, right? What happened?"

"I'll give you the short version. Calista asked me to be in a production back when I was 27. I think I was having some sort of post-partum confusion because it was a few months after I had Samoset." Samoset was Wanda and Brian's first child and they had given him the name of a well-known Wampanoag Indian who had been among the first to meet the Pilgrims.

"Why you?"

"I'm not exactly sure why. I ran into Calista when I was walking in the Punkhorn. She said she had heard of me and of my practicing what she called 'natural magic.' She said with my Cape Cod lineage and connections I was a 'young plant, but with a deep root.' She gave me this whole spiel about how I would be so right for one of the productions, that I would fit right in and I would learn so much more about natural energy and magic. I gotta admit it sounded pretty fantastic. And Calista herself is one of the weirdest, but somehow very persuasive, people I've ever met."

"So, you were in a production?"

"Two of them, in fact, though I never got to meet the infamous Moira. But, all I did at the full moon events was wear an old-fashioned costume and dance all night."

"Really," Faye said, "Ariella has been nattering on about nature spirits and some secret society called the . . . the Viridis Glas . . . uh—"

"Luminasti," Wanda interjected. "Yeah, I heard all about them, too. What a bunch of crap."

"Are you sure? I mean, all this stuff that has been happening and Calista gave me this old, old coin and I heard voices when I held it."

"Ah yes, the coin. That one had me going, too."

"They gave you a coin? Did you keep it?"

"No, they took it back when I refused to go along with their crazy, fucked up plans for me."

"Wanda, you're scaring me. I need you to tell me everything.

All the details, all the stuff you experienced and all the stuff they told you. Everything."

"Sure thing, dahlin. Where do you want me to start?"

"Well, tell me more about happened at the productions."

At that moment, there was a tap at Faye's bedroom door and Ariella's golden head appeared. She made a show of examining her wrist, even though she wasn't wearing a watch.

Faye looked at her wristwatch and saw it was 6:50.

"Wanda, I promised Ariella I would go for a walk with her before it got dark. Can we talk later?"

"Not tonight, babe. I'm planning on giving Brian a bedtime workout and I want to spend some time beforehand making myself sexually irresistible. You know, sometimes it seems he's more interested in talking about the cabin on the lake or four barrel carburetors."

"Okay, how about tomorrow?"

"Definitely. Just remember what I said about that girl and her mom. Don't believe everything they say and be sure to read the fine print."

As they walked out the front door, Ariella asked, "Who was that on the phone?"

Faye thought about whether she should answer a question Ariella had no right to ask, but considering what Wanda had said, she went with the truth.

"It was my friend Wanda Eldridge. She apparently knows you and your mom. She said she had been in two of the full-moon productions."

"Huh. I remember Wanda. She turned out to be a bogus loco, I must say. I heard she was really trippin'. My mom and Moira were very disappointed with her."

"Why do you say that? It was what, nine years ago, and you were only six years old." Ariella's immediate irritation was so obvious, Faye stopped walking. "What? Is this something else you can't tell me about?"

Ariella turned to Faye, her green eyes dark and deep. The cats, sitting at Ariella's feet, also stared up at Faye. "Yes, I was only six. But that was the summer Mom and I came to the Cape to meet my dad to check out the cottage. We stayed for four months and Mom was in all the full moon productions. I do know about Wanda because Mom tells me everything or almost everything. Plus I remember meeting Wanda that summer. But, also yes, I can't tell you all I know about her, not until after you meet Moira."

"O-kay," Faye said, drawing out the two syllables. "Let's go for that walk, shall we?"

"Did you bring the coin?"

"Uh, no, should I?"

"Yes, go get it, but don't hold it in your hand for long, at least not until I tell you to." Ariella opened the back door of the car for the cats to jump in, threw her pack after them, got in the front seat and shut the door. Faye waited for a second, then went back in the house and found Calista's pouch on her dresser top. She opened the pouch, saw the coin's dull gleam and wondered how Ariella would react if she didn't bring it. She shrugged, stuffed the pouch in her bag and headed back outside.

Chapter Twenty

They were quiet as they drove toward the beach until Faye suggested they could pick up sandwiches on the way back instead of cooking dinner.

"My mom would . . ."

"What? Your mom would what?" Faye had the wicked thought that Calista would grill up some road kill.

"Never mind. It's not important. Sandwiches will be great," Ariella said. Silence resumed.

Cruising along the twisty, hilly Route 28 in East Harwich and South Chatham, Faye was enchanted, as always, by the picture-postcard scenes which waited round each turn. It seemed every house was charming, cozy and surrounded by tasteful landscaping accented with glorious blooms which varied with the season - purple and pink rhododendrons, brilliant blue hydrangeas, swaths of deep orange tiger lilies and scented lilacs were common. It was hard to believe all of Cape Cod had begun as a big pile of sand and rocks deposited by a retreating glacier at the end of the last ice age.

She turned onto the road to the beach and stopped at a turnaround on the peak of the last dune before the water. Faye half-shut her eyes and peered through the veil of her lashes, which made the houses and roads near the ocean fuzzy. She could imagine the land the way it was before Europeans arrived. Something metallic and warm touched her bare arm. Ariella had thrust a Thermos at her.

"Take a sip or two. It's a refreshing tea and juice blend I made while you were sunbathing. It'll help us chill."

Faye took the Thermos, saying, "Is it as good as your mother's brew?"

"Better, much better."

As she lifted the thermos to her lips, Faye had a moment of disquiet, but then the liquid hit her tastebuds.

"This is delicious!" She took another, bigger sip. "This is

beyond delicious! What's in it?"

"Hey, Faye, it's like a Milky Way on steroids. Lots of bits of this and that. My special blend."

The warm liquid slid down Faye's throat and settled in her belly like a purring cat. She watched, bemused, as Ariella took a swig and then let both Midnight and Snow lap some from the palm of her hand.

"We're all going to be so happy," Ariella said and Faye grinned in agreement without knowing why.

When they reached the beach parking lot, Ariella and the cats were out and onto the sand while Faye was still retrieving her bag from the back seat. She watched the girl pause before turning to walk in the direction Faye wanted to go, toward the stretch of beach where the houses were few and far away. The stretch where the trees grew close to the water. The trees of the woods in which teenaged Wanda and Faye had built their magic hut.

Faye made no effort to catch up to Ariella, who made no effort to slow down or wait. The teenager had left her Indiana Jones' fedora in the car and her golden-red hair was loose and streamed out like a banner, blazing in the early evening sun. Her long, tanned legs in her safari shorts moved so effortlessly it was as if she floated over the sand. The cats trotted alongside her, black on one side and white on the other, tails fluffed out and held high.

Talking with Wanda had stirred Faye's simmering pot of anxiety. Were Ariella and her mother planning to manipulate or hurt her? As if in answer, she felt a rush of warmth and ease, which she attributed to Ariella's liquid concoction, and shook herself like a dog coming out of the waves. Why was she worrying? She had only committed to this weekend and she would see it through. For now, what would be would be.

As they reached Faye and Wanda's woods, Ariella slowed and looked around, like an animal sniffing the air. She stopped, stared into the thick growth of trees that started at the top of the beach and, as Faye walked up, asked, "Is this a special place for you?"

Faye wondered if Ariella would sneer at the dreams of two teenage girls who 20 years ago had built a 'magic' hut in which they could fantasize and pretend they had fairies and unicorns for friends?

"These woods were special to both Wanda and I when we were just about your age, in fact. We were into fantasy and magic and all and were tired of being made fun of, so we built a little hut. It was our secret place, where we could practice magic spells and pretend we had unicorns to ride. When it was hot, we would come down to this beach and bodysurf the waves, imagining we were mermaids. Pretty silly, huh?"

Instead of laughing, Ariella looked at Faye with something like respect. "I'm sure my mom mentioned you two once when she talked about kindred folk who had been in this area. She'd heard of two girls, known as the Fantastic Two, who had created a surprisingly powerful space in some woods which were already empowered by nature spirits. My mom said apparently something happened and the energy vortex dissolved and the girls disappeared off the radar. Was that you?"

"I guess so. We were also called Wanda the Witch and I was Queen of the Faye-ries, but together we were known as the Fantastic Two. But, it was all just pretend, we didn't know anything about nature spirits or an energy vortex." Faye giggled. "Energy vortex" was funny.

Ariella grinned at her. "Well, for sure, that's the way it almost always goes down. I bet this place must be gnarly with energy and spirit! Let me try something and see what happens."

The girl began moving her hands and arms in intricate patterns. After a minute, her long hair was stirred by a breeze Faye didn't feel. The cats began a low whine which rose and fell in time with Ariella's movements and Faye saw twinkles of light spark around the girl's body. She relaxed and closed her eyes. She could still see the twinkles. Opening her eyes, she glanced up and saw the stars were moving. No, they were dancing. Faye realized she was hallucinating. Ariella's special drink! Of course. She was going to speak sternly to her about it. But not now. Now just felt too good.

"Oooh! This is off the chain," Ariella whispered and began moving faster and swaying from side to side. Faye worried Ariella might be in trouble and stepped forward.

"No, no! Sit over there, right now." Ariella pointed at the tree closest to the water. "This could happen fast!" Faye waited a beat, but Ariella frowned at her so fiercely, she scurried over and sat down, her back against the tree's trunk. Her vision began to fill with light and dark streaks which combined to form a paisley, fractal pattern overlay hallucination. She concentrated on Ariella, feeling she needed a focus.

Ariella was gesturing ever more madly and started to dance in a tight circle. The breeze had freshened to a wind and her hair blew out into a huge halo. The sand combined with droplets of water from the nearby surf and began to twist up into dervishes. Ariella was muttering something Faye couldn't hear, though it sounded a bit like the rhyming rap she had performed in the classroom. The air around Ariella gave off a hum that rapidly increased in pitch and volume. The cats were now on their hind legs, dancing with Ariella and their whines had changed to full-blown howls. There was a tangy smell to the air, like spilled iodine.

"Pick up the coin! Now!" Ariella shouted over the tumult.

Faye fumbled the pouch out of her bag, twitched it open and felt around for the round piece of old metal. It seemed like she was moving in slow motion. Then she had the coin. It was warm. It felt alive.

"Hold it over your head with both hands," Ariella bellowed, almost obscured within a spinning tornado of sand, wave foam and whirling cats.

Faye held the coin high and watched it commence glowing and vibrating, sounding tones which rose and fell. Tones which made an unearthly melody when mixed with the sounds Ariella's whirlwind. *If only Wanda could see me now.*

Suddenly, there was a long drawn out whooshing noise and everything disappeared. Faye couldn't see. She couldn't feel her body. She tried to do deep breathing, but couldn't feel her chest move or hear her breath. But it was okay, it truly was. It was all going to be okay. She felt like she was a pebble tumbling underwater in a happy, bubbling stream that was somehow also an ocean that contained it all. She was part of the capital 'A' All, as was everything and everyone. If she could have laughed, she would've.

With a pop, it all returned and the sun was shining so brightly she had to squint. In a daze, she tried to make sense of what she now saw. Ariella was flat on her back, arms outstretched, with the cats curled up beside her. The wind was gone and the sand and water were in their proper places. But the beach was completely free of their footprints, the sky an astonishing crystalline blue and the waves were so perfect they seemed painted. Everything was overlaid with colors and paisley designs that were jewel-like, as if nature had put on her best hippie finery. More hallucinations. She had to confront Ariella about the drink. But not now. Perhaps not ever.

A tender breeze brushed by and Faye took a deep, deep breath, feeling her head and heart clear as if she had inhaled pure oxygen. It was wonderful to feel her lungs working and to see her hands, now in her lap, moving to her will. The coin was on the sand between her outstretched legs, but still had a glow, a presence. She didn't pick it up.

Ariella stirred, sat up and appeared unharmed. Faye leaned back to collect herself, but the expected tree trunk was gone and she toppled backwards into some soft moss and small flowering plants. She jumped up, spun around and saw the small woods was now a forest which stretched along the beach as far as she could see in either direction. And the trees were much taller, with oaks and maples and birches towering over the few scrub pines.

Something touched Faye's shoulder and she gave a squeaky scream and cowered. It was Ariella and the cats, all six of their eyes gleaming too brightly. "Wha . . . . what happened? Where are we?" Faye managed.

"Hey, Faye, it's all okay. I'm sayin' yay, cuz we went all the way. Wheres and whens, just throw 'em away. There's no dismay, we're not astray and now we can play." Ariella shone brighter than ever and it seemed to Faye the cats had matching Cheshire grins.

She mustered a semblance of her adult self and said, "Will you please stop talking in rhymes and riddles and slang and tell me what the hell just happened?"

"You really don't know? You hung out in these woods and never felt anything special? Nothing made you think there was something über going on? You never tested its possibilities?"

Faye stepped right up to Ariella and hissed, "Ariella, if you don't tell me what's going on right now, I swear I will put you and your goofy cats in the car and drive you straight to your grandparents in Boston. Is that what you want?" Faye stamped her foot, and the physical sensation sent shivers of pleasure to every corner of her body.

"Okay, okay. I keep forgetting you're still blind to what I take for granted." Ariella dropped to the sand and sat cross-legged. "C'mon, let's meditate for a few and see if we can, as you say, get our groove going again. Okay? Comprende?"

Faye glared down at this girl-woman who was either a world class wizardess or a very believable fake. She sputtered some malformed words, but gave in and collapsed down into a half-lotus. They sat in silence for what seemed forever. At one point, she felt Ariella's warm hand fall on her knee and felt reassured. It really was okay. The tea was clearly hallucinogenic, but she felt no panic, only a deep curiousity.

Faye kept her eyes half-open and began watching her breathing, which had a calming effect. Not that she needed much calming. Relaxing into the present moment was so easy, like sliding into a perfect, warm pool of love. Pool of Love. Faye snickered. *That would be a great name for a band.*

The light altered and she opened her eyes and saw the sun

travel across the sky at a walking pace, give way to darkness and stars, rise again, and speed up with each pass until it was flying, no zipping, from one side of the sky to the other. Each whizz-by of the sun was followed by an equally brief period of darkness in which the moon rose and set in a flash and the stars blinked on and faded. The effect reminded her of how moviemakers simulated time passing.

Faye wasn't alarmed. In fact, she thought the overall effect was cool. She was stoned, so what. She was hallucinating. Wonderful. *It's not like the first time I've been psychedelized.* As the day-night cycles strobed faster and faster, shadows flickered, clouds popped in and out of existence, the earth spun on its axis. She got the distinct impression time was melting, folding in upon itself and losing both definition and a connection to reality. *And what, after all, is time? Isn't it only a concept humans invented to comprehend a feature of the universe which was part of something much larger and connected with things like space and gravity? If I don't know what time is, then when am I? Where am I? What am I?* Faye played with these questions until they too lost coherence and meaning. She decided her sole purpose was, right now, whatever now was, to relax and just be. None of the rest mattered.

As she let go and mentally lay back, she slitted her eyes again and gave herself to pure sensation. It felt as if she was dissolving. As her bits fell away, she saw her center, where her identity was supposed to be, was empty, nothing there. She was idly curious to see what would happen if even the emptiness dissolved. *What will I be then or will I even be? Will I come back together in a new, possibly improved way?*

There was movement in her peripheral vision on the side away from Ariella. Faye opened her eyes wide and saw again the pristine beach, and the blue, blue sky, all in their proper place and not moving faster than normal. Something inside her settled back into place. Then what had caught her eye made her gasp. A group of people were proceeding up the beach in their direction. It was hard to see them clearly as the air was hazy and the group appeared and disappeared, leaving rainbow trails like the moving images one saw on color surveillance cameras. As they got closer, Faye saw the group numbered about 20 and they were all dressed in buckskin with lots of fringe and beading. Their hair was long and dark and many of the men were bare-chested. All of them had wonderful, reddish brown skin. Indians! Faye thought, and bit her lip to keep from giggling.

In the middle of the group, someone reclined on a bed or litter which was being carried by six others. She could see mouths moving and the individual on the litter, Faye was sure it was a woman, was gesturing and also talking. But Faye couldn't hear any sounds coming from the group. She glanced over at Ariella and saw she was slumped over, her chest resting on the cats snoozing in her lap, and her arms stretched out, one hand still resting on Faye's knee. Some meditator you are, Faye thought. She gently shook Ariella's shoulder and, when the girl sleepily opened her eyes, Faye pointed at the group on the beach, now only 30 yards away.

"What? What is it?" Ariella yawned and stretched.

"Shhh!," Faye shushed and yanked Ariella's arms down. "Either I'm hallucinating or people are coming! Indians!"

"What? No way." Ariella stared wide-eyed at Faye and then squinted toward where she had pointed. The cats' fur rose on their backs. "I don't see anybody or anything. You tryin' to punk me again, Ms Faye?" Ariella gave Faye a playful shove.

Faye peered hard at the group moving slowly toward them. As they got closer, the distortion in the air lessened and she saw more and more detail. This was no hallucination. "Will you be quiet? What if they notice us? What are they doing here?" Faye whispered.

Ariella studied Faye's face, then regarded the beach again.

"You're for real, aren't you? You see Indians coming toward us? That's off the chain!" She laughed in delight.

By now the group had come abreast of where Faye and Ariella sat in the shade beneath the first line of trees. The woman on the litter said something and gestured to the woods and then to the beach. The bearers set her down on the sand so she faced outward to the waves. The women in the party gathered round her and began fussing with her garments, which were more heavily beaded and had more fringing than any of the others'. She waved them off and spoke to one of the older males. He called to several other men and they set off down the beach and began picking up driftwood.

"Where are they, Faye?" Ariella got to her feet, brushed off her bottom and stepped out onto the sand.

"What are you doing, are you crazy?" Faye hissed and yanked Ariella back down. The cats growled and pivoted to face Faye, their fangs and claws showing.

Ariella held her hands up, palms out. "Okay, okay. Take it easy. It's okay, really. I believe you see Indians and I believe they seem real to you. But, let me tell you what's going on before you get all loco."

"Ms Cardona, if this is somehow your doing, you're getting a big fat F from this teacher. And you might even get suspended from the Bloomberg School of Friendship of which I am faculty *and* Principal!" Faye spat out, trying to keep her voice low. "First tell me, was there something 'extra' in that drink we had earlier? Am I on some sort of trip?"

"Well, yup and nope." Ariella guffawed.

"Will you please be quiet?" Faye got right in Ariella's face. "If they hear us or see us, who knows what they'll do?"

Ariella choked off her humor and said, "Listen, not to worry. They can't know we're here. That's not the way it works. They might feel a presence or even see a kind of ghostly afterimage, but they'll assume it's some of their spirits. They might even wind up praying to us."

"What do you mean? I can see them. Not clearly, but I can see them."

"Not clearly is exactly right. They're not truly of our time and we're not truly of theirs." Ariella peeked at Faye from under her golden eyelashes. "And yes, there was a little bit of a South American herb in what we drank. It's called the Veil Ripper because it helps you see through ego illusions. But, I only put in enough to give us a little lift, not enough for the kind of experience you're describing. You must be incredibly sensitive." Ariella thought for a moment. "And that's probably why Moira and my mom are so interested in you."

Faye shook her head and closed her eyes. It's going to be okay. It *is* okay. She'd taken mushrooms several times and LSD once, so she knew the effects of the herb or whatever would wear off and this would become an interesting, if not pleasant, memory. Meanwhile, she might as well enjoy the ride.

Fascinated, she watched the group on the beach. Individuals came and went, many bringing wood, which was set alight for a fire. Others moved around preparing what appeared to be food, though all action centered around the woman on the litter. Faye decided the woman must be their leader.

She turned to Ariella. "How can you be sure they can't see us?"

Without a word, Ariella jumped to her feet and trotted toward the Indians. Faye tried to grab her, but missed, so she got up and staggered after the girl. She had almost caught up when, to her amazement, she saw an Indian woman walk right through Ariella. As Faye approached, the woman slowed and glanced around, but didn't look directly at Faye, who jumped aside and let her go by. Ariella now appeared to be standing in the middle of the group and, in fact, had her feet and ankles in the leader's stomach, who reacted by waving her arms with her mouth opened wide in what must be a scream.

Faye sprinted the last yards to Ariella, took her by the arm, and towed her into the edge of the surf.

"What are you doing? Didn't you see how much pain that caused her?"

"Oops. Sorry. Remember, I can't see them, only you can.

But did any of them notice you?"

Faye realized no one had called out or noticed them. And now the Indians were gathered in a tight knot around the litter, swaying and mouthing something. A chant? When they stepped back, Faye saw the woman on the litter was smiling, the way one does after cramp has eased. Her buckskin top was open and women were massaging her chest and abdomen with ointments.

"Wow," Faye said. "Our footprints go right through where they're standing. But they aren't leaving any footprints. So they really can't see us or hear us. But, did you know you were standing on the leader's stomach?"

"I felt something, a tingle, and that's how I knew where to stop to prove to you they don't know we're here. But it was wack of me, you're right. I didn't realize the interaction between timelines could be so intense."

"So what do we do now? And how long do the effects of the Veil Ripper last"

"Let's chill and let the scene play out. Just keep telling me what's going on. And warn me if I'm about to step on somebody. Oh, and I think maybe another hour or less for the Veil Ripper, thought you'll feel generally good for a while after."

"Great," Faye said and leaned back against moss covered tree trunk.

Chapter Twenty One

After they had settled under the trees and the cats had cozied up, one to each lap, Faye kept up a running commentary on the group, who had set a circle of burning torches and within that circle they sat cross-legged, facing inward, focused on their leader. They started chanting again, accompanied by shaking rattles and drumming on skin drums.

Faye was now convinced more than ever Ariella was much more than a quirky teenager. This evening's events had blown away all of Faye's expectations. While part of her was still scared and angry, another, bigger, part realized this experience was a real-life fantasy, a fantasy both wonderful and strange. A pleasurable wave of curious wonder passed through her. Veil Ripper was still working, though the wild hallucinations had stopped. She again gave up trying to figure things out.

Finally, the Indians' woman leader stood up and pointed into the woods. The group gathered their belongings and, guided by torchbearers, started single file into the trees. When Ariella heard where the Indians were headed, she jumped up, dumping Snow to the sand, and said, "We could follow them. The nature spirits are totally stoked up about it."

"Stoked up nature spirits, huh? Are you sure they aren't 'toked' up too?" Faye began laughing and couldn't stop. She rolled onto her side, displacing Midnight, and continued snorting, doubled up with mirth.

"Ha ha. Really funnitive. But, c'mon, don't you want to see what they're going to do?"

Faye peered into the forest's dark leafiness and was just able to see the flicker of torches. She shuddered. "You know, I'm going to take a pass on that. I've had enough excitement for one evening. But, do you know anything about who these people are?"

"All I can tell you is —"

"Don't you try that again," Faye said, whirling on Ariella with true passion. "After what I've gone through with you today and before, I deserve to know everything. And I mean everything. If I think you're holding anything back, we're going back to my house. Pronto." When Ariella appeared to be about to equivocate, Faye spun toward what she hoped was the direction of the parking lot and her car and started walking.

She'd taken only a few steps when she heard Ariella sigh and say, "Okay, okay. I'll tell you what I can. I just wish my mom was here."

Faye came back to Ariella and put her hands on the girl's shoulders. "Listen, I hope you realize by now I'm trustworthy and I'm not going to deliberately hurt you. You do trust me, don't you?"

"For sure I trust you, especially what with the scallop locket and all." Ariella looked down and scuffed her foot in the damp beach sand.

Faye touched the scallop-shaped locket hanging near the top of her breast bone. "What's the locket got to do with it?"

Ariella didn't answer, but opened her matching locket and held it out. There was just enough starlight for Faye, by leaning close, to see her own face in one half of the scallop. She recognized the photo as one from the faculty section of the school yearbook.

"My mom said if you wore the locket today, then I could trust you. That our connection was strong and true-a-listic."

"True-a-listic? Really? I'm sure your mom didn't use that word. But, okay, whatever. The bottom line is you trust me and I trust you. Even if you did dose me with that herb."

"I didn't know the Veil Ripper was going to affect you that strong, honest. It only makes me and my mom feel a little extra happy and we laugh a lot. Kind of turns the lights up and the music sweeter, you know? Like drinking a glass or two of wine. Makes it easier to form a communicationship."

"Communicationship? Can we please stop with the mushing-words-together thing?"

"I'll try, but don't forget I'm 15 and incredibly hip." Ariella flashed a big, winning smile. "I'll tell you about the tribe on the way to the car, okay?"

As they started again walking back to the car, Faye felt a quick shift and held out her hands to keep her balance. Looking around, she saw the beach had returned to the way it had been when they'd first arrived. Footprints again marred the sand's surface and the tide line was a mix of seaweed, shells and man-made debris. Spinning about, Faye saw the forest had returned to a copse, a small smudge of trees compared to the verdant carpet which had existed in the Indians' time. The waxing moon shone on the water and its golden light was swept toward shore by the waves. Faye felt relief, but also a little sadness. The Ripper's effect was almost gone.

"So, the spirits are telling me these Indians were part of a larger tribe that moved here from the mainland centuries ago. The spirits say you wanted to see the Cape like it was back then. Plus they say their woman leader is connected to you."

"I told them? How's that possible? And why is the woman important to me?" Faye realized she had begun to accept nature spirits' might be real.

Ariella stopped, frowned and pressed her hands to her temples. Faye thought she might be getting a headache. The cats sat down and leaned in apparent sympathy against Ariella's legs. The girl's face cleared. "Hearing the nature spirits is like listening to the wind howl or a stream babble. But what I got was they knew you wondered how things were long ago on the Cape?"

"Wow. I *was* thinking about what this landscape was like before humans arrived when we stopped at the turnout at the top of the dune. They picked up on that?"

"Yup, and they said the Indians settled and lived in those woods for many years which made it source of extra natural energy. So, the hut you and Wanda built must have been on the site of the their settlement. The woman who was the matriarch of the tribe was called something like Still Pool of Wisdom and she lived for a long time."

"So, I'm connected to the leader of the tribe because of our hut?"

"I guess. There might be more, but the nature spirits are fading away."

"Can't say I'm disappointed," Faye said. Squinting at her watch, she was surprised see it was just 9:15. It felt like they'd been on the beach for days. "Do you realize it's only been a little over two hours since we left my house?"

"Things don't go in a straight line when the nature spirits are involved."

"Of course." Faye's back was stiff and a little sore, so she bent backwards as far as she could and then bowed forward and held that pose for 15 seconds. She straightened, brushed off her hands and said, "Righto then. Let's go grab some grub."

"The spirits did say they want to talk to you directly, but you need to hold the coin. Or at least the first few times. Do you want to try when we get back to the car?"

Faye shook her head. "It's got to wait. I'm wiped out." The bubbling amusement and relaxed ease triggered by the Veil Ripper was gone and all she could think of was getting something to eat and then crawling into bed.

"The spirits say that's okay, they think things are going to work out with you. They wish you sweet dreams. But they say you shouldn't eat any meat tonight. And perhaps not ever again. Meat eating messes up their lines of communication because the spirits of the animals you eat keep getting in the way."

"I'll do my best," Faye concentrated on keeping one foot in front of the other. Walking meditation was what it was all about at the moment.

As they reached the parking lot, Ariella asked, "Hey, Faye?"

"Umm?"

"'Member you said I could ask you some questions'? Like you did me?"

"Uh huh."

"So, why do you meditate so much? Why did you start? Who taught you?"

"I'll tell you once we're in the car and on the way home, okay? I need to chill out for a bit longer and make a call or two." Faye dug out her phone and checked her messages. One was a short text sent from Wanda around 8:30 saying *"feeling weird myself. call me?"* But nothing from Drake, which was unusual. She hit speed dial for his number and when he picked up she heard loud voices and music in the background.

"Hey," he said, "what's up?"

"You don't want to know. Or maybe you do. But where are *you*?"

"Me? Right now?"

"Yes. You. Now." Faye heard the weariness in her voice. She shouldn't have called.

"Well, I played tennis earlier and we decided to go out for some beers and munchies after. You know, the usual routine."

"Doubles or singles?"

"Singles."

"With . . . " Faye didn't want to pursue this line of questioning. "I mean, wonderful. Glad you're having a good time. We're still on for tomorrow, dinner at my house, right?"

"You bet. I can't wait. I want to hear all about your latest adventures with the wild child."

"I can't wait to see you either. I'm learning about nature spirits, if you can believe it." Faye wanted to add more, but knew now wasn't the time. "But I gotta go. Got a hungry teenager to feed. Love you."

"Okay! But, nature spirits?" There was a pause. "Love you too."

Faye ended the call and turned to Ariella. "How does pizza sound? Vegetarian, of course." At Ariella's eager nod, she called her favorite pizzeria and placed an order for pick-up. Then she noticed the cats staring at her. It had been a trying day for all of them. "And we'll swing by the supermarket for some fresh fish, okay?" She could swear both cats nodded their approval before turning and leading the way to the car.

Chapter Twenty Two

Once in the car and underway, Faye explained she had started meditating in her early 20s because "all the cool kids were doing it." But, unlike the others, who moved onto the next big thing after a few months, Faye discovered sitting on a cushion and watching her thoughts rise and fall helped with stress and gave her insights into how her mind worked. She began meditating every day, sometimes for an hour or more, but mostly 20 minutes or so. Eventually she went on retreats, usually for a weekend, but once or twice for a whole week. She would occasionally call a woman who taught at a Buddhist retreat center for advice on her meditation practice.

"Does that answer your questions?" Faye could have gone into more detail, but she was preoccupied with her post-high fugue and growing hunger.

"I guess. You were raised Jewish, right?" asked Ariella.

"Ah, another question, but yes, and I still consider myself Jewish, though I am far from being Orthodox. Like my parents, I'm what they call a Reformed Jew. That style of Judaism fits me because I don't believe women should be separated from men during services and I don't keep to the strict dietary restrictions. But, really, I may be something even less formal than Reformed as I don't go to services very often. I do usually participate in the High Holy Days with my mother and my sister."

"Are the High Holy Days like Christmas and Easter?"

"Sort of, though their origins are completely different."

"Is your boyfriend Jewish?"

"Drake? Yup, though he's better at going to services. But not much. He's Reformed too."

"Can you be into meditation and Buddhism and also be Jewish?"

"Not all meditators are Buddhists, though Buddha is probably the most famous meditator that ever was. He said meditation helps one to accept, work with and ultimately escape the suffering that's built into living. You've probably heard about mindfulness, right? Well, that came out Buddhism and meditation. Also, for some the goal of meditating is enlightenment, but I don't meditate to get enlightened. For me it's more about self-understanding and being present and mindful and loving in each moment. So, I'm Jewish and I meditate, but I don't consider myself a Buddhist, though I'm working with a meditation teacher who is Buddhist."

"What's enlightenment?"

Faye glanced over and saw Ariella wasn't joking. "Tell you what. I'm pretty beat and that's a very big question and I'm not sure I can give a good answer right now. So, can we hold that for another time?"

"Fer sure. And anyway, I asked way more than three questions."

"That you did, but it's okay, because I've got a bunch more for you."

At the supermarket they purchased some fresh flounder for the cats and a few organic items Faye wanted. The cats started yowling the second they got back in the car and, after getting the go-ahead nod from Faye, Ariella unwrapped the fish and began feeding bits to Snow and Midnight. Faye was impressed the cats didn't squabble or gobble, but gently nibbled fish bits from Ariella's hand.

Faye picked up the pizza at the pizzeria and set the box on the car's center console. The mouth-watering aroma of melted cheese and tomato sauce wafted up and, after an unspoken mutual question, to which both Faye and Ariella agreed upon the answer, they each grabbed a slice and began munching. And the first was so good, they each had a second, content to just sit in the parking lot and fill their bellies.

After their second slices, Faye shut the pizza box tight, even though Ariella had reached for the box again. The girl smiled, turned to the back seat, picked up Midnight and stood him up in her lap facing her. The girl and the cat stared at each other, then

Ariella put her mouth close to his ear and whispered something. Faye saw this out of the corner of her eye. More of Ariella's antics. But she was surprised when she felt paws on her right shoulder and whiskers tickling her cheek. Midnight was standing on the edge of her seat and had his mouth and nose almost touching the side of her head. He began licking her ear and purring, but not in a deep rumble, more in a sing-song. Faye fancied she could almost make out words, one of which sounded like "pizza." Intent on her driving, she risked a quick peek at Ariella and saw she was staring straight ahead and struggling not to laugh. Without saying a word, Faye opened the pizza box. Ariella grabbed her third slice and offered Midnight a bit of cheese.

"Everyone happy now?" Faye asked.

"Yup. Hey Faye?"

"Yes?"

"Can you teach me to meditate? I mean, the right way?"

"Well, I'm a teacher, right? I can teach you to meditate the way I do. But you should know there are many different techniques, so you may want to find your own eventually. And, in exchange for teaching you, you'll tell me how you got Midnight to sing in my ear."

"Ooooh, that's highly confidential. I'll need to ask the cats."

It was almost 11 by the time Faye pushed open the door of her house. Without waiting for Ariella and the cats, she threw her bag, the pizza box, and the leftover wrapped fish on the couch and plopped down beside them. She closed her eyes and let the relief of finally being home sink into her weary mind and body. Ariella came in from outside and Faye sensed she was watching her.

"Everything okay?" Ariella asked.

"Oh yes, just happy to be home," Faye didn't open her eyes.

"Me too."

Faye heard Ariella's footsteps recede down the hall to her room and felt good the girl thought of this house as home. After five minutes of letting the sounds, smells and feel of her house wrap her in their comfortable ambience, Faye took the pizza and fish to the kitchen and stashed them in the fridge. She took out a gallon jug of organic apple juice, and savored the sweet and slightly tart aroma as she removed the top. Her sense of smell seemed unusually acute, which she put down to the after-effects of the Veil Ripper. She drank two big glasses of juice, leaning against the counter and staring out the sliding door to the deck. So much was new and strange and she had so many questions. She grabbed another glass, filled it with juice and took it to Ariella, but her door was closed. Could she already be in bed? Like a good mom, Faye remembered to knock before she entered.

The cats were sleeping on the bed, but Ariella was hunched over the laptop, the light from the screen giving her tanned face a washed-out tone. No other lights were on and the windows were open wide, the curtains moving lazily in the nighttime breeze.

"Brought you some juice. Organic apple."

"Mmmm, sounds good." Ariella kept her gaze on the screen, but put out a hand for the glass. She took a sip. "Yummy. Where'd you get it?"

"BJ's Wholesale in Hyannis. They've got quite a few organic items." Faye watched as Ariella tapped the touch pad and a new webpage appeared. "Does your mother set a bedtime for you on weekends?"

"What?" Ariella pivoted to look at Faye. "Oh, you're punking me again." She smiled and turned back to the screen. "Good one."

"Yeah, got ya, huh?" Faye realized bedtimes in the Cardona household were likely personal and flexible. She turned to go but, as she was closing the door, she couldn't resist one more attempt at mothering. "Just remember to brush your teeth, okay?"

"Fer sure," Ariella said, and eyes still on the laptop, gave a thumbs up.

Faye left her bedroom door a bit ajar in case Ariella called for her, though she hoped to be undisturbed. She was bone tired, but her mind kept playing over and over scenes from the movie the day had become. She thought she might meditate, but she was still feeling small occasional tiny ripples of Veil Ripper effect. Calling Wanda was a possibility, but it was late and her friend would be either asleep or playing temptress to the mid-life, distracted Brian. She closed her eyes and, fully clothed, lights still on and without having brushed her teeth, fell asleep.

She was awoken by the doorbell ding-dong from her phone signaling a text message had arrived. She struggled to a sitting position and finally figured the phone was in her bag at the end of the bed. The screen said it was 1:30 AM and the text was from Drake, who never sent texts. Rubbing her eyes to clear them of sand and sleep goo, she read: "*i love u, really do. but, u need 2 kno i played singles w shandra this evening. we didnt go out after w the group. she wanted 2 go somewhere else. Shes acting like shes attracted to me. we didnt do anything but im confused. just wanted u 2 kno. luv*"

Faye reread the text three times. Talk about Jewish guilt, Drake had it bad. And since when did he even know how to text? And when did he learn shortcuts and abbreviations? Finally, she typed in: "*no worries mate. lets talk manana. luv 2 u 2*" and hit Send.

She turned the phone off in case he wanted to start a texting conversation or worse, call her. His text could be a manipulative attempt to make her reconsider her decisions about having a child and changing her life. She couldn't deal with all that right now. Stripping off her grimy clothing, she tossed it all in the general direction of the laundry basket in her closet and started across the hall to the bathroom. A light still shone beneath Ariella's door. Flexible bedtimes, indeed.

Ten minutes later, showered, shampooed and with her teeth brushed and flossed, Faye felt almost normal. She slipped into loose shorts and an oversize t-shirt, her usual sleeping attire, and went to Ariella's door. There was no response to her soft tapping, so she cautiously opened the door. Ariella was asleep on her back in some kind of old-fashioned nightdress, half under the covers, with her head turned sideways and propped against the headboard by pillows. Her long hair spilled around and over her face and glowed in the light from the TV, which was on with the sound off. The remote lay near Ariella's outstretched hand and the cats curled at the foot of the bed, each with one eye open, scrutinizing Faye.

Faye tiptoed closer and watched Ariella sleep. A surge of emotion almost brought her to tears. The girl was so beautiful and, despite her weird ways and her overuse of hip slang, very, very innocent. Faye felt an urge to kiss Ariella's cheek where it peeked out from beneath her hair. She bent forward, but stopped and instead pushed the hair off the girl's face. Ariella stirred, murmured something and held up her hand. Her eyes remained closed and her breath was sleep slow. Faye took Ariella's hand in both of hers. So warm, so smooth, untouched by the rough edges of life. Ariella gave Faye's hands a small squeeze before letting her arm drop back to the bed. After wiping the moisture from her eyes, Faye drew the covers up over the sleeping child, clicked the TV off, closed the laptop lid and went back to bed.

Chapter Twenty Three

When Faye awoke at 8:30 Saturday morning, the first thing she noticed was how clear her mind was. Had a bunch of elves or fairies had come through while she slept and swept away all the confusion and doubts, then scrubbed and polished her self-confidence until it gleamed in the bright light of her future? *Yeah, right.*

Whatever, Faye threw the covers back and jumped out of bed, ready for anything. But a muffled squawk from the end of the bed stopped her. She twitched the covers aside and saw an indignant Snow glaring up at her.

"Oops! Sorry. Didn't know you were there." Snow began licking her left front leg and paw. "Can I get you anything? Breakfast? Do you want to go out?" Snow glanced at her with mild annoyance and went back to her toilette. "Okay then. Guess I'll go find your boyfriend. Perhaps he needs something."

When Faye poked her head into the spare bedroom, Ariella was already typing into the laptop and the television was also on, tuned to one of the 24 hour news channels. She was dressed, like Faye, in t-shirt and shorts and her glorious hair hung down her back in a disheveled mess. The t-shirt was the one with the PETA logo. She gave Faye a brilliant smile and Faye's mother persona did a happy little two-step. The morning sun was shining in a clear blue sky and a light wind tickled the land. Today was going to be a great day.

"How did you sleep? Can I make you breakfast? I've got organic granola, organic blueberries and organic milk," Faye said.

Ariella stretched her arms above her head. "Sleeping here is nice. Your house has a much better vibe than the Punkhorn weirdos' dump. Plus it's awesome you let me use the laptop and watch TV as much as I want. I can totally chill here. And I already found the granola and all. Très consumptable."

"I'm glad you like my house and I'm glad you found something to eat. Please help yourself to anything in the kitchen.

Except for the beer and wine. But don't you mean 'consumable'?"

"Sure, whatever. What are we going to do today?"

"Well, I'm going to eat breakfast and then I thought we could meditate on the deck. Maybe after that we can answer more of each other's questions? And didn't you want to go to the Mall this afternoon?"

"Sounds . . . " Ariella was obviously searching for a word. ". . . groovy!" She smirked and pointed at Faye, who pointed back.

"Très awesomable!" Faye responded.

After breakfast, Faye changed into black Capri-length yoga pants and a white, cap sleeve, v-neck knit top. She found her extra meditation cushion in her closet and took it, plus her own cushion and two small woven mats out to the deck. Then she went into the kitchen, poured two glasses of apple juice, called to Ariella and went outside to settle on her cushion.

Minutes passed while Faye adjusted her position, lit some incense and set the timer. She was determined to not nag at Ariella about meditation. It was surprising a teenager even had an interest in practicing and Faye didn't want to make it a chore. She remembered a trick she had used to stay still when she first started sitting. She went to her bedroom and picked out 12 medium-sized beads from her collection.

As she left the room and turned toward the kitchen, she heard Ariella laugh and say, "That's off the chain!" Ariella laughed again, louder this time and said, "No way! Tell me more." She was obviously talking to someone, which meant she probably hadn't heard Faye call to her. Ariella's door was part way open, and Faye could see the teenager was wearing some sort of headset which was a combination of headphone and a microphone. The headset was plugged into the laptop. Faye stepped into the room and a quick glance revealed Ariella was in a video chat with a dark-haired young woman.

Ariella noticed Faye and said into the headset mic, "POS. Hold on a moment." She turned the laptop away and said, "Wassup?"

Faye couldn't stop herself. "You know, your use of teenage slang continues to be a bit irritating. Whether you believe it or not, I'm an adult and I like the way adults talk to each other. And not to stretch your imagination, but someday you're going to be an adult." Ariella's smile faded but Faye charged ahead. "I don't hear your mom using slang and acronyms."

"I thought you liked being cool and hip with me." Ariella now had her hand over the mic.

"I do like being cool and hip. I'm just not sure I want to be 'gnarly' and 'off the chain'." Faye sounded petulant, so she tried to reset. "Are we going to meditate this morning, like we said? And what does POS mean anyway?"

Ariella's uncovered the mic and spoke into it. "Hey, GTG. Need to learn to meditate. Talk later?"

After a pause, during which she was clearly listening to the caller, Ariella laughed, hit a button, closed the laptop cover and took off the headset. She came over to Faye and gave her a warm hug and spoke into Faye's shoulder. "Thank you so much for letting me use the computer. I know I've been obsessed with it, but it's all so new and exciting. And please don't be cranky with me about the way I talk sometimes. I want our relationship to be more like equals, not like the one with my mom. I'm talking to you like I would to my friends." After a pause, Ariella added. "If I had any friends."

Mollified, Faye patted Ariella's back and said gently, "I know and I'm sorry. It's just I'm trying real hard from my side to not treat you like a little kid. I want you to be my friend too, so don't worry about the slang." She held Ariella away from her. "Just remember I'm like a stranger in a strange land and don't always know the language. So translate. A lot."

"I will, I will. But, I gotta tell you." Ariella began hopping up and down in obvious excitement. "I've got a new gal-pal. I was just talking to her on Facebook Messenger. She's from my school, but she's in 11th grade and we're going to chill out, I mean, get together, tomorrow or next week." Ariella's eyes were gleaming, almost as bright as they had been on the beach the previous evening. "And POS means 'parent over shoulder' and GTG means 'got to go'. Okay?"

"Wow, you have a friend. That's great, I mean, awesome. How did you meet this person?"

Ariella's words came out in a rush. "I finally got to make a Facebook page. I couldn't ever do it at school because Facebook is blocked. So that's what I did this morning. I was up real early and figured it out. And once I was on Facebook I could search around for kids I knew from school and send them a friend request. And Sappho's Cat, that's her screen name, was the first to respond. So we messaged on FB and then she said we should video chat and she told me how to do it. So that's what I did. She's totally crunk, that's pretty much the same as gnarly, and I've been wanting to get to know her like forever. She's just like me. I mean she's different. In a good way. And now we're going to be BFs! That means 'best friend' and please don't tell my mom."

Faye felt multiple protests rising. This wasn't the self-possessed and confident young woman from last night. In fact, she sounded much like Faye had been when she was in high school, hungry for a social life and grabbing at any crumb the in-crowd might throw her way. This was a situation Faye might actually know more about than Ariella.

"Whoa. Slow down. Let me ask a few questions. First, why shouldn't I tell your mom you made a Facebook page? I mean, practically everyone has a Facebook page. I have a page and I'll be glad to be your friend, in fact."

"My mom thinks me getting involved in cultural cesspools, that's her description by the way, will just dilute what I can offer the world. And will hurt my future in the VGL. She says I'll lose sight of my true purpose and become just another cow in the herd. Meanwhile she has a website to advertise herself as an actress and model!"

"Okay, I'm not sure I want to keep anything from your mom. But, realistically, she knew you would get computer access at my house. So, how about you tell her about the page and let's see what happens?" Ariella nodded okay. "But, I want to know more about this new friend. What's her real name? Are you sure she's a student at our school? I'm only asking because people sometimes pretend to be someone else on the internet."

"Her name is Sorcha Novak and she said you knew her, that she'd been in your class."

Sorcha Novak. Faye remembered her well from last year. Black hair, cut punky short with gelled spikes, black eyes rimmed with heavy kohl, a nose that was probably been broken at least once, lips painted some awful shade of brown or black or purple and curled in a permanent sneer. Midst all this punkiness, two brilliant blue eyes glared out in constant challenge. Sorcha had been and, Faye assumed, still was a problem student. She had rarely been on time for Faye's class, scuffed her big black engineer boots as she made her way to her desk, and slumped into the chair and immediately looked bored. Every day she wore slight variations of the same outfit of tight black jeans, frayed at the cuffs and knees, a tight fitting black t-shirt with the sleeves cut off and a scuffed black leather vest which must have been once been owned by a Hell's Angel. Her hands and nails were always grimy, because she was always tinkering with her Harley Hog, a monstrous, thundering motorcycle that, when it was working, she rode to and from school, no matter the weather.

After the first week of classes, Faye had checked Sorcha's school records and wasn't surprised to learn she came from a family with big problems. Both parents struggled with addiction and had been arrested multiple times for selling illegal substances. Sorcha's father had been jailed twice and her mother once. Her two older brothers had dropped out before their senior year and gossip in the teachers' lounge was they were dealing drugs on the West Coast. To complicate the situation, Sorcha was older than her classmates because of some unnamed trauma which had kept her out of school for over a year.

"Ah, Sorcha. Yes, I do remember her. Definitely different,"

Faye said as she put her arm around Ariella and guided her through the house toward the deck. "Let's meditate and after we can talk about your making friends at school?"

"Does that mean you don't like Sorcha? She likes you a lot."

"I do like Sorcha and I consider her a friend. But, I think you need to know she's had a difficult life and has a different attitude, if you know what I mean."

Ariella's face tightened into a stubborn frown, so Faye quickly added, "I just don't want you to get hurt."

Ariella's frown deepened and she crossed her arms on her chest. "I don't know what you mean. I think Sorcha is awesome and she would never hurt me."

"Okay, okay, let's meditate and talk later. I know I can express myself better after a good sit. Now, where do you want your cushion?"

Ariella shrugged and pointed to a spot a bit behind Faye's cushion and near the edge of the deck. Faye gave basic instructions Ariella in how she herself meditated: sit with back straight, legs crossed comfortably and to tilt her head down at a slight angle. Eyes could be open or closed.

"Popular choices for where to put your hands are to clasp them in your lap or rest them on your thighs. And don't worry about shifting position if it gets uncomfortable." Faye gave Ariella a handful of the beads. "When I first started, I counted 10 breaths, then dropped a bead on the mat and then started over at breath number one. When all the beads were dropped I picked them up and began again."

With no fuss, Ariella slipped into a good approximation of the correct sitting position. The cats lay down beside her, one on each side, and did their black and white sphinx imitations. Faye went to her cushion and again settled herself.

"We'll sit for 20 minutes, okay?" Faye said and started the timer. Ariella didn't answer, so Faye glanced over her shoulder and said, "Okay?" Ariella nodded, but kept her eyes lowered.

As Faye began watching her own breathing, her thoughts returned to Sorcha Novak. Sorcha was qualified as Low Income, which meant she was entitled to a free lunch every school day. Given that Sorcha was gaunt by almost anyone's standards, Faye knew the school lunch could be the only real food Sorcha ate most days. And the girl often was so exhausted in class her eyes would close for several minutes before she jerked awake and glared at the other students, daring them to laugh. Faye imagined Sorcha was a starving, feral cat, ready to fight or, more likely, run away.

Faye had felt confident she could befriend Sorcha. Food was always an enticement, so Faye started bringing big batches of whole wheat muffins to share with the students in her classes. But Sorcha wouldn't come up to the desk with the others and grab a muffin. So, during times when the students read to themselves or took a written quiz, Faye would walk down the aisle and put a muffin on Sorcha's desk. The first few times Faye found the uneaten muffin left behind. She's beaten, but unbowed, Faye thought. Finally, on a day when Sorcha appeared both more bedraggled and more defiant, Faye whispered as she put the muffin on the girl's desk, "Just eat it. It won't bite. Or are you scared?"

By the time Faye got back to the front of the class, Sorcha had not only devoured the first muffin, but was making a big show of coming to Faye's desk and taking a second. As she did so, Sorcha looked right at Faye and gave her a pleasant, if enigmatic, smile. After that, things with Sorcha became much easier. Faye invited her to stop by after school to talk and, true to her reputation among the students, created a safe and private space for the strange girl. Sorcha was reticent, but did let on her parents pretty much left her to her own devices. Faye tried to gently raise the issue sexual abuse, but Sorcha shook her head and studied the floor. She did say she was glad her brothers had moved out and she'd finally gotten a room of her own. She also revealed she was a lesbian.

Sorcha turned out to be wicked smart. She had scored in the high Advanced range in all three of the required 10th grade standardized tests, English, Math and Science, and her course grades, while inconsistent, contained a significant number of A's. Sorcha became a regular attendee at Faye's informal after school book discussion group and revealed she was an insightful and voracious reader. Now in 11th grade, Sorcha continued to stop by Faye's classroom, but only once or twice a month.

"Hey Faye?" Faye realized she had been off on a " Sorcha thought vacation." Without turning around, she said, "Yes?" expecting Ariella to complain about aches and pains or want to know how much time remained in their sitting.

"Can I close my eyes?"

"Sure." Faye peeked over her shoulder and saw Ariella was just as upright and relaxed as she had been when she first sat on the cushion. No doubt a natural, Faye thought.

Should she say anything to Ariella about Sorcha? What would a "good" mother do? With a shrug, she let the thought go. Pay attention to the present and the future will evolve naturally. She began to hear small noises behind her and smiled to herself. *Poor kid is probably trying to shift around to ease her knees or back. Maybe not such a natural.*

Ten minutes later, the timer dinged and Faye stretched her arms high above her head and stood. As she bent to pick up her cushion and mat she said, "Was that too long for you?"

Faye looked to Ariella expecting some grumbling and her mouth fell open. Ariella was surrounded by creatures, either snuggled in her lap, leaning against her legs or just sitting or standing around her. Faye counted four squirrels, two rabbits, a half dozen birds, a chipmunk, multiple crickets, ants and a three grasshoppers and, of course, the two cats, who showed no interest in the other animals. Yellowfoot was there too, sitting on his haunches beside Ariella in a way that was a clear imitation of her meditation pose. Several monarch butterflies sat atop the teenager's head, their wings moving lazily.

Ariella's eyes opened a sluggish fraction and her head turned in Faye's direction. In a slow, deep voice, she answered,

"No." After a pause, she added, "I'm good." As her eyes closed, her head tilted down again.

Is she in some kind of trance? Faye thought. She had read about unusual meditation experiences, like levitation and out-of-body stuff, but this was different. Not wanting to scare any of the animals, she quietly put down her cushion and mat and went to Ariella. The animals shuffled out of Faye's way, but didn't seem at all disturbed. She knelt, heard her knees pop in protest, took Ariella's chin in her hand and gently lifted her head up.

"Ariella, are you okay?"

The green eyes opened, again slowly, but this time all the way. They stared straight ahead, pupils dilated and unfocused, clearly not seeing. Faye and put her hand to Ariella's cheek. Ariella shuddered several times, as if she was getting mild electrical shocks, and her eyes snapped into focus.

"That was off . . . I mean, wow, I really like meditating," Ariella smiled around at all her furry and winged companions. "Can I give them all some food?"

"Sure, but what —" Ariella jumped up and was in the kitchen before Faye could finish her question. With a sigh, Faye gathered up the cushions, mats, timer, and glasses and followed. She drank another glass of juice and watched as Ariella crouched on the deck with the animals and bugs, handing out nuts, greens, seeds, honey and water. The cats came in and sat gazing at Faye until she got it and fed them.

Chapter Twenty Four

To say Faye was feeling confused was short of the mark. She needed answers from Ariella. In her bedroom, she booted up her laptop and opened a new Word document, which she entitled "Questions for Ariella". She started a bulleted list and began typing. After fifteen minutes, she reread what she'd written, made a few changes and printed out the document. The door to the spare bedroom was closed and Faye could hear Ariella talking. Rather than interrupt another online conversation, Faye slipped the list of questions under the door.

In the bathroom, as she ran her electric toothbrush over her teeth, checked her face in the mirror and started reviewing everything yet again - Ariella at the beach, Ariella in the school bathroom bleeding from the welts on her thighs, Ariella on the deck with the animals, Drake and having a child, Sorcha, Wanda, and - wait a minute! Was that a zit on her chin? It was! Just starting to get red and become a real bump. Too much pizza? And was that another one on her cheek near the crease of her nose? Damn! Wouldn't you know this would happen when Drake was coming over. She started to yank her top off over her head, intending to give her face a good defoliating scrub and put something on the pimples.

Ouch! Her breasts hurt as she drew the top up over them. She held her top out with one hand and stared at her reflection, scanning her breasts as if they might contain a bomb. Was it possible? It was too soon wasn't it? She ran from the bathroom to her bedroom and, frantic, stared at the wall calendar until she realized she needed the date from the previous month. She tore down the turned-up sheet and saw that her last period had started 27 days ago. Great, just great.

Faye shuffled to her bed and fell backward onto it. This wasn't good. Drake was quite fastidious about not having sex when she was even close to getting her period. And she definitely didn't want fastidious tonight. But what could she do? Perhaps she could get Ariella to appeal to the nature spirits to intervene somehow, give her a day or two of reprieve? Whatever. She sniffed back tears and dragged herself back to the bathroom.

She was in her bedroom getting dressed, yanking on her tight jeans, when there was a tap at her door and Ariella walked in. Faye paused, her jeans around her knees, thankful she had her bra on. She started to say something and stopped. Faye knew she needed to get used to these semi-announced entrances.

"When are we leaving for the Mall?" Ariella asked. She was still in t-shirt and shorts and bare feet. In her hand was Faye's list of questions. "Hey, is that a thong?"

"No." Faye yanked her jeans all the way up. She hated panty lines. "How about we leave in 45 minutes or so? What did you think of my questions?"

"This?" Ariella flapped the piece of paper. "No problemo, senorita. But you didn't say there was going to be a pop quiz. Does this mean I can skip writing the wacked out essay you assigned in class?" Faye gave her a baleful look. "Okay then, do you want my answers now?"

"Sure." Faye put on a crisp, off-white, short sleeve blouse and began buttoning it.

"Okay. Question number one. Do I want you to talk to me about Sorcha? Answer is no. Question number two. What did I do last night at the beach to make all the weird stuff happen. Answer is I only got things going by tapping into the energies I felt. When the nature spirit energies are strong, I can actually feel them, like threads I can pull or pillows I can push. And the spinning just amplified everything, like a generator sort of. Question three-"

"Hold it. About Sorcha. You do know she's a lesbian?"

"Because her FB name is Sappho's Cat?"

"Well, yes, but I also know that from talking with her."

"So what's your point?" Ariella demanded.

"I just thought you should know. So you don't get hurt."

Ariella's expression was complicated, but it wasn't happy. "So I shouldn't be friends with her because she's a lesbian and she might hurt me? You've never had a friend who was a lesbian?"

"No, that's not what I said." Faye tucked her shirt into her jeans. This wasn't going well. Why was everything such an issue with Ariella? She went to her closet to pick out some shoes, aware of those green eyes following her like targeting lasers. "Look, just forget it, okay?" she said, tugging a pair of red flats from the pile of shoes, boots and sneakers, "You can be friends with whomever you want. I'm not your mother. I'm only trying to be a good friend. And Sorcha is my friend too."

"So you're worried I'll like her better than you?"

Faye spun around and her heart dropped. It felt like she was back in the hut when she discovered Brian smooching Wanda with the fear that everything she treasured and had hoped for was going to dissolve and be lost. Nothing was going right. Ariella, Drake, Calista – they all considered her someone to manipulate. And she knew she deserved their opinions, just a stupid nobody Jewish kid with dreams and fantasies of an exciting life. She had lifted her left foot to slip on her shoe and she stopped in mid-motion, balancing like a stork on one leg until it quivered and gave way and she collapsed in a heap. She was crying. Again.

As she sobbed into her hands, she felt Ariella's young, strong arms go around her and smelled a mixture of sun and cats and sweat and herbs. The teenager cradled Faye in her lap and made shushing sounds and said, over and over, "It's okay, it's okay. Don't worry. It's going to be okay."

"I'm so, so sorry," Faye managed to say. "I'm about to get my period and, with all that's going on, my emotions are taking charge. And Drake's coming over and it's just going all wrong."

"Your period? Really? That explains a lot. No wonder you were so sensitive to the spirits last night. If you want, I can make you something that will delay your period."

Faye managed a weak smile and nodded. "That would be good, so long as it's not the Veil Ripper."

"No worries," Ariella said and bent over to kiss her on the

forehead like Rhoda had when Faye was a child. Faye gave a little whimper. Ariella let her slide gently to the floor, where she curled into the fetal position. She heard Ariella go into the spare bedroom, then come out and head for the kitchen. Five minutes later Ariella was back with a steaming mug of aromatic liquid. Sitting up, Faye took the mug and raised her eyebrows at Ariella.

"It's a mix my mom uses if she's going to get her monthlies at an inconvenient time. Plus, I added a few ingredients to help you relax. No hallucinations, I promise."

Faye took a sip. The drink was hot, had a strong minty taste, but was also bitter, grassy and chalky.

"Mmm, good. Thanks, Mom," she said and raised the mug in mock salute.

"For sure. Just drink it all, okay? And I assume you don't want any more questions answered right now?"

Faye shook her head. It felt as if she was nine years old and didn't feel well and her mother was hovering about. Note to self, she thought, remember to be the adult.

"If you don't need anything more, I'm going to go get dressed. Try and rest, if you can. We can go whenever you're ready."

Faye felt tears prickle eyes again and could only muster a husky, "Okay."

After Ariella left, Faye went to her bed and crawled under the covers. She imagined she could feel Ariella's tea or drink or whatever it was circulating through her system, cleaning up the new mess and putting things back in order. She wasn't surprised when, after fifteen minutes, she felt a resurgence of the clarity and confidence she'd had when she first awoke. She called Wanda.

"I'm back in bed," she said in answer to her friend's query. "But I'm dressed. We're going to the Mall."

"Really? In bed at 11:30 in the morning? What a great life. I've been up since six, fed the brood, cleaned the kitchen, done two washes and was contemplating a quick shower before we all go on a hike with Sir Brian the Intrepid Explorer."

"He's still in mid-life mode, huh? How'd things go with him last night? It was wild in my corner of the world. We went to the beach."

"You know when I texted you last night I said things were weird? Well, it had nothing to do with Brian. It was around 8:15 and I was getting myself dolled up for some hot sex and, all of a sudden, the room started to spin. I'd had a couple of glasses of wine and a toke or two, but this was way beyond that. I put my head between my legs, but that didn't help, so I got into bed. Then I started smelling the ocean and forest and I heard a kind of windy, whiny sound, almost like someone talking after inhaling helium. And I kept getting the feeling you were in danger or doing something really strange."

"Strange is an understatement. But tell me more about what happened to you."

"The room got like real dark and fuzzy and I saw these flickering lights, like fireflies but bigger. I kept smelling leaf mold and other woodsy stuff. And I got a real strong image of the hut you and I built in the woods. Remember? Then I guess I passed out or something because the next thing I knew, it was 9:30 and Brian was kissing my neck."

"Wow." Faye debated what to tell Wanda about her Friday night at the beach.

"The sex was pretty awesome, by the way, probably the best we've had in years. I kinda went wild and Sir Brian was surprised, but rallied." Wanda giggled.

"Wanda, I need to tell you what happened last night to Ariella and I on the beach near the woods where the hut was. But you've got to promise to never tell anyone. I mean it. I could lose my job, or worse."

"My lips are super glued."

Faye tried to keep the retelling short, but the more she talked, the more she relished recalling all the details. Wanda egged her on by adding punctuation with comments such as, "OMG," "No way!," "Stop it!," and "She did what?"

Faye began to describe what happened that morning with Ariella and meditating and the animals showing up, but Wanda interrupted.

"Never mind about all that. You know what we're gonna do, don't you?"

"What do you mean?"

"We've got to go back to the hut site. You and me. And do some poking around. I mean, what if we made an archeological discovery or something?"

"I'm not going to dig up skeletons, if that's what you mean. And I'm not going to let you dig any up either."

"Okay, we won't do any digging, but we could snoop around for other stuff, like arrowheads or something. That way we'll know what you saw was probably real."

"I know it was real. And I now believe in the nature spirits."

"Ah, I see. My little fair maiden hath been magicked by the evil VGL." Faye noted Wanda was using her Prince Glorious voice, deep and commanding. The voice which made Faye shiver. "Methinks I must come to your rescue, my sweet?"

"No, this maiden isn't so gullible. It's Princess Ariella that's convinced me - with her actions and her words. Despite what you think, I find she's quite extraordinary and we're becoming friends." Though Faye was playing along with Wanda, when she heard herself say "Princess Ariella" she had the odd sensation of a puzzle piece clicking into place.

Wanda snorted. "She's just like her mother, who is an extraordinary actress. Beware, my lady, of green-eyed women bearing promises."

"Ariella hasn't promised anything. In fact, we've already had a few disagreements, so I know she's not trying to snow me. And what about you experiencing all that weirdness while I was tripping out last night? Doesn't that make you believe in some of what Ariella has told me?"

"Uh, no. All it tells me is you and I are tuned into each other. And our connection isn't surprising given all the fantasy stuff we did as teenagers. I don't think what I went through last night had anything to do with nature spirits or Ariella. You were on some drug and I got a long-distance contact high. It's all just about you and me. And that makes it even more important we go together to the hut, if only to see what remains and to see if we can sense anything. You know, use our magical powers."

"Magical powers. Right. We were amateurs then and we're probably less now. But, it might be interesting to just meditate at the hut site and see how it feels. When do you want to go?"

"How about tomorrow afternoon? I can beg off the kayaking adventure Brian has planned."

"Can't tomorrow. I'll still have Ariella with me. And I assume you don't want her along."

"Nah. Fool me once, shame on her; fool me twice, shame on me. How about after-school in a few days?"

"Sounds good. Have fun with Sir Brian and the kidlings today."

After she hung up, Faye stayed in bed and watched an unruly tribe of thoughts pad through her mind, their torches dimly lighting a path she might follow.

Chapter Twenty Five

When Snow and Midnight hopped onto the bed and began kneading her legs and walking on her stomach, Faye knew it was time to get it together to go to the Mall. Careful not to topple the cats, she slid out from beneath the covers and went to her dresser, which doubled as a make-up table. She brushed out her tangled, curly hair, understanding the effort would not produce any noticeable improvement.

What would happen if Faye brought Ariella to the hut? Faye knew Wanda would sputter and threaten, but would be too curious about the hut to leave. And perhaps Ariella could be persuaded to change her negative attitude to Wanda. If it worked out and no one threw a major hissy fit, Wanda would be a great resource in helping Faye understand Ariella.

Faye applied a vivid red shade to her lips, though her mood didn't match. As she started on her eyes, a suspicion hit her. What if Wanda stole a march and went out to the hut on her own? Was she devious enough to do that? Yes. Did Faye care? Most definitely.

Mascara wand in hand, she picked up her phone and called Wanda. "We'll go to the hut tomorrow," she said before Wanda could even say hello, "Let's go around 11 AM?"

"Really. What about your teenage witch? I thought you said you had to babysit her."

Faye hated lying to her friend. "I'll find something for her to do here. She's got lots of homework and she's become obsessed with the laptop I borrowed from school."

"I guess I could do tomorrow, so long as you're sure about Ms Teenage Nature Spirit. You know, as a devoted mother and wife, I would never recommend leaving a child alone." Faye was sure she heard a muffled snicker.

"She'll be fine." Faye thought about it. "Of course, you could relent and let me bring her. It would be so educational for her. And I know, as a devoted wife and mother, how much you value providing educational opportunities to children."

"Faye Bloomberg, if you show up with that brat, I will steal your unicorn, I swear."

"You wouldn't dare! C'mon, it would mean a lot to me as a devoted teacher and hopeful mother-to-be to see how an exemplar parent like yourself is able to put aside her petty feelings and do what is best for the children. In fact, why don't you bring your kids along? They could play with Ariella." Faye put a hand over her mouth to stifle her own snort of laughter.

There was a longish silence.

"Damnit, okay, bring her. And I hate it when you recite that educational bullshit."

"How wunnerful! You are just such a dahlin', I must say. Y'all take care now."

When she was satisfied with her makeup, Faye dropped the scallop locket necklace over her head, grabbed her bag, slipped on her shoes, went across the hall and tapped on Ariella's door.

"Entrez vous!" Ariella said and, as Faye opened the door, added "That means 'enter you'."

"Yes, I know. I took high school French too. Are you ready?"

"Yup. How do I look?" Ariella jumped up from the desk and spread her arms out at her sides.

"But, you're wearing almost exactly my outfit," Faye stared at Ariella's neat white blouse and tight blue jeans. Ariella's abundant hair was piled up and tied back in a way which mimicked Faye's loose mess. The only difference was Ariella had on red sneakers instead of flats and the ring with the large green gemstone twinkled on the third finger of her left hand. But she was wearing her scallop locket necklace.

"Yup. Everyone will think we're mother and daughter. It'll be gnarly!"

I bet she's nervous about the Mall and disguising herself as my daughter is a security thing. "If it works for you, it's fine by me. Now let's get going. And bring a sweater or something, because it's getting cool outside." Indeed, the sky was clouding over and, like many spring days on Cape Cod, it seemed Old Man Winter was sneaking in under the door with yet another faded bouquet of gray, icy forget-me-nots. Ariella nodded, grabbed a windbreaker from her duffel and stuffed it into her backpack.

"And I'm sure you know the cats can't come?"

"Yup, they already know that. I let them out earlier. They'll be fine."

As they neared the front door, Ariella stepped in front of Faye and put her arms out for a hug, which Faye gladly returned. Faye thought she felt a small tremor run through Ariella's body, but before she could ask why, Ariella took her head off Faye's shoulder, merrily met her eyes and kissed her softly on the lips. Startled, Faye drew back, then leaned forward and gave Ariella a return peck on the cheek.

"I really like you, Faye," said Ariella, and Faye felt a familiar lightheaded, spinning hollowness.

Faye had recovered her composure by the time they were belted-in and ready to go. She was trying to remember what had been said at a training on student-teacher relationships. Was it common for female students to develop crushes on female teachers? Certainly lots of teenage girls swooned over good looking male teachers.

"Guess what?" Ariella's voice was light and happy and Faye's stomach churned. *What now? She's going to tell me she loves me?*

"Sorcha is coming over tomorrow to give me a ride on her bike!" Ariella practically shrieked in glee.

"What?" Faye was confused. Sorcha was going to ride a bicycle all the way from Hyannis? She pictured Ariella perched on the handlebars as the bike wobbled down the road, Sorcha's slender, black-clad form struggling to keep it upright.

"Sorcha's coming over tomorrow. To give me a ride on her bike," Ariella enunciated each word slowly.

"Oh, her bike. Her motorcycle. I get it now." Faye started to say something cautionary and perhaps even forbidding, but then remembered how kind Ariella had been to her earlier, holding her and making a wonderful drink. And Faye remembered she also actually liked and trusted Sorcha.

"What time is she coming over? I'm asking because I thought we could go the hut site in the morning if the weather's good. Just to, you know, scout around. See what it's like now." Faye didn't mention Wanda.

"Sorcha said in the afternoon, so I'll tell her later is better, okay? I really want to go see those woods again in the daylight."

"Okay, but no conjuring up nature spirits, agreed?"

"For sure, for sure. You da woman."

"That I am, honey chile, that I am."

In the summer, the Cape Cod Mall's halls overflowed with the influx of tourists, who more than doubled the year-round population. Money piled into cash registers and pockets like a tide which keeps rising until it becomes a flood. But tides, no matter how high, always ebb and winter business was a fraction of the summers'. Now, in early June, the mall was quiet and the long, high-ceilinged main concourse echoed to the conversations and footsteps of the few shoppers. For the first half-hour, Faye and Ariella window shopped, with Faye acting as guide. She was amused that her "daughter" stayed close by her side and seemed almost shy about even looking in the glittering, merchandise-filled windows. She was reminded of those movies where the native from some lost tribe cowers away from cars, modern buildings and technology.

They wound up at the food court and Faye suggested they eat lunch and devise a "strategy" for Ariella's shopping. Several of the vendors were vegetarian friendly and Ariella brought an overflowing tray back to the table, including guacamole, Japanese soba noodles, vegetable spring rolls, organic potato fries, two large slices of pizza and a dish of frozen yogurt.

"Now everyone's going to think your 'mother' hasn't been

feeding you. Or worse, I'm allowing you to eat junk food," Faye said as she dribbled balsamic vinaigrette dressing on her modest salad.

Her mouth full and a smear of guacamole on her chin, Ariella just chewed and smiled, her cheeks round like a chipmunk's.

"Would your mom approve all of all that?" Faye reached across with a napkin to wipe off the guacamole.

Ariella stopped chewing, swallowed and said, "I think she would be okay with the organic fries and the spring rolls."

"Well, what happens at the mall, stays at the mall, okay?"

Ariella smiled and took another bite.

"But, you know if you eat all that it might be hard to fit into those new clothes you're going to buy."

Ariella's eyes went wide and she dropped the pizza slice she was devouring. "Really? What should I do? I can't throw all this away!" Faye got a Styrofoam container and a plastic bag from one of the vendors and, despite her obvious distaste for the artificial materials, Ariella packed up the remaining food, grumbling "the cats probably won't eat this."

"So what exactly are you hoping to get today?" Faye asked, expecting a list with earth sandals, modest and simply made cotton dresses, skirts and blouses and perhaps a sweater made out of organic wool. Instead, Ariella pulled from her pack a folded fashion magazine page which showed a photo of a model taken in heavy contrast shades of gray, black and white. The model was a young girl photographed against a pure white background, leaning forward with her long, long hair blowing out to the side and back, while gazing into the camera with the combination of provocation and mystery great models possess. Small, obviously pure metal, platinum or gold, earrings twinkled at her ears and a delicate, slender necklace of glittering diamonds contrasted with her smooth skin. For a top she wore a low-cut, loose, flowing blouse made of some shimmery material that, in the wind from the photographer's fan, molded to her skinny body. Her pencil skirt was pale, simple and straight, but clung to her non-existent hips and ended just below mini-skirt length. To finish the outfit, the model wore sheer black stockings and shiny stilettos with a heel so high Faye's toes clenched in empathic pain. The photo's caption was "Beauty Is Simple" in big letters with a smaller sub-title of "When you wear the right stuff". In the lower right hand corner there was a list of the designers and the cost of each item the model was wearing, including makeup and jewelry. Faye's eyebrows shot up at the prices, realizing it would cost her more than a month's salary to buy just the skirt and top, never mind the shoes, jewelry and makeup.

"Wow," how . . . uh . . . unusual. For you, I mean. This really is what you want to buy?"

Ariella nodded, her face turning pink in what Faye realized was the first time she had seen Ariella blush. "Plus, I want to get a bra."

"Of course you do." Faye thought of all the questions she could ask, like where the heck did Ariella plan to wear an outfit like the one pictured in the photo. If she wore it to school, she would stand out even more than she did in her usual bell skirt and Mary-Janes combo.

"Okay, then," Faye opened a map of the Mall on the table. "Let's identify a few stores which will probably carry something like what you want, though hopefully not at the prices in that ad. By the way, how much money do you plan to spend and do you want me to come along?"

"I've got lots of scrilla," Ariella reached into her backpack and produced a scratched, dark brown, worn pouch. She opened it and started pulling out bills and piling them on the table. Faye saw lots of twenties and tens mixed in with fives and ones.

"Whoa!" Faye said, shoving the bills back toward the pouch and glancing around to see if anyone noticed the heap of cash. "You don't want to get mugged. Put it back. Where'd you get all that?"

Ariella shrugged, "Babysitting mostly."

Faye arched a questioning eyebrow.

"For real. There's lots of folks in the Punkhorn who need babysitters." Ariella paused. "Okay, my mom gives me money, especially when she's feeling happy, like when she has a new boyfriend. It's not a lot, but I've been saving for over a year. And sometimes I read palms at school. Last September, when I first started public school, I hinted I might be a witch."

Faye ran her hands through her hair, clearing tangles with her fingers, then said, "Hmmm, I know I should ask you more about your money-making activities at school, but let's leave it for another day. Right now you need to get shopping. So, am I going with you or would you prefer to park your 'mother' somewhere and check back at regular intervals?"

"Let's try the parking and checking first. If I get stuck or some derpina in a store gives me a hard time, I'll come and get you? I'm going to leave my backpack and the food with you, though." Ariella jumped up, like a runner eager to start a race.

"Okay, lets meet back here in two hours? In the meantime, I might do some shopping myself."

Faye got back to the food court long before the two hours were up. She was quite pleased with her purchase and imagined Drake's reaction when he saw it on her. However, carrying her own bag, plus Ariella's leftover food and her backpack had been tiring. After purchasing a cup of tea, she settled at a table with collection of Emily Dickinson poems she had stashed in her bag. Though she'd read all the poems in this collection many times over, she never got tired of rereading. She liked underlining certain lines or verses, as she was fond of writing a new Dickinson quote on her school smart board and then letting the students debate its meaning for a few minutes at the start of each class. Emily was so way ahead of her time, Faye thought. So much of what she wrote resonated even now in the 21st Century.

She sat back in the plastic chair, the book of poems open in her lap, and tapped her teeth with her finger, savoring the various food aromas. Without thinking about it, she began watching her breath, gently brushing aside any thoughts about Ariella or poems or food. A blissful, blank, unworried state of mind crept over her until she heard Ariella's strained and shrill voice.

"Faye, Faye! I mean, Mom! Help!" There was a pause, then Ariella said angrily, "See, I told you she would be here!"

Faye leapt to her feet to see Ariella staggering toward her, her face an agony, trying to carry four big shopping bags and a shoe box, while a large man in uniform had a tight grip on her shoulder. All blissful feelings evaporated and Faye knew what a momma bear feels when its cub is threatened. She heard a growl rise up her throat, the hair on the back of her neck bristled and she bared her teeth.

Chapter Twenty Six

Though she was trembling with outrage, Faye pushed through and said, in her best posh Brit accent, "Sir, I must demand you unhand my dau . . . my charge immediately or I will be forced to take actions which will impact you in a most negative way."

The man was big, no, he was huge. He stood at least six foot four and must have weighed over 250 pounds. His head was shaved and he seemed muscular, but his gut preceded his belt buckle by several inches and his face, though mostly hard planes, had softened around the jowls. Faye guessed he was either ex-military or ex-football, perhaps in his mid-thirties, gone to seed with easy living, but still no one to take lightly. His mouth was a harsh, downturned curve and he stared hard at Faye, as if assessing her threat potential. That's right, Faye thought, I *AM* dangerous. In fact, I might just throw my tepid tea in your face and make a run for it with my teenage accomplice. She stood up straighter and pulled her shoulders back to puff herself up the way animals do when they want to intimidate.

Ariella, sensing Faye's attitude, shouted at the man, "That's right, you cretin, let go of me or it's going to go hard for you!" She tried to jerk away, but the man, who Faye now saw was a mall cop, just shifted his grip from Ariella's shoulder to her upper arm. He kept his eyes on Faye as he turned his head and spoke into a radio attached to his shoulder.

"I'm at the food court. Suspect and situation under control. Will be interrogating adult female associated with the young female perp." There was a crackly, staticky unintelligible response and the mall cop said, "Okay. Over and out."

"She's not a perp!" Faye's voice rose to a near squeak.

"Please be advised I intend to record this conversation. Do you have any objections?" the cop said implacably and pulled out a small voice recorder and put it on the table. Ariella stopped struggling and hung from his giant hand like a rag doll, her bags and packages now scattered at her feet. Faye could only shake her head, knowing if she opened her mouth so much vitriol would spew out she would probably wind up in handcuffs.

"Please say yes or no for the recording." The cop was a granite block, showing zero emotion.

"No, damn it, though I don't understand why you need —"

"Ma'am, I have to ask you to only answer my questions. Any other response could be interpreted in a 'negative way.'" The cop smirked and Faye understood he wasn't just one big, brainless muscle.

"Please state your name, address and occupation and please provide some ID."

"Faye Bloomberg, 22 Sunset Lane, East Harwich, and I'm a teacher at Bradford High School." Faye dug in her pocketbook and produced not only her license, but her teacher's ID on the lanyard she hung around her neck when she was at school. As an afterthought, she also handed over her library card.

The mall cop took the cards, gave them quick once over and said toward the recorder, "Adult female has produced ID showing Faye Bloomberg of Harwich." He then turned to his shoulder mike and said, "Hey, run a check on Faye Bloomberg, 22 Sunset Lane, East Harwich, 36 years old, Massachusetts license number S13571113."

"Are you the mother of this young female, who has self-identified as Ariella Cardona?"

"No, but she's my student and I'm taking care of her this weekend while her mother is away. May I ask why you apprehended her, . . . sir?" Faye decided to change course and try for respectful citizen, so she flashed what she hoped was a winning smile even while her urge was to give the cop a swift kick in the groin.

"Again, I will advise you to answer only my questions. What was your business today at the Cape Cod Mall?"

"We're here to primarily purchase some items of clothing for Ariella and myself. Is that a crime?"

The cop gave Faye the hard eye and she knew the ice was

getting thin. She forced another smile onto her face, trying to let him also know he was, without doubt, the biggest, baddest, dominant alpha male she had ever seen and she was just a silly, admiring adult female who couldn't keep her mouth shut. She let her eyelashes flutter a little and stuck her breasts in his general direction.

Mr. Big Authority leered and Faye knew she had touched his libido without having to kick him.

"Ma'am, this young female, who claims she is Ariella Cardona, was observed entering multiple stores at the mall and making purchases of high-end merchandise and paying in cash. When approached by mall security she couldn't provide any verifiable ID. When we attempted to take her in for questioning under suspicion of money laundering, she resisted. Violently. In fact, she bit the hand of another security staff and, had she broken the skin the charges would be much more serious."

Flabbergasted, Faye didn't know where to start. The radio speaker on the cop's shoulder burst into raucous life and he turned his head to listen.

He handed Faye's IDs back. "Well, Ms Bloomberg, you check out, but —"

It was Faye's turn to interrupt. "You do know how money laundering works, don't you, Officer?" she asked innocently. "And, just for the record, can you give me your name and badge number and the name of your superior?" Another sweet smile.

For the first time, a light of doubt appeared in the cop's eye. "Yeah, sure I know how laundering works. Criminals take the cash they get from crimes and spend it so it can't be traced. Just like the alleged Miss Cardona was doing. And I'm Officer Robert Slatterly of S & W Security Services. And we don't use badge numbers. And I'm sure my superior is not interested in talking to you. That's not the way we roll." He tried for a confident, superior smile.

"I see," said Faye, finding a scrap of paper and writing his info on it. "Not the way you roll. Well, for your information, money laundering indeed happens when criminals spend cash obtained through their illicit activities. But the trick is, they spend it where they can get it back after it's been spent, like in a seemingly legitimate business they own. That way they get to keep the money. You do understand the difference between that and what Ariella was doing today, which was simply making purchases at several real stores, none of which she has a financial interest in? Or don't you roll that way?"

Officer Slatterly's face started to color and he turned his back to speak into his shoulder radio, his hand falling off Ariella's arm. Realizing she was free, Ariella glanced around wildly, trying to decide which way to run, but stopped when she saw the Faye's settling hand gesture. Faye watched the back of the officer's neck get bright red and his shoulders slump.

"Yeah. Okay. Got it. Will do. Yes sir, no charges. Yes sir, apologize. Uh huh, gift certificate. Roger. Wilco. Over"

Slatterly turned back and, while examining the floor, perhaps for evidence it needed laundering, said in a low voice, "Apparently there's been a misunderstanding and, on behalf of S & W Security Services, I want to apologize for any inconvenience this incident has caused you. We will not be pressing charges against Ms Cardona. I've also been instructed to tell you a one-hundred dollar gift certificate good in any store in Cape Cod Mall will be sent to your address within two weeks. Please also be advised that any information gathered during this invest . . . incident will be immediately deleted. Is there anything else I can do for you today?"

Faye glanced at Ariella, her eyes vivid with mischief. "Why, yes, Officer Slatterly, there is something you can do. As I am sure you must understand, my charge, Ariella, is quite distraught at the way she has been manhandled by you and your fellow officers. And I'm quite sure neither you nor anyone else on the other end of that squawky radio wants us to pursue what would be our legal right to file official complaints or perhaps even criminal charges. Am I correct? Or do I need to call our attorney?"

Officer Slatterly glanced up from his inspection of the floor and nodded, his face as woebegone as it had been when he fumbled the ball in his college championship game and allowed the other team to score the winning touchdown.

"Good. So, first you will get down on one knee and apologize to Princess Ariella."

"Princess? What do you —." Faye cut him off with an imperious gesture and pointed to the floor. With effort, Officer Slatterly knelt on one knee, and, confused and shamefaced, said to Ariella, "I apologize, Princess Ariella, for . . . for . . . everything!" he finished in a rush.

Ariella shot a questioning look at Faye, who nodded, so Ariella stepped forward to the kneeling man in a most regal fashion and held out her hand with the big green stone ring on the third finger.

"You may kiss her Highness' ring, officer," Faye said, feeling so very Queen Mother.

Slatterly looked furtively around and saw the majority of the patrons of the food court and many in the nearby concourse had stopped to watch this little drama. He started to struggle to his feet, but stopped and slouched back down as Faye lifted her cell phone and mimed dialing a number. He leaned forward, took Ariella's hand and quickly touched his lips to the ring. As he did so, there was an audible snap and a bright green spark arced from the ring to his forehead. He shook his head as if to clear it, then stood slowly and, clasping his hands in front of his belly, gazed at Ariella with doglike devotion. The watching crowd applauded at what they took to be some spontaneous theatre or an internet promoted flash event. Both Faye and Ariella made sweeping bows to the audience, but Officer Slatterly kept his eyes on Ariella.

"Robert," Ariella said in aristocratic tones, "We're going to the car now. Do be a darling and bring the packages won't you?"

And so it was that the Princess Ariella and her Queen Mother paraded out of the mall, followed at a proper distance by the gigantic man, who struggled to balance all the packages and bags (including Faye's purchase, Ariella's backpack and the leftover food) while never letting his gaze stray from his Princess. At the car, Faye opened the Prius' hatch and Robert carefully piled in the boxes and bags and then turned to face Ariella, his eyes brimming with tears.

"I'll not be seeing you again, will I?" he managed to say.

"Oh, yes you will, my dear Robert. Watch for me in your dreams." Ariella gave a little laugh and stepped forward and reached up to touch the center of the giant's forehead. She also gave him a five-dollar tip. Robert stared at the money in his hand, shook his head again, then looked around, seeming surprised to find himself outside in the parking lot.

"Goodbye, Robert," Ariella said and got into the passenger seat as Faye started the car. As they drove off, Faye saw in her rear view mirror the mall cop rooted like a boulder, staring forlornly after the receding Prius. Faye waited until they were well clear of the mall, then turned and put her hand up for a high-five, which Ariella happily returned.

"Way, Faye," Ariella said, grinning hugely.

"You were fantastic back there," Faye replied.

"You were no slouch yourself. I loved the way you took charge of the situation. 'Unhand the damsel, you scoundrel!' and all that. And how did you know all about money laundering?"

"Not sure. I must've read about it somewhere or seen it on TV. But, you made a very convincing princess. And what's with the spark from your ring? Dear Robert was pretty stunned and willing after that."

"I guess now I can tell you about me being a princess, I mean, for real a princess. Ever since I was small and my parents got involved in the VGL, I've been groomed to become a "Princess" in the organization. And I might eventually become one of the queens. They aren't really royalty titles, BTW, but about how much authority and responsibility a person has. There's a lot to learn and it's a pretty big deal and I got exposed to lots of knowledge I wouldn't have in public school. That's why they kept me at home until this year, even though I've wanted to go to regular school since about sixth grade. The VGL wants to get more young people involved, 'specially as so many of their members are way, way old. I'll give you more details after you've met with Moira.

"And the thing with the ring is, I told you how when I'm in modern buildings I can't connect to the nature spirits that well? It's something about all the metal and plastic and the atmosphere is often clouded with greed and fear. So they gave me the ring because I can load it up with natural energy at home and then, when I'm at school or someplace like the mall and I get wiped out, I just touch the stone to get a charge up. And I can use it on other people, and even add some *intention* to it. So that's what I did to our dear Robert. Kind of changed his point of view."

"He certainly changed. Are you actually going to appear in his dreams?"

"Probably. When I make that kind of impression on someone they always think or dream about me after. Didn't it happen to you after we had our moment during the exam?"

"Is that what was? I remember feeling lightheaded and out-of-sorts after I went over to your desk. Did you zap me with the ring?"

"Yup, though I didn't mean to. I think it discharged when you bent down to talk to me about my missing pencil."

"About the pencil, was it actually lost or was that an excuse of some sort?"

"Hey, I thought you were going to submit your difficult questions in writing first. But, I'll be nice and answer. Because the exam seemed so silly and I couldn't get into it, I started playing around trying to contact the nature spirits, to see if they could do something like color in the circles on the answer sheet for me. I think they did try, but the connection was so weird my pencil vanished instead, I guess because they didn't want me to take the exam. They're so not happy I'm attending public school."

"Really." Faye grew quiet as she remembered the mad energy which had possessed her as she had filled in the blanks on Ariella's exam answer sheet. "But, why didn't you use the ring on Officer Slatterly before he dragged you to the food court? Couldn't we have avoided the whole scene?" she asked.

"Maybe, but the way I figured it was if I ringed just him he'd be wandering around all dazed and stuff and would draw more attention, so there'd be other guards on the lookout for me and the ring didn't have much charge left. I knew if could get back to the food court you'd be able to handle things, being an adult and all. And, you were awesome. I just added the final touch with the ring."

Faye smiled. "It was fun and, incidentally, thanks for answering my questions without resorting to teenager lingo or gangsta rap."

"Well, after you became the posh, almost royal, Brit back at the mall, I felt I should keep the linguistic standards high. And for sure after you claimed I was a princess. As the English say, that was 'brilliant'."

"Ever think you might try an acting career? Has your mom ever mentioned that to you?"

"I asked her once about acting in movies and plays and she said it was too 'mainstream' and 'dirty' for me, that my real destiny was to become a VGL Princess. She said I would have so much greater positive impact on the world as a representative and leader of the VGL. And, when I first asked why she still was an actor, she said it was her 'youthful addiction' and she's still acting and modeling because it allows her to influence people from inside the 'monster'. And it's also really good money."

"What about your dad? He's an actor too. Does your mom miss him?"

"Alberte's fine. Like my mom, he's acting because it gives him a chance to reach a wider audience than he could on the Cape. I mean, he's been in productions all over the world and many of them are plays and films which support the VGL's beliefs.

And yeah, I think my mom misses him, but she has boyfriends and everything. She says she and my dad have an understanding, whatever that means. And can we stop with the questions for now? I think the buzz I got from the scene in the mall is wearing off, cuz I'm getting sleepy."

"Absolutely. I'm feeling a bit weary myself," Faye said and meant it. She'd ask Ariella to brew up another cup of period-postponing tea at the cottage when they stopped to feed the cats.

Interesting that Calista was dating other men. Did it mean she was sleeping with them and did she bring them home to the cottage for overnights? What kind of man would be appealing to Calista anyway? She was so beautiful, exotic and her lifestyle so alternative Faye couldn't think of any man she knew who would be a good fit. Or did Calista just have liaisons for sexual fun?

The day's gray ceiling began to leak and spit. Raindrops polka-dotted the windshield and Faye turned on the wipers. As the sky shaded to a darker gray, the air grew heavy and it felt like they were under a big, smothering blanket. A quick glance showed Ariella's eyes were closed and her mouth slightly open. By the time they reached the cottage in the Punkhorn, the spits of rain had turned into a real shower, not pouring, but steady. Faye roused Ariella by rubbing her shoulder and watched the green eyes open and brighten like stage lights coming on.

As Ariella opened her door, Faye said, "Would it be okay if I stayed here in the car? I just need to take a little nap. You can feed the cats without me, right?"

"For sure. But you know you could come in and nap in my or my mom's bed."

Faye found the idea of sleeping in a cottage bed enticing, but shook her head. She had used up her capacity for new experiences.

"Okay, I'll be done in about half an hour. Do you need anything from inside?"

"A cup of the postponement drink you gave me this morning would be nice."

"You got it." Ariella started to leave, but turned back, flung herself across the middle console and gave Faye a quick hug, followed by another swift kiss on the lips, then jumped out the door and ran toward the cottage. Faye put her seat back, opened her side window a crack, closed her eyes and listened to the rain patter a jazz beat on the roof and hood. A cold breeze blew in and she could smell the rain and scent of wet vegetation. So earthy, she thought, so natural. So why was she sitting inside this technological marvel of a vehicle? Why wasn't she outside running naked through the meadow in the rain? Because she was too tired, that's why. And it was too cold. Faye sighed and squirmed to get more comfortable in the bucket seat.

As she felt sleep start to pull her under, she grinned at an offhand thought. I think my time with Ariella is turning my life upside down and emptying it, like a handbag which needs to be cleaned of all its junk. And someone's starting to refill it with lots of new, shiny, stimulating things. I wonder if I could write a story about my last eight days and make it believable. Faye lips quirked in a small smile and she slipped beneath the blanketing waves.

Chapter Twenty Seven

After 20 minutes, the rain sputtered to a stop, the cloud cover blew aside and the afternoon sun appeared to shine like a heat lamp on the meadow, the car, the woods and the cottage. Within a few minutes, plumes and clouds of evaporating water vapor were rising from the plants and ground. The sunlight made water droplets sparkle and, in places, shimmer into mini-rainbows. In the closed car, the humid heat built quickly and a sleeping Faye began to squirm in discomfort. She was dreaming.

She's at the beach on a hot sunny day, lying on a chaise facing the ocean watching her two young children play in the surf. Like her, their hair is curly, though the little boy, two years younger than his sister, has hair the color of dark honey. His seven year old, taller and skinnier sister, who has Faye's black ringlets blowing about her head in the wind, says something to her brother and they both turn their happy faces toward Faye and wave. Faye feels a surge of almost unbearable love and tries to raise her left arm to wave back, but finds her hand won't move. She glances down and sees another's hand holding hers. Both her hand and that of the other are browned by the sun. Whose hand is holding hers? It must be her partner's, her co-parent's? Her husband? She turns toward the owner of the hand but the person's outline is blurry and Faye strains to see any clear characteristics. Is that a smile? Is the person real? She feels a tingle of panic and tries to pull her hand away, but can't, even though the grip of the other's hand doesn't tighten.

Faye's came awake and gasped in the steamy air of the car's interior. She sat up, coughing and quivering, her heart twittering as fast as a bird's, and gazed dumbfounded at the sparkling landscape with the twinkling rainbows. The fog obscured anything beyond 20 feet of the car. *What am I doing here? Where am I? The dream. It was so real and in it I had children, beautiful children. Was this more of Ariella's doing, did she dose me again with some hallucinatory herb? Damnit, what's with that girl? How can she keep messing with me like this? And where is she? Can't*

I get a few hours of normalcy without being jerked into some weirdness?

Angry, she started the car and powered down all the windows. She was about to pop her seat up and drive away from wherever she was when a puff of cool air swept through and dissolved the fog. Faye now could see the meadow and the cottage beyond. She smelled again the damp earth and plants and memory returned. Of course. It had started raining and she'd fallen asleep and Ariella was inside feeding the cats. But the dream. So real. And the children, my children, she thought. She closed her eyes and tasted an echo of the joy she had felt in the dream. Was the dream a glimpse into the future?

Faye fell back against the reclined car seat and tried to relax, to fall asleep and resume the dream in which she was with her children. She did sleep and she did dream, though this time she was in a forest, perhaps near the hut site.

Through the trees, Faye sees at a distance a man facing away from her, standing in a sunlit clearing. Was it Drake? It could be him, tall and slender with wild dark curls. But something makes Faye hesitate. If only he would turn and she could see his face. The man begins walking away out of the clearing and Faye calls out, "Drake, Drake! Wait a moment. It's me, Faye. Wait!" But the man doesn't stop, doesn't even glance back, so Faye crashes after him through the thick underbrush, scratching her arms, her face and her legs. When she feels a thorny branch whip painfully across her belly, she realizes she's naked. But she forges ahead, knowing it's important to catch up to the receding man, knowing he's important to her. She reaches the clearing and is about to rush across when she sees on the ground ahead a gold ring with a large green, sparkling stone. She's wants to stop, but also knows if she does she may never catch up to the man. She keeps running and sweeps her left hand low as she nears the ring. By some miracle, the ring catches on the tip of the third finger of her left hand and, without breaking stride, she pushes it down over her knuckle and hurtles into the woods on the far side of the clearing. She gets a burst of energy and knows it's coming from the ring.

She fairly flies through and over the underbrush, no longer being lashed and scratched, but rather caressed and stroked. She's getting aroused and there's a heat growing between her legs. The man is still striding ahead. She calls out to him again, "Drake, please wait. I need you. I really need you. Please wait for me!" The man seems to slow and she increases her pace, barely touching the ground at all. The man has stopped. She comes up behind him in a rush and blurts out, "We need to make children! Please, they will be so beautiful." The man turns and there's something distorted, not quite right about his face. Are his ears pointy, like Spock's in Star Trek? She sees he, too, is naked and has a huge erection, much larger than Drake's. He reaches for her and she leaps into his arms, his hardness pressing against her belly like a tree branch. "Oh, Drake, finally, finally. Drake, Drake, I love you so." She falls backward, pulling him with her, wanting to feel him inside her, wanting him to plant the magic seed which will grow their child. He drops on her and she arches her body to give him easy access. But he doesn't try to enter even though he is so hard and she is so ready. He feels light atop her, not the coiled, muscular weight to which she is accustomed. She tries again to see his face, but he leans close and kisses her mouth roughly, his whiskers tickling both her cheeks, then slides his furry head down to her neck and sloppily kisses her there. "Just do it, please, get in me," she pleads. His surprisingly small arms go around her neck and his claws dig into her shoulders, but he still doesn't slide in. She reaches up to pull him into her and feels how his back is like a fur coat and she hears him start to purr.

Faye's lids fluttered open and she stared into a pair of enormous, loving golden eyes in an orange face that had pointy ears and stiff whiskers. She was nose to nose and mouth to mouth with Leaf, Ariella's big orange tomcat. Leaf gave her lips another rough swipe with his raspy tongue, humped her belly and gave a low, grunting purr of pleasure, his claws flexing on her shoulders. Faye began to giggle hysterically and turned to see Ariella in the passenger seat staring straight ahead, her hands primly folded in her lap.

Ariella gave Faye and Leaf a sidelong glance and said, in a sanctimonious tone, "Can't you two get a motel room?" Then she too broke out laughing.

"Did you tell him to get on me?" Faye said between giggles. As she lifted Leaf off her she noted his little red penis was sticking out of its sheath.

"No, Ma'am. I come back to the car with Leaf jus' a few minutes ago - he wants to come to your house for the rest of the weekend, if'n that's okay with you - an' we found you kind of wrigglin' an' moanin' in your seat. It seemed you was talkin' to Drake in your sleep. At least I think I heard his name couple times. Before I could reach over an' wake you, Leaf jumps in ahead of me and settles on your chest. When he starts lickin' your face, that's his way of kissing, by the by, you seem to like it, so I figured I'd just sit here an' let the two of you do what you're goin' to do." Ariella smiled at Faye when she finished, her eyes all wide and innocent.

For some reason, Faye blushed and Ariella said, "What're you turning red for? If you and Leaf got a thing goin' on, it's okay with me. I mean, out here in the boonies, we find love however we can. If'n you know what I mean." Again, Ariella couldn't keep a straight face and let go of a loud "Hoo-haw, that's rich!"

"I was dreaming," Faye tried for annoyed, but failed. "And I was with my boyfriend. Or at least I think it was my boyfriend."

"Sure appeared to be a good dream. Here's the tea you wanted." Ariella picked up a mug from the front seat floor and passed it over, having to reach around Leaf, who was sitting on the center console gazing at Faye with a worshipful expression.

"You're sure this isn't going get me high?"

"Nope. Just what's needed to postpone your bleeding for another day. By the way, you can't take this tea for days on end. It'd mess your cycle up pretty bad."

"I just need it for tonight, I promise," Faye said as she took a sip of the warm, fragrant brew. She popped the release on her seat back and sat forward. "Those were some weird dreams," she said, as if Ariella had shared them. Ariella nodded and stroked Leaf's back, though he refused to look away from Faye. As she finished the contents of the mug, Faye replayed the dreams in her mind. The feeling of having children had been so wonderful, she could dream of them every night and never tire of it. She glanced at her left hand, remembering a ring with a green stone and how much energy it gave her. Faye passed the empty mug back to Ariella and started the car.

When they began moving, Ariella said in a casual tone, "Uh, I called my mom while I was in the cottage and she said everything's going great for her. But, surprise, surprise, she won't be back until Tuesday, so she asked if you could keep me another night. If you can't, it's fine because I could just stay at the cottage Monday night by myself."

Faye sensed there was something Ariella's wasn't saying. She acted as if it didn't make a difference one way or another where she stayed, but perhaps she actually wanted to be alone at the cottage because . . . because . . . ah, of course, she could invite someone over. Quite possibly someone who wears all black and rides a motorcycle.

"I don't think your mom would be pleased with me if I let you stay alone at the cottage. Do you?"

Ariella's face took on the petulant and uncertain expression teenagers get when they are trying to negotiate with the adult world for something they want. They don't know all the rules and those they do understand seem pretty silly.

"No, my mom wouldn't be happy, but I'm pretty sure she wouldn't get all freaked out or anything. Especially because nothing bad would happen. You know I can take care of myself." Ariella grabbed Leaf off the center console and put him in her lap, though he immediately turned to watch Faye.

Again Faye saw it was difficult to know how to respond appropriately to Ariella. The boundary between being a teacher/parent surrogate and a friend was blurring ever more. *Well, I'm definitely not in a position to be the teacher right now. In fact, it seems my Princess is giving me lessons about things in which she's the expert. So, parent or friend? Friends can give advice to each other. And parents can be permissive. So maybe there doesn't need to be a difference this time. Maybe sometimes the best parents are also best friends to their children.*

"Okay, you know I trust you and you know I'm your friend, but I've got to say I'm not comfortable with you staying alone at the cottage, even with your many guard-cats. I'm not confident it would be risk-free, especially given all that has happened since last night. You could fall and be unconscious or someone you invite over could turn out to be not as nice as you imagined." Ariella turned her head away. "And if something did happen to you, I would be responsible and feel terrible. So, I'm being a little selfish in saying I want you to stay at my house the extra night. Is there something you can do at your house you can't do at mine? Or can't wait until Tuesday night when your mom's home?"

Ariella stared out the windshield, her frustration obvious. They were getting near the end of the long winding, mostly smooth dirt path which led from the cottage to the main, potholed, dirt road. Faye pulled the car to the side and turned off the engine. "Why don't we both think about it while I go pee?"

"You're really going to go in the woods?" Ariella's smile was back and her expression mischievous.

"Yup. I'm not the civilized wuss you think I am. When I ran with Wanda and we went to the hut almost every day, I got good at peeing outside."

"No way! What about all the creepy crawly things and . . . and the bears?"

"Ha! The only bugs I might worry about are ticks and there's been just one bear on the Cape in like forever. But don't worry, I'll be careful."

"Make sure you don't get your not-a-thong wet." Ariella was snickering.

"Very funny." As Faye opened her door, Leaf jumped from Ariella's lap and slid out of the car, brushing against Faye's legs.

He glanced back at her and started picking his way through the underbrush, his tail poking straight up.

"Guess he wants to keep you safe," Ariella said, "but be careful, this is the magic Punkhorn Forest, after all. You might attract the Boogie Man. He loves to ravish damsels."

Faye tossed her hair and pretended to ignore Ariella. She plunged off the road and followed Leaf as he wove around bushes and trees. The tip of his tail turned from side to side, like it was a periscope. He passed by several spots Faye considered okay, but finally, 50 feet in, stopped at a perfect round little patch of grass which was shielded from view. Faye glanced back the way they had come, realized she couldn't see the car, and felt a tremor of apprehension. Leaf prowled the edge of the patch and was focused outward. He looked back at Faye as if to say, "We're here, get on with it."

Faye slid her jeans and underwear down and crouched in the center of the clearing, her bare butt sticking out. As she started to pee, she felt a kind of ease, not sexual, but relaxing nonetheless. It felt so natural to do this in the woods. She watched her urine splash onto the dirt and leaf litter of the forest floor and wondered if she was drowning any bugs or microbes. On the bright side, she was giving the plants some needed nitrogen. Speaking of plants, Faye belatedly noticed lots of small, yellowish mushrooms poking their bulbous heads up around the edge of the small clearing. The phrase "Fairy Ring" popped into her mind as she saw the fungi did, indeed, make most of a circle. She smiled, thinking how apropos it was the ex-Queen of the Faye-ries should be peeing in a Fairy Ring.

As her stream slowed, a sudden cold draft scraped its icy fingers across her bare butt and thighs, while at the same time she heard an eerie, buzzing whine, like angry bees swarming. A strong, pungent odor assailed her nostrils. The odor evoked both rancid, spoiled honey and the dusty, desiccated husks of insects, like the ones you found inside outdoor lamps.

"Faye, I am here." The voice was hollow and high-pitched as

if the speaker was down a well and had inhaled helium. Faye immediately thought it was the man from her dream. The man she was convinced was Drake and whom she had pursued through the woods.

She yanked her jeans up and, unable to stop her flow, knew she was getting pee all over everything, including her thighs. Spinning around, she noticed Leaf had stopped prowling and the fur on his back stood on end. He glared into the depths of the woods, uttering a continuous and menacing low growl. Faye looked in that direction and saw, in the distance, a green, whirling cloud, all but obscuring the dim outline of a man. The voice sounded again, this time sounding like two branches rubbing against each other in a gale and she couldn't make out any real words. But Faye knew he wanted her to come to him, that her destiny was with him. She couldn't think clearly, didn't know what to do. The clouded man wasn't moving toward her and she hesitated. His voice or call or whatever it was came again.

"Faye, I am here." This time the voice was clear.

The strong compulsion to be with him shivered through her. But he wasn't Drake, he was something out of a fantasy or a dream. But she wanted fantasy, right? Yes, she loved fantasy. She had always loved fantasy, the odd, the different, the exotic. Faye took a step toward the man, not feeling Leaf's claw catch at the leg of her jeans. She took another step, her arms lifting up as if to welcome him to her body. The man cloud matched her step for step, moving toward her with the same hesitancy.

Suddenly, she had a vivid flashback to the dream of her two children and she stopped. How was this blurry outline of something which might be a man give her the children she wanted? She glanced back over her shoulder toward where she thought the car was. At her feet, his teeth now firmly clamped on the hem of the right leg of her jeans, was Leaf, still managing to growl through a mouthful of denim. There was no doubt he was trying to stop her, digging in with his rear paws and jerking at the cloth.

"Ariella?" Faye called, her voice a weak warble.

A dry, hot breeze, no, a strong gust, hit her in the back and she stumbled toward the buzzing green figure who was becoming more solid as she got closer. A sirocco wind, she thought absently, and felt the dampness on her inner thighs start to dry. She squinted and saw something that made her heart leap. In the cloud of swirling green there were now also two smaller outlines, clearly children, waving and jumping in excitement. She was sure she could hear their eager, piping cries above the whining buzz of the green maelstrom. She knew this was good. She made to run into the cloud, now only about fifteen feet away, to join her family.

A small, but quite strong, hand grabbed her arm. "Faye! Stop," said Ariella in a tone so commanding Faye halted with one foot in the air, lost her balance, and fell backwards into Ariella's arms. She struggled weakly, but Ariella was able to put her upright again and pivot her away from the green cloud.

"This isn't right, let's get back to the car."

"But my children . . . they're waiting for me." Faye tried to turn back to the green cloud, but Ariella kept her moving toward the road, with Leaf leading the way. With an effort, Faye wrenched herself out of Ariella's grip. But the cloud was gone and she realized she couldn't hear the buzzing whine any longer. The cries of her children were also gone. All at once, she was weak to the point of falling down and would have if Ariella hadn't grabbed her again.

"Where did they go? What happened to them?" Faye wailed

"I'll try to explain when we get out of here, okay? But don't worry, this isn't what you think it is."

"What was it then?" Faye was instantly indignant. Then she was angry, as angry as she had been when she had woken from the dream in her car parked at the edge of the cottage's meadow. "Did you have anything, anything at all, to do with what just happened?" She was screaming, she knew, but anger flooded her and she had to release it. "Because if you did, we will never be friends again and I'll never talk to you or welcome you into my house and I'll . . . I'll . . . " Faye spluttered to a stop, realizing how crazed she sounded. "You said something about the Boogie Man, so you knew this could happen, didn't you?"

"Faye, I swear I didn't do anything and I wouldn't have let you go into the woods if I thought you were in danger. I was just foolin' about the Boogie Man. In fact, I'm not even sure what happened just now. All I saw was some bugs buzzing around, like bees swarming to find a new nest." Faye knew Ariella was telling the truth. She slumped against a tree trunk and started to slide to the ground, but Ariella gently pulled her up and supported her as they walked to the car.

"Listen," Ariella said, "you tell me all about it once we're out of the Punkhorn and I'll try to make sense of it. I can tell it was something pretty serious. Whatever it was, it's influence must be extra strong around here. And, if my suspicions are correct, we need to get you away quickly. It could come back if we hang around."

"Okay. Whatever. I just know this kind of craziness has got to stop or let up soon. I can't take anymore." Faye said, her head hanging.

"For sure. I totally agree. We'll go straight to your house and get you back to normal. Do you want me to drive so you can rest?"

"You don't have a license!"

"So? I already know how to drive. I'm going to get my license when I turn 16 next month." Ariella flashed a big grin.

Faye shook her head, sighed, opened the driver's door, sat in the seat and started the car. She didn't object when Leaf jumped into her lap and settled there.

Chapter Twenty Eight

After the car brushed through the fan of foliage which obscured the path to the cottage, Faye turned onto the main dirt road. Her whole being, body and soul, felt as if it had been scrubbed with a coarse cheese grater. And her still damp pants and underwear were sticking to and chafing tender and intimate areas. Had all this happened because she wanted to change her life? She had wanted excitement and fantasy. And a baby. She just hadn't expected so much stress and emotional pain. *Just let me get home without incident. All I want is to do is make dinner, drink some wine and make glorious love with Drake, just like any normal weekend.*

She drove slowly, trying to minimize the jolts from the many potholes and bumps. I'll just roll along, like a kiddy roller-coaster in slow motion, no bumps, no bangs. She sighed, took one hand off the wheel and stroked Leaf, who gave a low rumble and kneaded her thighs with his claws. Looking at Ariella to see if she wanted to talk, Faye saw her friend was frowning, had turned around in her seat, and was staring out the back window.

"What are you looking at? Is the Boogie Man chasing us?" Faye barked a short, bitter laugh.

"For real, I think that's exactly what's about to happen."

"You're kidding," But in the rear view mirror she saw a green mist seep through the roadside foliage and start to coalesce on the dirt road. What was worse, she felt again the beginning of a tingling urge to merge, to allow the green mist's magical, fertile energy penetrate her. There was a buzzing whine in her head. She took her foot off the gas, letting the car coast, spellbound by what she saw and felt. Leaf left her lap and leaped into the backseat, where he stood on his hind legs to glare out the rear window. His growl was deep and angry.

"Faye, we've got to blast and fast. Step on it." Ariella voice was tight with urgency.

Wide-eyed, Faye gaped at Ariella, not understanding

anything. "I need to stay and be with it, don't I? It's for the children. I want the children to be safe."

"Faye, I said I'll explain all later. I'm finally seeing what you saw in the woods. I think the cloud back there is a Swarm and you don't want to get involved with one of those. You're not ready or strong enough to resist. Now let's go before it catches us." Ariella glanced back and gave an involuntary shudder.

"Wh . . . what? I don't understand. Why are you . . . " Faye trailed off, staring fascinated into the rearview mirror, seeing the cloud take firm shape and begin to move rapidly toward them.

Ariella jumped from her seat to straddle the middle console. She forced her left buttock and thigh onto the driver's seat, pushing Faye hard up against the door. She yanked Faye's hands off the wheel and kicked Faye's feet away from the pedals. Grabbing the wheel, Ariella stomped on the gas pedal with her left foot and the Prius lurched like a horse stung on the rump by a wasp. The motor howled and the car shot forward, accelerating harder than Faye had ever pushed it. The front wheels hit the top of a bump and bounced up, followed a moment later by the rear wheels. For a second they were airborne, then the car smashed down, halfway into a huge, water-filled pothole and the bottom of the car crunched into the mud with a metal bending bang. Ariella didn't flinch, despite Faye's squeaks of distress, but kept her eyes on the road and the pedal to the metal. Faye watched with fascination as the speedometer climbed steadily upward. Who knew a hybrid could go so fast so quickly? They crashed and smashed along the road, bouncing up and then bottoming out again and again, even though Ariella tried to swerve to avoid the worst parts.

The branches and bushes at the side of the road reached out to snag the car, scraping along its length. Faye's left shoulder and knee were getting squished against the door as Ariella's slim body took up more and more of the driver's seat, but Faye dared not complain, at last comprehending they were in real danger. If she tilted her head just right she could see in the side mirror the road unwinding behind the car and the bilious green cloud flowing after them like a gaseous tsunami.

After five minutes the car reached the first houses at the edge of the Punkhorn and Faye felt her head clear as if she had gotten a mega-injection of anti-histamine. In the mirrors, the cloud dropped back, shrank dramatically and became transparent. When they hit paved road a minute later, Ariella finally took her foot off the gas, pulled to the edge of the asphalt, stopped, and turned off the engine. Trembling from head to toe, she leaned into Faye, who managed to get her right arm free and around the girl's shoulders and hug her tight. We're like two wounded warriors, thought Faye, comforting each other after fleeing an intense battle with monsters.

They stayed like that until their heartbeats slowed and their breathing became less ragged. Leaf came from the backseat and snuggled again into Faye's lap. Eventually, the two sat back and just gazed at each other. Faye felt an extraordinary sense of connection.

Ariella smiled and said, "I thought you said you weren't going to do wild stuff anymore. That you needed to avoid crazy excitement."

"Yeah, well . . ." was all Faye could manage. "Nice driving, by the way."

"For sure. I learned that in Driver's Ed class." And they both laughed.

When they had settled down, taken sips from their water bottles and given some to Leaf, they got out and inspected the car's damage. It was hard to see all of it because the car was splashed and speckled with mud splotches. Both sides had long scratches and a multiple small dents. But along the bottom of all four doors there was some very crumpled metal. Faye became grimmer and grimmer as she circled the car, which she now imagined was some badly maimed, spotted creature. This was going to be expensive. She tried to remember what her collision deductible was.

"I'll help pay for the damage. I didn't spend all my money at the Mall. And I can do more babysitting or even get a part-time job," Ariella said.

"Don't worry about it. I'm pretty sure I've got good insurance for this. Besides, if I understand what just happened, you saved my life and certainly my sanity."

"It would've been bad, real bad. Those Swarms, my mom says they're nature gone wrong. All they want to do is absorb other life into them, sort of like The Borg aliens on Star Trek. And, like The Borg, they change to adapt to whatever beings they're hunting. They somehow know what you want to see and then suck you in and once that happens, you become like a zombie or something. It's truly bad."

"Whatever, can I send them the bill for the damage?"

"For sure. I think they're in the phone book. Call 'em up. They'll be happy to talk to you, probably invite you over for tea and crumpets, even if they're not real nature spirits. Speaking of which, I should probably wait until Moira or my mom give you the big picture, but maybe I should give you the Cliff Notes version on nature spirits and weird stuff like Swarms."

"Cliff Notes? You know about Cliff Notes? You better not use them for my class! And why are you giving me the abbreviated explanation? What is it that you're not going to tell me?"

"Do you want to know more details, good and bad, about nature spirits and Swarms or not? Believe me, my short 411 version is a zillion times less boring than Moira's four-hour lecture. And that's just her introduction. Plus, she hands out loads of reading assignments."

"Okay, okay. But can you talk me through it on the way back home? We still need to make dinner, and it's already 4:15."

They got back in the car and Faye pulled out into the driving lane. The poor Prius made all kinds of creaking, clanking and whiny sounds, as if it had aged 70,000 miles in the last half-hour. Faye decided she wasn't going to obsess about the damage. It had happened and she would accept it, though she dreaded having to explain it to Drake.

At Faye's prompting, Ariella launched into what she called "My Introduction to the Introduction to the Official VGL 101 Course on Nature Spirits. And Swarms."

"So, yup, nature spirits come in many different sizes and flavors. The major ones on Earth are involved with the planet-wide elements and forces of nature, like wind and water. They're generally trying to be helpful to all life, though they also do what they call . . . 'cleaning,' which means destroying stuff. And killing life, humans included. They just do it and don't give an explanation. Supposedly it's to restore the natural balance, but that seems a little ridonkulous to me.

"Then there's lots and lots of smaller spirits who are attached to a location or even to stuff like a tree or a pond or a sacred spot. They're not so involved with the forces the big element spirits are working with and the good news is you can, with a little practice, hear them. I mean, you can't actually have a conversation with them, but you can listen to what they're broadcasting. Like a radio.

"On the beach last night I started out reaching the local spirits in the woods where your hut was, but before I knew it, some medium-sized spirits from the nearby wind and the ocean got involved and things got off the chain. That's why we saw the Indians and all. I've only had something like that happen once before, when I was with my mom. I think last night happened because of you, because the spirits consider you muy importante."

"Really. Well, I guess that's a plus, right?" Faye was trying hard to not scoff.

"It *is* a good thing. You for sure want nature spirits pulling for you. But let me tell about another kind, the spirits that work with animals, from the smallest insects to the largest, like whales and elephants. And that includes humans. They don't take over the animal or anything, but sort of influence it to do stuff which benefits the planet's ecosystem. The Swarms are like these little spirits, but they actually do take over the animal or person.

"The big problem right now is humans, who my mom says were supposed to move life on this planet to the next big evolution, stopped listening to the nature spirits. Like for the past three hundred years or so. My mom says human civilization has strayed further and further from the roots of life until now many people are leading lives which are almost totally artificial. It's like we've forgotten something very vital."

Ariella paused and Faye chimed in. "I can believe that, what with global warming and all those species either going extinct or being threatened with extinction, we're absolutely not doing a good job of taking care of life on this planet. I think we're actually making it a more unhealthy place to live. And I can believe that's at least partially caused because we've stopped paying attention to nature.

At Ariella's encouraging look, Faye went on, " I'm sure you know many human activities have negative health effects. For example, pollution or radioactivity which accidentally gets released can drift around the world, causing all sorts of cancers and other diseases. So, it's a problem for everyone living on the earth. But, tell me how these Swarms came to be. Were they here from the start?"

"Nope. No one is sure what caused them, but they seem to be showing up more often and are getting stronger as humans do more bad stuff. The VGL says it might be because small insect nature spirits, who are often hive-based, get intensely entangled with receptive humans, especially humans who are weakened due to some manmade causes. The Swarms and the humans kind of merge and form a new kind of being, but not an evolved one, just a mixed-up, confused one. Their whole reason for living is to increase in size, but no one knows why. Swarms appear most of the time as groups of weird insects, but can morph into human-like forms in order to approach people. I mean, they can interact directly with people and, like I said, turn them into zombies, sort of. There's been reports of people found sitting in a daze under

trees and in fields and they don't respond except to make a
buzzing sound. And there's always lots of sting marks on their
skin.

"What's messed up is I had no idea there were any Swarms
around here. My mom and Moira put all sorts of protections in
place to keep that sort of thing away. So I think you must be
sending out strong vibes which attracted a Swarm into our
territory. Did the dreams you were having in the car contain
anything like the Swarm that showed up when you were peeing?"

Faye hesitated. The dream about the man she had chased
in the forest and wanted to mate with was almost too private, and
definitely too sexual, to talk about with Ariella. Instead she gave a
sanitized version, emphasizing the attraction she'd felt in the
dream was much like the pull she felt toward the Swarm. She left
out the dream man's huge erection and her own arousal. She did
confirm the Swarm in the woods was similar to the man in the
dream.

"That makes sense then," Ariella said. "The Swarm felt your
dream like a vibration in the atmosphere and came to investigate
you, disguising itself as your dream man. Was there anything
unusual about the spot where you stopped to pee?"

Faye told her about the mushroom circle.

"OMG! A Fairy Ring! And you peed in it! That's like
announcing yourself to all nature for miles around by screaming
through a 1,000 watt amplifier."

"Do you think I should worry about them coming after me
again? Can I go back to the cottage? Why did the Swarm
disappear when you grabbed me? Did you do something to scare
it off?" Faye again found it startling she could talk calmly and
phrase questions about such bizarre topics as nature spirits,
Swarms and whether her life might be in danger.

"Um. No, I didn't do anything special in the woods, but I
think the Swarm sensed the bigger spirits I'm connected to and
realized it was at risk. And that's bizarre because I didn't see it or
sense it until later when it came out of the woods onto the dirt

road. So, I'm not sure whether there could be more danger for you. I mean, if you made a big impression on this one, it might be possible for it to detect you again. We'll just be mega careful whenever we go to the cottage. I'll tell Mom what happened and she can probably make it impossible for Swarms to get close. And, just to be extra sure, I'll do some protective stuff at your house."

Faye shivered at the thought of going back to the cottage. The Swarm encounter had taken her into a decidedly unpleasant and scary place. But was backing out of spending time with Ariella even an option now? Could she walk away from this opportunity to change her life and add fantasy and adventure? Isn't that what she'd always wanted? *No, I'm not going to creep back to my "normal" life now. The Rubicon has been crossed, as they say. In for a dime, in for a dollar. Sink or swim. Whatever happens, happens. Que sera, sera! Just do it! Damn the torpedoes, full speed ahead. Well, not full speed, maybe half or quarter speed would be better. And why am I thinking of all these different ways to say I'm not going to be scared off?* Faye shook her head like a mare trying to dislodge a horse fly and saw Ariella was giving her an odd look.

"Oops, guess I was wool gathering. What did you say about protection at my house?"

"For starters, I'll do a smudge and then put some special, warding spell items out at the corners of your land."

"Smudge? You mean like wave around smoldering sage and the smoke gets into everything?"

"Yup."

"Well, let's wait on that until tomorrow, because Drake is sensitive to dust and pollen and smoke. And what things are going to be at the corners of my property?" Faye envisioned intricate constructions of rocks, animal bones, plants and crystals. What would the neighbors think?

"Okay, I'm sure it's okay to wait to smudge. And, I need to think about what to put around your property/it."

Faye shoulders sagged in relief when they pulled onto her street. Home turf at last. The Prius seemed to perk up, though it was still clanking and rattling. Dear old Mrs. Bennett, who lived three houses down, was gardening out front of her house and raised her head as the noisy car drove by. She saw Faye at the wheel and gave a tentative wave, her expression curious.

Faye waved back and shouted, "We did a little off-roading in the Punkhorn. It was muddy. And bumpy."

Mrs. Bennett just nodded and said, "Sounds like fun!" as if off-road driving in a Prius was quite ordinary.

Faye pulled the car as close to the garage as she could, hoping Drake might not notice the dents. She made a mental note to spray the mud off the car before he arrived. She wished she could put it in the garage, but it was full of overflow storage. As she opened her car door, she tried to pick Leaf up off her lap. But he dug his claws into her jeans and wouldn't let go. Faye tried rubbing his head and saying, in a sweet voice, "It's okay, Leaf honey, we're home and everything's alright. I just want to set you down for a minute." But, when she again tried to move him, he just hung on and gave a low growl.

Meanwhile, Ariella was at the rear of the car and asked, "Can you open the hatch so I can get the packages?" Faye reached down, flipped the switch to release the hatch and made one more attempt to tug Leaf off her. No luck. He was stuck as tight as a tick.

"Okay then," Instead of pulling at him, she gathered Leaf into her arms like she would a baby, and he was okay with that. Then she reached into the car, grabbed her bag and kicked the door shut. As she turned toward the house, Leaf stretched up and put his furry arms on either side of her neck and gave her lips a wet lick. Then he put his head on her shoulder. Faye wasn't surprised when she felt the stiffening twig of his penis on her stomach. On the other side of the car a fully-laden Ariella snickered.

"It's not funny, Princess friend of mine," Faye said, "How am

I going to ~~get~~ dinner ~~made~~ if Leaf won't let go of me?" At the sound of his name, the big orange cat squirmed in her arms and pulled himself even closer.

"Hey, not my problem. Leaf is obviously smitten with you. I had nothing to do with it. Could be worse, you know. And, I don't know what Drake looks like, but I think Leaf's pretty handsome, don't you?"

Faye gave Ariella a glare meant to silence a whispering student then huffed and led the way up the walk, trying to hold Leaf away from her and not peek at his equipment. She unlocked the front door and pushed it open and was turning to say something smart to Ariella when she heard screams from inside her house.

Chapter Twenty Nine

Leaf was the first to react. He leapt out of Faye's arms and trotted off to disappear down the hallway which led to the bedrooms. Faye, her heart thumping, dropped her bag and was about to follow when Ariella said, "Faye, wait. I know what's going on. It's okay."

The screams, howls really, continued and got louder and more frequent.

"How can you say that? Someone's in the house and they're screaming? How can it be okay? Should I call the police? Or 911?"

"Relax. It's just Snow and Midnight having some recreational funning." At Faye's blank expression, she added, "They're hookin' up, you know, bumping fuzzies. They do that a lot. Very loving, those two. And the louder they scream, the more they're enjoying it."

"What? Your cats are . . . are . . . you mean . . . they're having intercourse in my house?" Faye wasn't sure why she felt shocked. The screams reached an almost unbearable pitch and volume.

"Yup, absolutely intercourse, if that's what you preps call it, and they're probably doing it on your bed." Ariella chuckled at Faye's confusion. Abruptly the screams stopped, as if someone had finally found the off switch. Faye's breathing was rapid and she was trembling. Yet another shock to her already overloaded nervous system. This continuous stimulation and sense of danger appeared to be the norm in Ariella's world, where magic and fantasy were every day and ordinary. And, Faye reminded herself for the umpteenth time, she wanted magic and fantasy in her life, too. Damn the torpedoes!

"Oh, sure, my bed, why not? Am I supposed to do anything, perhaps bring them some après-coitus treats? Would salmon bits do?"

Ariella dropped the packages on the couch and gestured for

Faye to follow her down the hallway. They quietly entered Faye's bedroom and found Midnight atop a recumbent and clearly post-orgasmic Snow. Midnight was lazily grooming her, giving her ears and neck small bites, and still making little thrusts with his pelvis. The cats turned to look at them and Faye swore they both grinned. For some weird reason, she decided she was honored the pair had chosen her bed for their tryst. *No wonder cats sleep so much, I'd be exhausted if I had sex like that.*

Leaf was sitting on the floor a few feet from the bed and he glanced over his shoulder at Faye, as if to say, "See? That's how it's done." Then he pivoted and went to the kitchen, where he began meowing his demand to be fed.

"Let's leave them alone, shall we?" Faye said in what she hoped was a blasé tone. "I'm so thrilled they chose my bed. At least it was made up." She gave Ariella a pointed look. She had noticed the girl's unmade bed that morning.

"I'm sure that was a big consideration for them. They've always been a fussy pair." Ariella smirked and took her packages to her bedroom, while Faye put the takeout into the refrigerator. She opened a tin of cat food and held it out for Leaf's inspection. When he gave a sniff of approval, she spooned some out.

In her bedroom, under the lazy eyes of the reclining feline lovers, Faye stripped out of her smelly clothes, grabbed a robe and headed to the shower. A quick lather and rinse got rid of any lingering pee residue and, back in her room, she quickly dressed in workout pants and an old black t-shirt emblazoned with the Rolling Stones' logo of a big, red tongue. She'd change into something nicer after dinner was made. Back in the kitchen Faye was collecting the makings for the humans' meal when Ariella appeared in the doorway, accompanied by Snow and Midnight.

"What's for dinner? I'm starving. And these two love bugs are too," Ariella said.

"You're not starving, you're hungry. If you were starving you wouldn't be asking, you'd be grabbing. We, and that means you and I, are going to make a delicious vegetarian lasagna with garlic bread and a big, healthy tossed salad. For dessert there's Chocolate Lover's frozen yogurt. How does that sound?"

"Yummy, but I'm hungry now."

Faye glanced at the clock. It was only 5:00 and Drake wouldn't be arriving until 7:00 or so, which meant it was going to be at least two and a half hours until they sat to table. She knew most teenagers had huge appetites, except, of course, for those girls who were flirting with anorexia. She guessed she should be glad Ariella obviously loved to eat.

"Well, why don't you finish up some of your lunch leftovers? And there's pizza left from last night."

"Never thought you'd ask." Ariella took the Styrofoam boxes out of the refrigerator, saying, "I think Leaf is waiting on your bed. You know, he's been hunting for a mate for some time and none of the furry, four-legged types back at the cottage appeal to him. He's truly very advanced and doesn't see himself as," Ariella lowered her voice to a whisper, "a C-A-T. I think Leaf believes you to be a suitable match."

Assuming Ariella was joking, Faye answered in her proper English Miss accent. "Well, I'm afraid I'm going to disappoint him, don't you know? My boyfriend will not take kindly to another male in my bed."

"Okay, but be prepared for some hissing and attitude. And Leaf might even try to spray you, to mark you as his."

""Ha, ha, very funny. As for Leaf throwing a hissy fit, can you speak with him and make him understand, while I like him a lot, we're not going to be mating anytime soon?" Faye's mind wobbled around the idea she could really be discussing, with a 15 year-old, how to handle a suitor who happened to be a cat.

"For sure, I'll try."

Faye put a large pot of water on to boil for the pasta and Ariella took the takeout containers to the microwave. "Hey, can you take a picture of me using the micro? I wanna post it to Facebook. All the other yutes from school will be gonzo."

"The 'yutes' will be gonzo? Of course they will. Let me get my camera. Feed Snow and Midnight, will you please?"

As Faye went in to her bedroom, Leaf jumped off her bed and ran to her, uttering little cries of welcome and pleasure. Faye knelt and gave him a good, thorough petting and rubbing and he purred and nipped lovingly at her hands. She hoped he would be satisfied with that, but when she stood to get the camera from her bureau, he grabbed at her legs, much like he had in the woods. And, again when she tried to pry him off, he resisted, muttering low and dark. She called for Ariella who, with lots of stroking and sweet words, got Leaf to let go. She carried the feline paramour into the other bedroom and the moment Ariella closed the door behind her, Leaf began to moan and complain loudly.

"Don't worry about him," Ariella said, "he'll settle down. I told him you liked him and would see him later."

Faye had a flash vision of Leaf and Drake facing off, ready to fight for her. She wondered which one would win. "That's great, but can he stay in your room tonight?"

"I'll try, but he's pretty sneaky." She pointed at the camera. "I'm ready for my close-up."

Faye marveled at her young friend's ease and style in front of the camera. Ariella laughed and moved from pose to pose in front of and beside the microwave, sometimes holding a takeout container and sometimes pretending she was concentrating on the settings. She was still dressed in the, now wrinkled, clothes she had worn to the mall and her hair was unruly, but she carried herself with such poise it seemed the disarray was deliberate.

"Where did you learn to pose like that? You're a natural." Faye asked as they were reviewing the pictures. In one shot Ariella looked like she was puzzled by the microwave, in another she was playful, pretending to be frightened, and in yet another she was a Lolita, coyly innocent, while radiating a sexuality Faye hadn't noticed before. She's the proverbial farmer's daughter, Faye thought.

"Oh, Mom would bring back all these fabulous clothes she

got for free from the movies and her other gigs and she would dress up and show me how she had to act in them or, if was just a photo shoot, how she posed. Then I'd get to try on the clothes, though they were always too big, and I'd pretend to be her and imitate the walk and fake the attitudes. It was fun. We'd laugh and get silly. But, we haven't done that in a while."

"That sounds . . . gnarly. How come you stopped?"

"She said I'm maturing too fast. That now I need to learn to be careful of how I act and look, especially because I'm 'out in the world'. Sometimes I think she's punishing me because I insisted on going to regular school this year. Hey, can we load two of the pix onto the laptop so I can post them to Facebook?"

"First eat your leftovers and help me get dinner ready. Then we can do Facebook."

Faye added another pot to the stovetop and poured in several cans of organic crushed tomatoes and one of organic tomato paste. She like to make her own sauce for Italian dishes like spaghetti, pizza and lasagna. Cooking was like yoga or meditation, it calmed and soothed, no matter how trying the day had been. Now, making this dinner in her warm and cozy kitchen, in her home, with her new and special friend, Ariella, who was sitting at the kitchen table with cats curled at her feet, and knowing Drake would be here soon, Faye felt a rightness and a happiness which pleased her.

"Hey, what's that, cardboard?"

"It's whole wheat lasagna pasta. I like to use whole wheat whenever I cook Italian because it's more healthy and has more flavor. Are you ready to start helping with dinner?"

"Yup. I've got the right stuff when it comes to making food."

"I'm sure you do. Here, you can start with the tossed salad. And when you're done with that, how about you butter and season the garlic bread? And then you can set the table."

For a few minutes it was quiet as they both concentrated on their culinary tasks. Then Faye decided they needed some music

that

and, hoping Ariella would approve, tuned the living room's stereo radio to a station which played mostly Top 40 pop and dance music. Back at the kitchen counter, Faye did a couple of quick shuffle steps to the song's infectious beat and Ariella giggled. As they stood side-by-side, Faye working on the lasagna sauce and Ariella shredding lettuce and chopping tomatoes and green onions for the salad, Faye felt a hip bump hers. When, two beats later, it happened a second time, Faye saw Ariella doing her own dance steps and deliberately swinging her hips wide. Without a word, they both moved to an open space near the slider to the deck and began freestyle dancing with each other. Ariella was predictably wild and loose, waving her arms about, doing spins and even some pogoing. Faye's style was a bit more funky-hip, with repetitive moves and a little sultry bump and grind.

This is so much fun, Faye thought, I do love to dance. The day was finally settling into a nice groove. When the song ended, the station immediately segued into another danceable song. With a laugh, they kept dancing. A half-hour later, and with another break for dancing, dinner prep was finished. Faye slid the lasagna into the oven and Ariella put the large bowl of salad in the refrigerator. The foil-wrapped, sliced, buttered and seasoned garlic bread was ready to go in the oven a few minutes before dinner was served.

"All done?" asked Ariella.

"Yup," Faye said and held her hand up to be high-fived.

"Can we load upload those two photos now?"

After the photos were transferred and Leaf had been pacified with five minutes of petting, Faye lingered in Ariella's bedroom, wanting the good feeling to continue. But Ariella gave her the eye, so Faye started for the door.

"What time's dinner?" Ariella asked.

"Probably around 7:30. Drake's going to get here before that, but we'll hang out for a while before we eat. I haven't seen him all week, so we need to get reacquainted."

"That's good. Gives me plenty of time to change."

"Hey, don't worry. We're very casual when it comes to events like tonight's dinner. You don't need to make any special effort to dress up."

"Don't you want me to model my new clothes, the ones I bought today? I could do a runway number for you."

Faye's hesitated. What exactly did Ariella mean to do and how would Drake react? "Of course I want to see your new clothes, but I didn't realize you were planning that for this evening, I mean, what with Drake being here and all."

"You think he'll make fun of me? Is he some kind of male pig?"

"No, absolutely not. He's easy going, so go ahead, it'll be fun," Faye inwardly prayed Ariella wouldn't turn this into something weird and unexpected.

Faye went back to the kitchen and poured herself a glass of Pinot Grigio. It was only ten minutes after 6, so she could relax a bit before getting changed. She took her wine out onto the sunlit deck and sat on the steps leading down to the backyard. The birds were singing their evening songs and the smell of grilled meat from a neighbor's barbecue tickled her nostrils. She thought she heard Leaf's plaintive calls, and somewhere a car door slammed. Faye inhaled and exhaled, long and slow and closed her eyes.

The doorbell rang.

Faye's started. Who could it be? Wanda was the only person she knew who would show up unannounced. If it were Wanda, should she, could she, invite her for dinner? That would definitely put a difficult spin on things. From the kitchen she peered through the living room to see whether she could tell who it was. Her front door was open, but the smoky, tinted glass of her combination storm and screen door prevented anyone from seeing in. The afternoon sun was shining in through the door, so all she could see was the indistinct silhouette of a man. A tall, slender man. Faye's heartbeat immediately ramped up. The Swarm. Had it somehow found her? How was that possible? She remembered Ariella had said she was going to do some protection spells or something.

She was about to call for Ariella when the doorbell rang again and she heard a familiar voice. "Faye? It's Drake. I know I'm early, but I couldn't wait because I wanted to see you."

Chapter Thirty

Startled by the voice

At the sound of the voice at her front door, Faye jumped up and back a couple of inches. She landed on her toes and wanted to run. She wanted to believe it was Drake, but remembered the Swarm's ability to take the shape and characteristics of the person or thing you wanted most. Her heart beat even faster and she felt her hands go cold and her face flush. How could she be sure it was Drake? It was unusual for him to use the doorbell. Normally, he just came in unannounced, as she did at his house. Faye glanced down and realized she was still wearing the grungy workout pants and the tomato-sauce-bespattered Rolling Stones t-shirt. She had wanted to wear something cleaner and definitely more sexy for Drake. Should she go to her bedroom and do a quick change? But, if it *were* the Swarm at the door, would it come in if no one was there to stop it?

"Faye? Are you home? Can you hear me?"

Faye crept closer to the door. "I hear you. Can you just give us a minute?"

The silhouetted figure didn't reply, but turned away, either to pass the time surveying the neighborhood or to hide its features. She began to sweat all over. Faye remembered seeing a BBC America television series with vampires as main characters. The vampires kept saying they couldn't come into a house unless they were invited. Did that apply to Swarms? From the back, the figure certainly could be Drake – tall with broad shoulders and narrow waist. But wait, what about its clothes? Some kind of green, skin-tight shirt like the ones athletes wore when they wanted to show off their cut physique. Or was green its skin color? What she could see of the pants, black jeans she thought, were also form-fitting. And dangerously low-riding. Drake never wore tight clothes. His casual wear was almost always loose-fitting polo shirts and either shorts or khakis. Of course, he did possess an amazing, beautiful, sexy body, but he never flaunted it, at least not around her.

Faye was right next to the door, but the figure was still turned away. She reached for the storm door's handle, but stopped. "Hey Drake? Do you remember when we went on that wild, bouncy power-boat ride in Nantucket Sound and we wound up sopping wet and had sore butts afterward? What was the name of the boat company?"

"Huh? What is this, twenty questions?" The figure turned a bit toward the storm door as it spoke and Faye could see its profile, though with the late afternoon sun behind it, it was still mostly a silhouette. It was wearing wrap-around shades, also very un-Drake like. And Faye didn't see his usual wild mop of black curls.

"C'mon, open the door and invite me in. I'll remember in a moment." The man-shaped figure had stepped back as if to allow her to open the screen door. Unfortunately, the sun was then directly behind its head so a flaring halo put its entire face in shadow. It had actually told her to invite it in, just like the vampires! Faye could see it was holding two large objects, one in each hand. Clubs? Knives?

Her heart kicked into a tempo she didn't know it could reach and she began to feel lightheaded. She dropped her hand onto the storm door handle and suddenly saw herself from behind, as if she was in that predictable horror movie scene when the audience starts screaming, "Don't open the door!"

Faye wheeled around. Where was Ariella? Where was Leaf? Should she warn them? She needed to protect them, didn't she? "Drake . . . darling, just indulge me and tell me the name of the boat company. I . . . need it for a friend who wants to go out on the water." Faye was trying for coy and sexy, but, to her ears, she sounded scared and squeaky. "Please? I just know once you're in the house I won't be able to keep my hands off you and I'll forget."

The man-shaped figure gave a low laugh and said, "You're a nut, you know that? But, okay, give me a moment."

The moment stretched on and on. Faye, quivering, panting and sweating like she was running a race, could only stare at her hand on the door lever. It felt like her whole life, and perhaps the lives of Ariella and her cats, depended on what happened next.

She couldn't breathe right and black dots swirled through her vision.

"Alright, this isn't the exact name, but what I remember is Alex's Boat Rides and Rentals or maybe Alexander's Boat Rentals and Rides. They're based in Hyannis Harbor, as I remember."

With a rush of expelled breath, Faye turned the handle and burst out onto the porch like a bucking rodeo bull with a spurring cowboy on its back. She slammed into Drake, who had a bemused smile on his face and was holding a bottle of wine in each hand. One red and one white. How considerate, Faye thought, as she wrapped her arms around her lover. But her momentum unbalanced him and he staggered backward and, for a second, it seemed like they were going to tumble down the porch stairs. Instinctively, she dug in her heels and pulled at his right side so they pivoted and, instead of cracking their heads on the asphalt walk, fell onto an old rickety chaise lounge Faye used for relaxing and reading in the afternoon sun. Drake was able to retain his grip on the bottles as he and Faye fell and he raised one to either side as they landed. The chaise made an agonized sound and Drake wound up more or less in a sitting position with Faye sprawled across him diagonally. She quickly shifted so she lay atop him lengthwise and stared into his eyes. Nose-to-nose, they started to laugh. Unfortunately, the under-carriage of the chaise wasn't supportive of their mirth and, after giving a mighty screech of protest, collapsed beneath them and they dropped another foot and landed on the chaise cushions amid bent aluminum struts and vinyl strips. A wheel from the chaise broke off and roll-wobbled across the porch and down the stairs to fall on its side on the lawn.

Still laughing, Drake carefully set down the wine bottles, pulled Faye to him and began kissing her with amused passion. And her body, already buzzing with adrenaline, flared like with a super nova of pleasure, love and lust spreading through her torso and limbs at the speed of light. She enthusiastically kissed him back, loving the feel and smell of him. It had been so long - six days! But, was he wearing some kind of scent? She thought she recognized an expensive men's cologne. It was sharp and clean, like evergreens near the ocean, but mixed with other musky notes. It brought to mind English country homes and riding to the hounds combined perhaps with hint of a wooden ship riding the waves, its rigging singing and men heartily calling to each other as they swigged their measure of rum. She lost herself in the scent, squishing her nose into his neck and inhaling deeply, which made tingles flash through her nerves and especially in the endings in her nether parts. The parts she was now avidly rubbing against the bulge beneath and to the side of his fly. Oh my god, she thought, I think I'm going to orgasm! She started to go, but stopped.

This was madness! They were all but doing it on her front porch, in full view of her neighbors and any passing cars. And, furthermore, Drake never wore cologne! She pulled back, gasping like someone surfacing from the depths, braced herself on her with arms to either side and gazed down at him. He faced up, but the sunglasses were quite opaque. And he *had* slicked down his hair. What was up with that? What was he thinking, showing up like this? As if in answer, he reached hungrily for her again and she said, "Whoa, sailor. I know I may be morphing into a Class One Hussy and perhaps am on track to be quickly advanced to Slut Initiate, but I think we should take this inside."

Faye looked around. Was that Mrs. Bennett ducking behind a tree? No doubt the dear old thing was wondering what had happened to the sweet, young English teacher two houses down, who apparently had taken to driving off-road in her hybrid and then doing something naughty with her boyfriend on the front porch. Faye jumped to her feet, knowing she was madly blushing, reached down, grabbed Drake's hand and pulled him up.

"Are you okay?" Faye practically yelled at Drake, "That was quite the tumble you took."

Drake got it right away and replied in a loud voice, "Yes, I'm fine. Lucky I didn't get seriously hurt. And thanks for giving me mouth-to-mouth resuscitation. I definitely had the wind knocked out."

"Yes, you were lucky." Faye continued to bellow, "Let's get you inside in case you need a bandage or something."

Feigning stiffness, Drake bent down to pick up the two bottles of wine, hooked one finger through the door handle and held it open for Faye. As soon as they were both inside and the doors closed, she turned to him and was about to again rush into his arms, and he was ready for her to do that, when she remembered her houseguest. She put a finger to her lips and whispered, "Let me check on Ariella."

Faye took the two bottles to the kitchen, slowing to listen for sounds from Ariella's bedroom as she passed the hallway. She put the white wine in the fridge and the red on the table. At the start of the hallway, she glanced at Drake, whose expression was a mixture of lust and bemusement, and pointed down the hallway and mimed "Ariella."

"Thanks so much for coming by early, Drake. Those windows in my bedroom stick something terrible. Want to check them out before we eat?" Faye's raised her voice, though she could hear laughter and music from Ariella's bedroom. No doubt her young friend was online with her posse and oblivious to anything else.

Drake said in a similar, louder than ordinary voice, "Yeah, let me take a gander at those windows now. There's time before dinner, right?"

"We've got lots of time," Faye bum-rushed Drake down the hall and into her bedroom. As he stumbled in the direction of the bed, she confirmed Ariella's door was completely closed. Faye shut her door, grabbed a side chair and wedged it under the door knob. Too bad she hadn't considered installing locks on the interior doors. But the chair method worked in the movies. She turned to Drake and paused, struck by how beautiful he was. She was so hungry for him, though the aroma of baking lasagna was also tickling her appetite.

He stood at the foot of the bed facing her and the sunlight

from the windows gave his tanned face and arms a warm golden glow. Scrumptious, Faye thought, and tonight he's all mine. His slicked back hair was in disarray from their fun on the porch and she could now see he had a hint of beard shadow, which was a turn-on for her. He still wore the opaque, bug-eye black shades, but they somehow intensified his gaze, which she knew was focused on her. And his clothes, while way snugger than anything she had seen him wear, just accentuated the fine, sculpted planes of his lean, muscular body. Yummy!

And what's with his shoes? Could they be the pointy, expensive, leather, Italian-made ones all the young male celebrities and actors were wearing? No way! He never wore anything but tennis shoes, scuffed and stained. A disturbing thought clouded her excitement. The clothes made him appear way younger than 42, more like a hip dude in his early 30's. She shivered, imagining Drake drifting away from her, taking on a new persona with which her funky old, self didn't fit.

"Well, ma'am, p'rhaps you could do me the favor of showin' me yer problem? The one ya want me t'fix? Ya know, I kin't work on it if'n you don't show t'me."

"Oh, I'll show you everything!" Faye cried, cast doubts aside and ran into his arms, again knocking him backward, though this time they fell harmlessly onto the bed. Their lips met in more fiery kisses and Faye tried to get the green slinky shirt off him. But the fabric, while silky smooth and light, just stretched as she pulled and she couldn't get it over his head. And there weren't any buttons.

"Here, let's do this properly," said Drake and slipped out from under her to stand by the bed, bringing her up with him. He took off the sunglasses and gazed down at Faye so tenderly her eyes stung. But she wasn't going to cry, no way. Not after everything that had happened. But she would say something, something to clue him in to her confusion. What she wanted to say was, "*Why are you looking at me like that? What's going on with us? Why are you dressed like that? Where are your regular glasses? You're going to say something I don't want to hear, aren't you?"*

Instead, she said, "Are you wearing cologne? I like it. And what's with the new duds? Your shirt is so tight. But it's good, real good. I can't wait to peel it off you." She knew she was going too fast. "And the jeans are new, too, aren't they? Plus, those shades are bangin' and what cool shoes . . . you're awesomely gnarly, dude! Did you get a makeover or something?"

"You really are a big goofball, aren't you? But, yeah, someone told me I needed to achieve my total coolness before it was too late. Before I got too old."

"Ah, total coolness. Of course." Faye gazed down and scuffed the toe of her shoe on the floor. "Well, if these clothes and shoes are an example, someone has a cool definition of cool, that's for sure. And a very sexy definition to boot." She raised one eyebrow at him. She was not, not, not going to ask who that someone was.

Drake laughed and pulled her to him and kissed her hard. His hands quickly slipped beneath her stained t-shirt and gently lifted it off. She was wearing the now clean purple bra and panties set he'd given her and she saw his eyes light up as he dropped the t-shirt. He grunted in pleasure as he cupped both her breasts with his hands, his thumbs tracing circles around her nipples through the bra's lace. Her breasts, while tender, responded to his touch. He pushed his bulging crotch toward her and she pushed back with her pelvis, while sliding her hands under his slinky green shirt, marveling, as she always did, at how smooth and muscular his abdomen and chest were. She liked the sensation of her hands being trapped by the shirt. Her fingers found his nipples and began gently pinching.

They stayed like that for a minute, kissing and delicately stimulating each other, until their sexual heat rose and their need became urgent. Faye gave a little whimper and Drake growled, took his hands off her breasts and yanked his shirt off over his head. Faye marveled it didn't rip. Suddenly her bra was on the floor and his hands were all over her as they slid their bodies together, skin to skin, like they could melt into one.

While he held her tight, she reached down and smoothly undid his belt and pulled down his zipper. When his erection immediately popped into her hand like a thick pump handle, she realized he wasn't wearing underwear.

Faye stopped kissing and pulled away. "Commando? Really? Since when?"

"Jeans too tight. Didn't want panty line." Drake grinned, so she squeezed him just right and he gasped and pushed hard into her hands. He yanked on the drawstring of her workout pants and, with a shove, pushed them down to puddle at her feet. He put his hand between her legs and she felt her juices flood toward his fingers. Faye moaned when he found her clitoris and began teasing it. She struggled to push his jeans out of the way, but they were so tight she could only slide them down as far as his mid-thighs. Abandoning them, she grabbed his erection with two hands, holding it against her belly. Spasmodically, he began thrusting into the crevice formed between her hands and body.

"Damnit, I can't wait!" Drake cried and, after ripping her purple panties down, he lifted Faye up by the ass and lowered her eager wetness onto him. She felt every pulsing bit of him as he filled her, sliding in slowly like a snake into its den. Her mind went blank as if it was in a snowstorm whiteout. She felt weightless, only his stiff cock providing a solid and central reference for her. It felt so good, she almost swooned, but instead quivered from head to toe in a delightful, frothy, unforced orgasm.

She started to collapse against him, but he lifted her up again and began to slide her up and down his firm length and, in an instant, she was again burning and wriggling like fish on a hook. Her hands clenched together behind his neck and she got her legs up above his hipbones and locked her ankles behind his butt. Drake stood like some champion, his legs braced wide, holding her entire weight and repeatedly raising her, only to plunge her down onto him and him into her, deeper each time. He

seemed very much in control, small grunts being the only sign he
was exerting himself. Faye had the stray thought this position
could be a new part of the Olympic weight lifting competition. The
up and down went on and on, her head lolling back in orgasm and
then reviving to give him kisses of encouragement. They'd always
had good sex, but this was on another level, as good or better
than it had been the previous weekend.

Drake finally paused, held her steady, and said, in a low,
purring voice, "Okay. Enough fun and games. Let's do some
serious bonking." He paused, then said, "We're okay, right? I
brought some condoms. Wouldn't want us to make a mistake."

Faye felt an impulse to make a snarky comment that, for
her, a baby wasn't a mistake, but she withheld and said, "Ah, Mr.
Pragmatism is in the house. Don't worry. We're fine. I'm about to
get my period." To Drake's skeptical expression she added, "I
checked the calendar. And I've got the symptoms. Honest."

The mist of intense lust returned to his eyes and he lowered
her carefully onto the bed, never slipping out of her, and began
thrusting in earnest, sometimes hard and fast, sometimes
tantalizingly slow. Bracing himself on hand, he reached down
between to further tease her sensitive button. Faye's nose began
to run as his rhythm increased in tempo and intensity and she
shamelessly rubbed her face on his chest. He was hers, damn it,
and if she had to mark him with her "scent," she would. She
reached down and grabbed his tight buttocks and dug in,
imagining she had claws.

But Drake reached back to pull her hands away, saying,
"Easy tiger. Remember what happened the last time you used
your talons on me."

Faye laughed a laugh so unrestrained and joyous, she was
sure the whole world would hear it. Then she clapped her hand
over her mouth and, her eyes merry, pointed with the other hand
in the direction of Ariella's bedroom. She checked to see if Drake
got it, but his eyes were half-closed, lost in sensation.

"What is it you want?" he said throatily and thrust into her with extra power. Faye tried to answer, but could only manage an unintelligible "unh . . . unh" as another wave of sweet delight swept through her.

"I'm sorry, I didn't get that. What did you say?" Drake pulled back and stormed into her again. Faye saw his eyes were now open and filled with a mischievous lust. Again, all she could do was cry out, her limbs turning into wands of light and energy, her insides fizzing away with gentle fireworks.

"What's the matter? Is my tiger becoming a pussy cat?" Another powerful thrust that, like a rogue wave which knocks people wading in the surf off their feet, left her gasping and moaning. But why wasn't he more excited? Why wasn't Drake groaning like he always did when he was straining to hold back his orgasm. Faye had always been able to tell when his control was starting to slip and, on occasion, had been able to let go when he did. Mutual orgasms were the best. This time, she'd already lost track of the number of orgasms she'd had - three, four? He'd had plenty of opportunities to join her and she was already absolutely sated, but he was just forging ahead, like a man on a mission, with a far off goal he had to reach before he could rest. Faye grinned at that image, especially because they were in the Missionary Position and also because Drake still had his jeans, socks and shoes on. And she still wore her red flats.

"What are you smiling about, my little kitten?"

"Oh, nothing." she managed to say and began intensified squeezing with her inner muscles.

Now it was his turn to groan and arch his neck and she knew he was no longer a missionary, but rather a man holding on to the lip of a cliff with slippery fingers. She began to buck and thrust back to help him go completely over the edge. Then she remembered Midnight and Snow on her bed.

Without thinking, she pushed at Drake's chest so he slid partway out of her. "Wha . . . what are you doing? Is something wrong?" The smell of their sex was pungent and heady.

"So, you think I'm a cat, do you? Well, let's do what cats do."

It wasn't her most graceful moment, but after raising her feet so they were both on his left shoulder, she rolled over very slowly and carefully, without breaking their connection, and got on her hands and knees with Drake behind her. She realized in all their years together they had never tried doggy or, in this case, feline style. She glanced coyly over her shoulder and taunted, "C'mon you big tomcat, let's see if you can make me yowl." Drake seemed confused and dazed and he stared first at her face and then down to where they were joined, so she added. "Go to it, tiger!"

Finally, like a machine restarting, he began to move and it seemed like he was back in rhythm, but then he slowed and Faye felt him slip out. She saw he was scrabbling at his remaining items of clothing, pulling off the expensive Italian shoes and tossing them. He flopped onto his back and wriggled out of the tight jeans, kicking them toward where the shoes had landed.

Still on her hands and knees, Faye asked, "All better now?"

Drake gave her a wry grin. "Ma'am, I kin see this new arrangement, this new thang, will require full use of both m'legs." He got back on his knees between her thighs, grabbed her by the hips and slid back inside her. Then he leaned forward and put his arms around her, reaching one hand to fondle her breasts and the other down to tease her clit.

Faye twitched as if he'd zapped her with an electric prod. She began uncontrollably squirming against his hand and he began a relentless, steady thrusting, his pelvis hitting her buttocks with an audible slap. She couldn't help it. She started making noise, lots of it. At first it was staccato cries, ah . . . ah . . . ah . . . sounding out each time Drake rammed forward. But then he increased his tempo and her cries lengthened into two syllables, ah-unh . . . ah-unh . . . ah-unh . . ., and she knew she couldn't take much more. She squeezed even tighter around him to let him know she was about to spiral away. He took it up another notch and Faye's cries lengthened into sustained yowls similar to those Snow had voiced.

She had one last thought about how this was a truly mindful

moment, being totally present with her body, and felt all the anxieties about babies and Drake and Ariella and nature spirits dissolving in the flames of her sensory pleasure. Then, with one final piercing, drawn-out cry, she went beyond the beyond and felt Drake shudder and call her name and they spasmed together and her mind went blank, every nerve overloaded with bliss.

When Drake stopped twitching, he kind of collapsed onto her back and she, in turn, collapsed face down onto the bed. They lay quiet for what seemed like a long time and Faye was still, far, far away, not quite unconscious or asleep, but close. She felt the heat of Drake's long body atop her like the best blanket ever and his breath tickled her neck. As the curtain of sleep began to descend, she thought she heard a cat yowl and smiled at the coincidence. Then she heard the yowl again, longer, louder and closer, and then there was tapping, like someone knocking at her bedroom door.

"Faye? Faye? Are you okay? Leaf got all frantic and upset and started yelling at me and I thought I heard you screaming or something." Ariella's voice was a bit muffled by the closed door, but Faye got the gist. She heard the doorknob turn and it sounded like Ariella was trying to push the door open. Groggy, Faye rolled onto her side and Drake slid off her onto his back. She glanced at him to see how he was taking this interruption and realized he was sound asleep. And even snoring softly. Thankfully, the chair under the knob trick did work and kept the door from opening, though it did move a half-inch inward, but was still within the doorframe, not allowing a crack through which one could peek. But another good push would do it.

"Faye! Please say something. I can't get the door open. Are you okay? Did he hurt you?" Ariella's voice was strained and Leaf's howls got more demanding.

Faye knew Ariella would keep calling and trying to get in. They were friends, after all, and more than that, they were warriors who had stood side by side when danger threatened. She cleared her throat, not sure what her voice would sound like.

"Ariella, it's okay, I'm fine. Drake and I were just working on the windows in here that were stuck. It took a lot of effort and we were having fun making a lot of noise while we pushed and pulled." She paused, thinking pushing and pulling pretty much summed up what they had been doing. When Ariella didn't respond, she went on, "But we finally got everything loose and lubricated and opened and it's all . . .   good. No worries really. And right now I'm getting changed for dinner, so don't come in. We'll be out in a few."

After a pointed silence, Ariella finally said, "Oh, okay. Just let me know when you're ready for my fashion show. C'mon Leaf, back you go. C'mon, I mean it. She's okay and she'll see you later, I promise."

Faye heard Ariella's door close and Leaf's cries diminish. Her bedside clock showed it was 6:30. The lasagna needed to come out of the oven around 7:10, so there was time for a quick nap. She set the alarm on her phone for 7:00, making sure to change AM to PM, slid back next to Drake and put her head on his shoulder. She noticed the wonderful scent of his cologne had survived their exertions. That means it must be expensive, she thought as she closed her eyes.

Chapter Thirty One

Faye was on her back, her body still hot and sweaty, but her head was filled bubbles of pleasure, gently bumping and popping. Something hard was poking her left buttock, but she didn't immediately open her eyes or reach behind to see what it was. She wanted to bask in the residual smolder from their wonderful lovemaking. Opening her eyes would mean she was ready to return to the world of worries, fears and responsibilities. Like having to take the lasagna from the oven before it dried out or making sure Ariella did her homework or worrying about the Swarms. She rolled toward Drake and reached out blindly, wanting only the simple pleasure of touching him. Her hand landed on his chest and she was surprised to feel he was wearing a shirt. Had he gotten up and put it on because it was too cold? Not likely, because the bedroom was plenty warm. In fact, it was decidedly too warm. But not too warm for a short snuggle. Eyes still closed, she slid over to press her body against his and took a deep breath, anticipating the intoxicating mix of Drake's own pungent male, post-sex aroma with the hint of his new expensive cologne.

What she smelled was damp earth, crushed vegetation, leaf mold, and an animal muskiness. *Bloody hell! What's this then? More insanity leaking in through the Ariella connection?* Or had Drake, who had a fondness for practical jokes, awoken while she was insensate, carried her into the backyard and was now beside her feigning sleep? Being outdoors would explain why he had a shirt on. A breeze riffled across her body and, yipes, she realized she was still completely naked.

She sat up fast and squinched her eyes to the teensiest slits in the vague hope that if she only let in a little of her surroundings, she wouldn't be visible to someone nearby. Someone like her neighbor's teenage son gawking from his bedroom window. However, what Faye could see through her slitted eyes wasn't her familiar, scruffy backyard lawn. Wherever she was, it was filled with sunlight, lush greenery and it was hot, which explained why she was sweating. She opened her eyes a bit more and peered around. It appeared she was in a forest clearing.

Not again. Please not again.

In a vain attempt at modesty, Faye crossed her legs, put an arm across her breasts, and, with the other hand, rubbed at her eyes. Then she opened them wide. Yes, she was in a forest and yes the sun was hot and high in the sky, even though it had been falling toward the horizon when she and Drake started their lovemaking. Faye felt an agonizing twinge of fright. How many jolts and bumps and high voltage moments could she take before she burst? She shuddered. Her hands grew cold and her heart beat faster. She thought she might faint. Or scream. Then, it all stopped, as if something strong and raw had boiled up in her and grabbed the reins and yanked until she was as still and centered as she had ever been while meditating. Whatever was happening, wherever she was, she understood she was first going to accept it and second, she was going to work with it until normalcy returned.

She tried to get a clearer view of her surroundings, but no matter how she squinted or blinked, she couldn't seem to focus on much, either near or far. Most everything was green and smelled of forest. She thought she saw blue sky overhead though the air was too sparkly for clear seeing. She was reminded of times she had squinted through a prism or a kaleidoscope. Even her body was blurry, like an impressionist painting or a reflection in rippling water. But in some places the blur weakened and the trees and sky and forest floor of leaves and twigs seemed semi-transparent. *I must be dreaming again, and the dream is more realistic than most. There's nothing else possible, though I'm sure Ariella would produce some explanation. Please, please don't let this be her doing.*

She turned to the still figure lying beside her. It could be Drake, but because of her inability to focus, she wasn't even sure if it was a man. It had a head and what could be thick, unruly dark hair, but she couldn't make out the facial features. And, aside from the hair, the entire figure was green. Was it even alive? One thing was sure, if this was a dream, it was both the most fantastic and most realistic one she'd ever had. Even more intense than the dreams she'd had in the car at the cottage. She didn't feel threatened and wasn't worried this was another Swarm intrusion, but she wanted out just the same. I'll get centered and concentrate on finding reality, she thought. Forgoing modesty, she closed her eyes, pulled her legs up and rested her face on her knees. First, she tried to wake up, envisioning her bedroom, Drake sleeping in her bed, Ariella and the cats in the other bedroom, the lasagna baking in the oven. She felt a mental tug and thought she heard Leaf's signature cry and that was encouraging.

Hmmm. If I'm at least a little bit connected to the reality I was in with Drake, perchance I can call out to or somehow summon Ariella? If I'm still in my bed, she's might not be able to get the bedroom door open. Still, worth a try. Faye lifted her head and tried to make a sound, but all that came out was a weird drawn-out moan, like playing a recording at slow speed. She tried again, but this time made a squeaky, plaintive whine. I sound like a cat, no, a kitten. Or someone who inhaled helium. This is ridiculous. If I'm asleep and this is just a dream, I wonder if I'll remember it? But how could it be just a dream if I'm able to think logically about what to do? Is this is what they call lucid dreaming?

Frustrated, she turned to the unmoving green figure and was about to do something radical, like hit it in the middle of the chest or, better yet, slap what appeared to be its face, when she heard a clear sound. It started as a low rumbling and then rose to finish on a higher note, like Valley Girls' voices at the end of sentences. The sound had a questing quality and Faye knew it was directed at her. She searched to find the sound's source and saw a large, orange something moving toward her through the sparkling haze. She was about to try and scramble to her feet, when, as if he was pushing through the skin of a bubble, a big, orange feline head popped into focus about a yard from her. Leaf's golden eyes stared at her and his mouth was curled in a definite cat grin. Faye had a Alice-meeting-the-Cheshire-Cat moment. How apropos, she thought. Leaf rumbled out another low purr as his whole body came into view. As he got closer the sparkling haze shrank back so they were in a clear space about four feet in diameter. Faye wasn't sure whether to be alarmed or relieved to see Leaf and, after considering her situation, decided on the latter.

"Leaf! I'm so glad to see you? Do you know where we are or why I'm here? Can you help me get back to my bedroom? Can you get Ariella to help me?" She could talk again, or it seemed like she was talking.

In response, Leaf's purring got louder and he bumped her chin with his head without having to stand on his hind legs. In this dream or whatever it was, he was much bigger than normal, probably as big as a mid-sized dog, like a border collie. Could she be in Wonderland, where one dream made you larger, but she was in the one which made you smaller? Faye wished for the dream that didn't do anything at all.

As Leaf put his lips to hers and gave her an affectionate lick, Faye noticed he had something hanging from a green ribbon about his neck. Reaching down, she lifted a leather pouch, the same pouch she'd kept in her bag and which held the golden coin. She slipped the ribbon over Leaf's head and pulled the pouch open. Sure enough, there was the coin, dully gleaming, but there was also a bit of scrap paper peeking out from beneath it. Remembering what Ariella had said about touching the coin, she slid her fingers in and tried to pluck out the paper. But, she couldn't help brushing against the coin and, as she did so, she heard the recumbent man beside her make a guttural, inarticulate sound. Faye saw the being wasn't completely in Leaf's bubble of clarity and so was still distorted, but she could tell its lips were moving and its eyelids fluttering. She tensed, but it quieted and was still.

Faye turned her attention to the paper. It was a handwritten note which, in almost impossible to read light green cursive, said, "F. I think you're in the Between. Hold the coins in your hands. The green man will talk to you. And Leaf will help. Listen to him.

Now's the moment. Do it quick. A."

As Faye watched, the paper dissolved and was gone. Shades of Mission Impossible, she thought, and giggled. Wherever she was, in a dream or between realities, there was an undeniable element of freaky humor. Thinking back, Faye realized most all of what happened this weekend with Ariella had a quirky, surreal, almost silly, quality. As if originating in the mind of an entity with a weird sense of humor. Kind of like Ariella herself, Faye thought. She remembered her meditation teacher saying one could reach a level of awareness where nothing would seem serious and she could play with reality. Well, okay then, she would play.

Faye grabbed the coin from the pouch and held it tight with both hands. The green being, who might be male, began to jerk convulsively, as if someone had plugged it in. After a couple of tries, it sat up, turned what must be its face, eyes closed, toward her and gave a loud, sibilant squawk and waved its arms and long, slender hands in her direction. She was convinced the figure was male. Something about its movement and also, as it flailed about and the haze lightened, he reminded her of Drake. She certainly wanted it to be her boyfriend, even if it meant he was wearing green tights. But, after a minute, she knew it wasn't Drake. The air cleared and she saw a face she remembered. A beautiful, heart-shaped and almost feminine, stunning face which had a green sheen, with skin so smooth it reflected light like glass. A strong straight nose and unkempt black eyebrows and hair were in distinct contrast. His mouth was full, with wet lips begging to be kissed and his closed eyes accentuated impossibly long eyelashes. Faye's heart started to thump, but not in fear. It was the man she'd seen in a vision last Sunday morning after Drake left. The one who had called her name and whom she had chased through the woods. Completely different than the Swarm. Giddy gladness surged in her and she started to grin. She was, for some reason, so happy to see him.

And then he opened his eyes and she was completely lost, her body and her soul and everything else pulled toward those deep pools of green that saw the Faye she knew she was. She leaned toward him, then remembered she was naked. She tried to cover the important parts with her hands and arms and, glancing down to see what wasn't hidden, was surprised to see she was wearing an elegant pale green gown. It was an empire waist number which covered her quite well, though it was more revealing than she liked. Faye put her hands in her lap, and gave Green Hunk a brilliant smile of welcome, raising her eyebrows to let him know she was more than willing to hear what he had to say. His luscious lips moved, but the words, if that's what they were, came out garbled and truncated.

"Fff . . . igh . . . tay . . . ther . . . coy . . . en . . . aye . . . illb . . . abe . . . awk." He gazed at her expectantly, but she could only shrug in helpless bewilderment. She motioned for him to try again. He bent his head and Faye had the impression he was gathering his strength. Staring again at her, he tried once more, and this time the sounds were fewer and stronger in volume.

"Uh . . . uh . . . ther . . . coe . . . een. Geh . . . geh . . . tit." The green eyes swallowed her and she felt a twinge in the back of her mind. The sounds might make sense.

"Other . . . coe . . . een? Oh, other coin. And geh . . . tit? Ah, get it! Yes, I get it. I need another coin?" He nodded and smiled, the corners of his mouth and his slanted green eyes turned up. Faye felt like a high diver, about to begin a graceful arcing plunge into warm waters. A calm, observing part of her pointed out she had just had phenomenal sex with Drake and it was, at the least, peculiar for her to be responding to another male. *Well, he does resemble Drake a little, so it's no wonder I'm attracted. Besides, it's just a dream and a fantasy at that. Everyone fantasizes, right? What am I supposed to do when my fantasy is so super delicious? And who cares if his skin is more green than tan?*

"I only have one coin!" she exclaimed, holding up the piece of gold. "Where's the other coin?"

He raised his eyebrows. She so wanted to make him smile

Poor

again.

Something was pushing at her back. That darn cat, she thought, even in a dream he demands my attention. Faye swatted at the air behind her, not taking her eyes off Green Hunk. Then there were two paws on her back, pressing with force, as Leaf used his full dream-size weight to actually bend her forward a bit.

"Leaf! Cut it out! This isn't time for cat cuddles. This is very important." She smiled warmly at Mr. Green and again swatted behind her, this time making contact with Leaf's paw. She pulled at his leg, trying to get him off her, and felt a pinprick of pain on the palm of her hand. He'd stuck her with his claw!

She turned, furious, and was about to do something horrid to Leaf, when she saw he had moved back a foot or so and was sitting on his haunches wearing that feline grin. And, in the ground between his front paws she saw a dull gold bit, with dirt piled up where Leaf had dug around it. It was another coin and it was what had been poking her in the butt.

"Oh, sweet Leaf, I'm so sorry. Ariella said you're here to help." Faye reached toward the coin and, as she touched it, Leaf put his paw firmly atop her hand. Faye saw intelligence and awareness in his eyes. And devotion. A devotion of which she'd been making light.

As woman and cat gazed at each other, his pupils dilating to fill his irises, Faye heard a soft, but definitely masculine voice in her head and knew it was Leaf's. "I am yours," he said and lifted his paw.

Faye smiled at him. He was so much bigger in this dream, he seemed less like a cat and more like a person. She wanted to pet and rub him like she had earlier, but somehow that seemed inappropriate. Instead, she said, "Thank you for everything," and meant it.

As she took up the other gold coin, the Green Guy burst into verbal life. At first he sounded like he was spouting more gibberish, as if he'd pent up an entire conversation and it was erupting out in one long string. Then he paused, his face serious, and said quite clearly, "Faye, it's so nice to finally be in your presence and be able to converse with you."

"And it's a pleasure for me to speak with you. But, pray dear sir, you know my name, so shouldn't I know yours?" Faye wasn't sure if the knights and damsels tone was correct for this situation, but, at the least, it might make him smile again. She was sore for that smile. And he did smile and her heart went hippity hop down the bunny trail.

They were by now sitting cross-legged facing each other, their knees not quite touching. Faye was aware of Leaf's reassuring warmth pressing against her right thigh. She knew he was watching the Green Man intently. She wondered what would happen if Green Man made a pass at her or did some other untoward thing. Would Leaf leap snarling to her defense? She wondered what she would do if Green Man made a pass. Further down the bunny trail went her heart.

As if reading her mind, Green Man reached across and took her hands, so they both held the coins. His hands were green and as warm as the summer sun and he touched his thumbs to hers. She smelled blooming wildflowers, much like the ones at Ariella's cottage. A gentle zephyr lifted her hair and rustled the folds of her dress and brought a scent of lilacs and roses. When he spoke his voice was as clear as a stream on a green mountain which humans had never disturbed.   undisturbed by humans

"Faye, if I tell you my name, it will be the beginning of a bond-forging between us." He kept staring at her, his smile never stopping. Faye was at first unable to speak, not because of a freeze-up, but because she was dazed. She cleared her throat a couple of times and turned to Leaf, who smiled up at her.

"What do you mean, a bond-forging?" she managed at last.

"We will begin to become so connected, our fates so entangled, neither of us will ever be the same. I will know your consciousness nearly so almost clearly as I know mine and you will get similar access to my consciousness." His eyebrows went up and his green eyes shone with sincerity. "Though you may not understand much of me at first." Did a small smirk pull at his beautiful lips?

"Oh, is that all? Something like a Vulcan Mind Meld?" If he was smirking, Faye was going to goof. "I thought you intended something much bigger."

His eyebrows shot up higher than was humanly possible and his eyes widened until they were circles of white with huge green centers. "Surely, you jest? What could be bigger than a bond-forging between one such as I and one such as you?"

"Well, heck, how about we switch bodies?" She laughed, remembering all those movies about parents and kids, women and men, making a wish or doing some magic and waking up in someone else's body.

"You want to. . . ?" and he said something which sounded like a word, but was made up of such strange sounds Faye couldn't even make out a syllable. "Do you know what you're asking? Not once in all my long time has there been one who demanded such a bonding price. I am not able to pay such a price without permission from . . . " and again he said something that sounded more like parakeets squawking than words.

"Hey, don't get your knickers in a twist, I was only joking," Faye said, digging this 'playing with reality' business. "The bonding thing might be okay, but let me think for a moment." She gazed theatrically off into space, before reaching out to stroke Leaf, who was adoring her with his gold eyes.

"Whaddya think, Leaf? Should I bond with this green being who won't tell me his name until I do?"

Leaf's eyes shifted away from hers and went to the Green Hunk. She heard his cat voice in her head say, "Tell him yes, but you want to wait. And you need to know his name first. So you can trust him."

"Okay then," she said, all cheery and sweet, "I agree to bond with you, but not right now. And I need to know your name first." She saw Mr. Green's face become even more serious. She faltered, then added, "Sorry, this is all new to me. In fact, much of the past week has been new territory. To say I'm feeling uncertain and a bit scared would be an understatement. This little meeting with you, as delightful and full of promise as it is, just seems so bizarre and unlikely, especially after I just had sex with my boyfriend and —"

He shook his shaggy head to stop her. "I know all about what you've gone through and I know all about this boy you believe is your match, but who is, in fact, a minor sprite at best and far too seduced by his humanity to be suitable for you."

Drake a minor sprite? Faye couldn't hold back her irritation, she tried to pull her hands from his, but they were stuck. Beside her, Leaf gave a deep bass growl. Frustrated, she stood up, but he rose with her. She faced him and was opening her mouth to tell him off when he leaned in and kissed her.

Everything filled with green light, her mind, her body, the universe. Faye felt his lips on hers and that was all she knew. Electricity sizzled through her and she heard thunder blasting away nearby. Whatever surface she was standing on began to shift and sway like a ship's deck in rough weather. Without thinking, she began kissing him back and pressed her body forward, their locked hands between them, still holding the two gold coins. This was the most fantastic kiss ever. Time passed, her senses began to return, but still they kissed. She smelt roses and lilacs again and tasted sweet honeysuckle. Her body felt drenched and bathed in the warmest summer rain and her toes squished in fertile, rich earth. She heard the wind caress, then roar through the trees. A final huge clap of thunder sounded followed by the greenest, brightest flash of lightning and he broke the kiss and her hands fell away from his, but still clutched the gold.

Smiling, he said, "You may call me Verdant Sea and I am a representative of this planet's nature spirits. I can take physical form and have helped guide human evolution for a long, long time." His gaze never moved from her eyes and she dizzied as he again pulled her close, holding her upright.

"Keep the coins with you at all times. We will talk more soon. And then we will bond and when we do I will tell you my true name. And you will see me as I really am." With that, he kissed her once more and everything began to dissolve. As she faded to black she understood she was swooning. So appropriate.

Chapter Thirty Two

Faye woke to music. It was annoying because she wanted to keep sleeping, though it was a tune she knew she normally liked. Someone's arm lay heavy across her breasts and warm breath caressed her cheek. She was afraid to open her eyes. Then the arm moved, its hand maneuvering to cup her right breast, where it lingered, gently squeezing and stroking. Then the fingers slid to her nipple and, after a pause, pushed it in like a doorbell, once, twice, three times. She knew whose signature move that was. Drake. He was fond of pressing her nipples, especially while she was dozing, and then saying, "Hello? Anyone home?"

She put a name to the music. It was the song "Wake Me Up" by Avicii and she had programmed it into her phone as an alarm. Faye knew she was back safe in her bedroom - in Drake's arms, listening to a favorite song. She opened her eyes and saw him on his side next to her, gazing at her with bemusement.

"Faye? Faye? Are you home? Are you sleeping? Time to wake up! The song says so." He pushed her "doorbell" again and then his hand began sliding down her belly, tickling as it went. Warmth rose in all the usual places and she lolled back.

His fingers had begun playing with her pubic hair when Faye gently, but definitely, pushed his hand away, sat up, leaned down and kissed him, then swung her legs over the side of the bed. He reached to grab her around the waist, but she was too quick. She dressed in the clean and sexier clothes she had chosen for dinner – a tight, black, short-sleeve cotton sweater, slinky, deep purple harem pants and strappy, low heel, black pumps.

When she saw his fake pout, she snapped her bra shut, gave him another kiss and said, "Later, Mr. Fix-it man. I'm sure there'll be a problem you can work on after dinner. But right now I need to keep the lasagna from burning and check on my house guest."

It wasn't until Faye noticed the chair wedged beneath the doorknob that flashes of her interlude with Verdant Sea popped up front and center. Once more she felt the heat of his incredible kiss and blushed, glancing back at Drake, who was getting dressed. She wanted to replay the memories of Verdant Sea and for that she needed privacy.

"I'll be back in a few," Faye threw over her shoulder as she slipped out the door and closed it behind her. She paused in the hallway, her body aquiver with sensations both exciting and strange. Images of Verdant Sea, the feel of his lips on hers, the warmth of Leaf's body against her thigh. All so vivid. But what precisely had happened? *Was any of that real and am I in fact going to see him again? Was he serious about bonding with me? And what does it all mean?* She leaned her forehead into the wall, which was solid and real, and tried to quiet her thoughts. Taking deep breaths helped, as always.

"I am happy and peaceful, I am healthy and strong, I am safe and protected, I understand right from wrong," she whispered several times. Her lust cooled and her head cleared.

She could hear music and Ariella's laughter even through the girl's closed. Wow, Faye thought, she is certainly making up for her lack of computer access. At this rate she might even become popular. Faye tapped on Ariella's door. The laughter stopped and the music got turned down.

"Yo! Wassup, Faye?"

"Can I come in?" Faye put her hand on the doorknob and started to turn it. There was the sound of a chair being pushed back and then quick steps to the door.

"Whoa, pardner! Not yet! I'm not ready."

"Oh, I just wanted to tell you dinner will be served soon. Do you still want to do the fashion show beforehand?"

"Do I? Duh, yeah." Ariella exclaimed, but didn't open the door. "I just need a couple more minutes. But I gotta give you something first."

The bedroom door cracked open just wide enough for Ariella's left hand to slip through holding a CD. Faye noticed the nails of the hand were painted a startling red and she caught a strong whiff of perfume. She also noticed Ariella's ring with the large green stone, the one she used to contact and get energy from the nature spirits, was glittering, almost throbbing, with light.

"When I tell you, can you start this playing on your stereo? Let me know when you're ready, okay?" Ariella sounded nervous.

"Sure, but I need to talk with you about what happened in my dream while I was napping. It was —"

"Yup, I know about Verdant Sea and the bonding and all that. Leaf clued me in. No worries, we'll talk later. It's all good, for sure." From behind Ariella came a familiar feline whine.

"But Leaf was there and he was really big and we —"

"Uh huh, I know. We'll talk all about it, I promise." Ariella closed the door.

Faye raised her hand to knock again, but instead shouted through the door, "Ariella, please don't use the green ring to summon nature spirits or whatever tonight? Okay?" She thought she heard an agreeing sound from Ariella, so she turned away and almost bumped into Drake as he exited her bedroom. He was dressed in his new hip gear and was even wearing the wrap-around shades.

"Where are you going? We're about to have dinner. And why are you wearing shades indoors?"

"I know, I know. I'm just going out to get my extra clothes and toothbrush and to stash these ridiculous sunglasses in the car. If I don't, I'll forget them." He smiled at her. "Which, I'm guessing, might not be a bad thing."

Faye put her arms around his neck. "So, tall, dark and handsome and ever so slightly dangerous, I guess that means you're staying the night?"

"Well, ma'am, you did mention some post dinner, pre-bedtime, physical activities which sounded mighty enticing. And I figger when those activities are over I'll prolly be too tuckered to go anywhere." Drake lightly kissed the tip of her nose. "Plus, I expect the delicious meal I smell a'cookin' is going to also slow me down a bit."

"That's right, Sir Fix-it, there's a truly wondrous meal almost ready and I personally guarantee you will be thoroughly delighted by the post-dinner phys-ed activity, which will take place in that there bedroom we was just in. And, lest I forget, we also have a gala, pre-dinner entertainment planned, featuring the star known worldwide by only her first name, Ariella!"

Drake feigned astonishment. "Whooee! Ariella's performin' here tonight? By gosh, by golly, I musta died and gone someplace truly heavenly. How can I ever thank you for invitin' me?"

"A kiss would be a start," Faye pursed her lips and fluttered her eyelashes. Drake lifted her onto her toes and kissed her so completely she thought she might pass out. All thoughts and images of Verdant Sea were banished as she snuggled into the warm comfort of her love for Drake.

The lasagna was cooked to perfection, bubbling and wafting up wonderful aromas through its crisp coating of toasted Parmesan. Faye knew it would be best to let it cool before cutting into it, so she set the pan on top of the stove and pulled the salad out of the refrigerator and gave it a few final tosses, then put it, along with an assortment of dressings, mostly homemade and organic, on the table. After surveying the place settings and making a few small adjustments, but overall approving of the job Ariella had done, she put the foil-wrapped, garlic bread into the still warm oven. She figured in 10 minutes all would be ready. She puttered around in the kitchen for a little longer, thinking about Drake and wondering why she had thought Verdant Sea so hot. *It's like having a crush on a comic book character! How silly is that?* She opened the red wine Drake had brought, poured two glasses and carried them into the living room.

Drake had returned from his car and was sprawled on the couch with his head thrown back. She realized he'd dozed off again. Her heart purred when she saw he'd changed into his usual well-worn polo shirt, khaki shorts and tennis shoes. And he was wearing his regular wire-rimmed glasses. So much for the hip, young dude style. Kicking him lightly on the shin, she handed him the glass of wine and said, "C'mon, rouse yourself. The show's about to begin!"

Faye went to the hallway and called, "Ariella! We're ready when you are." The hallway light was off, so it was like shouting into a tunnel. Ariella's door opened and Faye saw the silhouette of tall, amorphous figure backlit by the light from the bedroom. She felt a quick frisson of fear, but realized she was being ridiculous. Ariella was no doubt wearing her new clothes and the heels added height. "Ariella? I'm going to put the music on, yes?"

The living room was cozily lit by the last bit of twilight and two low wattage lamps. At the stereo, Faye slipped the CD in the player and pressed play. A deep, sonorous droning began, accompanied by a throbbing drum. As she snuggled up to Drake on the couch, hand claps sounded from the darkened hallway in time with the drum. Heels clicked on the hardwood floor of the hall and the clicks and claps kept time with the drum, which gradually sped up. It was a little spooky.

Drake leaned over and whispered in her ear, "Do you know what Ariella's doing? That is her, right?" Faye shook her head and squeezed his hand in what she hoped was reassurance. The volume of the music swelled and the pace of the drum increased again. The dark, shadowed figure gradually emerged from the mouth of the hallway and Faye tried to understand what she was seeing. In the dim light, the figure was shapeless, like a cloud, or cotton candy, or a sculpture draped with a cloth. Rhythmic movements rippled its surface. Nervous, Faye winced, praying Ariella wasn't stirring up the nature spirits.

The music abruptly stopped and the shrouded figure jumped into the living room and stopped moving. There was a hint of menace in the air and Faye entertained the wild possibility it wasn't Ariella, that they were going to meet yet another weird character from the teenager's world. But, a closer inspection revealed the figure was covered with nothing more than a deep green, flat sheet Faye had stored in the closet in Ariella's bedroom. Faye was about to say something smart alecky when the music started up again, though this time it was a wild, hard-driven electric guitar accompanied by heavy bass and drum. The shrouded shape began whirling in time to the music's furious beat and, as the shroud lifted in wide swirls, Ariella's slim form emerged from the bottom up.

Ariella was, indeed, wearing high heels, though not so high as Faye had feared. The three inch stilettos gave even more definition to her toned legs, though the muscles definition waw softened by sheer black pantyhose. She was wearing a short, slim pencil skirt which almost exactly matched the color and design of the one the model in the ad wore. As the sheet rose higher with each rotation, they could see Ariella was holding the cloth's center above her head, and that contributed to her larger-than-life height.

By the time Ariella had the sheet whirling at the level of her shoulders, Faye saw she hadn't copied the model's blouse, but instead wore a loose fitting, deep green, silky and layered top which also swirled around her body, though in a smaller circle than the sheet. As the music reached another crescendo, the sheet lifted above Ariella's face and she flung it from her so it frisbeed briefly in the air before settling to the floor.

Again the music stopped and Faye and Drake tried to make sense of what they saw. It was Ariella to be sure, but Ariella transformed. She stood with her legs apart, her hands on her hips and her head thrown back exposing the fine line of her young neck. For a long 20 seconds she didn't move, then the music began again, a sultry, slow, pulsing of synthesized melodic moans, throbbing bass, and heartbeat drums. Slowly Ariella lowered her gaze until her enormous green eyes burned at Faye and Drake, though she didn't smile or acknowledge them. Her face was made up in a reasonable likeness of the girl in the magazine ad, though the used too much blush and the eye shadow was uneven. Faye smiled at Ariella's inexperience. You can take the girl out of the forest, but you can't take the forest out of the girl, Faye thought.

Ariella began to move with that detached, almost otherworldly, way professional models had walking on a runway, her long golden-red hair floating about her head. She strutted to one end of the living room, stopped and held her pose for a long beat, then pivoted and strutted to the other end, all in time to the heavy pulse of the music. Faye thought her young friend was magnificent, like a vision out of some I-wanna-be-a-model fantasy, both aloof and yet so tender and vulnerable. Faye glanced over at Drake to see if he was amused and was surprised to see avid interest on his face.

When Ariella turned and moved back the other way, she turned to glance at Faye and Drake and a small smile crept onto her lips. She halted in the center of the room, directly in front of the pair on the couch and her smile deepened. Her eyes were glowing, her gleaming lips were parted and Faye could see the rapid rise of her small breasts beneath the concealing top. With a start, Faye realized Ariella was concentrating on Drake and she heard his quick intake of breath. With the same imperious strut she moved toward Drake, right hand on her hip, leftt arm out in front and the index finger pointed directly at him. She stopped just in front of his knees and, still swaying to the music, leaned forward and tapped him lightly on the nose. Faye remembered how Ariella had touched the mall security guard and was relieved the ring with the big green stone wasn't on girl's left hand. Nonetheless, Drake started as if he'd been poked with a pin. Ariella, her eyes bright, the pink tip of her tongue showing between her scarlet lips, let her finger slide down Drake's cheek, then glide to the center of his lips. She then gently, gently pried his lips apart and deftly slipped the tip of her finger between his teeth.

Faye stared at Drake and Ariella like they were strangers. What was going on? Drake let go of Faye's hand and she watched in fascination as he moved to cover his crotch. Did he have an erection? Angry and frightened, she was about to shout at Ariella to quit it and pull the girl's arm away when the music stopped and, with a joyous shout, Ariella leaped back, kicked off her heels and began jumping up and down, squealing over and over, "That was so much fun! It was totally cray-cray!"

The transformation from sultry temptress to teenage goofball was instantaneous. Drake turned to Faye, his mouth still slightly open and his eyes clouded with confusion and lust. His eyebrows went up in question and Faye could only blink like an animal caught in a spotlight. Meanwhile, Ariella stopped pogoing and squealing and ran laughing down the hall toward her bedroom. Faye knew she should speak to Ariella about what was clearly inappropriate behavior. She would say something. But not right now. Maybe after dinner.

"Did you know what she was going to do? That she was going to be so, . . . provocative?" Drake asked, his voice low and urgent.

"No idea," Faye said, "I just thought she was going to model her new clothes for us. No way did I expect a full-blown performance. I'm sorry she made you feel uncomfortable. I actually don't understand her that well yet. She often seems so innocent, I just never expected she'd play sex kitten. But I'm going to say something to her when the moment is right."

"Wow," said Drake, apparently not hearing Faye, "Just wow, wow, wow. She's truly something. How old did you say she was?"

"Fifteen, but I guess her mother's taught her a lot about . . ." Faye trailed off.

Ariella burst back into the living room, still in her new clothes, still laughing and carrying Faye's digital camera. "Faye, Faye, thank you so much for letting me perform! It was totally off the chain!"

"That's pretty much the way I would describe it," Faye said dryly.

"Can you take a picture of me in my new clothes with Drake? He's such a hottie!"

"Uh, no, Ariella, I don't think that would be a good idea. Drake is a teacher, like me, and it wouldn't be good for photos of him with a fifteen year old girl to show up on Facebook."

"But, it's just for laughs! And I promise I won't post them, honest. I just want to see how I look, please, please?"

"No, and that's final, Ariella. I'll take a picture of you in your new clothes, but not with Drake. I'm sorry, but this is one of those adult things you need to accept, okay?"

Ariella's smile faded and her joyous expression was replaced by disappointment. She looked down at her stocking feet. Faye looked to Drake and he gave a nod which said he approved.

Then Ariella's face lit up again and her green eyes brightened. "What if we don't show his face? I'm way shorter than him, even in my heels. You could just leave his head out of the picture. Please?"

Faye understood well how desperate Ariella was to be seen as cool and hip by her school mates. And knew how the photos might help change her reputation from weird outsider to happening insider. Drake gave a "whatever" shrug.

Faye sighed, "Okay, all right, I guess it could work. But you must promise to never say who is in the picture with you. Tell your buddies it was someone your mom knows. You do understand it would make serious problems for both Drake and I if he was identified. We could even get fired." Faye made her voice resonate with a teacher's authority. "And if there were to be problems, there's no way you could ever stay at my house again. And, I'm going to decide which pictures are keepers. The rest we delete."

"Fer sure, Faye, I would never do anything to mess up you or Drake. It's just it would be so stylin' if there was a slick dude in the pix. But can he change into the gear he was wearin' when he got here? That was especial money!"

Faye looked to Drake, who was smiling. He blinked and said, "Sure, you want the shades, too, right?"

He's enjoying this, the jerk. Well, two can play. "Do you want him to take off his shirt? He's got some great abs." Faye reached over and rubbed Drake's stomach.

Both Drake and Ariella were taken aback. Drake managed to sputter out, "No, I think that's not called for . . . uh . . . no, let's not do that."

Faye barked out a laugh. "Whatever! But it'll all have to wait until after dinner because I'm sure the garlic bread will burn if we wait even another minute. Let's eat!"

Chapter Thirty Three

Dinner was, Faye thought afterward, bizarre and fraught with tension. But, the food was delicious, plentiful and, aside from the garlic bread being a little singed, was brought to table at exactly the right time. Ariella and Drake sat at opposite ends of the small kitchen table with Faye between them, facing the deck. The first ten minutes were taken up with the sounds of eating and exclamations of how good everything tasted. Faye praised Ariella for her tossed salad and garlic bread prep, but the girl seemed embarrassed and kept glancing at Drake. Faye supposed she was still buzzing from her licentious runway strut and tease and didn't want Drake to think of her as an ordinary kitchen wench. Get over it, thought Faye, noticing Ariella's mascara had gotten a bit smudged and her lipstick was disappearing with each forkful. Would the real Ariella, the crunchy granola one Faye knew from the cottage, re-emerge before the evening ended?

To Faye's surprise, Drake showed an obvious and real interest in Ariella, asking her about school-related stuff and which popular music she liked. Ariella blushed and gave detailed, albeit rambling, answers. Then Drake, smiling, prompted her to explain how she had come up with her choreographed and impressive performance. Ariella became animated, and, peppering her answer with urban slang, went on about file formats and sequencing and how to create a merged audio track. Drake, not really tech savvy, looked blank, so Faye asked what music software Ariella had used, knowing there was usually only a basic player on the school's laptops. Ariella waved her fingers with their painted nails and said she had, of course, downloaded and installed a music composition and CD burning program and not to worry because it was all open source freeware. This brought a sharp glance from Faye, who asked about malware and viruses and was Ariella confident she wasn't screwing up the laptop. The techs at school would give Faye the evil eye if she returned with a virus-infected machine.

"Oh, Faye, don't be—"

"Old-fashioned? Paranoid? Out of it?" Faye interrupted.

"No, no, don't be trippin' so bad," Ariella tossed back her waves of golden hair. "It's all chill, honest. Don't forget I've been spending hours in the computer lab at school. I'm truly exceedingly solid with this stuff."

"Whatever," Faye said, and also tossed her hair back. Ariella giggled and then went on to explain how she had patched together several short bits of music and timed them so she would know when to start and end each segment of the performance.

"You planned the whole performance in advance?" Faye asked, "Even the ending bit?"

Ariella peeked at Faye from under her lashes, as if she wasn't quite sure what was being asked.

"Well, the last part was def spontaneous, yuh, huh. It just seemed like the . . . zany way to end it. You liked it, didn't you Drake?"

Drake opened his mouth, then noticed Faye staring at him. He shifted a little in his seat and took a big bite of lasagna and began chewing vigorously.

Faye jumped in, "Zany, huh? Interesting word choice. However—"

Ariella cut her off. "My mom said I need to learn how to relate to men, that I should be either strong or sweet and both ways can make men 'manageable.' So I was being extra sweet!" She glanced at Drake, who chewed faster and only looked up for a moment.

"Ariella, I know your mom has told you a lot about how to be in the world, but here, in this house, we play by my rules. Or, rather, the rules Drake and I understand are appropriate. So, that sort of provocative, sexual behavior directed by a teenage girl toward a grown man isn't allowed. Right, Drake?"

Drake met Faye's look, gave a quick nod, studied his plate and swallowed. "Yes, it's not appropriate."

Faye smiled and was turning back to Ariella when Drake

added in a rush, "Even if it was just a fun performance and had no real meaning. No real intent. This lasagna is delicious!" He took another big mouthful of food and chewed noisily.

"Yeah, what he said. No biggee. Just funnin'," Ariella was frowning.

Faye felt her color rise and anger sizzled her frayed nerves. What a bastard Drake could be. He had enjoyed how Ariella had played with him! He fucking liked it. Confused, she stood suddenly, hitting the table top with her knee, causing her wine glass to topple. She lunged and grabbed it just in time so only a few bright red drops fell onto the tablecloth.

"Oopsy daisy!" Ariella snickered.

Faye straightened, held the glass to eye height and gazed into its dark red depths. If Drake was a woman, what would his menstrual blood would taste like? I know what my blood tastes like. He doesn't know what my blood tastes like. She became aware both Drake and Ariella had stopped eating and were waiting for her. What would happen if she threw the wine in Drake's face? Instead, she took a sip of the red liquid, swirled It around and swallowed in what she hoped was a controlled, deliberate manner. The wine was delicious and its warmth settled in her belly.

"Ariella, I just want to make it absolutely clear you're not to behave in a sexual manner toward Drake under any circumstances, fun or otherwise. It may have been 'just a performance', but it was still inappropriate. Is that understood?"

Ariella looked to Drake, who was holding his wine up to the light, and muttered, "My mom . . . I think . . . oh, never mind, okay, I won't be inappropriate again." The girl speared a tomato and forked it into her mouth. "All good then?" She paused and added, "It was fun, though".

"Yes, all good, but not fun for all." Faye touched Ariella's cheek. "And thank you for not objecting more strenuously. I applaud your maturity. But, the real reason I'm standing is I want to propose a toast with this excellent red wine Drake brought."

She raised her glass and was about to start the toast when Ariella piped up. "But I don't have any wine," she said, holding up her glass of organic apple juice. "Mom always pours me a glass when she has wine with dinner. It's the mature thing to do."

There followed another lengthy pause while the two childless adults, both of whom taught teenage students during the school year, wondered what was the right thing to do. Drake opened his mouth, but Faye wasn't going to let him take this one. The effect of the wine, combined with their sex and the interlude with Verdant Sea made her brave and reckless. *Fuck him and his contradictions. He loves me, but doesn't want children. Fuck him, yeah, fuck him.*

"Well, if it's okay with your mom, it's okay with us." Faye got another wineglass from the cabinet and poured half a glass for Ariella, who grinned up at her and she knew her cred had just gotten a big boost.

"So, what's your toast, oh Faye m'lady?" Ariella's green eyes glittered with mischief.

"I want to toast to old friends," Faye waved her glass at Drake and watched in amusement as he flinched backward as the wine sloshed but didn't quite go over the rim, "and to new friends." She made a gentler gesture toward Ariella and hesitated, not sure what it was she wanted to say.

"May we . . . may we . . . enjoy this dinner and let it foster the spirit of camaraderie which will arise . . . as it does among folk of good intention and warm hearts . . . and may we find our bonding . . . in friendship becomes even stronger." Faye raised her glass, thinking her use of "bonding" sounded a lot like Verdant Sea. "And that we use our friendship to help nature heal the planet."

"Yay!" said Ariella.

"To friendship!" Faye cried.

Drake and Ariella clinked their glasses, echoed her words and all took big swallows of wine.

Ariella sat back and beamed. "Mmm, that's good wine." She drank off the rest in her glass and held it out for more. Before Faye could say or do anything, Drake grabbed the bottle and poured Ariella another dollop. Faye sat down and studied him. He flashed her a quick smile and continued eating. There was something going on with him, something she didn't like.

"Guess what I called my performance?" Ariella asked.

"I can't guess because I'm sure it's something I would never imagine," Faye said, "So please, enlighten us."

"Young Woman Emerging from Nature's Shroud!"

"Nature's Shroud? You mean the green sheet?"

"Yup, it was symbolic. The whole performance was symbolic of how I'm trying to change, how I'm trying to stop being the pawn of the nature spirits, even though I totally respect them, and how I'm emerging as my own person and learning to play and exist in the normal world."

"Wow. You've obviously given this a lot of serious thought. Are you sure you want to make such a big change? What's your mom say?"

"My mom won't like it."

"Hey, what's this about nature spirits? What do you guys mean?" Drake's eyes flipped from Ariella to Faye and back again. "Didn't you mention nature spirits to me last night?" he asked Faye, who turned to Ariella with raised eyebrows.

Ariella took a sip of wine. "I could spend the next week talking about nature spirits," she said, again waving her red-tipped fingers, a gesture Faye was starting to find annoying. "There's so much to tell and it's pretty much not fun, cuz it can get so serious and boring. It's sincerely fake sometimes, you know?" Ariella took a bigger sip. "I don't want to talk about the NSA tonight. I think Faye should tell you what she's learned about nature spirits."

Ariella snickered at Faye's nonplussed expression, emptied her glass, then held it out to Drake for a refill. Faye started to object, but Drake held the wine bottle up to the light and said,

"There's only a little bit left and you're not driving tonight, are you?" He grinned at Ariella and poured the last inch of wine into her glass.

"Now, Faye, my love, talk to me all about the nature spirits," Drake said and gave Ariella a conspiratorial look, though she seemed entranced by the ruby liquid in her glass. "Didn't you say you had some adventures last night? Did they involve nat-ure spi-rits?" Drake drew out the last two words, with exaggerated emphasis.

Faye took a bite of lasagna, looked out to the deck, and ran her fingers through her hair as she chewed. She felt unusual. Not bad unusual, but more special unusual. It was strange, but after the Verdant Sea encounter she felt honored to be asked to talk about nature spirits. It was as if she'd been given the Talking Stick. She leaned back, wondering where to begin, wishing there was someone to help her. There was a shifting of air and she scented lilacs and roses, accompanied by a vibration, a low humming, as if something big and alive and powerful was standing next to her feeding her energy. She felt warmed and comforted and, well, believed in. It reminded her of the feeling she got when she was up in front of a class and knew she had the undivided attention of every student in the room. Looking over at Ariella, she saw only merriment. Faye cleared her throat.

"Well, to begin with, I've learned to believe in nature spirits. I believe they are real."

"Really? Really real?" Drake was pleased with his cleverness.

"Yes, real. Though they're not real like humans are, they're real like the wind is real, like the waves are real, like the earth spinning on its axis is real. Last night Ariella helped me see the effects of nature spirits in action and I understand she can, in fact, communicate with them. And she's assured me I'll be able to communicate with them eventually. Plus, you do hear a humming sound, right?"

Ariella nodded, but Drake shook his head and picked at the

bits left on his plate. The hunch of his shoulders told Faye he was
disturbed. She hesitated, knowing she had to keep going, but
understanding blabbering on about nature spirits would further
complicate the situation with Drake. He already thought she was
veering way into the weird.

"Go on, Faye, you know there's more you want to tell Drake.
And, yes, I hear the humming."

Ariella did that annoying finger wave thing again and Faye
felt a compulsion to please Ariella. Why, after all, is it so important
for me to talk about nature spirits? Doesn't she understand how
delicate my situation with Drake is? With a start, she realized
Ariella had been finger waving with her left hand, the hand which
now bore the large green gemstone ring. The ring Faye had asked
her not to use to summon nature spirits tonight. Ariella hadn't worn
the ring during her runway performance, but it appeared the little
witch had put it on afterward and had likely been using it to her
own ends during dinner. And what were Ariella's ends? Faye
quickly reviewed what had happened in the past half-hour and
saw how things could have been manipulated.

"I see you've got your ring on. You don't remember me
asking you not to wear it?"

"You said not to use it to summon nature spirits. And I'm not.
For real."

"But you are using it?"

"What's the fuss over her ring? Are you guys serious about
summoning spirits? Hey, that would be gnarly! We could do like a
séance or something." Drake laughed and got up to fetch the
bottle of white wine he had brought.

"No, I'm not using it in any way you would object to," Ariella
put a big piece of lasagna in her mouth and talked as she chewed.
"I'm just spicing things up and smoothing them over, sort of."

"Ah, let's discuss later what I would object to." Faye used
the voice reserved for students who hadn't done their homework.

"Fine! I won't wear it!" Ariella yanked the ring off, slammed it down on the table and drained her wine glass.

Faye immediately felt a kind of deflation, a loss of sparkle, like one felt when an angry friend stormed out of the room. The humming vibration faded. She took a deep breath and glanced at Drake. He appeared puzzled, as if he'd remembered something that bothered him.

"Hey, ladies, take it easy. Is this really such a big deal? I mean, nature spirits? And, what is that, some sort of magic ring? Did you get it in a box of cereal?" Drake's tone was teasing, but his smile didn't reach his eyes, which were dark with warning. "Can we talk about something else? Let's all drink this great white wine I brought."

Drake searched for clean wine glasses and Faye and Ariella ignored each other like two uneasy cats. They were all quiet as they sampled the white wine, though Ariella grimaced in mock dismay at the smidgen Drake poured for her.

Faye said, "Oh, this is good" and Ariella added, "Mmmm, deelish".

Faye gave Drake a placating, tentative smile. "Let me just tell you about our adventures since yesterday afternoon and perhaps you'll understand why I'm so hyped about nature spirits. And supportive of Ariella. Okay?"

Drake's made an expansive gesture "Sure. Whatever. Can't say it's not interesting."

Faye skipped over Ariella's masturbating in the car and instead started with her near naked run through the field of flowers at Ariella's cottage on Friday afternoon.

Drake's eyebrows went way up when she gave details. "Somehow, I can't imagine you doing something like that. Sure you're not going hippy on me?" Faye smiled and went on to describe the interior of the cottage and the cats and the old fashioned kitchen.

"Definitely hippy," Drake said dismissively. "No wonder you're seeing nature spirits." When he saw the dismayed glance

Ariella gave Faye, he added, "No offense intended."

Ariella tossed her hair and bit off some garlic bread, so Faye continued, mentioning the flowers and card from Moira and described the old woman as Ariella had portrayed her. Faye also touched upon the Viridis Glas Luminasti and their history.

"Viridis Glas Lumi-nasti, huh? Nasty, nasty, nasty, huh?." Drake chuckled and was unfazed when no one joined in. He scooped up the last piece of lasagna from his plate and held it on his fork before popping it into his mouth. "Yum".

Faye described the items Calista had given her in the leather pouch, items she was to place around the house to make Ariella comfortable. She held out the scallop locket for his inspection, saying, "And we're wearing identical lockets with the other person's picture. They help keep us connected."

Drake held Faye's locket and peered at the picture of Ariella. He dropped the scallop back between her breasts, pushed away his empty plate and drained his glass. Faye thought his hand was unsteady as he reached for the bottle and poured himself more.

"Faye, don't you think . . . don't you see . . . can't you comprehend what's happening here? I mean, how can you, in the space of a little more than a week, change so much? Doesn't it seem at all strange to you? Are you drugged or something? Didn't you say you've been drinking some new tea?" Drake shook his head. "I'm sorry, Ariella, but I need to speak plainly to Faye. You can go watch TV or something if you want."

Ariella shrugged. "I'm cool staying here. No biggee." She reached down to stroke Snow and Midnight, who had appeared beside her chair. Faye knew Ariella wouldn't leave unless ordered and, when she thought about, Faye wanted Ariella to stay.

Drake drank off the rest of his wine, set the glass down gently and said, "Faye. Listen to me. I don't know what's going on. You know I love you, but tonight you're showing me sides of you I haven't ever seen. Or noticed, I guess. I mean, magic cats, taking off your clothes in the woods, believing in nature spirits, full moon events, demanding we make a baby . . . it's all too much, too quick and I can't believe it's really you. Or that it's really real for you."

Faye started to reply, but Ariella broke in, "Faye was ready for a change, Drake, whether you like it or not," she said with heat in her voice. "She wasn't always a meek little English teacher, you know. When she was younger she had big dreams and fantasies which were precious to her. My mom and I are just helping her revive those dreams and fantasies and maybe even convince her she can find happiness by taking a new, more true to her, path in life."

Faye gaped and Ariella gave a quick thumbs-up gesture. But Drake, with another expansive wave of his arm, said, "Well, thank you Ms Cardona, for that well thought out riposte. But, you don't expect me to accept your statement on the basis of the evidence presented, do you? I mean, Faye and I have been in an intimate, loving relationship for five . . . or is it six . . . years and I believe I know her a lot better than you or your mother does." He lowered his hand onto Faye's and gripped it with some force. "Oh, and you do know what a riposte is, don't you, Ariella?" Ariella's uncertainty was obvious and she tried to cover her confusion by spearing and eating piece of lettuce.

"Ariella knows what riposte means. After all, she is taking French this year." Faye tried to pull her hand out from under Drake's, but he wouldn't let go and she noticed beads of sweat forming on his upper lip. He's not dealing very well, she thought. And, he really doesn't know how many years we've been together?

"Drake, listen, before you come to any malformed conclusions, will you listen to everything else that has happened this weekend? Perhaps when I get through it all you'll understand better how I'm finding it possible to believe in things like nature spirits. And how it isn't unreasonable for me to change so much. And, as Ariella said, maybe I'm primed for a change."

He pulled his hand back and the expression in his eyes made her shiver. She so wanted to reassure him everything was still okay between them, that she still loved him and still wanted to be with him. But, like retreating waves pull sand from the beach, she felt him sliding away. Or was she sliding away from him? He stood, gave her a long look, then walked toward the door.

"Drake, wait! Where are you going?"

He stopped in the kitchen doorway, turned, and said, "To the bathroom. Where did you think I was going?" With a rueful smile, he disappeared down the hallway.

Chapter Thirty Four

Faye and Ariella sat in silence and picked at the last bits of food on their plates. Ariella got up to clear the table and, in passing, briefly rested her hand on Faye's shoulder.

"Well, this is going swimmingly," Faye said. "Sometimes he can be so irksome. I mean, he acts like he's so cool and says 'whatever', but then he gets uptight because I wanted to run naked in a field."

Ariella pivoted from the sink, "He's a nice guy and pretty hot, if you ask me. But, he's also kinda limited in terms of relating to what is important to you. I think you deserve somebody better." Ariella spoke in a formal tone, as if she was reciting something she'd said many times before. To Faye it sounded like each word was a bullet hitting a bell. I'm the bell, she thought, and I'm vibrating to the impact of these words.

"You may be right, but now's not the time to talk about all that. I just want to get through the rest of this evening in as pleasant a manner as possible. Can you help me?"

"I could put the ring back on. That would make a big diff."

"Really? Let me think about that." Faye sat up straight and took some deep breaths. Her fatigue was catching up to her again. They heard the bathroom door open and watched as Drake turned at the end of the hallway and headed for the front door.

"Drake! Where are you going now?" Faye stood and ran after him. He stopped and she put her arms around him. "You're not leaving are you? I'm sorry if I upset going on about nature spirits and all that." She stood on tiptoe and gave him a quick kiss. "How about we just relax and talk about something else? And eat some dessert? I've got delicious frozen yogurt on the menu."

"Relaxing with yogurt sounds wonderful," Drake said, holding her close. "And, not to worry, because I'm actually interested in all the crazy stuff you guys are doing. I was only going out to my car to get my new duds so Ariella can get the pictures she wants. Plus, I need to make a quick phone call."

"You're calling from your car? Why?" Faye's intuition lit up.

"The call is kind of . . . private. I'll just be an extra minute or so." He kissed her lightly on the forehead and moved toward the door.

"Are you calling Shandra?" She bit her lip, wishing she could take back the question.

His eyes flashed and he nodded. "Yes, in fact, that's who I'm calling. She's not feeling well. I told her I'd call to make sure tennis is still happening tomorrow. Is that okay?"

"Oh, sure, whatever. Say hi for me."

Faye returned to the kitchen where Ariella, who had no doubt heard the entire conversation, gave Faye a quick hug and said she was going to her room to redo her makeup. Faye sat down at the kitchen table with a thump. She was tired, emotionally drained, and her period was rising in her like the tide. She wanted to cry, to just let it all out and be a sobbing mess. But Drake didn't like it when she cried. He didn't like it when she got her period. He didn't like it when she said she wanted a baby. He did like playing tennis. He liked playing tennis with Shandra. And he was surely not going to say hi from her to Shandra. Fuck!

She poured herself the last of Drake's white wine and drank it in three quick swallows. She would get through the rest of this evening. She would be loving and sexy and she would sleep with Drake in her bed. And she would not dream. And tomorrow would be another day.

Five minutes passed. Ariella ran in and held out mascara and eyeliner. "Can you do this part for me? I think I drank too much vino."

Faye pulled her chair close and began lining Ariella's eyes. She was tempted to blurt out how unhappy she felt, but held back. Ariella already had a lot to deal with. She didn't need to be burdened with her teacher's romantic problems.

"Drake's not back yet?"

"No, he's making a phone call." Faye started in with the mascara wand.

"You know, he's a lot like the guys my mom gets involved with. They're nice enough at the start, but they all turn out to be pretty self-centered and aren't very reliable. Though they seem to like falling in love. Mom's always getting disappointed. I sometimes think she wants my dad back."

Faye studied Ariella's makeup. She now knew to whom Ariella had previously given the "you deserve someone better" speech. "How does your mom deal with guys like that?"

"Oh, she kicks them to the curb and moves on. She always gets just as excited about the next one. In fact, I think she's met someone out on the west coast and that's why she wants to stay an extra day."

When Drake came back in he waved from the kitchen doorway and went down the hallway. "I'll be right there. Just gotta change into Hip Dude."

Faye sighed, glanced at the clock and saw it was 8:30. Early for her, but she was wiped out. She heard a meow from under her chair and, bending over, saw the big orange tabby curled up, one eye open, his cat smile plain on his face. Faye smiled and winked at him and he winked back.

"You think you can make things better for the rest of the evening with your ring?" Faye asked.

Ariella nodded. "Fer sure, I can make us all feel good enough to avoid getting upset. We'll feel like we're on the beach drinking wine and laughing on a warm, sunny day."

Faye sat and thought while Ariella inspecteded her makeup in a small hand mirror. "Made progress on your homework?"

"Duh, of course. Plus, Monday's a holiday so I have an extra day."

"Good, because tomorrow's going to be busy, what with us going to the hut and you taking off with Sorcha on her motorcycle. She has an extra helmet for you?"

"Yes, absolute. No worries, mon."

"I wish there were no worries." Faye slapped her palm on the table. "Okay, put the ring back on and use it as needed. But, no calling nature spirits or turning Drake into your servant."

"It'll be all good, I promise. You just relax and enjoy." Ariella slid the ring on her finger and gave it a quick kiss. At Faye's raised eyebrows she added, "Gotta activate it."

Drake appeared and leaned against the kitchen doorjamb. He was in full regalia, hair slicked back, wraparound shades, skintight shirt and jeans and pointy Italian shoes.

"Whooee!" exclaimed Ariella, and clapped her hands.

"Rather nice, Sir Fixit," said Faye with less enthusiasm.

Drake pointed both index fingers, like his hand were pistols, toward Faye, then went straight to her, pulled her up out of her chair and kissed her hard.

"Double whooee!" Ariella began clapping rhythmically as the kiss went on and on.

Faye leaned into Drake and let his lips tell her he wanted her. Her lady parts awoke, stretched and were more than interested. When she started to get lightheaded, she shifted her nose to his neck, hoping to catch another whiff of the wonderful cologne which was, she admitted, a real aphrodisiac. She smelled cologne, but there was another odor in the mix, a pungent, herbal, earthy odor, reminiscent of skunk. She had smelled it before.

Hold on! Faye pulled back and gazed up at Drake. She couldn't see his eyes through the shades, but the way his mouth quirked told her all she needed to know. He'd smoked some pot, no doubt when he'd gone to his car to 'make a phone call.' Drake occasionally got high, she knew, and she had joined him now and then. But this was definitely not a good time for him to be stoned. Ariella might be a world-wise teenager and loyal to Faye, but the girl could, with just a casual remark to another student, cause real trouble for both she and Drake.

Faye glanced over at Ariella, who was still watching them.

"Hey, why don't you two get a motel room?" the girl said with a laugh. "Joke! Seriously, you two don't need to be shy about being all physical in front of me. I'm used to seeing a lot of kissing and more. My mom's very open about her sexuality and, in fact, leaves her bedroom door open no matter what."

Faye and Drake stepped away from each other gawked at Ariella, who said, "Hey, lax. It's not like I'm some sort of voyeur. You do know what voyeur means, don't you, Drake?"

Faye turned to Drake, "You should brush your teeth. Your breath is . . . difficult."

"Brush my teeth now? Can't I wait until after we finish eating?"

"Yes, now and because I want to kiss you again before the meal is over." She pushed and turned him, then followed him toward the door.

"I'm just going to talk to Drake for a little while in the bathroom. Can you dish out the frozen yogurt?"

"Yup, fer sure, you two go and fun out. Just get back before the yogurt melts."

Faye closed the bathroom door behind her, put her hands on her hips and glared at her boyfriend. He stared back, toothbrush and toothpaste in his hands.

"What?" he said.

"You smoked pot. I can smell it all over you."

"Uh, yeah, I did, but so what? It's Saturday night, after all. Plus, I just wanted to get in the groove, you know, with the crazy jive you and Ariella were making."

"Crazy jive, huh? Well, she's not stupid, she's going to smell it on you and she'll know what it is. And then what if she tells somebody? Her mother probably wouldn't care and might even cheer us on. But, if any of the kids at school find out, it would backfire on us. Brendan Fitzgerald would surely hear of it and, even if I said it was only a friend of mine who got high at my house, he'll be upset because it happened when Ariella was here.

And, what if he feels compelled to inform *your* Principal?"

Drake looked into the mirror and started to put toothpaste on the brush, then stopped. He turned toward Faye and, for a second, with his bug-eye, wrap-around shades and slicked back black hair, his aspect was a bit alien or even MATRIX menacing.

"So this little bathroom tête-à-tête isn't about my breath, but my general odor?"

Faye nodded. "I have some essential oils we can smear on you which will hopefully mask the smell." She opened a small wall cabinet and picked out a vial. "Here, try this. It's eucalyptus oil. It's got a good clean aroma and shouldn't clash with your Hip Dude pheromone cologne. And please take off those glasses until we take the pictures?"

Drake made a big show of carefully removing his shades, then began dabbing the eucalyptus oil on his face, his neck, the front of his shirt, and in his armpits. But when he unzipped his jeans and made to put some on his privates, Faye grabbed his hand and laughing, said, "Okay, okay, that's enough!" She pulled him to her and kissed him. "Where'd you get the pot?"

"Um, Shandra gave me some. I just took a couple of puffs in the car while I was on the phone, honest. And I've got a little more if you want later. We can chill out in bed and do the hootchie-koo." He put his hand on her breast and squeezed until she stepped away.

"So you smoked in your car while talking on your cell with Shandra? How cute, you and she getting high together over the phone. Please don't tell me you had phone sex, too?" Faye struggled to keep her tone light.

"Whoa, nothing like that. She's home alone on Saturday night and feeling forlorn. She's just a nice kid who's having a tough time. Her boyfriend broke up with her like a month ago. When she asked if I had the pot with me I didn't realize she wanted to get high together. But, she asked and sounded so needy, I couldn't say no. We just goofed and giggled for a while, nothing more."

"Goofing and giggling. Of course. Just a nice kid. Right. A nice, forlorn and lonely kid who would like nothing more than to get in your pants. Speaking of which, tell me exactly what made you change your style so dramatically, from funky tennis jock to this." Faye gestured to his clothes.

He had the grace to seem abashed. "Well, yeah, it was Shandra. She gave me a hard time about people mistaking me for her fuddy-duddy uncle, so she took me shopping one night after tennis. I was flattered she even took an interest and, I gotta agree, the new look is killer."

"Killer? Right. I might kill her if she continues to exert such an influence on you." Faye managed a little chuckle. She had known it had to be Shandra. "But, I agree you're especially hot in these threads, so kiss me again."

Ariella was still at the kitchen table, both Snow and Midnight in her lap, and she was giving the cats little bites of frozen yogurt from her spoon. Faye's bottle of Pinot Grigio had been taken from the refrigerator and decorked. Ariella's glass had some white wine it. The big green gem in her ring gleamed.

"All good now?" Ariella asked, with a knowing smile.

Drake grinned, sat down and reached for the wine bottle, but Faye remained standing, feeling puzzled. Was it all good now? She was less tired and, yes, she did feel sort of relaxed, definitely not tense. She had the nagging sense she'd forgotten something. Something to do with Ariella? Drake's apparent intention to get drunk? Drake's growing friendship with Shandra?

Ariella waggled her fingers and said, "Sit down, Faye, and have some more wine. And tell Drake more about our adventures. I know he's just dying to hear all about it." Drake raised his glass in agreement and took a big swig.

Faye shrugged, poured herself some Pinot Grigio, took a nibble of yogurt and, on impulse, sipped some wine and swirled the mix around in her mouth. *Mmm, the mixture of dry wine and sweet, fermented yogurt is divine! Why didn't I try this before?* She took another sip and another spoonful. *Yummy!*

"So Faye, you've got more to tell me? More tales of naughty nakedness in the woods, I hope?" Drake said.

"There was another scary escapade in the woods, but that was today, this afternoon. But first, let me tell you what happened last night."

She launched into a detailed retelling of the time with Ariella on the beach - drinking the Veil Ripper tea, Ariella's invoking the spirits with her wild dancing, the appearance of the Indians.

"That's just so very weird, so very, very weird. And how dis . . . dis . . . ah . . . disorientat . . . ating for you, my love. I'm so very, very sorry." Drake seemed more woozy than was justified by the amount he'd had to drink. He got up and, swaying slightly, came to Faye and bent down to hug her. From the corner of her eye, Faye saw Ariella's huge grin and the green ring twinkling. But she couldn't help herself, she moved into his embrace and began leaking tears.

"And I'm so sorry, too. I know I've been difficult this past week." She put her arms around his neck and pulled his face down for her to kiss. "You know how much I love you."

The kiss got traction and felt incredibly good, though at one point Drake's swaying increased and he almost toppled them both onto the floor. Ariella coughed and Faye let go of Drake and glanced at the girl, who rolled her eyes. Faye laughed and mouthed to Ariella, "Too much with the ring!" When Ariella reminded Drake 'disorientatating' wasn't a real word, he giggled and waved his glass in her direction.

Faye told about how well Ariella had meditated Saturday morning and about the animals gathering around her on the porch, Drake lifted his glass in salute. "You really are something, ya know that, Ariella? Really, really something. I mean, you're the . . . the . . . kitty cat's meow!" He began laughing so hard a bit of snot came out of his nose. Faye, seeing this, laughed with him and then Ariella, who had frowned at first, chuckled. After the silliness ended, Drake dispensed more wine all around and held the empty bottle toward Faye, who made a face.

"C'mon, Faye, I know you've got some more booze stashed. Your wonderful houseguest, the Amazing Ariella, is lookin' parched. And, so 'm I!" Drake was slurring his words.

Faye was usually irritated when Drake got drunk and became funny-belligerent, but now she found it only amusing. But, was it okay for Ariella to drink so much? Something was nagging her about that. She shook her head like a dog trying to dislodge a fly. She was a bit tipsy and her vision started to blur. It looked like there were shadowy shapes around Ariella - perhaps a flickering crown and a pulsing green aura encircling her body. And, when Faye squinted, Ariella looked much older, possibly even older than Faye, with graying hair and wrinkles. *I must be drunk. Too, too much of everything.* She shook her head.

"What? Yer sayin' there's no more wine? No way! I know better. Yer such a wine hound!" Drake struggled to his feet, but rocked back on his heels and had to take a step to the side to keep his balance. "I'm gonna get some more."

"Sit down before you fall down, I'll get it."

Drake grinned when he saw another bottle appear, though Faye left it unopened, hoping that obstacle might slow him once he finished what he had in his glass.

"C'mon, tell me some more stories! I know you've got lots more to tell." Drake said.

Faye's retold what had happened at the Mall with the mall cop. Drake laughed and cheered and pounded on the table with his fist. Faye didn't mention the bit about Ariella using her ring on the cop. She hesitated before telling Drake the dreams she had in her car while sleeping outside the cottage. But, she thought, I think one of the dreams was about him, so . . . Drake became grimmer and grimmer as Faye described her dream of being at the beach, watching her children play in the surf and wondering whose hand was holding hers.

"Y'know that's gotta be my hand, Faye. I mean, c'mon, it could only be me, right? It's what you want, right, to make babies with me?"

Faye paused, then nodded, but Ariella broke in, "What about Verdant Sea? He'll give you children."

Stricken, Faye looked down at her lap.

"Huh? Who? Faye, what the hell is she talking about? Who or what is the ferddy n sea?" Drake's face flushed. "Why won't you look at me? What the fuck's going on?"

"Drake, listen. It was only a dream. I —"

"Verdant Sea wants to bond with Faye." Ariella waggled her left hand with the green ring as she spoke. "Now, Drake, you know you want the best for Faye, right? You wouldn't want to stand between her and true happiness, would you?"

Drake frowned and his voice softened. "Of course I want her to be happy. But with me, not with someone else. Surely you understand that, don't you?" He turned back to Faye and his anger again flared. "Now tell me what does bonding with the friggin' sea have to do with anything? What does it mean? Is there another guy? Because if there is . . .I can . . . I will . . . walk right now. I mean it!"

Perhaps it was because she was so tired and perhaps because she'd had too much to drink and perhaps because Ariella had used her ring, a wave of dizziness swept over Faye. Her throat grew tight, and her heart sped up. She wanted to get up and run to her bedroom or out the door into the night to anywhere but here, facing Drake's angry, bloodshot stare.

"Drake." Ariella said sharply and he swiveled to face her. "Listen. Verdant Sea is a semi-physical manifestation of the nature spirits. He appears in near human form to allow easier communication with people. He speaks for and about the spirits. And he's approached Faye because of her great sensitivity and talent. He asked her to bond with him so she can help the nature spirits heal the planet's biosphere. He will make her happy."

"What? You cannot be serious. Some spirit, some ghost wants to bond with Faye? Heal the biosphere? Make Faye happy? She was fucking happy before you came along! What kind of bullshit is this?"

Faye's eyes shifted between Drake, drunk and angry, and Ariella, articulate, clear-headed and mature. Both were behaving in ways which were so not typical. Ariella now the adult, while Drake, seriously inebriated, and Faye, exhausted, nerves flayed to the bone, also a bit drunk, were the children.

"Language, Drake? No f word, if you please," Faye put her hands over her face. She just wanted to hide somewhere. How had this simple dinner turned into a tragic-comic bit of surreal theatre? Ariella, again and always, it was Ariella. My life is not my own, she thought.

"C'mon, damnit! Tell me what's goin' on." Drake slammed his hand down on the table, making the dishes and glasses jump and the unopened wine bottle topple on its side. Ariella held her left hand with the green stone ring toward Drake. She muttered something and there was a snap and a bright green spark. Drake fell back in his chair and his eyes closed.

"Drake, don't you think it's a great opportunity for Faye to be bonded to Verdant Sea?" Ariella said.

Drake's eyes fluttered, but didn't quite open. "Yeah, sure, why not. If it makes her happy." His body relaxed and slid down in his chair and his head jolled back. He had fallen asleep.

"What did you do to him? I know I told you to use the ring, but this is too much. And why did you bring up Verdant Sea?"

"Faye, I had to chill him out. He was getting cray-cray. You saw how angry he was. But, don't worry, when he wakes he'll be a sweet pussycat, I promise. And, didn't you plan to tell him anyway about Verdant Sea?"

Faye brought the yogurt dishes to the counter. She rinsed them and put them, along with the spoons, into the dishwasher. She'd run it tomorrow. It was only 9:20, but she was done. She opened the freezer to get more yogurt and felt the icy air condense on her face. It was way more peaceful with Drake mentally absent. But, how would he react if she told him about the Verdant Sea dream?

Faye turned and said to Ariella, who was again checking her

look in her hand mirror. "Just so you know, I'm not convinced Verdant Sea has a place in my future. You say he's going to make me happy, but Drake was right saying I was happy until last weekend. Or, at least, I thought I was happy." She got down a clean dish and spooned in a little yogurt and waved the container at Ariella.

"No, I'm good on the yogurt." Ariella tapped her spoon on the tabletop. "I think you're missing the big picture in how you conceive happiness. Sure, as an individual, you may think you're happy. But, you said yourself the world is pretty messed up, especially when it comes to humans ruining the environment. Can't you conceive of a happiness which would also include you helping making the world a better place for all life?"

Faye took a nibble of yogurt. Needs white wine, she thought. Why is this 10th grade student of mine able to lecture me so eloquently about happiness? "Yes, I believe making the world a better place would bring a different, larger kind of happiness and satisfaction. But, like most people, I can't see myself being an agent for that kind of widespread change. I don't know if I've got what it takes." Faye paused to take another bite. "You know, Ariella, sometimes you look and sound so adult, like you're much older. Even older than me."

Ariella's smile said she knew something Faye didn't. "When you get the whole picture, you're going to see how you can help the planet and be even more happy. It's all a matter of changing your perspective. And, it's progress you can see me as older. I was hoping you'd see that in me. Now, don't be frightened, we're going to try something." Ariella stood up.

"We? You mean you and I?"

"Not exactly. I want you to meet someone. C'mon, get up."

"Listen, I said I didn't want nature spirits tonight and I meant it."

"Fer sure, but this is different, nothing like the wildness at the beach." Ariella pulled at Faye's arm.

Faye resisted, then pushed herself upright. She was tired

and her will was weak. Plus, she wanted to trust and believe in her new young friend. Ariella took Faye by the shoulders and gazed into her eyes and there was again a shifting in the air along with the rising of a low hum. Faye watched in fascination as, despite the overdone makeup, Ariella's face took on strong angles, losing the roundness of youth and gaining wrinkles. Her green eyes, normally full of youthful sparkle, became muddy and flat and her body slumped and tipped slightly to the side. It was as if all surface traces of teenage girl were being erased.

"Ariella, what's going on? Where are you?"

The face which was Ariella and also not Ariella just shook its head and said in a deep, mature voice, "No worries, Faye. Ariella is safe and we're both here now. I'm just in front, you might say."

"Who . . . what *are* you?" Faye stammered.

"You can call me Epifania." The voice was low, melodic and resonant. "Suffice it to say I am like Verdant Sea in that I am a connection between the nature spirits, humans, and other mortal life forms. When the child you know as Ariella was born, I bonded with her. She has grown up with me as her teacher and guide."

"But where is Ariella now? What did you do to her?"

"Ariella has stepped aside and allowed me to emerge. We have practiced for just such a moment as this. Surely you've noticed how adult she sounds sometimes? Normally I only supply her with words, but this is a critical time for you and for us and I need to be fully here. Rest assured, Ariella is safe, watching us, and will completely return when I recede."

"This is ridiculous! And I don't like it. I need to talk to Ariella now, so return her or step aside or whatever it is you need to do."

At first it seemed as if nothing was going to happen, but then Epifania/Ariella let go of Faye's shoulders and the face, eyes and body again wavered and changed. Then Ariella was back. Her green eyes were intense, but not with humor.

"Faye! What are you doing? I told you I wanted to try something and yet you messed with it. Eppy and I worked on the switch for years and tonight was our first ever attempt to do it for a regular person. It was going great and I'm fine. For me, it's no biggee, like watching a movie. So, can we get on with it?"

Faye tried project the her teacher's confidence, but couldn't make it happen. She slumped into her chair and glanced first at Ariella and then Drake. He was still out, but looked uncomfortable sleeping with his head propped against the chair back.

"Ariella, this is really too much. I'm overwhelmed and exhausted. Plus I've been dealing with my own personal issues, particularly with Drake." Drake stirred at the sound of his name. "He and I are both very tired. Remember, we're both just 'regular persons,' as you put it. We work all week as high school teachers and need to relax and take it easy on the weekends. I really, really need to get to bed. But, I'm not saying I don't want to try again with Epifania or whatever that was. I mean, I truly want to learn more about nature spirits and all, but we have to do it another time."

Expressions of frustration and stubbornness flitted across Ariella's face, but she nodded and sat down next to Faye. "Fer sure, I'm sorry things got crazy. If it was only up to me, there wouldn't be any nature spirit stuff this weekend. But, they've become pushy about getting you involved. It's hard for me to resist them." She learned forward to give Faye a quick hug. "Go ahead and take Drake to bed. I'll clean up here. But Eppy wants to know if we can we try again tomorrow?"

"Tomorrow, as they say, is another day. If I get my period I may not be up for much more than reading, eating frozen yogurt and sitting in the sun. Thanks for cleaning up. Oh, and remember to put aluminum foil over the lasagna before it goes in the fridge."

Faye roused Drake by rubbing his shoulders and giving him little kisses on his ears. His eyes opened and he glanced around like he didn't know where he was. After a moment, he got up, still a bit unsteady, and leaned on her as they shuffled toward the bedroom.

Just before they went through the kitchen door, Faye turned

and asked, "So is Epifania a woman or a man?" Faye didn't know why this was important, but it was. It was just too creepy to think a man took over Ariella's body.

Ariella laughed and came over to take Faye's free hand. "It works better if we're in physical contact."

Again there was a shimmering around Ariella and, perhaps quicker than last time, her face shifted and Epifania appeared. A quick glance at Drake told Faye know he wasn't freaking out, but was puzzled, his bleary eyes going first to Epifania/Ariella and then looking around the kitchen.

A small smile cracked Epifania's stern visage. "In nature spirit terms, I am neither man nor woman, but, in your terms, I am female, a true daughter of Mother Nature." Epifania/Ariella let go of Faye's hand and Drake jerked as features of the familiar teenage girl reappeared.

"Who the heck was that old woman?" Drake asked as he and Faye reached the bedroom.

"Uh . . . sort of a friend of Ariella's. It's complicated. I'll tell you more after a good night's sleep."

As they undressed for bed, Faye remembered they hadn't taken the pictures of Ariella and Drake in their new finery. Drake was sitting on the bed, bending over and struggling to untie his new pointy Italian shoes. He nearly fell over, so Faye went and helped. The photos will wait, Faye thought. She was getting comfortable under the covers when she recalled the present she had bought herself at the mall, the present which was actually for Drake. She contemplated him. He was still wearing the skintight green t-shirt, his curly black hair spilled over his pillow and his eyes were open, staring up at the ceiling. He was sexy, no doubt about it, and her lady parts warmed. She sighed, got out of the bed, grabbed the bag from the mall and headed for the door.

"Don't fall asleep just yet."

When she came back from the bathroom he looked asleep. "Drake? Are you awake? Want to see something?" He turned his head toward her and peeked from under his eyelashes. When he saw she was wearing a skimpy purple satin teddy with oodles of black lace, his eyes went wide. Then he sat up and gave a lewd grin.

"Wow," he said as she walked provocatively toward the bed and did a little spin. "Wow, wow, wow."

She got back in bed and, after some kissing, he scooched over and she felt his hardness press against her thigh. She winced a little when he put his hand on her breast and squeezed, but it still felt good. He had taken off the tight jeans. She turned on her side and kissed him.

"I thought you were too tired and drunk for this."

"I'm never anything but ready for this." He began kissing her with more intensity, his tongue teasing her lips. "You know I'm really not a Hip Dude, right?"

"Uh huh, but you're my Lovely Lover."

The sex was slow and tender and neither wanted or tried for an orgasm. When he rolled off, Faye felt like crying. Damn period, she thought.

"I love you, Faye Bloomberg."

"And I love you, Drake Fixit Man."

They were both asleep in less than a minute. Faye woke once in the night and went to the bathroom to pee and take two aspirin to ward off a hangover. Leaf stayed away and she didn't dream at all.

Chapter Thirty Five

Sunday morning, after almost nine hours of sleep, Faye left the bed at 7:00 AM, free of hangover and feeling refreshed. At Drake's muttered request, she brought him some aspirin and water and closed the curtains.

"I'll be up soon, babe," he croaked.

"Take your time. I may need a Fixit Man in a bit."

He rolled over and looked at her with heavy lidded eyes. "You mean all my labor last night didn't get it working?"

"Oh, it's working fine. Just might need a few tweaks to make it truly hum."

"No rest for the wicked. Or is it the weary?" Drake flopped back on the pillow.

Faye dressed quickly in yoga pants, no bra, and a clingy, v-neck t-shirt that showed a discreet bit of cleavage. She had plans to get Drake back to bed after his breakfast. She went to the kitchen and took eggs, bread, and butter from the refrigerator. Ariella walked in rubbing her eyes and gulped down the organic apple juice Faye handed her. The teenager was wearing only flip-flops and a grey, oversize t-shirt bearing the logo of a professional football team. Ariella's messy hair partly obscured her face and also tumbled down her back. Faye hoped she was wearing underwear. The cats, Leaf included, milled around her feet.

"Where did you get that shirt? And you're still wearing the makeup from last night!"

"So? My mom still has makeup on the next morning when she has a guy stay overnight." Ariella went to the refrigerator for more juice. "The shirt belonged to one of Mom's many boyfriends, I think he played football. They tend to leave stuff behind when she kicks them out."

"Listen, always wash your face clean before you go to bed and put on moisturizer. If your pores get clogged, you could develop pimples."

"I don't get pimples. What about the pix with Mr. D?"

"You never get pimples? What about when you get your period?"

"Nope, never. You wanna know why? Cuz I'm in tune with the nature spirits. They've enhanced my biologics."

"Your biologics? Seriously?"

"Yup. You'll see when it happens to you. Now what about the pix?"

Faye reluctantly agreed the photos could be taken once Drake woke up. As she began making breakfast her mind pondered Ariella's claim of being enhanced. More stuff she needed to ask more about. They fed the cats, ate eggs and toast, and then spent a silly, happy 45 minutes in Ariella's bedroom, playing with makeup and getting Ariella dressed again in her new clothes. Faye even let Ariella put some lip gloss and eye shadow on her and, despite misgivings, Faye had to agree she looked "gnarly."

Faye's heard the shower running and knew Drake was up. She wanted to quiz Ariella about Epifania and other nature spirit subjects, but Ariella surprised her by insisting they meditate first. Out on the deck, Faye suggested a little yoga first and demonstrated a few poses, such as Salutation to the Sun and The Plow, and then smiled when Ariella slipped into them as easily as a yoga instructor.

The morning was cool, but the sun was bright and the sky was blue. It promised to be a rare glorious spring day on Cape Cod. Faye's head felt clear and clean, and life seemed simple. She was confident things would somehow work out – with Drake, with Ariella and yes, even with the nature spirits. She settled herself on her cushion and, after a quick check to see if Ariella had the right posture, began watching her own breathing. She also did a quick body scan, noting her left shoulder was sore, probably from being squished against the car door during their mad escape from the Swarm. Aside from that, she was good, both physically and mentally. Faye knew her period was still going to happen, but, for now, it was like thunder on the distant horizon.

Surprising how okay I am after all the excitement. All the stress and plain old craziness now seems to have been both needed and believable. It's been cray cray, as Ariella would say, but isn't it what I've been craving? Rhoda said I needed change and I'm certainly getting it. She shook her head and conceded a small smile. So cray cray. Faye entertained the thought that everything which had happened in the past nine days was only a dream. Or was her life before Ariella a dream?

"Faye!" The authoritative voice came from behind her. She turned and what she saw was both extraordinary and funny. Epifania's stern face was again perched atop Ariella's young body, which was sitting, legs crossed, hands clasped in her lap. Belatedly, Faye realized Ariella was wearing the least likely clothing for meditation - the tight pencil skirt, pushed high up on her thighs, was too confining, and the knees of her black pantyhose would surely catch on the rough wood of the deck. With Epifania's face crowning it all, the image was incongruous, like a Frankenstein experiment gone awry.

"What?" Faye struggled to not erupt in laughter. How could this be real? And, if it was, it was still funny!

"Stay with your breath!" Epifania/Ariella thundered.

That did it. Faye couldn't hold it in. She starting snickering, pressing her lips together, then opened her mouth and began laughing full on, her rowdy laughs driving back her fear and confusion. She rolled off her cushion and onto her back, holding her sides. The Epifania face pinched with effort as it struggled to maintain control, but then, with a glare of frustration, it shimmered out and Ariella popped back in, already laughing.

"That was ridonkulous!" Ariella said, and began tickling one of the squirrels curled in her lap. The squirrel squeaked and squirmed and, when it got free, started running circles around Ariella. The other animals shrank back at first, but then started chasing after the squirrel, making a mad, woodland version of Ring Around the Rosie. This only made Faye and Ariella laugh more.

"Eppy is 'quite irritated,' as she puts it, with you," Ariella said between giggles. "She feels you should understand why there is, all of a sudden, so much interest in you, why you're getting notes from Moira, why Verdant Sea is visiting you in your dreams, and why the Swarm was attracted to you. One of the reasons the nature spirits want to recruit you is because of your willingness to see through the illusions of your desires, aversions and non-stop thoughts and allow your true nature to arise and expand into Nature, with a capital N." Ariella spewed all this out and grinned when she was done. The animals stopped circling and settled down, pushing at each other for space in the girl's lap.

Faye wiped tears from her eyes. "She actually said all that?"

"Yup. I'm good at repeating what she dictates, almost as quick as she says it. Oops, wait a min, there's more."

Ariella's face went blank and Faye thought Epifania was going to re-emerge, but instead Ariella again began speaking quickly.

"Epifania says she studied Eastern Religions when she was incarnate, which means here in human physical form. So she understands what meditation is all about. She wants to talk about all that with you and about your becoming an integral part of the nature spirit cadre. She thinks when you see how ready and perfect you are to be part of the movement you'll agree and go along with everything. She wants to be your friend."

"Integral part of the nature spirit cadre? You've got to be kidding." This second-hand means of conversing with Epifania, whoever or whatever that really was, was creepy. It was almost like Ariella was shifting back and forth between her normal self and her Epifania self, like she had two personalities. *Wait a minute. Could that be it? Might Ariella be suffering Multiple Personality Disorder? Or Epifania's an imaginary friend whose personality she can assume at will?*

"Nope. No joke. She says she's sorry she interrupted our meditation, but she's asking again if she can talk to you today."

"Let's wait and see. We both have plans for today. And my

period is definitely looming. So, tell Eppy maybe, okay?"

After meditation, Ariella came in from the deck and grabbed some food to take out for her animal and insect friends while Faye brewed herself a cup of Calista's energizing tea. She knew it wouldn't forestall her period, but it might make the cramps and fatigue easier. And it might help her think more clearly about all the new developments in her life.

Faye had awoken with her rational, normal self restored and all that had happened felt like it was someone else's experience. But, the Epifania phenomenon, happening right in her house, was more real and immediate. Was it all just an elaborate charade produced by Ariella, who had already proved herself an accomplished actor and choreographer? If so, what was Ariella's motivation? And was her mom, Calista, supposedly a professional actor, involved? Faye entertained the possibility Ariella was innocent of guile. Perhaps she was just a tool in her mother's manipulations. And where did the old woman named Moira fit in? There was so much Faye didn't know.

Faye stared at the kitchen ceiling. Am I in some sort of enchantment? I mean, is it possible Ariella mesmerized me with her waving hands Friday night on the beach when I was stoned? What else could be faked or be a believable illusion? I hope not the dreams I had in the car. And the Swarm appeared when I was alone in the woods. Leaf's reaction certainly seemed authentic. But Ariella showed up at just the right time to save me.

Faye brought her laptop to the kitchen and Googled "involuntary hypnosis" and found evidence it might be possible to hypnotize someone without them knowing. She tapped her front teeth with her fingernail. *I've been drinking Calista's tea practically every day without being completely sure how it could change my perceptions. Real problem is I've charged ahead without getting all the facts. In addition, my PMS has been unusually intense, which could make me more susceptible to illusion.*

"Whatcha doing?" Ariella came in from the deck, trailed by the cats. The other animals were drifting off into the trees and woods

"Oh, just some internet research." Faye put her hand on the laptop lid and started to close it, but stopped. Perhaps the best strategy was to let Ariella know she had doubts and questions, to be honest and confront her directly. They were friends weren't they? And friends could be open with each other.

"About what? Nature spirits, dreams and visions?" Ariella's eyes held a challenge.

"Yes, more or less. You know there are still tons of questions I want to ask and we haven't had a chance to sit down to just talk about all the stuff you've brought into my life." With a miaow, Leaf jumped up into Faye's lap. "Including wonderful magic cats." She stroked Leaf's silky head and watched Ariella's face, trying to find some reassurance there.

"Okay, let's talk. Right now," Ariella said, dropping into the kitchen chair opposite and making room for Midnight in her lap. "Ask away, Ms Faye."

"I've got the list of questions I typed up, but I think the most immediate ones are about Epifania."

"Okee, I'll let her answer."

"No! I want to talk to you, to Ariella."

"What do you mean? She can answer better than I can."

"I'm sure she can, but I'd like this first part to just be you and I, okay?"

Ariella rubbed at a spot on the table top and examined her fingertips. "Fer sure. Whatever."

"Let me try a different approach. How real is Epifania to you?"

"Very real! Why are you even asking that? She's been with me since I was small. I hear from her almost every day." Ariella waved her hands in agitation, then stopped and stared at Faye like she was a stranger. "You don't think Epifania's real? How can you say that? You saw her! Don't you believe me?"

"Slow down, I mean, chill. I didn't say I didn't believe she was real. I'm just not sure. I need to know how she fits in your life. And how she came into your life." Faye took a deep breath and added in a rush, "I mean I was just thinking maybe you made Epifania up when you were small and didn't have a lot of friends your age. And now she fits into this whole nature spirit thing and helps you make sense of all that."

"I absolutely didn't make her up. She came to me because Mom wanted me to grow up with nature spirits and the Viridis Glas Luminasti and 'all that,' as you put it, as normal parts of my life. Mom set the whole training thing up and keeps me on track with it. And Eppy has helped me over and over, especially when my mom's been gone."

"And that's exactly why I'm suggesting Eppy isn't as real as you believe. If you were alone a lot as a kid it would be very natural for you to make up friends with whom to play and talk. I think almost every kid has imagined a special friend. But, most grow out of them as they get older."

Ariella stood up quickly, dumping Midnight onto the floor, and leaned toward Faye over the table, her face angry and her eyes blazing. "Listen, Faye, my mom was the one who introduced me to Epifania. She was the one who got me into this whole stupid nature spirit thing in the first place. And it's Mom and Eppy who are grooming me for an important future role in healing the growing rift between humanity and the rest of this planet's biosphere. Eppy is real, not real like you and I, but she's an actual being. And you would know that if you'd only let her talk with you."

Faye suspected Epifania was again feeding words to Ariella, who, she knew, would be unlikely to mention the "planet's biosphere." Faye decided to change tack.

"Okay then. I'll agree to talk with Epifania, but later. And, as your friend, I'm going to be honest and let you, and her, know my skepticism is pretty strong."

"Fine, but you'll see. Just wait." Ariella sat down and crossed her arms across her chest. "What else do you want to ask about?"

Faye checked the time. It was 9:30. Drake must have had

gone back to bed after his shower. Did that mean she should remind of his tennis match with Shandra, whenever that was? Then again, wasn't that his responsibility? Besides, he needed his rest after such a tough night. And perhaps he actually didn't want to play tennis, maybe he wanted to stay in bed all day and be her sex slave.

"Ha!" she said and Ariella started. Faye got up and began to pour herself another cup of Calista's herbal tea. Then she stopped and instead got a glass of apple juice.

"Okay, let's start with the cats. I know I've never seen any like them. How did they get that way? Did you train them?"

"When I was small, the cats just started coming to me. Eppy said it was because my energy had been 'tuned' by my association with nature spirits. She says most animals recognize humans as beings to be fearful of, but also capable of providing food and shelter. And, though their sense of concepts like evolution is primitive at best, animals also recognize humans are the current end-product of evolutionary life. So, when someone like me comes along, someone who they see as radiating an energy they can understand, animals, and insects, are drawn in, mostly out of curiosity."

"Did Eppy just tell you what to say?"

Ariella squirmed in her seat, picked up Midnight, rubbed her finger again over the spot on the table. "Yup."

"Is it possible for me to talk to you without having Eppy running your mouth?"

Ariella looked out to the deck where three squirrels were sunning themselves. Faye wondered how Yellowfoot, the Squirrel of the Future, was doing. She hadn't noticed him among the creatures gathered round Ariella that morning and she made a mental note to check her peanut supply.

Ariella patted Faye's hand. "I'll try, though Eppy is very anxious."

"Good enough. So, tell me about the cats."

"Yup. At first they were my playmates, I guess, because you're right about me not having many kids my age to hang with back then. So, I started making little games the cats and I could play. And I know lots of people think cats are difficult to train, but I was able to get them to understand what I wanted. Eventually, I understood them, too."

"So, they talk to you?"

"Sorta, but not like you and I talk. They talk more in attitudes and images. Like when Leaf wanted me to know he was hot for you he sent me an image of him mating with you." Ariella laughed. "It was pretty funny. You were on your hands and knees and he —"

"Okay, I get the picture. I'm sure it was quite amusing." As if he understood, Leaf chose that moment to stand on his hind legs and put his front legs around Faye's neck and give her lips a thorough licking. Even as she gently pushed him back down into her lap, Faye felt an odd pleasure. "But, can they teleport or whatever? I mean, after I visited the cottage last Sunday it seemed cats were showing up everywhere around here, sometimes even inside my house."

"Oh, that was me and my mom! What happened is Moira came over to the cottage right after you left last Sunday and said you had great potential. That's what she said, Eppy isn't telling me to say that. So, Moira told us to do everything possible to get you interested. And that the cats would be a good introduction. So, we wound up driving cats to and from your house for a couple of days. We'd drop them nearby and I told them where to find you. And then we'd come back and pick them up. It was pretty cray cray, for real."

"Okay, I believe you. But what about the cats I almost surprised inside your bedroom? I heard them jump off something and there was a warm spot on the bed. I searched the room. Did they teleport out somehow?"

Ariella snickered. "No, not really, though they do spend time in other realities. That's why they sleep all the time, so their spirits are free to roam about. But, no, they hid under the computer desk and you didn't check there. They can squeeze into really small spaces. And then they snuck out when you were in the bathroom. Apparently, you had left the slider a little open?"

Faye nodded. "Hmmm, I did run back into the house from the backyard and I could've left the slider open. The whole cat appearance, cat disappearance thing was the first sign I had something unusual was coming my way." In her mind she pictured her list of questions. "Okay, then, are you up for one which might be a little embarrassing?"

"For sure. It takes a lot for me to get embarrassed."

"Well, you masturbated on the way home from school on Friday afternoon. What was that all about?"

Ariella glared at Faye like she had spit in her face. "You're joking, right? That is such a mondo bizarre question. Why did I masturbate? Really?"

"I'm sorry. I hoped it wouldn't get you upset, but —"

"I'm not, not, not upset!" Ariella threw her hands up and stamped her foot. "Why don't you get it about me? You're supposed to understand me by now."

"Hold on! I'm not your mother, I'm your new friend so, no, I don't entirely understand you. Yet. And, more importantly, I'm your school teacher. Let's not forget that, okay? I certainly understand you better than I did a week ago, but, considering how complex your life can be, I know there's so much more for me to comprehend." *could come out to feel*

Faye reached across and took one of Ariella's hands, which was, she was surprised to note, trembling. The girl was looking down, her heavy red-gold hair falling forward and obscuring her face. "Listen, we don't need to talk about . . . what you did in the car. I was just curious, that's all."

Ariella was silent. Her head stayed bowed. Than her hand flipped over and gripped Faye's.

"Okay, okay. My mom . . . I know . . . I know she's weird

from a conventional POV. That's 'point of view' BTW. And that's 'by the way.' And she gets away with being weird in the so-called real world because she's an actress and model. People don't challenge her on stuff like masturbating whenever she feels like it. I've watched her do it lots of times. And I admire her and want to be like her in that way. But, I also just want to be a normal prep, y'know? Just goin' to high school and hangin' with my posse and doing Facebook and texting and gossiping and all that junk. So, I need to know when I go over that invisible line between being quirky, but cool, and just plain psycho. Okay?"

"That's fine. No problemo, as you would say."

"So, yes, I buttered the biscuit in the car because it had been a spastic, stupid day at school and I was tense and frustrated and just wanted to feel good, y'know? You were wearing the scallop necklace, so I figured we were tuned. And, I never imagined you'ld even think twice about it."

Faye contemplated Ariella, who lifted her head and stared back. The girl's eyes were a muddy green and she seemed simultaneously defiant and anxious.

"What are you two talking about? Buttering biscuits? Whassup wit dat? As my students always say."

Drake leaned against the doorframe. His black curls were tousled and damp from his shower. And he was wearing the skintight, green t-shirt with a pair of baggy tennis shorts. His bare legs and feet were tanned and lean. He's so damned sexy, Faye thought. She started to stand to give him a love hug, but Ariella jumped up and ran to Drake and clamped onto him like a limpet.

"Drake! You're so smexy!" she said and jumped to give him a quick peck on the lips, then wrapped her arms around him again.

Chapter Thirty Six

"Smexy? What does that mean?" The flush on Drake's face showed through his tan. Faye rose from her chair, stilled for an instant, and then sat down. What was Ariella doing now? Was this more inappropriate behaviour? Drake gently took Ariella by the upper arms and pushed her back a step.

"It means smart and sexy, silly!" Ariella wrapped her arms around Drake. She turned her head toward Faye and said, "He reminds me of my dad."

Faye had one of those infrequent clear insights into human behaviour. Of course! Ariella has been without a dad for years. And perhaps it wasn't an issue when she was living with her mom out in the woods. But now, going to public school for the first time, mingling with kids her own age, listening to them talk about their families, Ariella must be feeling the lack of an at-home dad like never before. Her mother's habit of taking frequent lovers can't help.

Over Ariella's golden-red head Drake's expression asked a question. "Ariella, Drake needs to get some breakfast. And then we'll see about taking pictures for Facebook," Faye said.

Ariella pulled away from Drake and began doing her jumping up and down in place. "Yippee! Yippee! Can't wait!" She poked Drake in the chest. "You're going to change into your Hip Dude duds, right?"

"Absolutely." Drake sidled away from Ariella and came stand near Faye.

Ariella smiled at the two adults. "You guys want some alone time, right?"

How can she go from being teenage inappropriate to adult-needs sensitive? Was Epifania again in play?

"Yes, that would be nice. Thanks."

"Okee, call me when you're ready." Ariella ran out the kitchen door and headed for her bedroom.

As Drake settled at the kitchen table, Faye asked, "Want me

to make you some eggs? I've got some organic, free range if you want. And there's organic wheat bread to toast and spread with organic butter."

"Nah, that's okay. Don't go to any trouble. Some of your granola would be great."

Faye brought the granola container and milk to the table and asked, "What time's tennis?"

"One."

"Oh, great, you've got oodles of time. You could even stay for lunch." Faye figured she could put off the visit to the hut with Wanda.

"Uh, I've got a bunch of American History essays to read and grade, plus two quizzes to prepare."

"You could do them later. Or, you know, this is a long weekend, you could do it tomorrow."

Drake gave Faye a look she could read like a children's primer, but she had to say something. "My period hasn't started yet, just in case you're wondering."

Drake took a big spoonful of granola and munched noisily. When he spoke it was in a whisper. "Listen Faye, I kept my promise and came over for dinner with you and Ariella, but I think I need to stay away while Ms Cardona is your houseguest." He glanced toward the kitchen door. "The whole experience last night was very unsettling and this morning hasn't improved things, so my original attitude hasn't changed. In fact, my attitude is probably worse. That girl and her wacky world are way more than I think you should be involved in. And, the longer I stay, the more upset I get."

"But —"

"Not now. We can talk more privately in your bedroom when I change clothes. But, I'm leaving after the pictures are taken, so let's not argue about it, okay?"

Faye felt tears tingle at the corners of her eyes. To cover, she got up and poured him a glass of apple juice and some for herself. "Fuck you!" she said under her breath with her back to him. Then clapped her hand over her mouth.

"What? What did you say?"

She pulled her hand down and turned to him, then set the apple juice on the table. "I said 'good luck to you'."

His right eyebrow went up. "Right."

Faye sipped at her juice and Drake crunched his granola.

"By the way, I meant to ask you what happened to your car. It sure is all banged up."

Faye gave him an abbreviated version of what happened in the woods after she and Ariella left the cottage yesterday. Drake stopped chewing as she described the Swarm and being chased down the dirt road with Ariella driving.

"I didn't want her to drive, honestly, but I was sort of out of it. She did a pretty good job, all things considered."

"Faye." Drake's voice was low and almost menacing. "This has to stop. Surely you see that. Not only is it completely unbelievable, it also sounds like you're actually putting yourself in danger to help this weirdo."

Faye went to the kitchen door and looked down the hallway. Ariella's door was closed and she could hear the bass thump of some hip-hop. She came back and put her hands on Drake's shoulders, gently turning him so she could give him a kiss. He tasted of milk, brown sugar and toasted oats.

"I'm fine, really, it may sound dangerous, but I don't think it is. I did some research this morning and I think I'm getting a handle on what's going on in her teenage head. She's totally into fantasy, much, much more than I was at her age. She has some real issues around her parents. And, I think she might have an imaginary friend. But I still believe I can help her."

"So now you're a psychologist and you're diagnosing her? I thought you said it wasn't a mental thing when we discussed taking Ariella's problem to the guidance counselor. What you're doing simply isn't right, both from a personal point of view and from a professional point of view."

"Trust me, if I thought Ariella needed to see a counselor, I would back out of everything. But, as of this moment, what I see is a very intelligent and talented young woman with some extraordinary abilities, who is struggling to find her way at a difficult time of life of her life. And she's asked for my help. Yes, her situation is different than what I usually encounter at school, but, because of her fascination with fantasy, which I share, I think I relate more to Ariella than a guidance counselor could. Plus, it gives me a chance to also grow and change." Faye had five seconds to be proud of her little speech before Drake stood up and put his hands on Faye's shoulders.

"I'm going to say it one more time. I think you're wrong all the way around. I think this is a bad situation and I think you're fooling yourself about what's going on with Ariella. And, most importantly, I think you're fooling yourself about how you're changing. The only opportunity I see is the one where you ruin your life." He kissed her on the forehead. "You know I wouldn't be saying this if I didn't love you, right?"

Faye nodded and, much like Ariella had earlier, wrapped herself around him and held him tight. He smelled so good, his arms around her felt so right, she wanted to stay like that forever. She rubbed her face on his chest. It was all too complicated. *I want to be with Drake and make our time together wonderful. Nothing more.*

In her bedroom with the door closed, Faye sat on the bed and watched while Drake changed into his Hip Dude clothes. Her legs were crossed at the knee and the top leg was swinging wildly, while her hands in her lap kept shifting positions around and over each other. She so didn't want him to leave. When he took off his tennis shorts and bent over to pick up his skinny jeans, she could see the outline of his tight butt through his underwear. It was too much. She leapt to her feet and came up behind him, pressed herself against his lean muscles and reached around to slip her hand in the front slit of his jockey shorts. She felt him respond right away and he gave a little groan.

"Ya gotta admit, Mr. Fix It, the sex has been pretty extraordinary since Ariella's been around. Sure you don't want to stay a bit longer?"

Without turning around, Drake said, "Yes ma'am, the sex has been wonderful. Yes, ma'am, I could stay a bit longer."

He groaned again as her hand got more traction on him. With her other hand she moved him toward the bed. He stumbled in that direction, then stopped, snatched her hand out of his underwear and turned to face her.

"Are you implying our great sex has something to do with Ariella coming into your life?"

"Well, yes, I —"

Drake stepped away. "That's just madness. I know you were excited after meeting Ariella and her mom, who, by the way, sounds pretty self-centered and on the verge of abandoning her child, but the sex has been all about you and I. It had nothing to do with the Punkhorn Pair. Why would you even want to believe that?"

As he spoke, Drake pulled on his jeans and Faye gave a little sigh. She watched as he searched for and found his shoes and put them on without socks.

"Did you see where I put those stupid sunglasses? I've got to get going."

"Did you leave them in the car? I'll get them for you if you want."

"Never mind, didn't we say the photos weren't going to show my face?"

Faye nodded. "Hey, I've got an idea! How would you feel about me coming to watch you play tennis? I haven't done that in a long time. It would be fun."

Drake put on his regular gold wire-rimmed glasses and blinked at Faye as if trying to bring her into focus. "Not a good idea."

"Why? Because of Ariella? She doesn't need to come along. She'll be fine here by herself. She's got homework to do and besides, she'll be busy chatting with her new internet friends. And I plan to be home by four o'clock, before she goes for her motorcycle ride."

Drake started putting his normal clothes into his duffel. "I don't think so."

Tears again threatened and Faye busied herself making up the bed.

"You don't have any school work to do before tennis, do you?"

He stood there, so beautiful and sad, his duffel in his hand. She had a fantasy flash he was some explorer about to embark upon an adventure in an exotic locale, armed only with his good looks and his tennis racquet.

"Faye —"

"Just tell me, okay?"

"Listen, it's nothing. I didn't want to say anything because I knew you'd get upset."

"What the fuck are you trying to say?" Faye again covered her mouth with her hand.

He began to laugh and she started to sniffle. He took her in his arms and stroked her hair.

"Hey, it's okay, really. I'm just meeting Shandra at noon for a light lunch before tennis. She wants my advice on her ex-boyfriend. She says it's 'très cool' to have an older man to talk to, that I possess unique insights into male behavioral patterns."

Faye snuggled into Drake and gave a little laugh. "She actually said 'unique insights into male behavioral patterns'?"

"Yup, like I said, no big deal. Shandra is way into relationship theory and believes those lists of ten things you should do or not do."

"So, you're acting as a psychologist and a relationship counselor now? Aren't both roles outside your legitimate, licensed role as a teacher of Social Studies?" Faye said with a smile.

"Yes, it is. You and I, we're like total rule breaking, outlaw, badass high school teachers."

"Hey! I've got another great idea."

"Uh oh, what now? Rob a bank?"

"Ha! Ariella will be gone on her motorcycle ride for at least a couple of hours, so why don't you come back over then?" She pulled his head down and gave him a kiss full of promise. "We could conduct some experiments on whether our hot sex is due to Ariella."

"Okay, whatever. Call me when the coast is clear."

The photo shoot with Ariella was predictably unsettling, though, once again, Faye couldn't deny the girl was a natural at posing. She moved around with the grace and assurance of someone much older. But, what was disturbing was the confidence and daring Ariella exhibited around Drake. One minute she was hanging off his shoulder, staring adoringly up at him, and Faye had to tell him to tilt his head back to hide his face because he kept watching Ariella as one would at an unpredictable, dangerous animal. For another shot, Ariella hugged him with full frontal contact, smiling back over her shoulder, her expression telling the camera, "He's mine."

Drake was acting bored, but it was obvious to Faye he was getting more and more agitated. At one point, after Ariella had moved his hand to her stomach, just beneath her breasts, he leaned down and stage-whispered to her. "You know you're beautiful, and we both know you're smart, so what are you trying to prove? Why are you trying to convince your schoolmates you're just as tawdry as they are?"

Ariella glared at Drake as if he were a store dummy who had started talking. Then she gave an obvious fake laugh, tossed her hair and took his arm, swinging around so they both faced Faye. Without breaking eye contact with the camera, Ariella reached across and pulled Drake's head down so his face was buried in her hair. Faye grimaced. In a way, this was her fault. Time and time again this weekend had been hijacked by Ariella and the whirlwind that was her life. Why did Faye think this photo session would be any different? She sighed and took the picture. But, when Ariella crouched down alongside Drake and put one hand on his thigh near his crotch, something snapped in Faye.

"No, we're not taking that photo. Stand up. I believe we're done."

Ariella smiled her inscrutable winsome smile, straightened, and stood on tiptoe to give Drake a kiss on the lips. "Was that fun for you, Drakee darling?"

Drake pushed Ariella away. "It was interesting, but I wouldn't call it fun."

Ariella pouted. "You didn't like it?"

"It's not a question of liking it. It's a question of not understanding why you're doing this. And, if there is some justification, then it's a question of you acknowledging boundaries. I think you need to learn how far is too much, especially if you plan on 'managing men,' as you said last night. Making people, men or women, feel uncomfortable is rarely a good idea." He reached down to grab his duffel and turned toward the door.

Ariella waved her hand with the green gemstone ring at him. "You'll learn." She pranced off into the hall leading to her bedroom. Without turning back, she added, "Faye, I don't think he's going to work out."

Drake stood rock still, his eyes open, but unfocused. He dropped the duffel and took a step to follow Ariella.

"Ariella! Get back here this minute! Undo your green ring spell or I'll ground you for the rest of your stay. And I'll tell your mother everything, especially about Facebook and Sorcha, and I won't ever allow you back at my house!" Faye was boiling.

Ariella came running, laughing like the delightful 15 year old she could be. "It was joke! Chill." She fluttered her ring hand at Drake and bounded over to hug Faye. "Can we put the photos on the laptop now?"

Drake shook his head, looked around, then slowly bent to again pick up his duffel. He blinked and blinked as he glanced from Faye to Ariella.

"First, apologize to Drake. Then say thank you to him for being such a good sport about the photos."

In her turn, Ariella became unfocused. I bet she's listening to Epifania, Faye thought.

"Fer sure! Uh . . . Drake?" Ariella began, "I'm sorry if I was . . . too forward and . . . uh . . . confusing." She gave a weak smile and did a little Namaste bow to Drake.

"And?" Faye asked.

"And what?"

This is like herding a butterfly! "The photos? How grateful you are to Drake for participating?"

"Oh, yeah. Drake, I am so grateful to you for participating in the photos." Ariella looked to Faye, who nodded.

"Okee! See ya! Dokee!" Ariella raced down the hallway.

Drake was studying the floor. His shoulders were slumped.

"Are you okay?

He raised his head. "I guess so, though I don't know what just happened. I think I must still be a little stoned. All of a sudden I was in this brightly colored fog and I could hear Ariella calling to me and I wanted to go to her, like she was my beacon. Or savior. Really important to me. It was strange and weird. What's that about?"

Faye thought. Should she obfuscate? Try to make a joke and laugh it off? Or was it time, now Drake had his own "Ariella Experience" for reference, to tell it to him straight? "Well, you see, Ariella has a magic ring which draws energy from the nature spirits? It's on her left hand mostly. And when she waves it at people they get disoriented and tend to focus on her."

"Ha! Good one! No, I did drink a lot of wine last night. And the pot didn't help. Hope I can still play tennis."

"You did drink a lot, so maybe you should skip tennis? Wouldn't want to faint on the court, now would you? Though I suppose Ms Phys Ed teacher is probably CPR certified and would be more than willing to give you mouth-to-mouth resuscitation."

"You crack me up, you know that?" Drake came over and gave her a warm one-arm hug. "Call me, okay? Or, wait, can you text me?"

"I thought you didn't do texts."

"Ah, I don't normally, but you know, . . .um . . . Shandra's been texting me, so I kinda learned it. No big deal. It's kinda fun."

"You and she text a lot?

"Oh, I wouldn't say a lot. Couple times a day, at most. She genuinely does need my help."

"Did you text her while you were here? Along with talking to her on the phone?"

Drake's face lost all traces of amusement. "Yes, I did, as a matter of fact. So what? I've already told you several times, it's no big deal." He eyed her and she looked away. "Unless, of course, you want to make it a big deal."

Faye shook her head and collapsed backward onto the couch. Her left eyelid began to twitch. She picked up a book from the side table, opened it, and gave him a little wave. "See you later. Play well. Don't faint."

When the door closed behind Drake, Faye put down the book and gave in to the tears. She didn't get hysterical, just sort of let them slide down her face. When they stopped, she blew her nose and wiped her cheeks. She knew her period was almost here and she'd be compelled to tell Drake and then he wouldn't want to come over. Wait a minute. He was texting now? And, in fact, he'd sent her a text just last night. Something about Shandra. Faye ran to her bedroom, grabbed her phone and flicked through her text messages.

Her breathing sped up as she read: "*i love u, really do. but, u need 2 kno i played singles w shandra this evening. we didnt go out after w the group. she wanted 2 go somewhere else. Shes acting like shes attracted to me. we didnt do anything but im confused. just wanted u 2 kno. luv"*

That bloody jerk! Shandra just wants his advice? Right. What kind of fool does her think I am? Faye started to throw the phone across the room, but thought better of it and stopped her arm in mid-throw. However, that didn't keep the phone from sliding out of her hand and falling onto a small area rug near the bed. She stared at it, hoping it was broken and, if not, thinking how she would love to jump up and down on it. Instead, she lay back on the bed, turned on her side and brought her knees up, her hands held tight between her thighs. The center of her chest ached, as if something vital had been ripped out.

Her phone rang and she didn't move, just closed her eyes. It was probably her mother with more advice, which she didn't need right now. But, it might be Drake. Maybe he changed his mind about tennis. She rolled off the bed and kneeled down to check the phone's display, noting it was almost noon. It was Wanda. Faye had completely forgotten about their plan to go to the hut.

"Hello, Wanda. I'm sorry, but I'm not feeling well and I can't go to the hut. Hope that's okay and I didn't screw up your day. Can we do it tomorrow?" Faye couldn't stop a whimper from escaping when she stopped talking.

"Babe! What's wrong? Who do you want me to get angry at and beat the shit out of, snarky little Ariella or Mr. Wonderful, aka Drake the Snake?" Faye felt a giggle rise through her sorrows. Wanda always knew what was going on with her.

"Neither and both, if you know what I mean. This has been the weirdest weekend of my life. I could write a book about this weekend, it's been so complicated, and up and down, and just plain wild. But, the biggest reason I don't want to go to the hut is Madame Sangre is arriving any minute." Back when they were teenagers they had taken to calling getting their period 'a visit from Madame Sangre' and thought themselves quite sophisticated for doing so.

"Ick, the dreaded Ms Sangre. Or, as your beloved Brits might say, the bloody witch." Wanda chuckled and Faye gave a little bark of amusement. Wanda was the best.

"Well, I guess the good news is you're not pregnant, right?"

At that, Faye felt the fragile bottom drop out again and she began sniveling into the phone.

"No . . . no . . . I'm not pregnant . . . and . . . but I love Drake and I want . . . I want . . . oh, fuck, I don't know what I want." She fell carelessly back and banged her head against the leg of the bedside table. She began crying in earnest.

"Oh, honey, I'm so sorry. I forgot you now want a baby. Please forgive me. Shall I come over and rub your back and say nonsense stuff to make you feel better? Or, if that doesn't work, I've got a bottle of vodka on ice which will freeze your sorrows in their tracks and also make you numb. Whattya say?"

Faye sniffed and hiccupped. "That sounds great, really it does. But, as you know, my houseguest is a young, impressionable teenager and I wouldn't want her to get the wrong idea about her English teacher."

"That girl got the wrong idea a long, long time ago. Don't let her facade fool you."

"Mmmm, you may be right, but I don't want to take a chance on another scene. So, I'm going to play it safe. Can we go to the hut tomorrow?"

"Yeah, sure, the kids will be fine and I think Brian has plans to rebuild an engine or something."

They chatted for a bit about Wanda's children and husband and Faye gave a short synopsis of Saturday night - how Drake had gotten drunk and stoned, how Ariella had given a sultry performance as a runway model wannabee and how she had pushed boundaries in the photo shoot.

"I told you she was trouble. And I don't know why we should be worried about getting snockered on vodka in front of her. But, let's cut to the chase. How was the sex with Drake the Magician?"

Wanda was the best tonic ever. "The sex was . . ." She realized she didn't know how to describe last night's wild coupling. "It was magnificent!"

"I knew it! I could feel the disturbance in the force. And I knew it was a good disturbance."

"Yeah, it was good. Very, very, very good." They said goodbye after promising to talk in the morning.

Faye got up from the floor and sat on the bed. After a minute of letting her thoughts swirl, she decided to meditate again. But this time she would stay in her room, where she was less likely to be disturbed. Even as she felt the first twinge of cramping, even as she felt the dread at Drake's predictable reaction, she understood she wasn't ready to give up on her dreams, even if she wasn't exactly sure what she wanted. See closed the bedroom door, positioned her meditation cushion so she would be facing the wall beside the bed, sat down, and crossed her legs.

Chapter Thirty Seven

Faye decided to sit until she got tired or her cramps became impossible. Or Ariella inserted herself again. At first she couldn't get comfortable on the cushion. Between her thoughts jumping about like monkeys in the jungle canopy and the mounting physical symptoms of her period, she kept twitching and shifting position. She deepened her breathing and concentrated on identifying what she really needed. Examining her life, both past and present, she looked for what had made her happy and what wasn't in her life now. Then it was certain, as certain as a sunrise. Real true love. She needed love, unconditional, constant love. And she wanted to give unconditional love. But from and to whom? A baby? Drake? Ariella?

Faye felt sure such all-encompassing love and commitment wasn't possible in her relationship with Drake? They said "I love you" a lot, but it had become more a habit than real declaration. Their stability as a couple was based upon certain mutually understood conditions, but primarily that the relationship remain uncomplicated. She tried to imagine continuing with Drake, which meant giving her dream of having a child, for a child would be the ultimate complication. She pictured herself sitting on the couch with Drake watching tennis, year after year, smiling and trying to please him, feeling frustrated, but unwilling to leave the safety of their relationship. This image was followed by a cramp which made her moan.

She rocked back and forth on her cushion while rubbing her abdomen until the pain eased. What about a future without Drake, which meant giving up the great sex, the status of having a hot boyfriend and probably living alone? What would that be like? Who would she be without Drake? A spinsterish teacher with a cat? Imagining this future was very unsettling, though it didn't prompt a cramp. Could she do it? Strike out on her own at age 36?

As if in response to her question, she sensed movement, inside and around her. Suddenly, there came a deep wrenching from within combined with a high pitched, animalistic whine as if a piece of organic machinery was going out of true. She smelled something bitter and sour. Frightened, Faye tried to stand up, but felt dizzy and collapsed back down. She tried again, but her muscles wouldn't obey and she started to panic, feeling everything was going out of control. It was as if she was trapped in a tornado, getting whirled around, shedding bits and pieces, not knowing where she would land. Then she smelled lilacs and roses and remembered Verdant Sea. At once, the atmosphere calmed, ~~like~~ as if she'd found the eye of the tornado, and she knew for sure her biggest problem was her inability to give up the attachment to Drake. She had to let go, but just couldn't now, no matter how painful it was. She screamed in anger and frustration

"Faye? Faye! Are you okay?"

From somewhere near, Faye heard Ariella's voice. What had Drake said when he was in a fog and heard Ariella? That she was a beacon, that she seemed like his savior? Whatever, Faye was happy to hear the teenager calling her. A hand first touched, then gripped, her shoulder. Faye turned her head with difficulty, as if part of her was stuck in some other space or dimension. Ariella crouched beside her, concern writ plain upon her face.

"Hey," Faye smiled. "Glad you're here."

"Yuh, me too, I'm glad I'm here. But are you okay? You were screaming, like someone in a nightmare."

"I'm not surprised. My meditation was so intense I couldn't stop, though I think Verdant Sea helped me. Ouch!" She bent forward, her hands covering her lower abdomen.

"Surprise, surprise, my period has arrived," Faye said when the pain eased. She checked the bedside clock. It was 1:15, which meant Drake had just started playing tennis with Shandra. "Wonderful timing, I must say." She allowed Ariella to help her stand and then move her to the bed. She absently noted Ariella was dressed in white shorts and an off-white, simple tank top which nicely set off her tan. Her golden red hair was down and she was barefoot. Her scallop necklace gleamed.

"Hey, Faye, I don't know what you mean by timing, but please tell me you're okay? Do you want something to help your cramps? I've got the ingredients for a super tea." Faye gazed at the girl's anxious face and knew she *was* truly pleased Ariella was here. Right now, right here, she was glad there was someone who wanted to help her and be with her.

"Oh, don't worry, I'm okay. Just cramps, you know. But, yes, I would love some tea."

After Ariella left, Faye rolled onto her side into a fetal position. She felt so crampy she gave a little grunt. That felt better. So, she grunted again, louder. And that felt better yet. She switched from grunting to moaning, each time getting louder. She sat up and opened her mouth as wide as she could and screamed. OMG, that was so good.

Ariella came running and stopped in the doorway. She reminded Faye of a white candle with a red-gold flame. She really is a beacon. What a mess I must seem to her and what is she going to think of her English teacher now? I can only hope she doesn't tell anyone at school. They peered at each other, Ariella's face pinched with concern and Faye's red with the effort of screaming.

"Awesome, that was a good one." Ariella came to the bed. "My mom screams sometime, not only when she's got her period. Don't they call it primal scream?" She pushed Faye gently onto her back. "Let's get you settled and I'll bring the tea in a moment."

Ariella lifted Faye's legs and tugged the covers out from under her, pulled them up to Faye's chin, then moved Faye's head to plump the pillow. She put her hands on either side of Faye's shoulders and leaned down, so their faces were just inches apart. Looking up into the gleaming green of Ariella's eyes, Faye felt something inside ease and a warmth spread through her body, while a bubble squeezed up her throat and her eyes got wet.

"Do you own a heating pad or hot water bottle?" Ariella asked.

"Heating pad on shelf in closet."

"You're going to be okay. It's going to be okay. Fer sure."

When Faye had drunk her tea and the heating pad was on her belly, Ariella sat down and took Faye's hand. "You know, I don't need to go riding with Sorcha. I can stay and help keep you comfortable."

"Don't be silly. Of course you should go. I'll be fine. Remember, I've been getting my period for decades." To counter Ariella's doubtful expression, she added, "I've got a routine, don't worry. I'll do a lot of napping today, catch up on my reading, mayhap do the schoolwork I brought home, maybe yap on the phone with my mother and, at worst, I'll veg in front of the TV."

"Okee then! Speaking of schoolwork, I need to go put the finishing touches on the amazing essay I'm doing for my English teacher." Ariella gave Faye's hand a squeeze. "If you need anything, holler. I'm just across the hall, you know."

Faye stared at the ceiling, trying not to question everything again. But it was all Drake, Drake and more Drake. As she shrank away from thoughts of him and their relationship and the complication of Shandra, her mind stalled and she yawned big. Must be the tea, Faye thought. Thank goodness for the tea. When her eyes started to close, she felt the impact of something on the end of the bed. It was Leaf, his golden eyes bright and tail high.

"Hey, you," Faye said and reached for him. "Am I back on your good side?" Leaf walked up and butted her nose with his head. Faye scratched behind his ears and was rewarded with purring rumble. "I'm glad to see you too." Faye yawned. Leaf put his paws on her chest and began licking her face. At first she tried to turn away, but then stopped and just let it happen. Then he tried to squirm under the covers, but was too big and only made the sheet and blanket bunch up. He looked at Faye.

"Okay, I'm really sleepy, so let's settle down." Faye patted a spot next to her pillow, but Leaf pawed at the covers. "You want to get under there?" Faye lifted the bedclothes and Leaf slipped under, but, instead of settling, he gently pushed the heating pad off Faye's abdomen and then curled up in its place. His rumble penetrated her innards and his warm body was so much better than the heating pad. She dropped the covers over him, but left a tunnel for him to breathe and so he could see her face. As she drifted off she thought, "I could get used to this."

Chapter Thirty Eight

Ariella woke her in mid-afternoon with another mug of tea and Faye got up to pee, being careful to ease Leaf off of her. In the bathroom, she saw the bloodstains in her panties, so she took them off and scrubbed them in cold water. After sliding in a tampon, she pulled her yoga pants back on, squeezed the wet panties in her hand and went back to her bedroom. Faye hung the damp panties over a hanger in her closet and some remnant of adolescent modesty compelled her to slide the door shut. She paused a beat or two, considering whether she should text or call Drake to tell him her period was here and he wasn't going to be a father. *Ugh, that sounds so final.*

Leaf watched at her from the bed, where the bright mid-afternoon sunlight gave him an orange aura. She knew he felt more sleeping was the way to go. When did a cat not want to sleep? Getting back into bed, Faye curled on her side and was pleased when Leaf settled in the angle formed by her belly and thighs, his warmth soothing. Faye closed her eyes and wafted away, pushed along by Leaf's hypnotic purr.

Something terrible was happening and it was horrible and loud. Faye struggled to wake, hearing huge thunder somewhere nearby. Some monstrous machine was tearing the world into shreds and exploding concussively as it did so. She sat up and peered out the window. Leaf shot from beneath the covers with his back fur up and his tail bushed out. The sky was still blue and the sun was still shining. Yet the banging, booming thunder was getting ever closer. Faye and Leaf jumped out of bed and ran into the hallway.

"Ariella, do you hear that? We've got to take cover or something! Get under your bed."

Then the thunder cloud roared right in front of the house, blasting and grumbling so loud Faye had to put her hands over her ears. Ariella popped out of her bedroom, laughing. She was wearing very tight, faded black jeans, a figure hugging, red cotton top under a ratty, fringed, short black leather jacket. Her face was free of makeup with the exception of some lip color and a hint of eyeliner. She had on her hiking boots. Something started to click for Faye.

"No worries! It's only Sorcha's bike!" Ariella shouted over the din, which suddenly dropped to a throaty puttering. Faye stared, first at Ariella, then at Leaf, then down the hallway to the living room. Outside, the noise stopped and the ensuing silence was profound. Ariella pushed past Faye, ran to the living room and turned left toward the front door. Faye stumbled after, while Leaf slunk back into her bedroom. The doorbell rang and she heard Ariella give a little squeak.

"You made it!" Ariella shouted. The screen door opened and closed.

"Yeah, your directions were perfect." Faye recognized Sorcha's voice, but hearing it without seeing her, she realized how neutral it was, definitely not girly feminine.

"Yup, considering I've only been here since Friday." Ariella's voice was shrill, as if her throat had constricted.

"Wow, babe, you look great!" Sorcha said. Faye flinched at Ariella's nervous giggle. She hurried into the living room and turned to see the familiar rail-thin figure, dressed, as always, in black jeans, frayed and patched dark t-shirt with the sleeves cut off and a disreputable black leather vest. Heavy duty black, scuffed boots completed the picture. Next to Sorcha, Ariella looked like a upper middle-class preppy, though Faye now saw she had made an effort to dress for a motorcycle ride.

"Hey, Ms B! Nice place you got here." Sorcha ran her right hand through her black, spiky hair, which looked as if it had been styled with automotive grease. In her other hand she held a somewhat bedraggled bunch of flowers. Ariella whirled around and Faye could see how pink her face was. Faye thought she looked as jumpy as any girl going on her first date.

"Sorcha, how nice to see you again. That's some raucous motorcycle you've got. I thought the world was ending." Faye smiled. She wasn't going to get all adult on them. "Would you like something to drink or eat? There's some lasagna leftover from last night."

Sorcha eyed Ariella, who squirmed and blushed, then noticed the flowers. "Oooh, are these for me?" It was Sorcha's turn to color. "C'mon to my room first. You can eat later." Ariella grabbed the flowers and pulled a smiling Sorcha toward the hallway. As they passed Faye, Ariella thrust the bouquet toward her. "Can you put these in some water?"

Bemused, Faye watched the pair, so different on the surface, yet in other ways so similar. A lingering odor of gasoline and tobacco hung in the air. Ariella's door closed and music started up. Faye wondered at the wisdom of leaving two teenagers alone, but then she remembered her own mom's laissez faire attitude when she had had girlfriends over. She put the flowers in a vase and decided, if the girls didn't emerge soon, delivering the flowers would give her an excuse to knock on their door.

She found her phone and sat on her bed, reading yet again the text Drake had sent Friday night about Shandra. It was now after 4:00 PM. Should she text him to say Ariella was going to leave soon? Should she tell him she'd gotten her period? What would happen if she didn't tell? Leaf rubbed his head against her arm and she stroked his handsome head. She tapped the little phone icon in Drake's contact page. He picked up on the second ring.

"Hey," she said.

"Hey, yourself. How are you? Are you free of your charge for a bit?"

"Sorcha's here. They're going to leave soon, after they eat some lasagna. How was tennis? And Shandra?"

"Tennis was fun. So, shall I come over?"

"Yeah, sure, why not? I'm not getting pregnant this month."

"What's that supposed to mean?"

"You know what it means." Despite her resolve not to cry,

Faye felt the familiar pre-tears sting and, if in concert, a cramp gripped her abdomen.

"You got your period?"

"Yes."

"Ah, I'm sorry. So how are you? Is it hurting a lot?"

"Yes." It wasn't awful, at least not yet, but she wanted Drake to feel bad - guilt or shame - something like that.

"I'm so sorry. Guess you're not up for company then." Faye took a couple of deep breaths while her mind spun around upon itself. "Faye? Are you still there?"

"Drake, I know you're squeamish about my period, but it would be so great if you came over and just hung out with me. Held me, that kind of thing." He didn't respond right away. Faye pushed the hair back from her face. She felt sweaty and grimy. If, by some miracle, he said he'd come over, she would need a shower.

"You remember the first time I was with you for your period?" Drakes voice was low and edgy.

"Yes, yes I do."

"Then you remember what happened to me."

"Yup, you fainted and fell off the bed when you saw my blood."

"Well?"

"You mean you haven't gotten over that? The sight of blood still makes you pass out?" She could hear his breath speed up. "Okay, okay, I know it stems from when you saw your mother get hurt when you were small, but, . . . but, that was so long ago! C'mon, you're a big, grown man now. And we don't need to do anything that would expose you to blood." Faye felt the ache between her breasts return. Why was she pushing him? She'd never done this before. He was quiet.

"It's because you really would rather spend more time with Ms Shandra, isn't it? If so, fuck you and you're a bastard. I hope she's bleeding too. I hope you get blood all over you!" Faye's words spilled out as if she ~~was~~ were vomiting them.

Drake made a strangled sound. There was more rapid breathing, gasping, really. "I gotta go. Sorry," he said and hung up.

Faye stared at her phone, willing him to call back. He didn't. She walked to her bedroom door and closed it, then ran to the closet, went in and slid the door shut. Leaning back against the wall in the dark, ~~her damp panties~~ almost touching her nose, the tears came in a torrent. She slid to the floor and put her head to her knees. How had the whole lot become such crap? Everything was in flux and in danger of irreversible change. And all in one week or so. Why wasn't Drake doing what she wanted?

She stopped trying to think and gave in to the crying. Time passed, seconds, minutes? Faye didn't know or care. She heard a scratching. Leaf. She opened the door a crack and he came bounding in, clearly worried. He immediately began to lick her face and, as his tongue caught her tears, her sadness eased. She put her arms around him and gave him a quick kiss.

"Leaf, you're absolutely the best." She giggled at the same time the final sob was rising and got the hiccups.

"Faye? Are you in there? We're going to eat the leftovers. Do you want some?" Ariella said, for once calling through the bedroom door, rather than just barging in.

Faye scrubbed at her face and crawled out of the closet, Leaf at her side. "Yeah, I'm here. Food . . . hicc . . . sounds great. Just give me a few minutes."

When she knew Sorcha and Ariella were in the kitchen, Faye zoomed to the bathroom, washed her face and armpits, ~~replaced her tampon,~~ and brushed her teeth. Back in her bedroom, she changed into loose white shorts and a baggy gray t-shirt, put on some lipstick, added a touch of mascara, and applied a dab of sheer foundation beneath each eye. She still had the hiccups, but so what? She was in her home, she could do whatever she wanted.

Ariella and Sorcha were standing close together in front of the humming microwave, laughing, while each tried to talk over the other. "So, you're sure you set this right?" Ariella said. "If it's still cold when it stops, that's the way you're going to eat it, Ms Know It All." She gave Sorcha a gentle shove and the older girl caught her arm. Faye stood in the doorway, knowing the girls were so absorbed in each other they hadn't noticed her. She watched as Sorcha pulled Ariella close and lifted golden hair away from Ariella's upturned face. Was Sorcha going to kiss her?

"Hey! How come the food . . . hicc . . .isn't ready yet?" Faye said brightly. The girls turned to her. Ariella's face was pink again, but Sorcha's gaze was calm and measured.

"It's almost ready," Sorcha said, her voice husky. "Little Ms Woodstove Vegan tried to program the microwave at 45 minutes on high to heat the lasagna."

"Well, I'm glad the two of you figured that out. Don't want . . . hicc . . . cold or burnt lasagna, do we?" The two reminded Faye of slinky cats, examining her like she was an interesting, but definitely inferior, being. "I'll set the table," Faye said and began banging open kitchen cabinets, clattering plates and grabbing silverware. Behind her she heard a little fake shriek from Ariella and what sounded like a light slap. The microwave dinged and Faye turned to see Sorcha's hand drop from Ariella's waist.

"Here, set the table, will you?" Faye thrust the plates at Sorcha. With some strategic maneuvering, she managed to sit between the two teenagers. When she hiccupped again, Sorcha told her to take a spoonful of sugar and drink a glass of water. It worked.

"So, where are you two cool, gal pals headed on Sorcha's big, old, jammin' hog? Try not to freak my neighbors by roaring out of here, okay?" Both girls smiled.

"Ms B, you're so funny!" Sorcha reached over and grasped Faye's hand and let go. The quick touch was so unexpected and the hand so warm and rough, Faye shivered.

"Yup, no worries, Faye," Ariella piped up. "We're going to just ride around for a while, then probably head to that big beach in Dennis. I think it's like a mile long. And then we're going to the cottage and feed the cats and so I can show Sorcha around."

"That sounds like fun, but I would like you back here by 7 PM, okay? And, call me if anything at all comes up."

This time there wasn't any laughter. Ariella glanced at Sorcha, who was staring stonily ahead. "But, Faye! It's almost 5 o'clock already. That doesn't leave us any time to really hang out. How about 9 PM, that's more reasonable, don't-cha think?" Ariella's tone suggested she'd negotiated curfews before. Faye was reminded of her teenage self.

"Listen, sunset is going to be at eight and I don't want you out after dark. So, 8 PM is the latest I'll agree to, take it or leave it." Ariella again turned to Sorcha, who looked away. Faye knew Sorcha's parents exerted little control over her, much less insisted on a curfew.

"Okay. But, if it gets to be later you'll come and get me, right?"

"Yes, I will come and get you, but just remember, I'm not feeling that well. And, I want to talk to you privately before you go." From the expression on Ariella's face, Faye could tell she'd won this round.

As they ate, they chatted about school and motorcycles and Faye went on at length about some books she thought the girls should read. Ariella grabbed a pencil and paper from the magnetized pad on the front of the fridge and wrote down the names of the books. Then, on a second piece of paper, she wrote out names of bands and songs she said were "gnarly" and beyond "unbelievabubble" and gave it to Faye.

After helping clean up, Sorcha said, "I'll be outside, I need to check something on the bike," and went out the front door.

Faye seized the moment. "Listen, Ariella, I'm not sure it's cool for you to bring someone to your house when your mom's not there and without telling her. And, I know you don't have any problem with Sorcha being a lesbian and I don't either, but she obviously likes you."

"My mom wouldn't care and so what about Sorcha? I can handle myself." Ariella pulled a strand of her hair forward and examined the ends.

"Did you tell your mom? When did you talk with her last?"

"Yesterday afternoon, when we were at the cottage."

"Did you tell her about Sorcha?"

"Yup." Ariella grabbed more hunks of hair and pulled them forward until they almost hid her face. Faye knew she was lying.

"Oh, good. So when I call her after you leave and she asks where you are . . . "

"Faye! C'mon, don't be trippin' on me. I'll call her now, okay, so just chill." Ariella stomped out of the kitchen and down the hall. Faye heard the bedroom door slam. After a few minutes, Ariella came back with the backpack she'd adorned with the cat stuffie.

"Okee, she didn't answer, so I left a message. If she calls me back and says no, I won't go to the cottage. Of course, then you and I will have to go feed the cats. Is that what you wanted? Do I get an A plus, teacher?"

"Sure, but I might still call her, just to chat, you know, shoot the breeze." Faye went to the sliding screen door to the deck and gazed out.

"Go right ahead." Ariella tossed her hair, turned and started toward the front door. "So wack!" Faye heard her say under her breath.

"Is Epifania going to be with you while you're away?" Faye called after Ariella.

"No!" Ariella shouted, "This is my private time."

Sorcha's motorcycle started up with a roar and a bang, but then settled into a rough, not unpleasant rumble. Faye went to the front door and watched as the teenage pair rolled sedately away, the bike's engine just purring. Faye was pleased Sorcha had heeded her request. They made an intriguing couple, the dark, thin-as-a-knife older girl in front, and bright Ariella behind with golden hair leaking out from underneath her helmet, her arms encircling Sorcha. Faye turned from the door and was thinking of what she wanted to do next, when something like a sustained explosion made her start. She whirled back toward the door and listened as the roar quickly faded into the distance. Of course, Sorcha had waited until she got to the end of the block before gunning the engine. How considerate.

Chapter Thirty Nine

As the rumble of Sorcha's motorcycle faded, Faye stood in the living room and relished the quiet. She realized this was the first time she had been completely alone since early Friday morning. What she cherished about weekends during the school year was the solitary downtime and the complete break from the din and chaos of teaching. She had thought this weekend would be filled with greeting card, lovely mother-daughter vignettes, but it had become probably the most hectic and stressful of her life. This couldn't be normal for mothers of teenaged old girls, could it?

Of course, if she had her own child there wouldn't be much alone time, at least not for the first three or four years, especially if she chose to be a stay-at-home mom. How long was paid maternity leave anyway? Probably not long enough, so she couldn't afford to not work unless the father provided support. Ugh. Having to rely upon that was not attractive. Anyway she loved her job and wanted to keep working, which meant she would need to rely upon a babysitter or daycare. Her mom? Faye shook her head. Unlikely.

Would there still be time to read and dream between working and caring for a child? And, when the child got older, became a teenager, would the demand for energy and time become even more intense, like it was with Ariella? She shuddered and brushed at the front of her shirt, reminding herself to try and stay present and not get caught up in the ego-driven, anxious, false reality her thoughts created. Leaf came running up to her and pawed at her leg for attention. It was past his feeding time. She picked him up and cuddled him like a baby, face up.

"What kind of mom will I be if I can't even remember to feed a furkid like you? Huh?" She stroked the soft hair on his chest and he reached up one paw and lightly touched her lips, then touched his lips. "I know, I know. You're hungry. Let's go get you some vittles." She went to set him down, but he gave a squawky meow and wriggled back into her arms.

"What? What is it you want? Are you having separation

anxiety?" Again he touched his paw to her lips and then his. Realization dawned. "You want a kiss?" Leaf began to purr. "Oh, what the hell." She lifted Leaf up to her face and put her lips to his and quickly pulled back.

He waved his paw at her and again brought it to his lips. Cat and woman studied each other. Faye could feel the affection, no, it was something more, flowing her way. She lifted him again and really kissed him. It was weird, no doubt about it, not the least because he had tuna breath, and his whiskers tickled her cheeks. But, when she just focused on the feeling, it was okay, actually quite nice. His two paws rested softly on either side of her face and she felt loved. When she did put him back on the floor, he glanced over his shoulder at her and she knew he was smiling. He led her to the cat bowls, tail held high. Faye called for Snow and Midnight, but they didn't appear. They had probably exited when Ariella left. She sat at the table and watched Leaf eat while she sipped another cup of period tea. How had it come to be that she was not only talking to a cat, but also kissing him?

"Hey, how about you can be my baby?" Faye snickered. But, Leaf turned his head and his expression was quite serious. "Okay, then. Bad idea."

She thought about getting some sun on the deck, but it was turning cool, so she wandered and wound up in Ariella's bedroom. Instead of the normal teenage mess of unmade bed, clothes on the floor, books and CDs piled everywhere, the room was as neat as it had been before Ariella arrived. The only evidence of the girl's presence was the dreamcatcher twirling slowly above the well-made bed. Had Ariella packed up and run off with Sorcha? Faye hurried to the closet and saw, with relief, the battered duffel on the floor. The duffel was secured with a padlock. How interesting. And why? To keep prying English teachers out of secret stuff, no doubt. Hmmm. She could cut a small slit in the bottom and then sew it shut before the girls returned . . .

Faye stepped back from the closet. Her ego was having a field day with all these imagined realities - about Drake, about

Leaf, about Ariella. She knuckled her forehead. Let it all go! But, on the way out of the room she just had to stop at the laptop. She stared at it. *None of your business, Faye Evelyn*, she could hear her mother say. *You're her teacher, not her parent.* But, wasn't she acting in loco parentis this weekend? Isn't that why Calista wanted her to watch Ariella rather than hand her over to the sketchy Punkhorn neighbors? Her imaginary mother snorted. *Loco parentis? Really? Isn't that Latin for crazy parent? I've told you before, keep your own nose clean and don't try and pick somebody else's.*

"Fuck it," Faye relished the sound of the profanity and imagined her mother's glare. She opened the laptop and turned it on only to discover it was password protected. That little minx! How dare Ariella lock a computer that was school property? But, Faye wouldn't confront Ariella because to do so would reveal she had been snooping. What was on the laptop that was so important? Didn't Faye have enough to worry about?

What if, after I drop Ariella at the cottage after-school on Tuesday, I decide I want nothing more to do with all her weirdness and the teenage attitude? What if I forget about nature spirits and full moon productions? What if I want to try and get back on track with Drake and just forget about having the baby? What if . . .? Once more Faye stopped her racing thoughts. What did her body feel right now? Despite the tea, she was achy and tired. And bloated. The solution was obvious. Ensconced in her bed with her fantasy novel, Leaf curled next to her, and a cup of hot chocolate within easy reach, Faye sighed and snuggled into her pile of pillows. No one around to disturb her or demand her attention. Though, if Drake appeared, that would be great.

She didn't know she had dozed off until her landline phone rang. Full of dream remnants, she reached across and fumbled the receiver. It dropped on Leaf and he protested.

"Mrs. Bloomberg? Mrs. Faye Bloomberg?" The voice was officious. Was it the police, calling to tell her that something had happened to Ariella?

Faye sat up, again eliciting an objection from Leaf. "This is *Ms* Faye Bloomberg. What is it? Has something happened?"

There was silence, then, "Uh, this is Officer Robert Slatterly?"

"Yes? Please tell me what's going on." Faye had a sudden image of a very angry Calista firing lightning bolts from her fingertips at Faye for failing as a surrogate mother.

"Uh, nothing has happened. But, we met at the Mall yesterday? You were with Princess Ariella?"

"Oh, thank goodness, I was afraid . . . but, why are you calling?"

"Uh, is the Princess there? Can I talk to her?"

Faye waited for her heart to ratchet down before replying. "Well, no, the Princess is not in residence at the moment. May I take a message?"

"Do you know when she's due back?"

"Officer Slatterly, I'm sure someone in your profession knows information about the Princess' schedule is classified."

"Oh, sure, of course. But, you'll tell her I called?" Slatterly sounded sad, as if something precious had slipped away from him.

"I absolutely will. Now, if you'll excuse me, there are some important people . . .um . . . waiting for an audience with me."

Faye bent over laughing after she hung up. Poor Officer Slatterly, caught in Ariella's glamour. She hoped the fascination with which Ariella had infected him would wear off before he became desperate enough to come to the house seeking his Princess. Thinking of spells and glamour and other ways Ariella could manipulate "normals," Faye again wondered if she, herself, was bespelled. How would she know? She grabbed Leaf under his front legs and lifted him up to her face, so he was standing on his rear toes. He looked uncomfortable with his shoulders hunched, but his love for her shone in his eyes.

"Leaf, am I under some sort of enchantment or spell that

Ariella or Calista or Epifania or Verdant Sea laid on me?" Leaf glanced away, toward the door. Faye gave him a light shake.

"Leaf? Please answer me! C'mon, you could talk to me when we were with Verdant Sea." With a twist, Leaf slipped out of her hands and jumped from the bed and trotted into the hallway.

"Damn!" Faye fell back on the bed. After five minutes of staring at the ceiling, she grabbed her cell phone and called Drake. He didn't answer. She hung up when his message started. After another five minutes of trying to accept and understand her panicky confusion, of trying to breathe normally, of trying to dispassionately observe how her desires and imagination were making her crazy, she called him again. He answered on the fourth ring.

"Faye?"

"I need you."

"What? Are you hurt? Did Ariella do something to you?"

"I think she put me under a spell or at least that's what I got from Leaf and I don't know which way is up anymore, but I still do think I want a kid, but I'm thinking it might just be more enchantment and I miss you and need you to be here with me so . . . so . . . oh, you know what I mean. Please, please come over and just be with me?" Faye held her breath during the silence that followed.

Finally, Drake said, "Faye, you know I love you and want to support you."

"Yes?" Faye said, "So you're coming over?"

"Ah, no, I just don't think I can handle anymore right now."

"What? Why not? Where are you? Is somebody with you?"

"I think a little break would do us both good, for a few days or so, until your . . ."

"Until my period is finished? For real? Is that all you can offer? What, am I so unclean you can't be around me? Do you want me to go to the Women's Tent or something? Not go out in public? Damn you, Drake Hershfeld and the whore you rode in on.

And you can tell her I said that."

"Faye —"

"Fuck you! I'm going to make a baby whether you're involved or not, even if it means I advertise online. You bloody asshole!" Faye was panting. "And I'm going to dance naked in wildflowers and communicate with nature spirits!"

She waited for his reaction, then realized the line was dead. Screaming obscenities, she threw the phone so hard it cracked against the wall and fell tinkling to the floor. Then she grabbed the small vase with Moira's flowers and threw that. Her meditation cushion, her shoes and a hairbrush followed.

Sobbing, she fell face down on the bed. *Am I going crazy? Have I gone over the edge? What am I going to do?* She punched Drake's pillow a few times and it felt good to do so. She punched it again. Then she held it in front of her and said, "Yes, I called you a bloody asshole, you jerk." She pushed the pillow into her face and smelled Drake. The pillow got damp from her tears. Leaf jumped back on the bed and pawed at her. Her landline phone rang. She grabbed at it the way a drowning woman reached for a life preserver.

"Ha! Changed your mind, Sir Fix It? It's going to take a lot of work to fix this problem."

"Faye Evelyn, are you all right?"

"Mom? What? Why are you calling me?"

"Never mind, are you all right or not?"

Faye thought how she should answer. "Well, I'm not physically hurt, if that's what you mean. I've got my period."

"Okay, that's good. But what's the matter then?"

"Wait, Mom, before I tell you anything, how did you know to call?"

"Well, you know that mothers possess this extra sense so we know when our children —"

"Mom!"

"Okay, okay, I just —"

"Did Drake call you?"

"Yes, my dear sweet daughter, he did."

"Oh, fuck, he's such an asshole, fuck!" Faye didn't think she could cry anymore, but she was wrong.

"Faye Evelyn! Language!"

"Oh, Mom, everything is shreklekh. Nothing is going the way I want. I think I might be losing my mind. And Drake, too."

The conversation went better after that. Faye cried, her mother chided, Faye wailed, her mother exhaled and said the things she knew would calm her daughter. She reminded Faye of what Rabbi Nahamn of Breslev had said: "If you believe breaking is possible, believe fixing is possible."

"You know I've never been a big fan of Drake, Faye Evelyn, but he was a mensch to call me and let me know you were hurting. And, for all his faults, I think he truly cares for you." Rhoda sighed. "Though I still think you could do better."

"If he's such a mensch, why can't he come and be with me when I need him, instead of playing games with that Shandra Cohen bitch?" Faye whined, but the fight had left her. Just talking to her mom was soothing her wounds and cooling her fever.

"Okay, what about what your meditation teacher told you, something about Noble Truths and how to live is to suffer and we need to learn to understand and accept suffering? I remember well how you would be quick to trot that stuff out whenever your sister was having boyfriend problems."

Faye sat back on the bed and cuddled Leaf in her lap. Her mother was right. "Yeah, something like that. You're right. I'll be okay." Faye blew her nose. "And, before you ask, you don't have to come over with chicken soup or anything."

"That's good, because Alice and I are going to go a poetry thing tonight."

Alice had been her mother's best friend for ten years and was always inviting Rhoda to events featuring poetry, music or art.

When it came to literature, Faye had an edge over brilliant sister Dr. Clara, The Doctor, so she perked up and had a good chat with her mother about poets and poetry. But, just before she hung up, Rhoda said, "Oh, I almost forgot. Drake said to tell you to stop drinking those herbal teas. He said he thinks they're getting you stoned."

"He's a fine one to talk about getting stoned!" Faye retorted.

"What do you mean, dear?"

"Never mind. Thanks for calling, Mom. I love you. Say hi to Alice for me."

Faye stretched, rubbed Leaf's tummy and realized she didn't feel so bad. Nothing like a good dose of Mom Juice to reset one's internal states. But what about screaming at Drake on the phone? The last time she'd gotten so emotional with a lover was in her twenties and the jerk had also been screwing her best friend.

Like their mad sex, it had felt empowering to vent her pent up energy and frustration at Drake. Perhaps something good would come out of all this. It was possible she was truly changing, moving to a new plateau, "leveling up," as the gamers said. But, if Drake wasn't part of it, was staying back, was it going to continue to feel so great?

Faye considered calling Drake's mom to inform her what a schmuck her son was. See how he'd like it. She scanned around for her cell and spotted it's crushed self on the floor near the wall. Well, then, she would use the landline. Then she realized she didn't remember Drake's parents' number, she always just used the one stored in her cell. She sat for a minute with the landline receiver in her hand, her other hand mindlessly twirling the hair on Leaf's back. What to do.

She *did* know Drake's number by heart. She punched in the number and, of course, he didn't pick up. Probably giving some mature man advice to Shandra the Slut. Faye quelled her anger and left a remorseful "please forgive me, I've got my period" message which, she realized when she hung up, was so, so very wimpy.

Faye cleaned up the mess of smashed phone, vase, water and flowers. Then she tidied her entire room, considered more meditation or more reading, before settling on doing her makeup until it was perfect. Although she looked great when she was done, she still felt ill at ease. Leaf meowed and led her to the kitchen and stood in front of the sliding screen door.

"Ah, so now you need me for something? You can't tell me about the spells I might be under, but you want me to open the door for you? Can't you do that for yourself?" Leaf didn't react, so she sighed and opened the door. "Don't do anything I wouldn't do and, if you do, be careful. Don't forget to tell your feline buddies how great I am. And give a good report to the nature spirits."

Calling the auto insurance company proved to be tiresome, especially when she tried to explain how her car had been damaged because she had to drive super-fast over a very bumpy dirt road while fleeing a dangerous person. The insurance rep asked several questions about where, what day and time, whether anyone had been injured, had she reported it to the police, etc. When asked, Faye said she had been driving, figuring that remaining in the driver's seat made her a driver of sorts. The rep said they would send an adjuster out to estimate the damage.

Then she got on the Internet and tried to figure out which new cell phone she could afford. That was also tiring, so she decided to bake some cookies and, while they were in the oven, to zone out and watch some TV. Once she was on the couch, however, she put her head back and stared at the ceiling some more. The doubts, fears, questions were still here and she had little confidence she could find any clarity. The only possible conclusion was she was changing. And, the changes likely meant something or someone was probably going to exit or something or someone would become a new fixture. Or all of the above.

The oven timer dinged and, when she got up to pull out the cookies, she let Leaf in from the deck. He rubbed against her legs as she slid the cookies off the pans and into a bowl. Faye felt an unexpected sense of secure, tranquil domesticity. Just a girl and her cat, some freshly baked cookies, nothing else required. She smiled down at Leaf and he smiled back up at her.

"I forgive you," Faye said, stroking his head, "but please, when you're able, tell me about any spells or other enchantments I might have been or am under?" Leaf licked her hand.

She sat down on the couch with the bowl of cookies and checked the time. It was 8:15. So, Ariella was pushing it again by missing curfew, though Faye had little energy left to get angry. The period tea's effect was wearing off and her bloaty ick factor was rising. She pulled Leaf into her arms and hugged him to her chest and kissed the top of his head. His loud purr was reassuring. It was tough being an adult when all she wanted to do was get naked and romp through a meadow of wildflowers with her cat.

Chapter Forty

Faye munched one of her cookies. She held it to Leaf's nose and he dutifully took a sniff, but showed no interest in eating it. "You know, Leafo, these organic oatmeal raisin cookies are all the rage here at 22 Sunset Lane, East Harwich. Better grab some before they're gone." Leaf licked her hand.

Be sure it isn't a real actress

"Now, what shall we do about our dear mischievous buddy, Ariella, who has missed her curfew? If we had a working cell phone I could call. Or we could call her on my landline, provided I could remember her number. And, if we had a working cell phone or we remembered her mother's number, we could also make that call. But, guess what? My cell phone is broken and I don't remember either number." Faye felt guilty relief about not being able to reach Ariella. Smashing her cell phone had some beneficial side effects. She wondered *whether* if Drake was trying to contact her. Maybe he was getting worried? If so, good.

"Wait. Do you remember their numbers? Can you tap them out with your paw?"

Leaf's smirk was big, but he made no attempt to tap out numbers. Rather, he squirmed even closer in Faye's arms and turned his head into hers and gently nipped her lower lip. She swung her legs up onto the couch, pushed a couple of pillows behind her head, placed the bowl of cookies within easy reach, leaned back and sighed. She pulled Leaf away from her breasts and pushed him further down so he rested on her lower abdomen, where his heat and purring worked so well.

She would wait until 9 PM and then call the police on her landline or, better yet, let Officer Slatterly know his Princess was in trouble. Faye giggled, snagged another cookie and picked up her fantasy novel. At 8:45 she heard the rumble of Sorcha's bike coming up the street. She got up from the couch and, standing back from the picture window so they couldn't see her, watched the two teenagers dismount and take off their helmets. Ariella looked impossibly beautiful, her hair in artful disarray, her eyes bright and her cheeks flushed. And Sorcha was standing tall, not in her normal slouch. Uh oh, Faye thought. Her suspicion was confirmed when the two girls put their arms around each other and shared a passionate kiss. Faye spun away to flop back on the couch with her book, the cookies and Leaf. She was going to be casual. She was not going to say anything now about the kissing, even if it was in full view of the neighbors, but she would talk to Ariella later, after Sorcha left.

The two girls came in the front door laughing. "Ms B!" They both cried in unison. "Wassup?" Their mirth increased.

"Ha, ha. You do know it's way past the curfew we agreed upon?"

"But, we tried to call you like three times and you didn't answer. So, it's not my fault," Ariella said, hands on hips. "Sorcha's bike stalled out at the cottage and she had to take out the spark plugs and clean them. We got here as soon as we could." Ariella looked to Sorcha, who stood close behind her.

"That's right, Ms B. I've been having problems with bad gas." The girls snickered.

"You guys are a riot. And, the reason I didn't answer is my cell phone is broken. So, you got lucky this time." Faye gestured to the bowl of cookies. "Hungry?"

The girls took handfuls of cookies, which made Faye wonder what had given them such appetites. Both of them devoured their first cookie in three bites. "Starving teenagers," Faye said, "You're living up to stereotypes."

"These are really good, Faye," replied Ariella. "Almost as good as the ones I bake."

"Hear that Leaf?" Faye poked the cat in his side. "You don't know what you're missing. Ariella says the cookies are good. But, Ms Cardona, before you run off, how's that English essay going?"

"Oh, it's almost done and going to be dench, fer sure. So don't be trippin now, just chill. I'll finish it later, after me and this Hell's Angel spend some quality time in my bedroom." Ariella took Sorcha's arm and steered her toward the hallway.

"Uh, wait a moment. Is Sorcha planning to stay overnight?"

The two gazed at Faye, and she knew they were calculating odds. Ariella opened her mouth, but Sorcha spoke first. "No, Ms B, I'm not. I gotta get someplace later, so no worries." Ariella elbowed Sorcha, but the older girl just put her arm around her and turned her into the hallway.

"I wasn't saying Sorcha couldn't stay. I just wanted to know so I could open up the couch and get some blankets and pillows for her," Faye shouted at their retreating backs, but they didn't stop, though Sorcha flashed her a smile as the pair turned into Ariella's bedroom. The door closed and the music started up. In the living room the shadows deepened. Faye recognized she was a little jealous and more than a little sad. As tumultuous as the weekend had been, she and Ariella had connected, not so much like mother and daughter or teacher and student, but more as friends or sisters or, when they were fleeing the Swarm, like the Amazon warriors of Faye's own teenage imagination. She had been looking forward to more deep spiritual and fantasy-themed conversations with Ariella, but it was clear Sorcha had taken top billing.

Plus, Drake hadn't tried her landline, assuming he had first called her cell. Faye knew her period magnified her melancholy, but she couldn't stop a few tears from welling up. In her mind's eye she saw, in quick succession, Ariella kissing Sorcha, then Shandra kissing Drake and then, incongruously, her mother kissing Alice.

But, it was the memory of Wanda kissing Brian when they were teenagers that opened the flood gates. She felt again like the shy girl she'd reverted to in high school after the split with Wanda. She had braved going to a few dances, but nobody, not even the other girls, hung out with her. Faye turned on the couch so her back was to the room and put a pillow over her head. Leaf squeezed in between her belly and the couch back and she stroked him while she sniffled over all the lost opportunities, for the excitement and romance she missed because of her anxious

freeze-ups, for the chances to have a child. And for whatever else
had she foregone by falling for Drake and settling for a
relationship based upon sex and convenience. Her cramps
increased in frequency and intensity and she wallowed in misery.

After ten minutes, sadness morphed to anger and Faye
surged up from the couch, spilling cookie crumbs onto the floor.
Leaf turned to her as if to say, "What now?" Speaking as much to
herself as to him, she said, "Okay, I'm tired of being cranky. I'm
tired of crying. I'm tired of this day. I'm going to bed." Leaf's ears
perked up at the word "bed."

In the bathroom, she swallowed three extra-strength
ibuprofen tablets. She'd drink no more of Ariella's herbal tea today
and none until she knew if it was magicked. As she brushed her
teeth in front of the mirror, she saw a woman who was tired and
red-eyed, with smeared makeup and tangled hair. She gave her
reflection the middle finger and stomped off to her bedroom,
leaving her door unlatched in case Ariella needed her. As she
yanked up the covers she realized that maybe Ariella would never
again need her and, to her dismay, moisture formed in the corners
of her eyes once more. To compound her distress, her tortured
thoughts started their nagging buzzing and, like mosquitos
attacking from all angles, and wouldn't let her sleep. She
thrashed, throwing off the covers, then pulling them back and Leaf
complained each time. When she had flipped over for the tenth
time, he stood up and, as she watched by the glow of the
nightlight, he hopped off the bed and went out the door. The pain
between her breasts, the one she called her "Relationship Ache,"
intensified and blew away her remaining angry defiance. Faye
was fated to be the Weeping Loser, maybe for the rest of her life.

She was still snuffling a half hour later when she heard
Ariella's door open. The two girls were talking in loud whispers,
but Faye couldn't make out what they were saying. Then Sorcha
said, in a husky voice, "I had a great time. See you tomorrow for
sure." After a pause, she added, "My motor's revvin' for you, you
know." Faye's eyes popped open. This was insult added to injury.
She wanted to say something, but couldn't find the words.

"And I like you a lot, too, Ms Biker Chick." Ariella giggled. The ensuing silence was punctuated by the small sounds that Faye recognized as being produced by two people enjoying a lengthy kiss.

"Good night, Sorcha." Faye called out, managing to put some teacher quality into her voice. Ariella gave a little squawk and Sorcha huffed.

"Oops, sorry Ms B. We thought you were asleep. Good night," Sorcha said as she moved away. Faye heard the motorcycle grumble into life and then growl into the distance. Somehow, Sorcha's departure made her more gloomy and she began to weep yet again. Through her funk, she heard noises first from the kitchen, then the bathroom, then back in the kitchen. No doubt Ariella was getting a snack and brushing her teeth.

She turned on the bedside light and grabbed one of her books on Buddhism. She read about the First Noble Truth of Suffering: "What is the Noble Truth of Suffering? Birth is suffering, aging is suffering, sickness is suffering, dissociation from the loved is suffering, not to get what one wants is suffering: in short the five categories affected by clinging are suffering."

And she read about the Second Noble Truth of the Origin of Suffering: "What is the Noble Truth of the Origin of Suffering? It is craving which renews being and is accompanied by relish and lust, relishing this and that: in other words, craving for sensual desires, craving for being, craving for non-being. But whereon does this craving arise and flourish? Wherever there is what seems lovable and gratifying, thereon it arises and flourishes."

Reminding herself that everyone was suffering in one way or another brought some relief. Faye turned on her right side, turned out the light and made a vow to try and let go of all the unmet desires she knew were creating her personal torment. It was difficult to accept that her desire to love and to be loved could cause her to suffer, but she knew it wasn't so much the loving, but rather the expectations that came with loving. How difficult it must be to love without expectations or attachments to expectations.

Pondering these concepts brought a further lightening of her mood. At least she wasn't still bemoaning all her lost opportunities. As she settled back on her side, still turned away from the room, she felt the bed behind her sink under a weight.

"Leaf, honey, is that you? Are you coming back now I'm a bit better?" Faye reached behind and lifted the covers so the big orange tabby could cuddle up to her. Instead, she felt the covers taken from her hand and a larger-than-a-cat warm body slide up against her back. She thrilled at the thought it could be Drake, but that fantasy was short-lived.

"Faye. Here drink this. It will help you sleep," Ariella said in a soft, caring voice. "And, no, it's not going to put you under any kind of spell."

A fragrant cup was in front of Faye's face. She surprised herself by taking it without hesitation and drinking its contents in three big gulps. "Thank you, Ariella. I truly appreciate it." Faye reached back and patted the girl's arm.

"Yer welcome, fer sure," Ariella said and snuggled up against Faye's back, one arm draped over her teacher's waist. Just like Wanda used to, Faye thought, then truly comprehended it was one of her students in bed with her.

Faye raised her head from the pillow. "Is this okay? Are you going to sleep in my bed with me? I mean, I appreciate all you've done, but—"

"Shush," Ariella said, "this is what sisters do. They comfort each other, they take care of each other, nothing more. You need to feel safe and loved tonight."

"Oh, of course." Faye felt sleepiness wash through her, no doubt the tea was kicking in. "I guess you're right, we are like sisters now," she said and closed her eyes. A memory prodded her back awake. "Officer Slatterly called, asking for you. I told him your schedule was classified, but he asked me to tell you he called."

"Poor Robert, he should be fine tomorrow."

As Faye put the empty cup on the nightstand she felt a smaller weight jump up to the bed in front of her. This time she was sure it was Leaf as his loud purr preceded him. He burrowed under the covers and fit himself against Faye's lower abdomen. She thought more about love, how it usually found you rather than you finding it. And, sometimes, the one you wound up loving was not who you expected. Like a cat instead of a boyfriend. She remembered the Stephen Stills song "Love The One You're With." She rephrased it to "Love The *Ones* You're With" and smiled.

Faye wasn't pregnant and she may have lost a lover, but she still felt loved. And, she loved in return.

NOT THE END!

My original intention was to write a single novel about Faye and Ariella. However, as the story developed and the characters wandered about like ping pong balls on the deck of a ship in rough seas, I kept having to add chapters. As a result, I wound up with a first draft of almost 250,000 words, which is more than twice the number of words in the average novel. I knew it wasn't practical to publish a first book of such large dimensions, so I made a Solomon-like choice to split the manuscript into two novels. *Nature's Kiss* is therefore the first book of what is now the "Nature Series" and *Nature's Love* is the second.

The good news for those readers who liked [enjoyed] *Nature's Kiss* but feel they were left up in the air at the ending [with too many unanswered questions], is that *Nature's Love* has already been [is in editing] written and answers all the questions. It will take me a few months to edit *Nature's Love*, but I expect it will be published sometime in the summer of 2017.

Send me an email at bemindful22@comcast.net and I'll be sure to let you know when *Nature's Love* is available.

I will say if you enjoyed *Nature's Kiss*, *Nature's Love* is more of the same, except crazier and more fantasy driven. Faye's life continues to change at an amazing pace, especially after she meets the mysterious Moira, the older woman who organizes the full-moon productions. Plus, Faye's relationship with Drake is put under even more strain, especially when a young female Physical Education teacher takes an interest in him and makes him over into a Hip Modern Dude. Faye hangs out with Leaf, Ariella's big orange tomcat, who decides Faye is his mate, with unpredictable results. Ariella is also transformed after she makes her first real friend from the public high school – an older girl named Sorcha who dresses all in black and rides a Harley Hog.

And, of course, we learn all about the nature spirits and the Viridis Glas Luminasti and the continuing threat from the Swarms. Verdant Sea makes several vital appearances and who is Epifania? There's lots more, but I'll leave it for you to discover when *Nature's Love* gets published.

REMEMBER: Send me an email at bemindful22@comcast.net and I'll be sure to let you know when *Nature's Love* is available.

41649794R00193

Made in the USA
Middletown, DE
19 March 2017